Lorelei Shannon

POSSUM KINGDOM

This book is a work of fiction. Any resemblance to actual events or persons, living or dead, is entirely coincidental.

"Possum Kingdom," by Lorelei Shannon. ISBN 978-1-60264-460-1.

Published 2009 by Virtualbookworm.com Publishing Inc., P.O. Box 9949, College Station, TX 77842, US. 2009, Lorelei Shannon. All rights reserved. No part of this publication may be reproduced, stored in a retrieval system, or transmitted in any form or by any means, electronic, mechanical, recording or otherwise, without the prior written permission of Lorelei Shannon.

Manufactured in the United States of America.

For my mom,
who loves me even though I write stuff like this.

And for everyone who was ever kind to a possum.

ACKNOWLEDGEMENTS

As always, I want to thank my husband Daniel and my sons Fenris and Orion for putting up with me while I was obsessed with writing this book.

Thanks to all the folks who helped me with the intensive research on the funeral industry that went into *Possum Kingdom*. Among them are Tony Bones, Ella Brackett, Lisa Carlson, Ann Schiefelbein, Karen J. Sonnenberg, and Stacy Stevens, not to mention the many people who answered questions for me on various funeral industry bulletin boards.

Thanks to the KiloMonkeys for reading and critiquing this monster. 'Specially you, Kij and Wolf.

Thanks to Alan M. Clark and Yvonne Navarro for helping me with Tennessee historical and mythological research, and for general moral support. And extra thanks to Alan for letting me listen to his dialect until I'm pretty sure I made him nervous.

Thanks to the many wonderful musicians whose music inspired me while I wrote. To name a few: The 9th Wave, Bobby Bare Jr., BR5-49, Johnny Cash, Nick Cave and the Bad Seeds, The Cherry Poppin' Daddies, The Cramps (Can't wait to go surfing with you, Lux), Cult of the Psychic Fetus, The Damned, Deadcats, Deadbolt, The Deep Eynde, The Dirty Birds, Dragstrip Riot, Freakwater, The Ghastly Ones, Ghoultown, The Handsome Family, Unknown Hinson, The Horrorpops, House of Freaks (Miss you forever, Bryan), George Jones, Los Straitjackets, Th' Legendary Shack Shakers, Shane MacGowan, The Meat Purveyors, Mr. Badwrench, My Life With The Thrill Kill Kult, Psycho Charger, The Rednex, The Revenants, The Reverend Horton Heat, Stan Ridgway, Social Distortion, Sons of Perdition, Southern Culture On The

Skids, The Supersuckers, The Toadies, Those Poor Bastards, Tom Waits, E.J. Wells, Hank Williams, and Hank Williams III. Extra special thanks to E.J. Wells for letting me use the lyrics of his song "Downstairs at the Funeral Home" in this novel. Like Robbie Jo, I think it's just about the Bestest Song in the World.

Huge thanks to Holly Burke, the amazing artist who created the *Possum Kingdom* cover, and most of the tattoos on my body. You rock!

Thanks to all the possums who've blessed my life and the lives of others: Spooky Fey Moonbeam, Spike, Velcro, Splat, Conan, Toesy, O-Ren, Trooper, and Marsi.

Thank you, Michael McDowell, for being my Southern Gothic inspiration since I was very young. One of the biggest regrets of my life is that I never got to meet you.

And finally, Thank you, Nick Cave, for inspiring this novel. Your song "The Curse of Milhaven" started this process in my head. You might say it's all your fault. Okay, it's a little bit your fault, anyway.

Lorelei Shannon
July 2009

Visit Lorelei on the web:
www.psychenoir.com

PROLOGUE

*P*ossum Kingdom, Tennessee hides itself away from the world, enfolded in the woods and water and mists of the Appalachian Mountains like an unspoken secret.

If you could soar over Possum Kingdom with the red-tailed hawks who make it their home, you would see a tiny town surrounded on all sides by wild, unspoiled nature; a jewel in the heart of a rose in full bloom. The wooded slopes of the mountains like the sides of great, green-furred beasts. The sapphire blue and ghost-white froth of Two Fox Creek, spilling down lichen-coated rocks, swirling like clouds, filling the unblinking, blue-green eye that is Virgin Pond. Main Street, dug into the green like a corn furrow, the slow but steady heartbeat of a little town.

Swoop down, now, closer to the earth, and fly along Main Street. See Tanner's General Store, where you can get flour, fishing tackle, fresh butter, and chewy, juicy gossip. The Sweet Hereafter Funeral Home with its Old Southern splendor, all creeping vines and columns and acres of front porch. The blue brick schoolhouse. The newly whitewashed Southern Baptist church. Possum Pete's Café, where you can get the best fried chicken and custard pie in the state.

A lovely little town.

A charming little town.

Although it lies no more than five miles west of State Highway 23, Possum Kingdom appears on no map. When lost tourists stumble into it, they don't linger. They never stay overnight. They're pushed away by an overwhelming strangeness that creeps into them like water bleeding through stone cellar walls. They stop, sometimes just past the "Welcome to Possum Kingdom" sign, sometimes in the middle of town, and turn around. Split. Get the Hell out of Dodge.

When their minivans and RVs and sport utility vehicles leave Old Possum Kingdom Road and pull back out onto the highway, they feel a sudden relief, as if the air were somehow easier to breathe.

No traveling salesmen stop to show their cosmetics and vacuum cleaners.

Busses don't even slow down at the turnoff.

Possum Kingdom doesn't belong to the people who live there. They belong to Possum Kingdom. It guards them jealously, and does its best to steer all others away.

Except for the ones it wants.

ROSE AND THE SKINNY DAWG

R ose Heron, seventeen years old, riding in the back of a near-empty Greyhound bus and on the edge of wild panic for the past two hundred miles. Heart pounding. Mouth dry.

Rose stood up. Sat down. Stood again. Switched seats, taking her bloated tapestry shoulder bag with her. Tried to sit still, and found herself rocking, rocking.

The driver asked her to sit down a few times, after she got on in Atlanta. He had long since given up, although she saw him glance in the mirror at her and shake his round, bristly head. Another passenger, a woman with the pink nose and moist eyes of a rabbit, turned around to stare. Rose pressed her forehead to the window.

Green, green and green. *So beautiful*, thought Rose, *like a deep-green sea*. Spiky treetop waves, high above. Rose wanted to be submerged.

She groaned, drew her legs up against her belly. It was strong again: the chewing pain in her stomach, the physical, twisting fear that drove her to run. It never went away, but sometimes it was bearable. Not now. Rose panted, her hands clutching at the strap of the bag. Her lips peeled back from her teeth. If it got much worse, she'd start screaming. Then she'd be put off the bus for sure.

"Please…," whispered Rose, jaws clenched, palms starting to sweat. Eyes wide, she stared out the window, hoping for something to distract her from her terror.

There was something ahead on the side of the road; an old wooden sign, split and grayed with age. There was an animal painted on it; a rat? Gray furry body and a thick pink tail. Faded letters the color of rust:

Possum Kingdom 5 miles

The possum's tail was pointing at a narrow dirt road leading into the woods.

Rose gasped, dropped her bag.

The pain was gone. Her muscles went limp for a moment, and she nearly fell out of her seat. One hand grabbed the seat in front of her, the other slapped the glass as the wooden sign flashed by.

"Driver! Stop!" Rose called, trying to stand. He didn't hear her, or ignored her. The pain began to gnaw again.

"Stop!" she yelled, staggering down the aisle. The bus lurched. Rose bumped into the rabbit-woman, who squeaked and clutched her purple plastic handbag. The other two passengers, the old man with the grimy yellow beard and the boy who couldn't seem to stay awake, were looking at her. The old man's mouth hung open. The boy rubbed his pointed nose and grinned.

"Driver, stop!" Rose yelled, now right behind him.

"Miss, I can't—"

"DRIVER, STOP! DRIVER, STOP!"

Rose was screaming, she knew. She could no more stop it than she could freeze the sun.

"Jesus!" from the driver. The hiss of brakes, and the bus swerved to the shoulder. Rose grabbed a luggage rack to keep from falling.

"You got family in Possum Kingdom?" asked the bus driver, his small blue eyes fixed on Rose. She shook her head, not trusting herself to speak.

"You got luggage under the bus?"

Rose blinked. She thought the man looked like a shaved pug dog.

"I said, do you have—"

"Open the door please." Rose began to shift from foot to foot.

He did, without another word.

Rose Heron jumped from the bus and began to run.

The sound of her own footsteps, her breath loud in her ears. Rose heard the bus idling for a moment, then the rumble and crunch as it pulled away. She didn't look back.

There was the possum sign. Rose reached up and touched the wood. It was oddly smooth, as if it were made of driftwood. The painted possum, towering over her with a great big toothy grin, was a silly-looking thing. It was looking right down at her, winking one round black eye. With its scaly tail of faded pink, gray fur like ragged grass stubble, dinner-plate ears weird little humanlike hands, it looked more like a cartoon rat than one of the creatures of nature.

Or did possums really look like that up close? Rose realized that she didn't know. She never saw them in Miami, where she was born and lived all her life. All the possums she'd seen since she left were flattened, gray and red smears on the highway.

Rose stood on her tiptoes, touched the painted possum's teeth with her forefinger. "You wouldn't bite me, would you?" The possum had no answer.

She took a deep breath, then another. Looked down at her grubby blue canvas sneakers. Crossed her arms over her belly, marveling. It didn't hurt. Nothing hurt.

For the first time since she started to run, the fear wasn't shrieking and yammering in her head. She no longer felt—no, *knew*—that *he* was right behind her.

Rose didn't know why. She didn't care. It felt too good. Rose grinned, and started down the road.

And as she did, fifty snakes in the Reverend Primus Reylark's Church of the Holy Blood reared back and rattled their tails.

And a corpse on the embalming table in the Sweet Hereafter Funeral Home sat bolt upright and scared the bejeezus out of Sam Dunwiddie

And a cloud of steam hissed up from the guts of the roadkill raccoon that Joe Reechur had just split open

And dogs howled

And cats shrieked

And Miss Reenie Rackham stirred her huge pot of brown, bubbling rabbit stew and wondered what the hell had just floated up from the bottom.

In the back of a rusted-out Chevy Nova on Highway 23, a black she-dog cringed in fear. There was something going on, something far worse than the fearful howls and shrieks coming from the woods. She pressed against the Woman as the car ground to a halt.

The Woman was sobbing, as usual. The Man was screaming, as usual. The dog knew, somehow, that he was screaming about her.

"Please," said the Woman. "Please don't." The dog knew those words. They were the ones the Woman said before the Man hit her. The dog pressed closer still.

She picked out a few words in the Man's raging torrent of sound. "Out," he kept screaming. "Throw the little fuck out." She knew he was talking about her, because, although the Woman occasionally called her Sweetie, her name was You Little Fuck. It was all the Man ever called her.

"No!" screamed the Woman. "No!"

Fast as a rattlesnake, the Man's fist lashed out and hit the Woman in the face. The salty tang of blood joined the ever-present stench of fear and anger.

The dog yelped and ducked her head. A hot squirt of piss spattered the Nova's ratty gray seat.

"KILL YOU!" the Man roared.

The dog knew what that meant. She fell to the floor of the car, scrabbling around in the fast-food wrappers and spent rubbers and snotty tissues, trying to duck the blows the Man hammered down on her. She knew better than to roll over and show her belly in submission; he'd stomp her, like he did before. She just screamed instead.

The Woman threw open the car door. "GO!" she shrieked. "Go, he'll kill you!"

The dog whined and licked the Woman's ankles. The Man crawled halfway over the front seat. He hit the dog so hard that she vomited thin bile, her mind a jagged haze of pain.

She would have died there, under the Man's fists, if the Woman hadn't grabbed her and thrown her out of the car.

The dog hit the hard-packed shoulder of the road with a grunt, then scrabbled to her feet.

"Go!" shrieked the woman. Pain, as the Man bounced a beer bottle off of her shoulder. Confusion. The dog whined, shifted from foot to foot.

"Sweetie, please! GO!"

The Woman's red, snot and tear-streaked face. The Man, wallowing back over the seat, opening the door, death in his eyes. With a miserable howl, the dog turned and ran.

Toward Possum Kingdom.

Rose walked. She moved fast, kicking up dirt, not thinking about much of anything other than how pretty it all was. It was like a tunnel, this road, massive old oak trees rising up on either side to form a canopy overhead, letting the light through in ragged stripes and leopard spots. The woods seemed impossibly dense and dark, although it was late morning. The forest floor was higher than the pounded dirt of the road, like the spongy dead-leaf banks of a flat, brown river.

Rose smiled at a lumpy black boulder, spotted green with moss. "Giant frog! Aaaah!" She paused to stroke the leaves of a riotous fern, busting up from the ground next to the frogstone like a fountain in a formal garden. She opened her mouth and breathed in the rich, moist, wild-smelling air. It tasted like freedom.

This was nice. Yes, this was just fine.

Except it turned out that five miles was a long way to walk, and Rose was hungry, and it was getting really hot. The sun didn't have a clear shot at her, but it turned the humid air into a sauna. Rose's thin Cramps t-shirt stuck to her narrow back and sharp ribs. Her hair seemed to be trying to swallow her face, and she pushed back the damp strands over and over again.

Rose grinned, blinking salt from her eyes. She still wasn't afraid. That was worth a little sweat.

"Possum, possum," she sang under her breath, striding along. "Awesome possum. Possum blossom…"

Pause. A fork in the road. Rose shifted her weight, first left, then right. Which way to go? She dug a quarter out of her dusty khakis.

"Possum toss-em," she sang, flipping the quarter in the air.

She dropped it. The quarter bounced off Rose's right palm, hit her left shoe, and rolled down the road a ways before spiraling down a rathole.

"Well, damn," she said, peering down the little hard-packed tunnel mouth. She cocked her head, certain she could hear tiny feet scrabbling, happy little squeaks.

"You're rich! You're rich! You're socially secure!" Rose told the rat. That's when she noticed the three drops of blood on her left shoe.

Rose touched the rust-colored spots. Where did they come from? She didn't remember. A nosebleed? A cut in the kitchen? Rose gently touched her swollen lower lip, the cut on the inside where her teeth had torn the tender flesh. Could that be it? *Hell, I don't even remember how that happened.* She shuddered. Perhaps not blood at all, but tomato juice? Ketchup? Kool-aid?

No, no. Definitely blood. Rose looked at the three dark drops on her left shoe, and went right.

The skinny black dog who thought of herself as You Little Fuck ran madly through the woods, tongue lolling, eyes bulging, tail between her legs. She wanted desperately to run back to the Woman, but she knew, somehow, that the Woman was lost to her forever. Besides, even if she went back, she knew the Man would kill her. The smell of it was all over him. Could she still smell it? Right behind her? She ran faster, whining.

Then, another smell. Rich and meaty, foul with shit, sweet with rot. Ahead of her. The insides of another animal. The smell of ripe, blown-open death made her terribly afraid. It made her terribly hungry. Slavering, trembling, she ran toward it.

ROSE AND THE SKINNER-MAN; THE DAWG HAS A SNACK

Rose had made a mistake. The road became a path. The path grew narrower and narrower still. The oaks and hemlocks and tall, gangly maples closed in on her until there was no path, just a thin strip of dirt cutting through the woods like a part in a wild mane of hair. Rose was slick with sweat; she felt as if she were slipping greasily through the trees that brushed at her shoulders. Her feet hurt. She had the uneasy, ridiculous feeling that she was sliding down a gigantic green gullet, into the steaming belly of the woods.

"Well, son of a bitch," Rose muttered. "Time to turn around, honey."

She pushed the lank hair from her face and blinked. She was starting to turn on her blood-stained left foot when she saw something ahead of her through the trees.

A little house. More of a shack, really, the raw boards bent and silvered with age. But the shingled roof was solid, the dirty windowpanes unbroken, the weeds cut back from the base of the walls. Someone lived there.

Rose's first thought was to go knock on the door, to rest for a little while, maybe get a glass of water.

Her second thought was that Leatherface and the entire cast of Deliverance might be bunking there.

She stood there and stared, her skin damp, her mouth dry, her head pounding with hunger and the heat. She took a step forward, then another.

Rose walked toward the shack, humming "Dueling Banjos."

The dog crept through the woods, belly low to the ground. She stared through the trees, eyes fixed on the prize. There it was, its overpowering scent driving her nearly mad. Glistening red and gray and yellow and pink, flies buzzing around it in a spotty haze. Dog heaven. Dog nirvana.

A pile of guts.

The stuff on the bottom smelled the strongest; some of it was practically liquid. The stuff on top smelled lush and meaty. Bloody. Chewy.

There was a tiny house, too, with the skins of animals nailed to the walls, but the dog could hardly see it. It faded away, pushed out of existence by her hunger. And by that *smell*.

The black dog crept forward, drooling.

Oh, dear. Oh, shit. There was something badly wrong here. Rose knew it even before she smelled it. Then smell it she did. The stink got worse and worse as she edged toward the shack. Something very dead.

Turn around, turn around, turn around, chanted her brain in a buzzing monotone. But her feet didn't seem to listen. Rose's every sense sharpened to painful clarity as she crept around the side of the building. The snap of a twig under her cat-quiet step, like a gunshot. The green of the trees was too bright. The animal hides nailed to the wall drew her eye like neon. Deer. Possum. Raccoon. Squirrel. Chipmunk. Even little, tiny things; mice or shrews? Stretched out with as much care as the others, and somehow that was just wrong. Who in the hell skinned mice?

Rose reached out with one finger, but stopped short of touching. *Ick. Yuck. Nasty.* The hides were gross, with their glossy fur and their shriveled edges. But they weren't the source of that stink. That reek. That *stench*.

The stench was vile, unbearable, making her mouth water with nausea. Rose pulled her t-shirt up over her nose and mouth. *Get out*, said her brain, almost conversationally. *Run run run run runrunrunrun…*

But dammit, she had to see.

Joe Reechur shook the bloody raccoon skin and held it up to admire. It was a fine one, the fur thick and nearly two inches long. Joe looked at the carcass on his skinning table.

"Ya fat bastid," he muttered, dropping the pelt on the table with a wet plop. Nothing could hold onto its skin like a coon. It took plenty of sweat and sharp knives to coax one out of his hide, that was for sure. This one had been particularly stubborn. Even now, lying there all sticky and bare, it seemed to be grinning at Joe with all those pointy white teeth.

Joe grunted. He jammed his hand into the hollow chest cavity and grabbed the coon by the rib cage.

He froze. There was something outside. He could hear it, snuffling, chewing, gulping.

One side of Joe's face twitched up in a grin. The pile of guts had worked its magic one more time, luring some critter to his doorstep. A walking hide. A pelt on the paw.

"Better than a French hoor's per-fume," whispered Joe. He picked up his rifle with his free hand.

Rose walked, quiet as a ghost, around to the front of the building, and then froze in her tracks.

She just stared.

I have never, she thought calmly, *seen anything that repulsive in my whole life.*

She stood and watched a scrawny black mutt, no more than a pup judging by her big feet and floppy ears, eat from a pile of animal guts like it was gourmet chow mein.

Or maybe gourmet spaghetti.

Rose gagged as the dog wolfed down something that looked like a small animal's stomach. The mutt heard her and looked up warily, a loop of intestine dangling from its muzzle.

Before Rose could pull herself together enough to puke, the front door of the shack flew open. A skinny old man, arms bloody to the elbow, hair like wild white feathers, stepped outside. He had a rifle clutched in one bony hand. In the other he held something that looked like a skinless demon from the pits of Hell.

The demon grinned at Rose with white, pointed teeth.

The old man grinned at the dog with broken yellow ones, and raised the rifle.

Rose screamed. The old man's arm jerked and the gun went off, sending a shower of leaves down onto the dog. The dog whirled and ran like hell, long gone before the last leaf hit the ground. The old man cursed in a rusty-hinge voice and threw the wet, dead thing down like a spiked football.

It bounced.

The man with the bloody hands spun around and glared at Rose. The whites of his eyes were as yellow as his teeth.

Rose's feet started running long before her brain realized what was going on.

Hot as she was, tired and hungry as she was, Rose didn't stop running until she reached the fork in the road again. Then she sat down in the dirt, sneezed twice, and started laughing.

ROSE AND THE NICE OLD COUPLE

The walk to Possum Kingdom was endless. Eternal. Rose picked up her feet and put them down like a metronome. Not fast, not slowly. She tried to imagine what Possum Kingdom would be like, smell like, taste like, who she would meet there. But it was hard to keep her mind off her aching feet and pounding head and growling stomach. Was five miles really this far?

Her shoulders sagged in despair when she saw that the road ended in a T-intersection. When she saw the weathered road sign, she nearly danced for joy.

It was one of those old-fashioned dealies; three boards nailed to a central pole. The whole contraption was warped and cracked with age. But the letters had been carved into the boards, and Rose read them easily.

She discovered she had been walking down Old Possum Kingdom Road. That made her smile. The road it intersected with, also dirt, was called Big Jesse's Walk. The bottom board, bless it, said "Possum Kingdom" and sported a nice, big, clear arrow pointing to the right. Shifting her bag, which seemed to have gained twenty pounds since she got off the bus, Rose turned the corner.

She did her damndest not to think about the old man and his Shack of Horrors. *Those were just animal guts, of course. That was just animal blood, of course. The thing in his hands was just some poor skinned woods beastie. That's all.* A name popped into her head.

Ed Gein.

Hot as it was, Rose shivered.

There was a path leading off the main road, to her left. She didn't even consider taking it.

Almost there, thought Rose. *I must be.*

And she thought about the dog. *Poor thing.* It had been so skinny, so desperate. She was glad the old fruitcake hadn't managed to shoot it. *What kind of creep shoots at a dog, anyway?*

Rose grimaced, kicked an acorn in the road. Surely the people of Possum Kingdom weren't all like that, a bunch of trigger-happy redneck psychos. Like in all those movies, where some poor girl stumbles into a little Southern town and immediately gets arrested, raped, sent to women's prison, and raped some more. Or just plain killed. Or killed and eaten with black-eyed peas and turnip greens.

"Oh Jesus, shut up," Rose told her wayward brain.

And then she stopped walking.

Although Big Jesse's Walk continued on, curving into the woods, there was a paved road joining it from the left. A small wooden sign named it as "Main Street." At the base of the sign was a low obelisk of black stone, almost like a gravestone.

"Welcome to Possum Kingdom," it said.

After hesitating a moment, Rose walked past it, to take her first look at Possum Kingdom, USA.

"Holeeeeey crap."

Rose had never seen anything like it, outside of old movies, and maybe 1950s TV shows. Main Street was beautiful. Perfect. Buildings, old but in good repair, lined the street. A little glass-fronted store, a fine old mansion, a café painted a cheerful red, a faded blue baby-Victorian house. There were more, of course, but they were obscured by the towering old oaks and maples that grew along the street, between the businesses. The woods surged up behind the buildings, the Red Sea parted by asphalt, looking as if they would crash in at any moment and reclaim Possum Kingdom as their own. There were no cars visible on the street. No people on the sidewalks. No dogs. No kids.

A little wet shiver ran up the back of Rose's neck. Her eyes narrowed. "What the hell...?" she muttered. This was not right. This was like some goddan Twilight Zone episode, where everybody in town has been kidnapped by aliens. Or the town is really an alien zoo. Or the hero comes back from a walk in the woods and everybody's been dead for a hundred years. Just dried-up stick figures, dusty, wasted corpses…

"Oh, bullshit." Rose wiped her face on the shoulder of her t-shirt, spit on the ground, and started walking down the middle of Main Street.

The mid-June sun was high, yellow as an egg yolk, revealing the heart of Possum Kingdom in crystal detail. Rose could now see that the store had pots of white daisies on either side of its heavy screen door. The mansion was a funeral home. The blue house down the way sported a hanging wooden sign in the shape of a dog which read "Veterinarian." A cool breeze swept by Rose's back and set the sign to swinging, just a little.

Almost even with the store; Tanner's General Store, according to the sign, and Rose stopped to look. She peered in through the big glass window, at jars and bottles and barrels, and an old-fashioned wooden counter.

She smiled with relief. There was someone in there. A plump older woman in a pale yellow dress, short gray hair, smooth mocha skin. She was looking down; maybe reading a book behind the counter? Rose tentatively raised her hand, and waved.

The woman looked up. Her full, pretty mouth opened in what looked like surprise. Then she smiled, and waved back.

There was a roar; muted at first, then suddenly very loud, coming down Big Jesse's Walk. Rose whipped around in time to see a long black hearse blasting along the dirt road. It was old; shiny as a beetle's back, glittering chrome and huge, sweeping fins, coach lanterns and white lace curtains.

The hearse pulled a screaming brake-turn and hit the pavement of Main Street, jumping like the strike of a snake. It came down with a crash; the whole hearse shuddered, but didn't slow down. In fact, the driver gunned it. What the hell was wrong with the driver? Rose couldn't see him; the glare of the sun turned the windshield into a wall of fire.

The engine snarled, the hearse lunged. It looked pissed off. It looked *hungry*.

Screaming down the middle of the road.

Straight toward her.

Rose leapt. Like a snapshot, she saw the horrified face of the woman in the General Store. She looked like she was screaming.

Rose hit the sidewalk hard, and rolled. The hearse blasted by, blowing her hair back in its wake. It didn't even slow down.

The dog. The scrawny black dog, it was the same one, it had to be, and it ran out from the woods and into the path of the hearse. The dog didn't stop, it was still running, but the hearse was going to hit it anyway, and it was going to be bad, and Rose wanted to shut her eyes but she didn't have time.

The dog was fast, but not quite fast enough. It would have been pasted all over Main Street if the hearse hadn't slammed on its brakes; not to avoid hitting the animal, but to pull a squealing left into the driveway of the Sweet Hereafter Funeral Home. Instead of being turned into jelly, the dog was clipped by the hearse's right rear whitewall tire and thrown into the air. It hit the pavement with a thump and a pitiful yelp, then scrambled to its feet. There it stood, head hanging, looking utterly confused.

Possum Kingdom came alive.

A young man in a white linen suit jumped out of the hearse and slammed the door. A tall old man came boiling out the front doors of the funeral home and started yelling at him. An upper floor window flew open, and an old woman started screaming at the young man, too. People came out of the café to stare at the dog and the fight. A tall guy in a white coat came running out of the vet's office and headed for the dog. The dog seemed to come awake; its head snapped up, its tail went between its legs, it cowered. The man in the white coat knelt, held out his hand. The dog backed up slowly, and then bolted into the woods behind the café.

Someone had Rose by the arms. Someone was helping her to her feet. It was the lady from the store, and a slim, fine-featured old man Rose guessed to be her husband.

Rose realized that the woman was talking to her.

"Oh, honey! Are you all right? That Sam! That Sam Dunwiddie is going to kill somebody one of these days. It was almost you, sugar. And that poor dog! Poor old thing was almost flattened. You should see how many possums Sam hits in that big ol' hearse. It's awful. Just awful. Are you okay, honey?"

Her voice was low-pitched and velvety, and the words poured out in a soft, sweet drawl that was pure magnolia and molasses.

"Uh...yeah, I'm fine..." There was a nasty burning on Rose's right elbow. She touched it, and her hand came away bloody.

"Oh, sugar! You've scraped off half your hide! Come inside for a bit, me and Owen will get you fixed right up. Would you like something cool to drink? Are you hungry? You sure are a skinny little thing, sweet pea."

"Don't talk the poor girl's ear plum off, Naomi," said the old man, and then slipped the woman a little smile that packed all the love in the world. Rose felt a tiny needle pierce her heart. *If anyone looked at me like that, just once*, she thought, *I could lie down and die happy.*

"Oh, you," smiled Naomi, and her love was like the sun.

The man had his wiry arm around Rose's waist, steering her toward the general store. She was surprised at how shaky her legs felt, and suddenly, her stomach started to flutter like a closet full of moths.

I was almost run over.

I guess I'm just lucky I didn't pee my pants.

It was cool inside the store. Well, if not, it was at least cooler than it was outside in the sun. A big swamp cooler labored away in the corner, but it was a losing battle.

Tanner's General Store was a weird collision of old and new. Barrels of dried rice and beans next to a rack of Doritos and Ruffles. Jars of stripy candy sticks by a display of packaged Rice Krispy Treats. Sasparilla and Coke, homemade cookies and beef sticks in plastic.

Rose was desperately grateful for the presence of those sugar and fat-laden mass-produced goodies. They meant that she was still in the present; she hadn't, in fact, slipped into some kind of time warp. There was no way to tell otherwise, looking at the elderly couple who had saved her.

The old man, who was helping Rose into a heavy wooden chair near the counter, wore slim striped pants, a white short-sleeved cotton shirt, and button-on suspenders. He could have stepped out of the 1920s. Naomi's long, flowing, short-sleeved dress could have been made yesterday or seventy years ago.

The man opened a bottled Coke for Rose. She clutched it with both hands, loving the cold. Naomi vanished for a moment and returned with a cool, damp cloth. Instead of handing it to Rose, she began to gently wipe down the girl's face, tenderly as a mother might. Or, how Rose guessed a mother might, anyway.

"Good God, honey. That was some welcome you got to our town, wasn't it. Are you all right? Looks like your lip's a little swollen. You're not gonna have a sinkin' spell, are you?"

Rose had no idea what a sinkin' spell might be, but she didn't feel in danger of having one. "No, ma'am, I'm fine," she answered.

"Well, that's good. What's your name, darlin'? I'm Naomi Tanner, and this here's my husband, Owen. We own this little store. It ain't much, but it's ours, bless it. We love it so. Can't you tell?"

Rose nodded, smiling. "Yes, I can, Mrs. Tanner." She took a long, blissful drink of her Coke. The woman grabbed her other arm in a firm, warm hand and began dabbing at the blood on her elbow with the cloth.

"Oh, for heaven's sake, call me Naomi, child. And you can call that old buzzard Owen. But say it loud, though, or he won't hear you. He's as deaf as a gopher with mud in its ears." She fished a big Band-Aid out from behind the counter and slapped it onto Rose's elbow.

"From all your talkin', honey. That many words could burn the ears off a rabbit." Owen gave her another one of those smiles.

He was a handsome old guy, in a fine-boned, almost delicate way. Sharp cheekbones, bow-shaped lips, strong nose with a little bump on the bridge. Much darker-skinned than his wife, Owen's deep chocolate skin had a dusty, bluish cast to it that Rose found fascinating.

"You sure you're all right, little girl? You're starin' at me like you seen a ghost." Owen touched Rose's forehead, as if checking for fever.

Rose laughed. "I'm sorry. I think I'm still a little stunned. I—my name's Rose. Rose Heron."

Naomi smiled. "Why, that's a lovely name. Where you from, Rose Heron? What on earth are you doin' in Possum Kingdom?" Her brow knit. "And what are you doin' travelin' around all by yourself, anyway? How old are you, honey?"

"I'm eighteen," said Rose. *In about three months, anyway.* "I just graduated high school." At least that part was true.

"Mm-hm. And why are you out in the big world all by yourself? Where's your family? You don't have kinfolks here, do ya?"

Rose was suddenly nervous. She knew Naomi was just being friendly, but it felt like the third degree. And there was no way she was going to tell a complete stranger what she was running from. Rose opened her mouth, and lies spilled out as easily as water, just as they had always done.

"Oh, I'm just taking a trip across the country to, you know, find myself. I didn't want to start college right away, not when I hadn't seen much of anything."

"A free spirit," Owen smiled. "A young adventurer on the road of life."

Naomi's frown deepened. "Well, if you ask me, it just isn't safe for a young lady to go runnin' all over heck and half a' Georgia all by herself. Not in this day and age. What do your mama and daddy think of all this, honey?"

Rose's teeth ground together, just for a second. "They're...they're worried, of course, but I call them all the time. They know I can take care of myself."

"Mm-hm." Naomi sounded skeptical.

Rose drank her Coke and pretended to be terribly interested in the stock of the store.

"You're just passin' through, then?" Owen asked.

"Well, actually, I'd kind of like to stay in Possum Kingdom for a few days. It looks like a nice little town." *And it's evidently the only place on Earth that my stomach doesn't try to turn inside out and eat itself.*

Naomi and Owen looked at each other, seemingly very surprised. "That's okay," said Rose, "Isn't it?"

Owen laughed. "Of course it is, Rose. We just don't get too many visitors here, that's all. We're not exactly a hot tourist spot, if you get my meanin'."

Rose nodded. Disneyland it wasn't. "Is there a, uh, motel around here or something? Or a bed and breakfast?"

"Nope, not a one," said Naomi. "But you can stay with us, honey. We've got a whole upstairs floor that we just about never use. Old feeble folks like me and Owen don't do so well with stairs, you know."

The couple looked about as feeble as college baseball players. And why were they being so nice to her, anyway? Rose bit her lip, thinking.

"You'd even have your own bathroom!" Naomi went on. "The plumbin's old, but it works just fine. You can have breakfast and dinner with us. We usually have lunch at the café. Hey, sugar, are you hungry? You look hungry to me."

Rose's stomach let out a fearsome roar. Owen burst out laughing. Rose blushed, and laughed too.

"I can pay you," she said. She had eight hundred and sixty-one dollars in her pockets and her big, floppy bag. That would last her a little while, anyway. Maybe she could get a job somewhere in town when it ran out.

"Oh, we'll talk about that later," said Naomi.

The screen door banged open, and two girls came into the store. They both looked a little younger than Rose. One was skinny and mousy with short, brown hair. The other, taller girl had long, glossy hair the color of an old penny, pulled back in a high ponytail. She glanced at Rose. There was something weird about her eyes, something different.

"Hello, Nancy. Hello, Robbie Jo," said Owen with a smile.

"Hi, Mr. Tanner. Hi, Mrs. Tanner," said the taller girl. She smiled at Rose. "Hey. Who are you?"

"I'm Rose," she said, still trying to get a good look at the girl's eyes. "Who are you?"

"I'm Robbie Jo Ridgemont. This here's Nancy Plum. Wow, we don't get strangers in town too often. Are you lost?"

"I don't think so," said Rose.

Robbie Jo's copper eyebrow shot up and her mouth quirked in a little smile. "Oh, geez. You're the gal Sam just about ran over, aren't ya. You gonna be all right?"

"I'll live." Rose crossed her arms over her stomach, for fear that it would growl again.

Robbie Jo leaned in closer. "You sure are a pretty thing, Rose. Sam wouldn't a' tried to flatten you if he'd gotten a good look at you."

And Rose got a good, clear look at her eyes. They were a deep, fiery russet, almost the same color as her hair. Fringed with long dark lashes. Beautiful. But weird. They almost made Robbie Jo look like one of those dogs, those Weimer-heimers or whatever they were, whose fur was the same color as their eyes.

Rose blinked, then smiled. "Um, thanks. You're pretty too, Robbie Jo. You have gorgeous eyes. I've never seen eyes that color."

Robbie Jo grinned. "You like 'em? Most people think they're a little spooky."

"Nah," said Rose, although they were, in fact, very spooky.

Naomi cleared her throat. "Ladies, I hate to break up your little sewin' circle, but poor ol' Rose here is just about to starve to death. We need to get her to Pete's before she just plain keels over."

Robbie Jo laughed. "Well, we can't let that happen, can we, Mrs. Tanner. Tell you what, me and Nancy'll be happy to take you over to the café, Rose. We can have ourselves a chat, get to know each other. You stayin' in the Kingdom awhile?"

"I think so," said Rose.

"Well, that's just fine. When you're feelin' better, I'll be happy show you around. There's not a lot to see, but it's all ours!" Robbie Jo tossed her pretty hair and laughed again.

Rose stood up, stretched her back. Nope, nothing broken or even that badly bruised. She turned to Naomi and Owen.

"Thank you both so much. You've been so nice to me."

Naomi patted her hand. "Well, sugar, that's the way folks in Possum Kingdom are. I hope you won't let Sam put you off of us."

"No, I'll just stay out of the road," Rose smiled.

"Good girl. When you're done with your dinner, honey, you come on back here, and we'll show you the room, okay?"

"Okay, Mrs—Naomi."

To her surprise, Robbie Jo linked her slim, cool arm through Rose's. "I think we're gonna be great friends, Rose," she said with a grin. "I just have this feeling about it."

Rose felt her whole body relax. It was such a luxury, being around such nice, caring, friendly people.

Such normal people.

ROBBIE JO

My name is Robbie Jo Ridgemont, I'm fifteen years old, and I'm lucky enough to know exactly what I am. That's more than most folks can say at twice my age.

It's not like anybody up and told me. I had to find out for myself. The signs were all there, I guess. I used to set fires all the time when I was just a little girl. Damn near drove my mama to distraction. I took apart a mouse or two in my time, not to mention all the squirrels I shot. Oh, I know what you're thinkin'. Ever'body shoots squirrels. Well, not ever'body shoots 'em in the ass, then nails 'em to a tree to watch 'em squirm and bleed. And I'm a little ashamed to admit that I peed my bed from the time I was four until the summer I was ten. I always figured I was different, I reckon. I just didn't know how different.

But awhile back, somebody sent money to little ol' Possum Kingdom High School for some brand new computers. (Bless you Bill Gates, you geeky sumbitch.) All of us backwoods teenage rednecks were introduced to that incredible constellation of ideas called the Internet.

Of course, I had to look up most of the good stuff when the teacher wasn't around. So I volunteered to work in the library after school. Good ol' Robbie Jo always got her nose in a book. That's what they all said. And nobody thought about it twice.

Now, just imagine how lonely I'd be if I didn't have the Net. I woulda figured out what I am; I'm not stupid. But I mighta thought I was the only one. Even if I knew better, who would I have had to look up to? Husband poisoners and baby smotherers. Black widows and angels of mercy. Women enslaved by evil men; helpless victims in the clutches of all-powerful masters.

Take Caril Ann Fugate, for instance. You know, Charlie Starkweather's dumbass babychicky girlfriend. A fourteen-year-old tootsiepop so weak and pitiful that she followed a squirrel-brained, bandy-legged, four-eyed garbageman with a lisp all around the country, helpin' him shoot eleven people. Girl was so dumb she couldn't spell "flu." Really, she got it wrong in the note she left on her parents' door after Charlie shot 'em fulla holes. Girl was so ignorant she named her black dog "Nig." Is that who I wanna be? Shit, no.

Or the one they said was the first, that alcoholic, drug-addicted, bulldyke whore in Florida. Pickin' up yahoos and morons at the truck stop, drivin' 'em out into the woods and blastin' 'em fulla more holes than a buckshot chipmunk. Probably screamin' at her daddy the whole time. "You'll never hurt me again! You'll never hurt me again!" BLAM! BLAM! BLAM! BLAM! BLAM!

Forgive me, Aileen honey, but I wanna be a little more than that.

They say knowledge is power. It's more than that, by God. It's a weapon. It's a shotgun to blast your way out. It's a meathook to climb over the dead-alive mouth-breathin' motherfuckin' idiots that life piles in front of you like a damn compost heap. And the Internet? It's pure, undiluted, eighty-proof knowledge shot directly into your vein through a telephone wire.

It was the Internet that told me about Jane Toppan. Just four years after Jack the Ripper killed a measly five prostitutes in London, A nurse in New Hampshire named Jane confessed to poisonin' thirty-one people. Turned out her total was closer to a hundred; she was just bein' modest. Another misguided angel, you think? Puttin' old folks out of their misery? I'm afraid not. As Miss Jane put it: "This is my ambition: to have killed more people—more helpless people—than any man or woman who has ever lived." Well, you didn't quite manage that, Jane, but it was a damn good try.

But she was just a poisoner, right? Women just don't have it in 'em to really whack somebody. Well, tell it to Belle Gunness. She dosed, burned, bashed, hacked and dismembered her way through forty-five adults and four kids before she was found out and had to blow town. But you know what? She got away, that Belle. Who knows how many more she got before she died a free woman. Did Ted Bundy manage that? Did that fat ol' jackass John Wayne Gacy?

Let's talk sheer numbers. Let's talk about Countess Elizabeth Bathory. Back in medieval times, life was pretty cheap, but the Countess racked up a total that would impress just about anybody. She killed six hundred and ten peasant girls, torturin', cuttin', bitin', rippin' and slashin' 'em, dancin' in the rain of their blood like a moonstruck coyote. If you'll excuse me sayin' so, I think that's a higher score than any of the boys have ever hit (unless you count political leaders, and ever'body knows they have an unfair advantage). Elizabeth made Andrei Chikatilo and Henry Lee Lucas look downright pathetic. Made 'em *look* pathetic, hell. They *were* pathetic. A limp-dick ol' pervert and a white trash bean-brain with a droopy eyeball, for God's sake.

But the world's packed with bean-brains, isn't it.

People are so ignorant it just makes me sick. How stupid they are, not to realize how dangerous women can be. When we're bad, we're not just mean. We're bone-vicious. You better be afraid of us, you. Watch your back. Watch your front. Watch your food and your water and the brakes on your car.

Or better yet, don't. Just stay ignorant. It'll make things so much easier for me. I've only got one under my belt, but I'm gonna have more. So many more. And let's face it, people suck. I'll be doin' the world a favor.

I still can't get over Caril Ann namin' her dog Nig. I just can't get my brain around how some folks hate others for the color of their skin, or what church they go to, or who they like to do sex with. It just doesn't make sense. You don't have to hate folks because they look or act diff'rent. Just hate 'em because they're people, and people, to quote the Cramps, ain't no good.

I hate ever'one equally. People are all the same to me.

After all, ever'body on Earth is just as wet and red and juicy as a cherry, on the inside.

ROBBIE JO, ROSE, AND NANCY

"Isn't that just somethin'?" Robbie Jo giggled, pointing at the scene painted on the window of Possum Pete's Café.

"It's somethin', all right," said Rose. The painting showed a big, fat possum with a checkered bib around his neck, grinning ear-to-ear, holding a knife in one pink paw and a fork in the other. The possum was poised over a plate heaped with what looked like meat loaf and peas. The whole thing sort of looked like a Tex Avery cartoon, right down to the crazy look in the critter's eyes.

"Don't worry," said Robbie Jo. "The food looks a mite better than that." She held the door open for Rose and Nancy.

The lunch hour had passed, and the café was nearly empty. A lone diner sat in a corner booth, reading from a thick book. He didn't look up when the girls walked in.

Robbie Jo plopped down on the red vinyl seat of a booth by the window. Nancy sat down next to her. Rose realized that she hadn't heard Nancy say a single word.

There was a moment of awkwardness. Rose looked around, at the green faded plastic tiles, the much-repaired booth cushions, the tablecloths with little barns and chickens embroidered around the edges. She was relieved to find an "A" health card behind the cash register.

"So," said Rose. "Does a guy named Pete really own this place?" She immediately cursed herself for her own lameness.

Robbie Jo shook her head. "He did, but Pete died a long time ago. Now his son Jake runs it. Hey, JAKE!"

Robbie Jo had a yell like a pro-league cheerleader. The guy in the corner just about jumped out of his skin.

"Sorry, Rev," Robbie Jo smiled.

The man smiled tightly and raised his hand. He was young, in his late 20's, but his round, smooth face looked tired and strained. His smile didn't reach his pale blue eyes. He ran his hand through his thin dark hair, and went back to reading.

"That's the Rev'rend Thomas Rye," Robbie Jo whispered, none too quietly. "He comes in here to read his Bible every afternoon. I think he's hooked on the biscuits."

"He doesn't look very happy," Rose mused.

"He's not. He just opened the Wounds of Christ Baptist Church a few months ago, and nobody's goin' there."

"Why not?"

"We've already got a church. Church of the Holy Blood. Rev'rend Primus, now, he can belt out a sermon. When he gets goin', you can just about feel the flames of Hell lickin' at your backside. And then there's the snakes."

"…Snakes?" Rose had the feeling she had lost the thread of this conversation somewhere.

"Holy Blood's a snake-handlin' church. You know, folks get the Spirit, and then they dance with rattlesnakes, and the critters don't bite 'em. They drink poison, and it doesn't hurt 'em." Robbie Jo shook her head. "Let's face it, Rev'rend Thomas is nice and all, but it's pretty damn hard to compete with rattlesnakes. They're downright entertainin'."

Rose let out a snort of laughter, and immediately regretted it. "I'm sorry. It's just that, well, we don't have anything like that where I come from."

"And where is that?" Robbie Jo leaned across the table, looking Rose in the eyes.

A middle-aged man with a pot belly and slicked-back blond hair slapped a couple of one-page menus on the table. He regarded the girls with eyes the color of dried mud, then started to turn away.

"Just a minute, Jake. We're ready to order." Robbie Jo smiled at him. Rose frantically scanned the menu.

"I'll have a basket of fries and an ice tea," said Robbie Jo.

"I want a piece a' peach pie." So Nancy had a voice, after all. It was thin and high, as if she had to work to make any noise whatsoever.

"Um…I'll have the cheeseburger, and fries, and a Coke." Rose looked up at Jake and realized he was staring at her. Had he just noticed that she was a stranger in town? Suddenly irritated, Rose locked eyes with him. He turned and shambled into the kitchen.

"Sorry, Rose, honey," said Robbie Jo. "I didn't mean to rush you, but if we'd let ol' Jake get away, it'd been suppertime before we saw his fat ass again."

Nancy laughed in her mouse-voice. Rose grinned. There was something funny about hearing Robbie Jo curse, with her soft, southern accent.

"So. You were about to tell us where you're from!" Robbie Jo's weird eyes sparkled.

"I'm—I'm from Miami."

Rose was shocked to hear herself telling the truth. *Oh well. What could it hurt? None of these people know me.*

"My goodness, really? It must be so wonderful to live in a place like that. A big city, I mean. It must be just like livin' on a TV show."

"Robbie Jo loves TV," Nancy piped. "She only gets to see it at my house. She doesn't have any 'lectricity in hers."

Robbie Jo sucked in air. Her eyes cut sideways at Nancy with a razored glint of anger. It was then that Rose noticed Robbie Jo's clean but almost-worn-out overall shorts, her thin, holey white t-shirt. And Nancy's brand-new yellow sundress. She felt a pang of empathy for Robbie Jo, and suppressed the urge to kick Nancy's skinny butt.

I'll just change the subject.

"Miami's okay," Rose said, smiling at Robbie Jo. "It's hot."

"But you can just go to the beach when you get hot! Just jump right in the ocean, wearin' a tiny little bikini. Are there really people in bathin' suits on roller skates, like on—" Robbie Jo cut herself off, glancing at Nancy.

And Rose wanted to tell her. She wanted to tell Robbie Jo all about the sights and sounds, about the spicy smell of Cuban food in her neighborhood, the impossibly tall, skinny palm trees, the beach at night, the taste of salt in your mouth when the wind blew. She searched for the words, and they swirled around her, but wouldn't come together and dance. She didn't have the words to describe Miami. How could she, when she'd never really seen it, except through the black bubble of misery that was her life there.

"Yeah, there are. There sure are."

"Wow," Robbie Jo sighed. "I'm gonna go places someday. I'm gonna go all over the world, and meet all kinds of people."

"Me, too," said Nancy, looking at Robbie Jo.

Rose recognized the look on her face, the longing in her small brown eyes. Hero worship. Nancy wasn't a rich-bitch; not on purpose, anyway. She was a not-so-bright little girl who wanted to be Robbie Jo more than anything in the whole world. A little smile quirked Rose's lips.

"I love your t-shirt," Robbie Jo grinned. "I'm a big Cramps fan."

"She's got three Cramps tapes," said Nancy proudly. "I got her a tape player for her birthday. It runs on bat'rees, 'cause she can't plug it into the wall at her house."

Robbie Jo stared at the table.

Jesus, thought Rose. *Why does she put up with that dipshit?*

"Which one's your favorite?" Rose asked.

Robbie Jo looked up. "A Date With Elvis."

"Mine too! What's your favorite song?"

"How Far Can Too Far Go," said Robbie Jo without hesitation.

Rose nodded. "I love that one too. And 'What's Inside a Girl'." She immediately blushed.

"Ha! You're somethin', aren't ya. Who else you like, Rose?"

"Well, the Reverend Horton Heat. I think he's the best guitarist alive."

Robbie Joe grinned. "And he sure is sexy! I'd take a ride in his big blue car anytime." She waggled her eyebrows, making Rose laugh.

Jake rolled up with their plates of food balanced on his hairy arms.

The cheeseburger looked terrific; big and thick, lots of lettuce and fresh tomatoes. In fact, everything looked pretty damn good. Rose noticed Robbie Jo eyeing the cheeseburger with an unreadable expression.

"What is it? Are these made of ground possum or something?"

"Nah," said Robbie Jo. "But there might be a little bit of chipmunk in there. They were nice and fat this year." She didn't so much as crack a smile.

Is she serious?

"But, um, really, are they any good?" Rose had no intention of biting a chipmunk.

It was Nancy who answered. "Robbie Jo wouldn't know. She doesn't eat meat. She's a vegetarian." She took a ladylike nip of her pie. Robbie Jo nodded and drowned her fries in about half a bottle of ketchup.

"Wow, really? Isn't that, well, kind of unusual in this part of the country? I mean, I thought you had to eat several gallons of sausage gravy a year just to keep your Tennessee membership card." Rose smiled, hoping she hadn't offended Robbie Jo. Once again, her smartass reflex had fired off without her permission.

Robbie Jo laughed. "I keep a funnel under the table, so I can sneak mine to the dawg." Rose cracked up.

"You don't got a dawg, Robbie Jo," said Nancy, looking perplexed.

"It was a joke, Nance," Robbie Jo sighed. "And yeah, I guess people think it's pretty weird, my not eatin' meat. I just have strong feelin's about it."

"You're into animal rights?" Rose took a huge bite of her burger. It was wonderful; juicy, greasy, just right.

"Well, not exactly. I just think that death has its place, but not in my mouth."

Rose swallowed, and the burger seemed to have gone dry.

Robbie Jo laughed again, tossing her shining ponytail. "I'm sorry, honey. I didn't mean to gross you out. Good lord, sometimes I let my mouth just run away with me." She dug into her basket of fries, getting her fingers all red and sticky.

"No problem." The burger was good again, and Rose ate like a starving coyote. When her stomach stopped howling, she spoke again.

"So, um, tell me, Robbie Jo, do you know of a guy out in the woods who, uh, skins animals?"

Robbie Jo cracked up, as if Rose had told the funniest joke in the world. "Don't tell me you ran into Joe Reecher! What did that ol' reprobate do to you?"

"Nothing, really, but I came across his house…and there were these animal skins nailed up all over the place, and this dog was eating a pile of guts in the front yard, and he came out with a gun and tried to shoot it…"

After a few minutes, Robbie Jo finally stopped laughing. "I'll bet he just scared the jumpin' bejeezus out of you, girl! But don't you worry about him. He's a harmless ol' coot. Unless you happen to be a fur-bearin' mammal, that is."

"What does he do with all those skins?" Rose wondered, thinking of the tiny ones.

"Well, he tried sellin' 'em at the general store, but Mr. and Mrs. Tanner didn't like havin' 'em around much, and nobody ever bought 'em anyways. So he started goin' around and tradin' 'em for food. Nobody wanted the damn things, but they didn't want Joe to starve neither, so they gave him the food and took the hides anyway. Then he started given' 'em to ever'body as presents. There's not a house in Possum Kingdom that doesn't have at least one critter hide moulderin' away in a closet or attic."

"We don't," said Nancy, sounding hurt.

Robbie Jo smiled at her and nudged her with her shoulder. Nancy lit up like a hundred watt bulb.

"How about the Tanners? Are they as nice as they seem?" *Can anybody be that nice?*

"Oh, yes, I'm afraid so. Just ever'body likes 'em. All the kids hang out in the store, and they don't even care. Sometimes Mrs. T. gives us free sodas and stuff."

"That's cool," said Rose. *Want a piece of candy, little girl? Want a ride in my car?*

"How old are you?" Nancy asked.

Unbelievable, she thought of a question by herself!

"I'm seventeen." *Oh, shit. I told the Tanners I was eighteen. Oh well…*

"Are you a senior? Me and Robbie Jo are fifteen. We're gonna be juniors next year."

You're gonna be dull for the rest of your life, thought Rose. "I just graduated." Her eyes stole to her tapestry bag on the floor beside her. She remembered in a series of flashes; standing in a huge line of other students, sweltering in her purple nylon graduation gown. Smiling and taking her diploma under the football field's glaring phosphorus lights. Slipping out behind the bleachers instead of sitting down with the rest of the new graduates, hearing the monotonous litany of names being called as she sneaked into the girls' locker room. Tearing off the gown and stuffing it into the tapestry bag, already packed, hidden under a changing bench. Heading for the highway. Hoping to God he hadn't noticed her leaving.

Did he look for her? Did he walk through the oceans of kids, squinting, scanning, getting angrier and angrier...

"Well, that's marvelous," said Robbie Jo. "I'm jealous. I can't wait to get out of high school. I want to get on with it, you know? I've just got so many plans."

I wish I had just one, thought Rose. Robbie Jo was watching her, almost studying her. It made Rose nervous. Next would come the personal questions, the ones she had no intention of answering. So, a preemptive strike.

"Who in the hell was that guy who almost turned me into roadkill? Does he always drive like that?"

Robbie Jo grinned. "He sure does. That was Sam Dunwiddie. He's the son of the folks who own the Sweet Hereafter Funeral Home. Oh, he just drives his parents insane."

"What, they don't approve of vehicular homicide?"

"You wouldn't think they'd mind, would you? I mean, it *would* increase their business..." Robbie Jo smiled mischievously. "But it's not just that. He's their only son, and he's not exactly what they bargained for. Oh, he's smart and all. He went and got himself a degree in business over to Memphis. But he drinks some, and he's always tryin' to change the way they do things in the mortuary. Old Mr. and Mrs. D. just hate that. Worst of all, he's twenty-five, and still not married!"

"He drives like a goddam psycho," Rose grumbled.

"That he does, but you should see the man! He's just gorgeous. He's got eyes as green as new grass, and this curly black hair just like a Greek god. He's tall and he's got these shoulders—he looks just yummy in those black suits undertakers have to wear. And his smile could melt butter in January." Robbie Jo and Nancy giggled. Rose was surprised at the greedy look in Robbie Jo's eyes.

"I don't care if he looks like Brad Pitt's baby brother. He almost pasted me, and he hit that poor dog!" Rose bit a French fry savagely.

"Oh, that ol' dawg will be okay. I know he scared you to death, Rose, but try not to judge Sam too harshly. He's not so bad, once you get to know him."

SAM, SAM'S FOLKS, AND THAT POOR OLD DAWG

"You almost killed someone, you God-forsaken eedjit!" thundered Ephram Dunwiddie at his only son. "You act like a common hoodlum, boy! Don't you have any respect for your family name?"

Sam glared at his father and strode through the parlor of the Sweet Hereafter Funeral Home. He threw open the door to the casket showroom and stomped in. Ephram was right on his heels.

"Don't you have anything to say for yourself, Samuel?"

Sam rested his elbow on the shiny silver Heaven Cloud 600 Luxury Casket. "She shouldn't have been in the road. Ever'body 'round here knows enough to stay out of the road, for Christ's sake." Scowling, he toyed with the coffin's frothy, creamy silk lining.

Ephram drew himself up to his full six-foot-six and glowered at Sam. His eyes were like ice-blue lasers. "I see. So it's fine to run over strangers, because they're too ignorant to live. Is that about the long and short of it? And stop fondlin' that casket. You'll get your greasy fingerprints all over the satin."

Sam sighed and rubbed his temples. His father was such a pain in the ass. He'd just tell him to fuck off, but then he wouldn't inherit the Sweet Hereafter. "Give me a break, Daddy," he mumbled.

"We've given you nothin' but breaks, Sam. And you just take and take and take." The two men stared at each other.

Ruth Dunwiddie strode through the parlor door. She stood next to Ephram, the two of them forming a wall of chilling disapproval. Sam found them amusing; two tall, well-bred, well-dressed, old-time Southerners. His father with his black suits and ridiculous string ties. His mother with her gray Gibson Girl hair and long lacy dresses. Dinosaurs who refused to admit their extinction.

"Do you have any idea what you put your father and me through?"

Well, that was original, thought Sam. "I don't mean it, Mama. I'm just who I am, that's all." He gave her a charming smile, and managed to keep the sarcasm out of his voice.

"Oh? And who exactly are you, Sam? Why don't you tell me, because I'm sure I don't know any more." Ruth Dunwiddie raised one razor-sharp eyebrow.

"Oh, Mama," Sam sighed, shoving down a heaping pile of epithets.

"And that poor dog! You ran over a poor dog and you didn't even stop to see if it was all right. Is that the way we raised you, Sammy? Is it?"

The disdain in his mother's voice could cut steel.

"It was okay, Mama. It got up and ran off, didn't it?"

"To die, most likely." Ruth looked heavenward, as she did whenever she wanted Sam to know just what a disappointment he was.

Ephram put his arm protectively around his wife's bony shoulders. "We built this business from nothing, Sam. It's our whole lives."

How fuckin' sad, thought Sam, *to have death be your whole life.*

His dad wasn't finished. Not nearly.

"You're our only son. Our heir. When we die, the Sweet Hereafter will be yours. We just want to know that you'll take the responsibility seriously. That you won't soil the name that we've taken fifty years to build."

"'Course not, Daddy. You know I love the business too."

Ephram's stare was relentless. "I know you love money. You're a smart boy, Sam, but you're capable of being as shiftless as a stone."

Sam's teeth gritted together. "I'm sorry, Daddy. I really am. I'll drive careful after this."

His mother raised her chin, so she could look farther down her nose at him. "I would certainly hope so."

"Okay… I'm gonna go help Jimmy in the embalmin' room. We're gonna try out the new machine." Sam tried another smile. It bounced off his parents like rubber on concrete.

After an awkward moment, Sam left the showroom through the door marked "Employees Only." He walked down the long, L-shaped corridor to the embalming room. Jimmy wasn't there; he had a habit of going outside for a cigarette break whenever the Dunwiddies started screaming. Not that Sam blamed him a bit.

Sam was mad. He hadn't even managed to squash that ugly dog in the road. It wasn't much, but the crunch it would have made under his wheels would have made him happy, for a little while. But then his folks would have screamed at him even more, for getting innards and hair all over the front end of the hearse.

He crossed his arms and narrowed his eyes at the naked corpse of a fat old man on the embalming table. "Couple a' stupid, high-toned, stuffy ol' assholes," he growled. "And you know what? They'll prob'ly live forever."

The corpse didn't say anything, so Sam hauled off and punched it in the gut.

Thud.

The black dog had never felt such pain in her whole life. All the Man's beatings, all the kicks and punches and cigarette burns, could not compare. One side of her body was hammered with a deep, agonizing hurt that throbbed in her bones and filled her brain with red. The other side was on fire, where the skin of her shoulder had been scraped off on the unforgiving pavement. She ran and ran, but she couldn't get away from it.

And then her legs wouldn't work. She stumbled and fell, scraping her raw shoulder on a fallen log. She howled in misery.

The black dog lay there, somewhere in the deep woods. Eyes wide open. Panting. After awhile, she mustered enough energy to drag herself under a rhododendron bush and curl up into a tight little ball. It hurt too much to stay awake, so the dog went to sleep.

She didn't move for the next two days.

ROSE'S ROOM

ose walked slowly back to Tanner's General Store, enjoying the delicious breeze that caressed her face and hair. She was alone; Robbie Jo had gone off to Nancy's house, "to socialize a bit." Rose guessed that meant to watch TV.

Rose slung her bag over her shoulder, turned a little circle in the middle of the sidewalk. Her emotions were whipsawing between delighted gratitude and downright suspicion. People just didn't offer total strangers a place to stay, did they? People didn't ask you to lunch five minutes after you'd met them, did they? Rose wasn't used to taking anything at face value. Her own family life had been like a lovely porcelain mask on the face of a rotting corpse.

"Maybe they're just nice," she muttered. "There *are* nice people in the world, y'know."

Or so I've been told.

When she opened the door of Tanner's, Naomi beamed at her like a long-lost relative. "There you are, honey! Did you get enough to eat?"

"Sure did. I'm stuffed! They sure make good burgers over there."

"That's the truth, little girl. Are you ready to see your room?"

"That'd be great. I could use some washing up."

"Well, bless your heart! Come on, then." Naomi hung a, *Back in Ten Minutes,* sign on the screen door and lead Rose around to the back of the store.

Yup, this is it, thought Rose grimly, wondering why her feet were still walking. *Owen's back there waiting for me with a big old ax. I'll turn up in the meatloaf at Pete's tonight.*

But of course, he wasn't. There was nothing behind the store but a rake leaning on the wall, a broken wheelbarrow, and a graveled path leading through the trees. "This way, Rose, honey," said Naomi, smiling over her shoulder.

A little walking, then a house rose up through the green. "Well, there it is. It isn't much, but it's home."

Not much! Rose grinned. Nobody she knew had ever owned a house like that. It was a two-story, faded gray, semi-gothic looking farmhouse, with lots of windows and wooden shutters and scalloped trim on the roof. Sure, it was old, but it looked as solid as the hills.

"It's lovely," Rose said.

Naomi grinned. "Thank you, baby! You're a dear one. Come on in, now. Everything should be ready. I sent Owen home to change the sheets and air the room."

The Tanners' home, like the Tanners themselves, could have come from another era. Victorian floral wallpaper, wooden floors, antique furniture, and a parlor as warm and friendly as a hug. Rose smiled at the framed photos on the walls. Owen and Naomi in wedding clothes, grinning like the kids they were. Owen and Naomi and a fat, smiling baby. The baby a toddler now, with twin baby sisters. Another baby boy. Children at five, at eight, at twelve. High school graduation. The oldest son's wedding. A daughter's wedding. More babies. The other daughter's handsome groom. Rose was filled with a swelling, bitter-tasting envy.

Naomi sighed. "The kids all live out of state now. We surely do miss 'em. They drive down to see us pretty often, though. Of course, I think it could always be more often." Naomi laughed. Unsure of what to say, Rose nodded.

"Now listen here, young lady. You don't let your folks worry, all right? You can call 'em on our phone, if you want to. We don't mind."

"Are you naggin' that poor girl, Naomi?" Owen stuck his head into the parlor, grinning. "Come on upstairs, Rose. We've got ever'thin' all set for you."

Thank you, thank you, thank you, Owen, Rose thought, as she followed him up the wooden stairs. She was too tired to think up a plausible brush-off for calling home.

She closed her fingers around the banister, and found it worn so smooth it was almost glassy. It was fascinating.

Nothing in Rose's world had been so old, so well-built, so loved. Just run-down and cheap.

"Will this be all right, then?" Owen asked, eyes serious.

Rose looked around, at the antique cherrywood vanity, the big window with cream-colored curtains tied back just so, the carved cherry bed with sheets so white they glowed, the deep, richly smooth cherry wardrobe.

"Oh," she said. "Oh, yes." For a moment, she thought she would cry.

Naomi had bustled up the stairs behind her, and after fussing over the bedcorners, pointed out the door of the little bedroom. "The bathroom's right down the hall, last door on the right. The bathtub's nice and big, but you be careful, it's porcelain and a mite slippery. We put in a shower last year, and it works pretty well, but sometimes the pipes rattle. I'm tellin' ya, it can scare the beans out of a body at six in the mornin'!"

Owen patted his wife's shoulder. "We should let the girl rest."

"Of course we should, darlin'. Now Rose, there are three more rooms up here, two other bedrooms and a nursery. If you like one of the bedrooms better, you can sure stay there, but we'll have to change the beddin'."

"This is fine, Naomi. This is wonderful. Thank you." Rose sat down on the bed and dropped her bag.

"All right, then. Dinner's at six, if you're hungry for it. Just come on down to the kitchen."

Rose nodded. She stretched, rubbed the back of her neck. Suddenly she wanted nothing in the world as much as a hot bath.

"Let's go, sugar. We might have a whole line of customers at the store by now." Owen winked at Rose, and escorted his wife down the stairs.

A half-hour later, soaking in a clawed bathtub big enough to hold three of her, Rose leaned her head back and marveled at her good fortune. Her mind roved lazily over the day, skipping over the bad parts, savoring the good.

Robbie Jo. Robbie Jo was something. Smart, funny, pretty. Despite the age difference, Rose felt like they might become good friends. Real, true friends.

But what in the world was the deal with Nancy? Rose couldn't begin to figure out why Robbie Jo would hang out with a drip like that.

Charity, perhaps. Robbie Jo was a nice kid. Maybe she just felt bad for Nancy.

"You're a better woman than I am, Robbie Jo," Rose laughed, splashing her toes in the suds.

ROBBIE JO

Y 'know, some folks just need killin'. Ever'body knows it's true. It's just that most folks aren't willin' to admit it.

My daddy was one. He needed killin' for a long, long time. He probably needed killin' before he stuck his little pickle in my mama and made me, but what the hell, here I am!

I was ten years old when I murdered him.

Damn. Isn't "murder" just one melodramatic motherfucker of a word? In my daddy's case, I guess I prefer "exterminated," since that's what you do to bugs and rats. Or, I guess I could get technical, and say "drowned."

He'd been stickin' his big rough fingers in my itty bitty hole ever since I could remember, for the first ten years of my life. When my mouth was big enough, he started stickin' his dick in it ev'ry chance he got. I still get the horrors when I think about it. I couldn't breathe, I was chokin', he'd have me by the hair so I couldn't get away and he'd be whisperin' to me the whole time, callin' me his darlin', his angel, his little baby whore. Even his cum tasted like cheap alcohol.

I have no idea why he waited until I was ten to try to stick it in my pussy. But on my tenth birthday, he took me out to Two Fox Creek, you know, a couple miles upstream from the pond, where the grass is so soft and green and the water just kind of giggles over the rocks. He lay me down on my back and yanked down my little panties, tellin' me that he was gonna make me a woman, and how much I was gonna love it.

I don't know what was diff'rent this time. I started to just go away, to let my mind float off to somewhere nice like I always did. He was kneelin' over me, his cock hangin' down like some ridiculous, ugly, purple fruit. He was already breathin' fast, pantin' that repulsive, moonshine-and-rotten-teeth breath in my face. Then he spit on his hand and started rubbin' it on his pecker, and I just snapped.

I kicked him in the balls. I was barefoot, but it still musta hurt, 'cause he fell over sideways, howlin' like a snap-trapped coyote. I jumped up and started to run, but the creek was right there, and he was between me and the woods, so I stepped into the water and started hoppin' over the stones like a little ol' goat.

Daddy got up, and he was plenty mad. He was bellerin' and hollerin' and tellin' me he was gonna kill me, which I purely didn't believe. He never had the guts to do anythin' like that. Then he started yellin' that he was gonna beat me with his belt, which he did all the time, so I believed that part. I didn't much feel it anymore, cause I'd just go away like when he was pokin' and proddin' at me, but I was mad, too, and I wasn't about to give him the satisfaction of whuppin' on me, so I kept hoppin' over those stones.

Daddy hauled up his pants and started out after me. But he was drunk, like always, and clumsy even on a good day. He slipped on one of those rocks and fell face first into the creek. He knocked his head pretty good, but he was still awake. He was blowin' bubbles and tryin' to push himself up on his arms.

I'm not sure where I got the idea to sit on his head. But it seemed like a pretty fine thought at the moment, so I did. I just plunked my little bare ass down on the back of Daddy's pointy skull, and put all my weight on him.

Well, he took to thrashin' then, but I wouldn't get off his head, and he couldn't manage to get his feet under him. I started laughin'. I reared back and smacked his face against the rocks a few times, just for good measure. It was interestin', how fast the water could sweep away so much blood.

At first it was like ridin' a buckin' bronco. Then it was more like sittin' on a grounded catfish; just little twitches and shivers and such. Finally, he stopped movin' altogether.

I sat on him for a long while, still laughin' and gigglin' away. I'm not sure how long, but it might've been a whole hour. When my feet got numb from the cold creekwater, I got up and rolled Daddy over on his back. He looked just as stupid dead as he had when he was livin'.

Well, I worked up some tears, and went out to the tobacco field where Mama was workin', and told her there'd been an awful accident. I told her how Daddy fell and hurt his head, and how I tried to pull him out of the water, but he was just too heavy. Mama made a noise like I've only heard dyin' rabbits make.

Mama. There's another one who needs killin'. She let my daddy do all that stuff to me from the time I was a baby. She may not have thought she knew, but she *knew*. It's all over her face ev'ry time she looks at me. But when you're floatin' around in a haze of liquor all the time, it's easy to tell yourself you don't see the blood on your little girl's panties, or your husband lyin' in a puddle of his own puke.

She tells me Daddy had a job once, pickin' lettuce over in Jonesborough. And you know what? While he was off doin' that (supposedly), my mama was pickin' tobacco on the outskirts of town. And where was I? Where was little Baby Robbie Jo?

In a coffin on fuckin' stilts.

Mama's brother made this *thing* for her. It was supposed to be a crib, but it didn't have any bars on the sides, just wooden walls. It stood up on legs that were four feet high, and each leg sittin' in a coffee can fulla water, so's the rats and the bugs wouldn't get to me. My mama would put me in that thing, with a blanket and a bottle, go out to the fields at the crack of dawn, and leave me there until her lunch break. Then she'd change my diaper, give me another bottle, and fuckin' *put me back in* until she got off work.

I would scream my guts out, but we live in the middle of bumfuck nowhere. Nobody heard me but the varmits. After awhile, I started clawin' at the box all the time and my fingers would get all bloody and full of splinters, so Mama'd wrap my hands in rags before she left. Eventually, I just gave up. I'd just lie there and stare at the ceilin' until somebody came to get me out.

That all came to an end when I was a year and a half old, and I crawled over the wall of the box and broke my arm in two places.

You might not think a person could remember that far back, but I'm tellin' ya, I do. I remember it as one long, lonely, achin' hollow in my chest. I remember it as shriekin', throat-tearin' anger. I remember it as total and complete despair.

And if that wasn't bad enough, Mama kept the damn thing. She shoved it in the corner, and put laundry and stuff in it. It stood there, loomin' over me like some goddam monster, until I was eight years old. Then I drug it out into the woods and burned it to the ground. I danced around the flames, pretendin' that Mama was sittin' up there in the box, gettin roasted like a scrawny ol' chicken.

I ask you, what kinda person would do that to her baby girl? A worthless, brainless, slack-jawed, heartless whore, that's what kind.

I'd kill Mama today, right now, but she makes really good biscuits.

And who else needs killin'? Nancy Plum, and her fat mama too. Good lord, I'd be doin' the world a favor if I took that pathetic, watery-eyed girlie outta the gene pool. The best thing she can hope for is meetin' some sappy rich boy just as stupid as she is, and grindin' out one ugly, sappy kid after another until her ass grows to be the size of her mama's and her titties are as flat as flapjacks.

Though Nancy's mama's got a little money from her dead daddy's life insurance, she didn't have any friends, not one, until I sat next to her one day and smiled. I could smell her desperation like fresh baked bread—yum yum!

But I'm in a bit of a puzzle here. Y'see, I go over to Nancy's house all the time to watch TV. I watch ever'thin' I can, on every subject. My particular favorite is the Forensic Detectives show on the Discovery channel. Also "First 48" and "Most Evil" are a hoot. And then there's videos. I've seen "The Silence of the Lambs" fifteen times now. And how can I give all that up?

If I killed Nancy, her mama wouldn't let me come over anymore, now would she? I could kill 'em both, I guess, but then I'd have to hide the bodies, and I don't relish the thought of draggin' Mrs. Plum's gigantic severed hocks around the basement. Nancy I could just stick down the garbage disposal, she's such a scrawny little rag. Sure, it'd be fun, but I'd just have a few days to watch videos before somebody noticed they were missin', and the police would be all over the house. I can't even swipe the VCR and the TV, since, as Nancy so kindly pointed out to Miss Rose, we don't have any electricity in our house.

So what's a gal to do? Nothin', I guess, for now. But I'm puttin' my mind to it.

Back to that Rose. She's interestin', that one. So smart. So pretty. But she's hidin' somethin'. I see it, buried deep behind her eyes.

I suspect it's somethin' awful.

I'm gonna dig it out.

ROSE AND ROBBIE JO VISIT THE SWEET HEREAFTER

Rose awakened with a start and a cry, clutching the sheets, completely disoriented. For a long, scary moment she had no idea where she was. Then it all poured back in, and she slumped down in the bed with a smile on her face.

Goooooood morning Possum Kingdom!

She hadn't gone downstairs for supper last night, although she'd intended to. After her bath, she'd stretched out on the bed, just intending to rest for a few minutes. Instead, she sank like a rock into inky, velvety sleep.

Rose stretched extravagantly. She looked out the window at the deep green woods, bathed in pale morning light. Went to the bathroom, washed her face, and brushed her teeth for ages. Put on her only other pair of jeans and a clean t-shirt, and headed down the stairs, feeling outrageously happy.

The delicious smells of bacon and scrambled eggs wafted up to greet her. Her mouth watered like mad.

Rose poked her head into the kitchen, where Naomi stood in front of a huge old iron stove.

"Well, hi there, honey! Did you sleep well?" Naomi smiled over her plump shoulder.

"Sure did. I'm really sorry I didn't come down for supper. I guess I just crashed."

"Well, goodness, don't you worry about that. You must've been so tired! I'm sure you're just starvin' by now, though. Sit yourself down in the dining room and I'll be in directly with some breakfast for you."

Rose grinned. "Sounds fantastic. Can I help?"

Naomi chuckled. "Aren't you the sweet one? No thanks, honey, I've got it under control."

Rose ambled into the wood-paneled dining room. Owen was sitting at the table, looking at some papers. He smiled as Rose sat down. "Good mornin', sleepin' beauty."

Rose blushed. "I was tireder than I thought."

"And no wonder. Travelin's hard on a body. Are you hungry?"

"Starved," said Rose, hoping that she didn't actually drool on the lovely hardwood table.

Naomi came in with big platters of bacon and eggs. She set a smaller dish of eggs next to Rose. "Now, I made these for you special. They don't have any brains in 'em."

Rose's mouth opened, then shut again. "Um...excuse me?"

"We usually have brains 'n eggs on a Friday mornin', but since you're not from around here, I wasn't sure you'd like 'em. So I made you some eggs with no brains. Oh, you're welcome to eat the other too, if it appeals to you. But some folks just don't care for it." Naomi beamed. "Toast?"

Rose blinked, Twilight Zone music playing in her head. "Uh...sure."

Owen was grinning. "It's not as odd as it sounds. When they're scrambled, you can't really tell the brains from the eggs. They've got such a nice, rich flavor! Too much cholesterol, but what the hell."

He was right; the larger platter just seemed to contain only a mountain of yellowish egg. Rose squinted at it, trying to find gray matter.

"Eat your breakfast! Don't let it get cold, for heaven's sake." Naomi began busily dishing up food.

It was all delicious. Rose didn't work up the nerve to try the brains, but she finally managed to stop staring at them. The bacon was salty and crisp, the toast thick and buttery. *If I ate like this every day, I'd have a coronary by the time I was thirty,* thought Rose, chewing happily.

She was finishing her second glass of orange juice when somebody knocked on the back door.

"Well, who in the world?" said Naomi, getting up. She didn't peek through the curtains, didn't even ask who it was before she opened the door.

"Why, good mornin', Robbie Jo! Come in, darlin'! What brings you here?"

Robbie Jo stepped into the kitchen, looking a little self-conscious. "Well, Mrs. Tanner, I thought I'd see if Rose wanted to take a walkin' tour of Possum Kingdom with me."

"You bet!" Rose grinned. "Can I help with the dishes first, Naomi?"

"You're just an angel from heaven, Rose!" she chortled. "No, no, run along with your little friend. There's not much to clean up."

"If you're sure..." Rose stood up, feeling full and contented.

Owen kissed his wife tenderly on the mouth, brushed her cheek with his fingers. "I'm gonna go open the store, sugar."

"Be there soon, honey." Naomi looked into his eyes, and it was obvious that for that moment, they were each other's whole world.

"Let's go, Rose, and leave these lovebirds alone," said Robbie Jo with a grin.

"You sassy thang!" Naomi called after them.

Robbie Jo and Rose, walking down Main Street. The sun was shining, the air was warm and sweet, and Rose felt as clean as a newborn baby.

"Hey Robbie Jo, you know what the Tanners were eating for breakfast?"

"What?"

"Brains and eggs! I couldn't believe it!"

Robbie Jo nodded. "Oh, sure. Lots of folks like that stuff."

"Um...what kind of brains are they, anyway?"

"Chicken. It's really hard to fix, 'cause you need so darn many chickens for just one servin'. And gettin' the brains out is such a pain! You have to put all the chicken heads in a bowl and crack 'em one at a time, just like pecans."

Rose stared at her. "Really?"

Robbie Jo's pretty lips compressed. Then she burst out laughing. "'Course not, silly. They're usually cow brains, sometimes pig brains."

Rose shook her head. "'Scuse me for saying so, but YUCK!"

"Oh, I agree with you. I just can't stand the idea of eatin' somethin' that somebody's been thinkin' with. Even if that somebody's a cow."

Rose grinned. "You'd think that eating cow brains would make you start, I don't know, mooing in your sleep or something!"

"No doubt! And grass would start to look mighty tasty…"

"You might grow some horns, or an extra stomach or two…"

"Or lots of titties!"

The girls howled with laughter.

"So what are we going to see today, Robbie Jo?" Rose asked, when she could breathe again.

"People. I thought we'd go visitin'."

Rose frowned. "Visiting…but I'm not really dressed for it…" She looked down at her black Nick Cave t-shirt and dirty old sneakers.

Robbie Jo laughed. "Have you taken a look at me, girfriend?"

Rose hadn't, actually. Robbie Jo twirled around, holding out the hem of her threadbare, home-made blue sundress. She pointed the toes of her mangy-looking green canvas sneakers like a ballet dancer. "I'd say we look just fine, Rosie. I'd say that anybody'd be thrilled to have a visit from two such lovely and stylish young ladies. Wouldn't you say?"

Rose laughed. "I guess you're right. Hey, at least I had a bath. I don't know how you and Nancy could stand sitting across from me yesterday."

Robbie Jo nudged Rose's shoulder with her own. "Well, you might have noticed that we did sit upwind of you…"

The girls' laughter blended in with the shouts of children, the barks of dogs, the friendly shouts of one neighbor to another. Possum Kingdom was alive and kicking this morning. It seemed impossible that it had looked so deserted yesterday, even for a short time.

"Where to first?" asked Rose.

"The funeral home's right across the street…"

"Where that wacko is? The creep who almost ran me over? No way!"

"Oh, don't be such a fraidy-cat. Sam didn't mean to scare you. Besides, his mama and daddy will be there too. They'll protect you."

Rose shoved down a flash of anger. "I didn't say I was scared of him. I just don't want to see him."

"Well, if you're really gonna stay in the Kingdom for awhile, you're gonna run into him. You may as well get it over with now."

"Oh, all right," Rose grumbled. Her fine mood was fading.

The Sweet Hereafter funeral home could have come from the pages of a Flannery O'Connor tale. It was a true Southern mansion, antebellum style, both majestic and creepy. Rose thought it looked a lot like the one in that old Bette Davis movie; the one where Joseph Cotton tries to drive her crazy.

"Hush hush, sweet Charlotte, Charlotte, don't you cry," sang Rose, as they stepped onto the enormous porch.

"I love that movie!" Robbie Jo laughed, ringing the doorbell. "'Specially the end, where she drops the planter on those two and squashes 'em flat! CRUNCH! And then she gets away with it!"

"Go Bette go," said Rose, and then the door was opening, and there was this tall—*really* tall, handsome, imposing old guy looking down at them. Somehow, he fit his surroundings perfectly. He smiled, just a little.

"Well, hello, Robbie Jo. What can I do for you?" His voice was deep and rich, like an old-time movie actor. *And the part of the undertaker will be played by John Barrymore…*

"This is my friend Rose. She's new in town. I just thought I'd take her around to meet folks."

The old man sucked in air. "Rose—you must be the one my son nearly hit with the hearse yesterday. Young lady, please accept my apologies. I am deeply ashamed of Sam for doing such a thing."

Rose was suddenly very uncomfortable. "Oh, geez… it wasn't your fault, Mr. Dunwiddie."

"Nevertheless. Would you ladies like to step in for a moment?"

"We'd love to!" Robbie Jo beamed.

Yikes.

Rose had never been inside a funeral parlor before. She didn't know what to expect. She sure as hell didn't want to see any dead people. *Noooo way.*

The room she stepped into took her breath away. It was a parlor, complete with antique velvet couches, carved hardwood coffee table, and deep, inviting armchairs. Poppy-patterned rugs. Delicate knick-knacks on the walls. Not a coffin or a corpse in sight.

"Do sit down. I'll fetch my wife."

Robbie Jo flopped down on one of the couches like she belonged there. Rose sat down too, uneasy, embarrassed at feeling that way. Mr. Dunwiddie had vanished up the stairs.

"Isn't this just amazin'?" Robbie Jo whispered.

"It's lovely." Rose shifted to the edge of the couch. "Um, where do they keep the dead people?"

Robbie Jo giggled. "Oh, they're in the back part of the house; in the embalmin' room, or in a really big fridge. I've never been back there, but Sam told me all about it. Sometimes they're in the chapel, too, if they're gettin ready for a funeral." Rose pointed to a door with a stained-glass panel.

"Mm. Okay." Rose felt a little better, anyway.

"Breathe in through your nose, real deep."

Rose looked at Robbie Jo, then did it. The air was scented with something sweet and floral. Underneath that, though, there was something else.

"Can you smell that? It's formaldehyde." Robbie Jo chuckled. For a moment, in the light of a Tiffany stained glass table lamp, her eyes glinted a deep, liquid ruby.

Okay. That's it. I'm outta here.

Rose started to stand up, but then Mr. Dunwiddie and his tall, angular wife were there, smiling down at her.

"Miss Rose, this is my wife Ruth. Ruth, this is Rose—beggin' your pardon, young lady, but what is your family name?"

"Heron." Rose reached out for Mrs. Dunwiddie's offered hand. The woman's handshake was like limp celery.

"Pleased to meet you, Rose Heron. I'm sure Ephram has already expressed it to you, but we are deeply sorry about our son's shameful behavior yesterday. I hope you won't hold it against us." Ruth Dunwiddie sat fluidly down on the couch opposite Rose and fixed her with a pointed stare.

Rose took her in. She was a tall woman (nowhere near as tall as her husband, of course), and elegant in a displaced, old-fashioned way. Her gray hair was swept up in an elaborate style that hadn't been popular for a hundred years. Her dress was long, loose-fitting, high-necked and long-sleeved, a pale sea-green color. With her husband next to her, they looked like a turn-of-the-century tinted portrait.

Rose realized that Mrs. Dunwiddie was waiting for an answer. "Um...no, of course not. Forget about it." She did, in fact, want to forget about it. She wished everybody would stop bringing it up.

"Rest assured that we've spoken to Sam about it." Mr. D's voice was grim, his eyes hard.

Rose nodded. There was a long silence.

"Can I get you anything, Rose, dear? Some lemonade from the kitchen, perhaps?" Ruth Dunwiddie smiled, and it looked odd on her tightly-stretched face.

"Uh, no thank you—kitchen? You, um, live here?"

Mrs. D. nodded. "Oh, my, yes. This old place is huge. The business just takes up half of the bottom floor."

My. God. I don't care if it's the size of Rhode Island, they live in the same house with dead people.

"Daddy, listen, we need to order some more Abdo-Seal, and we're runnin' low on Viscerock—"

Sam Dunwiddie burst into the parlor, then stopped short, seeing the girls on the couch. A slow, lascivious grin crept over his outrageously handsome face. "Why, Robbie Jo. It's always such a pleasure to see you."

Robbie Jo smiled like a housecat full of cream. Rose's eyebrows went up. There was clearly something going on *there.*

Ephram Dunwiddie stood up to glare at his son. "Sam, this is Rose Heron, the young lady whose life you nearly ended yesterday. I think you have something to say to her."

Sam shot his father a barely perceptible poisonous look, then turned his megawatt smile on Rose. "Oh, dear. I am so very sorry, Miss Rose. I just didn't see you in the street there, you're such a delicate little thing. Will you accept my most sincere apologies?"

He was standing right in front of her now, hands folded contritely, giving her blatant puppy-dog eyes.

Sam was certainly everything that Robbie Jo had said he was. His hair was as glossy as black satin, his eyes a luminous, shining green. Lips curved and sensual as a satyr's. He was strangely pale, but the contrast with his jet-colored hair was striking.

What an asshole.

But Rose was sitting in his parents' parlor, and they were looking at her expectantly. Instead of saying "Fuck no, I don't forgive you, you lunatic," she mustered up a weak smile.

"Sure."

Sam seized her hand in his, and by God, brushed it against his lips. "Thank you. I don't deserve it, but thank you."

Oh, puke. Rose quickly slipped her fingers out of his cool, firm grasp.

Robbie Jo stood up. "Well, Rose, we'd best get goin'. We've got more folks to meet today."

Mr. and Mrs. Dunwiddie ushered them to the front door, with many pleasant words and nods and smiles. Rose caught Sam giving Robbie Jo a snaky look that could ignite wet kindling. And just before the door shut, she caught a glittering spark of anger in Ruth Dunwiddie's eyes, not aimed at her son, but at Robbie Jo Ridgemont.

ROSE AND ROBBIE JO VISIT THE DOGGIE DOC

Robbie Jo started laughing before they reached the end of the Dunwiddies' walk. "Was that just bizarre or what?"

Rose nodded. "Oh, yes…they actually live in that place? With the dead people?"

"Yep. And you know what? There's a crematorium not a hundred feet behind the house. You wouldn't believe the smell it makes, all that black oily smoke and all…"

"Yech!" shouted Rose.

Robbie Jo cracked up. "Oh, it's not as bad as all that. They don't sleep anywhere near the embalmin' room. And it's such an amazin' house! It has twenty-two rooms, Sam told me. The Dunwiddies are one of the richest families in East Tennessee."

"Then why do they run a funeral home? That can't be where they got their money."

"Oh, hell no. They're an old tobacco family. Mr. D's father opened the Sweet Hereafter some fifty-five years ago, because—get this, Rosie—it was his dream. I think Mr. D. took it over because his daddy wanted him to. He sure doesn't have to work."

"So why is Sam planning to take it over? So he can have someplace to get rid of the people he flattens in that death car?" Rose glanced at the hearse, lurking in the shaded driveway like a black, glossy predator.

Robbie Jo giggled. "That may be part of it. But he really loves the business. He's brought in all kinds of new equipment and stuff. He's started advertisin' in all the newspapers. They've already gotten business from Erwin, Jonesborough— even Johnson City! Ever'body knows the Sweet Hereafter is the finest funeral home in East Tennessee." Her eyes shone with pride.

Rose scowled. Robbie Jo was smart, nobody's fool, but she was awfully young. Sam had looked at her like a starving dog at a rare steak. And with looks like his, he could probably get Robbie Jo to do anything he wanted her to. She hated to see anyone—any young girl—taken advantage of in that way. A series of ugly memory flashes lit up her brain. Rose winced.

It's none of your business. Leave it alone.

Besides, Rose barely knew Robbie Jo. She didn't want to piss her off by telling her that the guy she was obviously crazy about was a phony, creepy, possibly homicidal little puke. Hopefully, Robbie Jo would figure that out for herself, before Sam ate her up like the Big Bad Wolf.

Robbie Jo tapped her shoulder. "Would you look at that?"

"What?"

Robbie Jo was pointing at the roof of the Sweet Hereafter. "That! You know what that is? It's one of those little bitty satellite TV dishes!"

"Oh. Yeah, I guess it is." Rose glanced at Robbie Jo, and took a step back. The other girl's eyes were glittering in the oddest way.

"Well, come on, Miss Rose. Let's get ourselves to the vet. I think I may be rabid." Robbie Jo giggled.

A little bell on the door of the veterinarian's office announced Rose and Robbie Jo's arrival. The waiting room was surprisingly big; a startling contrast to the fussy, gingerbready exterior of the mini-Victorian clinic. Somebody must have knocked down a few walls, Rose realized.

The waiting room itself was full of contrasts too. The newish blue formica tile floor and the delicate floral wallpaper. The modern receptionist's counter and the fan-shaped, Art Deco wall sconces. The pleasant look on the elderly receptionist's face and the sour, pinched expression sported by the obese woman on the waiting bench.

Jesus, thought Rose. *Even her canary looks pissed.*

"Hello, girls," said the receptionist, blinking owlishly. Her voice was like a rusty hinge. "Can I help you?" The woman's small, wet eyes were so clouded with age it was impossible to tell their color.

"Hi, Miss Lyndon," said Robbie Jo. "This is my friend Rose. She's new in town. Is Doc around?"

"That's what I want to know," snapped the woman on the bench. "I've been waiting here for forty-five minutes."

Robbie Jo looked over her shoulder and gave a pained little smile. "Hi, Mrs. Granger." The woman narrowed her black eyes and said nothing.

"Doc should be out any minute," rasped Miss Lyndon. "He's been operatin' on a poor little cat he found caught in a snap-trap." Her mouth bowed up into a yellow-toothed smile. "It's nice to meet you, Rose."

"A stray," Mrs. Granger spat, before Rose could get out a word. "I said it before, and I'll say it again. A stray shouldn't come before Mr. Tweet-Tweet." She held up the small, square cage and gave it a shake, causing the ratty little canary inside to fall off its perch with an angry chirp.

Rose covered her mouth and pretended to cough, covering up a snort of laughter. Robbie Jo chewed her lower lip, eyes sparkling.

A door at the back of the room swung open, and a tall, slim guy stuck his head out. "All done," he said, taking off his glasses and rubbing the bridge of his nose. "I think the little fella's gonna make it."

"That's lovely," said Miss Lyndon.

Mrs. Granger surged to her feet. "It's about time."

"I'll be right with you, Mrs. G." He looked curiously at Rose and Robbie Jo. "What can I do for you, ladies?"

Robbie Jo took a step forward. "Hiya, Dr. Yeats. This here's Rose. She's new in town."

The vet crossed the room in a few long-limbed strides and held out his hand to Rose. "Dr. Michael Yeats. I'm very pleased to meet you." His grip was firm, and pleasantly warm.

Rose's heart did a weird flop-thump. Doc Yeats, she realized, was seriously cute. His eyes were a deep, soulful brown; intelligent and gentle. His hair was brown too; the color of walnuts, and silky as a child's. It was cut short in the back, but hung in soft bangs over his forehead. His face was long and fine-boned, his mouth wide and humorous.

"Ah—nice to meet you too," she stammered. He smiled at her warmly, making her mouth go dry. He almost seemed to be studying her, as if she were a critter on his exam table.

"That, um, that was really nice of you to try to help that dog...who was hit..." Rose bit her lip, suspecting she sounded like an idiot.

Dr. Yeats gave a solemn nod. "Poor little thing. She took a nasty bump. I wish she hadn'ta run away."

His voice was soft, light, and soothing. Rose imagined how it must calm his animal patients. The lazy accent of Possum Kingdom was starting to sound quite natural to her, as if she had heard it all her life. She wanted to hear more. "Do you think she made it?" Rose asked.

"Oh, I think so. She looked like a tough one to me. If she doesn't get an infection from all that hide she lost, that dawg ought to be okay. I just hope somebody finds her and takes her in."

Rose nodded. "Me, too." She locked eyes with the vet and something passed between them, although Rose wasn't sure exactly what.

"This is real sweet an' all, but I've been sittin' here for a goddam hour and I think you need to look at my bird right now, Doc, not later, *now*!" Mrs. Granger stomped her foot, causing her entire body to quiver.

Dr. Yeats blinked. Irritation flickered over his face and vanished. "Certainly, Mrs. Granger. Bring him on back. See you later, Rose." He gave her another smile, turning her insides to jelly.

Shee-it. What the hell's wrong with me?

"Let's go!" said Robbie Jo, patting Rose's shoulder.

"Bye, girlies," Miss Lyndon called after them.

Robbie Jo didn't wait until the door shut to start ribbing Rose. "And just what was *that*, may I ask? Your tongue was practically hangin' out of your mouth."

"It was not," said Rose, blushing hotly. She had never, literally never, reacted to a guy like that before.

"Well, I don't blame you. Doc's awful sweet. He's nice-lookin', too, if you like those tall skinny types. And he's not that old, either. I don't think he's even thirty yet."

"Oh, geez, Robbie Jo, I'm not gonna marry the guy."

"You never know," Robbie Jo laughed.

"Who was that total bitch with the skeevy bird?" Rose asked, changing the subject.

"Effie Granger? Oh, she's just pretty much what you said. An ol' bitch. She was always foul, but when her husband died four years ago, she got downright impossible. Ever'body said he died of a heart attack, but if you ask me, she just plain bitched him to death."

"At least Miss Lyndon seems nice."

Rose grinned, not too pleasantly. "Oh, she's nice, all right. But she's also about a zillion years old. She can't see worth beans, and she's half deaf. She's always double bookin' appointments and losin' critters' charts and stuff. But Doc's just too nice to let her go."

"Well, that's pretty cool of him."

"Yeah, he just patches up her mistakes like they never happened. He pretty much runs the clinic by himself. Oh well, Miss Lyndon's not gonna last too much longer, prob'ly. Then he can get himself a real receptionist."

Rose let out a surprised little cough of laughter. "That's not very nice, Robbie Jo."

The other girl giggled. "Maybe *you* can go work for him after she croaks, Rose, honey. Then you could stare at him and moon all day long."

"Shut up!" Rose laughed.

"Well, come on, Juliet, the day's a-wastin'. We've got us more visitin' to do."

"Mm-hmm. What's next? Town hall, to visit the mayor?"

Rose laughed. "This half-ass burg is unincorporated, darlin'. The closest thing we have to a mayor is Tobias Thurber, the town manager. He's also the high school math and science teacher."

"Is that big blue building the high school?" Rose pointed down the road.

"Yep. Also the junior high, the elementary school, and the kindergarten."

"You're kidding!"

"'Fraid not. We only had two high school classes last year. They just put the freshmen and sophomores together, and the juniors and seniors."

"Amazing."

"Amazin' but true. You really have moved to Dawg Ass Nowhere, Rose, honey. We don't even have any cops. Mr. Tanner is the actin' town constable, but he never has to do anythin' but occasionally break up arguments over somebody's goats eatin' somebody's crop of carrots."

"Well, geez, what do you do if there's a murder or something?" Rose was having trouble wrapping her brain around all this.

Robbie Jo laughed so hard Rose thought she might hurt herself. "Well, damn, I don't think nobody's kilt anybody in Possum Kingdom for the past fifty years. At least not that anybody's found out about. I don't think folks in this town would recognize a murderer if one reached out and bit 'em like a snake." She "bit" Rose on the shoulder with her hand, making her laugh, too. Then Robbie Jo turned and ran down the street. Rose ran giggling after her.

Robbie Jo, as she put it, made Rose "walk her legs plumb off." They visited old Doctor Vanguard Poteet in his tiny office. Once they got past Miss Verbena Combs, his large, rock-faced nurse, the elderly doctor was all smiles and warm Southern greetings. Rose had never seen anyone who resembled a crane so completely, with his long, skinny legs in highwater pants, cannonball-round belly, and long beaky nose.

They visited the Reverend Thomas Rye in his Wounds of Christ church, which was so new it still smelled like paint. The young preacher, not so stressed today, greeted them warmly and invited them to Sunday services. Rose couldn't take her eyes off the huge, garishly painted crucifix behind the altar. Jesus looked like Tim Roth with gas pains. The blood on his hands, feet and gaping side wound was an odd color of glossy orange.

They greeted ladies in sunhats, men in workboots, scabby-kneed children. Robbie Jo seemed to know everyone. Of course, it would be hard not to, Rose thought, in a town the size of Possum Kingdom. She couldn't decide if that was cool or creepy.

After drinking gallons of watery iced tea at the home of Mr. Tab Sasso, the short and dapper school principal, and sharing eternal, uncomfortable silences with Jerry McGraw, who delivered the mail and had one big eye and one little eye, Rose had decided the day would never end. That's when Robbie Jo stopped mid-step and declared herself starving to death.

"Have we visited everyone?" Rose asked, dreading the answer. She had never been much of a social butterfly.

"Yep," said Robbie Jo. "Let's get some dinner."

"Dinner? But it's only twelve-thirty, Robbie Jo!"

The other girl laughed. "Nobody eats lunch around here, ya damn Yankee. We eat breakfast, dinner, and supper! It's one of those redneck semantic thangs."

"I'm not a Yankee! I was born and raised in Miami!"

"So you claim, missy. Ya hungry, Bluecoat?"

"Sure," said Rose, when she was struck with a thought. "Robbie Jo, what about your house? Aren't we gonna visit your folks?"

Robbie Jo looked down at the sidewalk, her face turning pink. "Naw."

Rose bit her lower lip. "Robbie Jo—listen—I don't care if you don't have a lot of money. I don't, either. You should've seen the shithole where I lived in Miami."

Robbie Jo cut her eyes at Rose. "It's not that."

"Then what?"

The girl heaved a sigh and looked up, chin tilted at a defiant angle. "My mom's a goddam drunk, that's what."

Oh shit, thought Rose. *Poor kid.* "You know, my dad is, too."

I've never told anyone before.
Is he looking for me?
Is he?

To Rose's surprise, Robbie Jo grinned. "Damn. We're just sisters under the skin, aren't we."

"Looks that way," Rose answered, looking over her shoulder.

"Well, since you got an alkie in your family, you know what they're like. You don't really wanna go look at another one, do ya?"

Rose shook her head. "Shit no." For a brief, horrible moment, she thought she could smell his rum-soaked, too-hot breath.

"Then let's go eat, for God's sake, girlie!"

Possum Pete's, of course. It wasn't like there was much choice. There were a few patrons in the diner today. Jake was nowhere in sight, but at least there were menus on the table. Robbie Jo plunked herself down like she owned the place.

Rose picked up a menu, really reading it this time. She found herself alternately baffled and horrified. Corn pudding? Pork cracklin's? Fatback? Poke salat? Beans, beans, and more beans. Biscuits and gravy and an ice-cold co-cola.

Possum, in season.

These people are aliens. Rose shook her head and grinned.

Robbie Jo scanned the little restaurant with narrowed eyes, like a lion searching the veldt for something tasty. "Lessee…who's worth pointin' out…most of these people are just Joes and Joe-ettes, y'know what I mean?"

"That's rather uncharitable of you, Miss Ridgemont."

"Do I look like the fuckin' United Way to you?"

Rose was still laughing when Jake appeared, looking about as bored as a human can get. "What'll it be, girls?" he droned.

"My, my! You just purely snuck up on us, Jake, you stealthy thing!" Robbie Jo actually batted her eyelashes at him. A blotchy blush crawled up from his collar.

"Grilled cheese and a coke," said Rose. Surely they couldn't find a way to hide some possum meat in grilled cheese. Rose ordered fried green tomatoes.

"That guy," said Robbie Jo after Jake's loris-like departure. "There's somebody kind of interestin'". She pointed discreetly at a pudgy young black guy sitting by himself. He had a goatee; not exactly standard facial wear for Possum Kingdom. He rubbed one hand over his close-shaved head as he read a paperback with battling starships on the cover.

"That's Jimmy Liggett. He works for the Dunwiddies, over to the funeral home. He may be the smartest damn guy in town."

"What's he do for them? Accounting?"

"He's an embalmer."

"Yuck! Why would anybody want to do that?"

Robbie Jo laughed. "I just don't have him figured out. I mean, I think he gets paid well and all, but I can't understand why a guy with his brain power stays in a little pisshole like Possum Kingdom. Or why he plays with dead folks, for that matter."

She raised her hand and hollered, "Hey, Jimmy! What'cha readin'?"

The guy jumped, slamming his book shut. With a faltering smile, he held it up. "*Galactic Firefall*. It's pretty good."

"Got aliens in it?"

"Loads of 'em."

"Good deal." Robbie Jo laughed. "This here's Rose, Jimmy. She's new in town."

"It's a pleasure, Miss." Jimmy looked almost grave, as if he were meeting a foreign dignitary. Rose noticed that his coffee-colored eyes were very big.

"Me, too."

"We'll let you get back to your space war now!" Robbie Jo waved, and looked away.

Jimmy Liggett watched the girl for a moment longer. There was something strange in his eyes; an expression that didn't belong there.

If it weren't so ridiculous, Rose would have thought it was fear.

"Well," said Robbie Jo with a sigh, "I'd best be off. I'm s'posed to go to Nancy's tonight and watch the TV." She looked about as pleased as someone disclosing the date of her own execution.

Rose nodded. "I should check in with the Tanners, start learning about the store. I'm gonna start working tomorrow." She shook her head. "I still can't believe how nice they've been to me."

Robbie Jo smiled, long and slow. "Sometimes the world's a pretty special place, id'n it."

ROBBIE JO, NANCY, AND NANCY'S MAMA

So there was Robbie Jo, sitting on the grungy gold carpet in Nancy Plum's ugly living room, brain full of blood and murder. Nancy braiding Robbie Jo's hair, chatting happily about boys who would never look at her, girls who snickered behind her back, exotic places she'd never have the nerve to go. Robbie Jo was doing a fine job of tuning her out.

Instead she focused on the television, on the genial voice of the medical examiner, on the ruined, bloated hunk of flesh that was once a woman's torso sitting on the steel autopsy table. The medical examiner explaining how the killer of this woman had cut through her joints cleanly, with a hacksaw, about how that was easier, if you knew what you were doing, than sawing through solid bones. Robbie Jo was taking mental notes.

Nancy glanced up at the screen and cringed. "Jeez, do we have to watch this stuff?"

"It's almost over," said Robbie Jo. She knew Nancy wouldn't insist she turn it off. Nancy wanted her to stay there, to be with her. Nancy would let her do whatever the hell she wanted to.

Nancy's mother Sherleen waddled in from the kitchen. Robbie Jo's eyes narrowed at the neon glare of her tackiness; purple stretch pants, lipstick like bright red axle grease, huge, slick, polyester floral top that wasn't quite big enough to conceal the fact that the woman had rolls upon rolls of fat under there, like the bulging segments of a hairless caterpillar.

"You girls havin' fun?" Her voice had the same high pitch as Nancy's, but with an awesome lung power that made every word come out just shy of a screech. Sometimes Robbie Jo thought she'd rather have a hole bored through her skull with a rusty hand drill than hear that voice just one more time.

"You betcha, Miz Plum," she said sweetly.

"Well, good. I'll just bring you some co-colas and popcorn. Then I'm gonna tuck in."

"That'd be great!" Robbie Jo knew that "tucking in" meant that Mrs. Plum intended to drink a liter of root beer, eat a bag of chips and maybe some ice cream, take a Valium and pass out. Soon they'd hear her thick, gurgly snoring, loud and relentless as a hydraulic motor.

Nancy's cat Goober rubbed his side along the wall behind the TV, leaving even more black fur on base of the snot-yellow curtains. With a pop, the screen went black.

"You stupid cat! You unplugged the TV!" Nancy dropped Robbie Jo's hair and stood up.

"Aw, don't be mad at him. He's just bein' a cat. I'll get it." Robbie Jo stretched and crawled across the carpet. Goober emerged from under the TV stand and rubbed against her hands, purring noisily.

After she got past her early, childish compulsion to tear up anything capable of emitting blood and screams, Robbie Jo decided she liked cats. What wasn't to like? They were fantastic hunters, utterly without conscience. No morals. Despite what their owners might think, no loyalty. Whoever held the can opener held the key to their little hearts. Robbie Jo was certain that, if cats became the size of elephants overnight, they would hunt humans like they once hunted mice, pinning them shrieking beneath daggerlike claws, pulling their guts slowly and delicately from split, steaming abdomens, crunching their skulls like crispy kibble. The thought made her smile.

Robbie Jo scratched Goober's fat head and gently set him aside. Then she peered around the TV stand. Her nose wrinkled. She blew a mass of cat hair off of the electrical outlet before reaching for the loosened plug.

The outlet had a six-plug adapter in it, and it sprouted wires like an anorexic octopus. A couple of them lead to extension cords, which had even more plugs in them. Lamps.

Nintendo machine. VCR. Vacuum cleaner lurking dusty in the corner, evidently never used, but plugged in just the same.

Robbie Jo giggled. Did her brain look like that? Too many wires, plugged into all the wrong places? What would happen, she wondered, if her wires and plugs happened to overload? Oh, it would be spectacular, she knew that much. She took in a deep breath through her nose and smelled blood and smoke and sweet, burning flesh.

Robbie Jo replaced the plug and the TV came back to life. The autopsy show was over.

"Shall we watch the MTV channel?" asked Nancy timidly.

"Well...this movie comin' on next looks pretty good," said Robbie Jo. "It's called 'Freeway.' Okay?"

"Whatever you want, then." Nancy's expression was placid, resigned. Pathetically grateful.

Robbie Jo had the sudden, powerful urge to jump on her and snap her reedlike neck.

But that didn't happen. Nancy survived the night, somehow. Later, walking home through the woods in tarry darkness which her russet eyes pierced like lanterns, Robbie Jo felt something building up in her, behind her eyes, filling her mouth with drool.

She couldn't deny it much longer. She didn't want to.

I have to kill someone, she thought, hands shaking like a junkie's. *Soon.*

I have to.

I have to.

THE BLACK DAWG AND THE HANDSOME STRANGER

The sun was high before the dog stirred, whining, licking her nose with a parched tongue before ever opening her gluey eyelids.

She'd still be sleeping, if she weren't so terribly thirsty. Her whole body was a dull ache. She stretched, eyes squeezed shut with the pain, and got to her feet. At least she could walk.

The dog slowly bent around to lick the scab which covered one entire shoulder. Her mouth was so dry that her tongue stuck to it, taking away little bits of blood and skin.

She could smell water, not too far away. Stiff and slow, she walked toward it.

The pool was, at that moment, the most wonderful thing she'd ever seen or smelled. She shivered with pleasure at the cool of the water in her mouth, on her hot, dry nose. She drank and drank and drank, eyes closed in contentment.

At last she raised her head. Her nose was suddenly filled with the powerful scent of another dog. Growling, teeth bared, she whipped around.

He was standing at the edge of the woods, head lowered, staring at her. A little smaller than she was, maybe, but strong and healthy. Thick, thick fur. Eyes like the moon. Tail swishing slowly, ears back. He smelled like a dog, but not quite.

And he smelled like something else.

The black dog whined. She became aware of a strange heaviness low in her belly. A swollen warmth somewhere below her tail.

There was something wrong. Nothing like this had ever happened to her before. She wanted to run, but the weirdly compelling scent of the strange not-dog kept her rooted to the spot.

He walked toward her, slowly, tail still wagging. It was clear that he didn't mean to hurt her. What, then? What could he possibly want? The black dog flinched as he nuzzled her cheek, but he didn't bite.

The stranger buried his nose in the fur of her neck, licked her muzzle, nibbled at her chin. Irritably, she drew back, wiping her nose with her paw where he had tickled her.

While she was doing that, he crept around behind her.

She hated that. It made her afraid. The Man used to creep up behind her and kick her so hard she vomited. She wanted to run. But, to her horror, something else entirely began to happen.

Her tail moved aside, all by itself.

And then the not-dog landed heavily on top of her. Her sore joints screamed, and she grunted in pain. But it got worse. He jammed something inside of her body, and started shoving it back and forth.

The black dog tried to run, but the stranger gripped her tightly around the waist with his forelegs. She turned around to bite him. He was panting, eyes staring, tongue hanging out. She chomped one of his oversized ears. He didn't seem to notice at all.

And then she couldn't bite him again, because she was panting herself, overwhelmed with a strange feeling. This was something she had to finish, physically had to, like when she squatted and shit. Her head hung down, and everything was blank until the pumping of the stranger's hindquarters stopped. She breathed a deep sigh of relief when he got off of her.

Dazed, disoriented, the dog started to walk away. To her horror, she couldn't move. Whatever was inside of her was still stuck, and it had somehow glued her to the not-dog, butt to butt. She glared at him. He gazed back at her with an embarrassed, toothy grin.

She tried to sit down. She couldn't do it, and it made the stranger yelp with pain. She tried again to walk away. The not-dog growled, digging his claws into the soft earth.

The black dog licked her nose, closed her eyes, and waited for it to be over.

After what seemed like a terribly long time, the thing slipped out of her, and the stranger melted into the woods like a ghost. She wished he would come back so she could bite the hell out of him.

Exhausted, confused, and sore, the black she-dog sank down onto the grassy bank of the pond, and drifted into a heavy sleep.

She dreamed of resting her chin on the Woman's knee, of a soft human voice whispering love to her, of gentle hands stroking her head and ears.

SAM, ROBBIE JO, AND A DEAD GUY NAMED BOB

Someone surely would have died in Possum Kingdom that bright Saturday morning if Robbie Jo's mama Lureen hadn't made her biscuits with honey and sweet butter for breakfast. But she did, smiling sweetly at her daughter, swaying just a little from the fifth of gin she'd been nursing since daybreak. And because those biscuits were so good, all warm and flaky, and the butter so cold and creamy from the springhouse, and the honey so sweet and wild, Robbie Jo found herself in a fine mood. Instead of creeping through the backwoods in search of a stray hunter to dismember, she decided to have a walk through town. She'd smile at everyone she met, wondering how, exactly, would be the best and most fun way to kill him or her. Sort of like window shopping.

She was peering into the Baptist Church at the Reverend Thomas Rye as if he were a prime cut of steak when someone put a hand on her shoulder.

Robbie Jo spun around, teeth bared.

"Why, are you fixin' to bite me, pretty girl?" Sam Dunwiddie, smiling like a fallen angel.

"I've considered it." Robbie Jo transformed her snarl into a big, wide grin.

He took a step closer to her, giving her a snaky look through sooty lashes. "Are you flirtin' with me, honey?" Such a husky whisper.

"I suspect you know I am." Robbie Jo locked eyes with Sam. Lord, but the man was pretty. She didn't give a good God damn about him personally; in fact, she thought he was a weasely asshole. But he was sure something to look at, and with all the girls in town falling all over him, she was certain he'd had plenty of practice at sex. She'd decided long ago to use him to get rid of her virginity.

Today's as good a day as any, thought Robbie Jo.

"Mmm. I wonder if you know what you're gettin into," said Sam, brushing her hip with his hand. That was so funny Robbie Jo had to laugh.

"Should I be scared?" she whispered. "Are you the big bad wolf? Are you gonna eat me up?"

"Oh, my yes..." He bent his face down to hers, starting to slip his arms around her waist. Before their lips met, something started chirping in his pocket.

Robbie Jo drew back, mouth quirked up at the corners. "And what would that be, Sam Dunwiddie?"

He grinned hugely. "That's the grim beeper, baby."

Sam Dunwiddie couldn't believe his luck. He'd had his eye on the little Ridgemont girlie for months. She was so goddam cute, with her short, ragged dresses and long legs and sassy, fuck-me eyes. But he'd figured her for a cock tease, just another high school chickie full of talk but too scared to spread 'em. But she was looking at him right now in a way he'd seen before, in older girls, girls who stood before him naked and willing. She wanted his boybone, the little slut. And he was more than willing to share it. He'd give her all she wanted, and then a little bit more.

She was smiling at him like a hungry possum, all teeth and a little red tongue. "And what do you do, Sam Dunwiddie, when the Grim Beeper calls you?"

"I must answer, sugar. It means there's a stiff for me to go pick up in the ol' black bonewagon."

She looked at him from under lowered lashes. "Take me with you?"

Oh yes. The girl was his. She was as good as impaled on his dick.

A half-hour later, they were headed for Jonesborough in the big old Cadillac hearse. Normally the Sweet Hereafter would send two people to make a pickup in a private home, but Sam had talked his dad out of coming along. He could wrangle the grieving relatives himself, no problem. In a single story house, moving the dead meat around was no big challenge, either. Sam just hoped that Robbie Jo wouldn't freak out at the sight of a gen-yoo-wine corpse.

He watched as Robbie Jo wriggled her sweet little ass on the fine leather seat and played with the air conditioning vent. It was like the girl had never been in a nice car before.

Of course, she may not have been. If you looked in the dictionary under "Po' White Trash," you'd find a picture of the Ridgemonts. But that didn't matter, not really. Sam had long ago figured out that no matter how you dressed it, in rags or silk, pussy was pussy.

Sam began to chat with Robbie Jo, asking her about herself, her family, the past school year. It wasn't that he gave a good God damn. But girlies just loved it when you acted like you gave a shit about them, like you thought they were special. Besides, Sam loved to talk. He was a fine talker, possibly the smoothest talker in Possum Kingdom, and he liked to stay in practice.

To his surprise, Robbie Jo wasn't so bad at it herself. The girl was sharp as a pin, and funny. She had an edge to her sense of humor that Sam liked a lot. It reminded him of himself. But she wasn't *too* smart, not a brain or anything, and he could tell by the way she laughed at all his jokes that he had totally charmed her.

"Well, here we are," he said, pulling up to a little green house at the end of a quiet residential street. "I gotta go pick up the croaker."

Robbie Jo smoothed down the frayed hem of her baggy yellow dress. "You want me to wait here? I'm not exactly dressed for it…"

"Nah. Folks in the throes of grief have their heads so far up their asses they can't even see daylight. They prob'ly wouldn't notice if you walked in there naked." Sam patted her knee, experimentally.

She put her hand over his and arched her back, showing him the shape of her high little breasts. "Wanna bet?"

Oh, that sexy babybitch. He could almost taste her.

Sam jumped out of the hearse before his budding boner could gain a mind of its own. He opened the door for Robbie Jo, then opened the back of the hearse and pulled out the collapsible rolling gurney. He made sure the nice, white, starched sheets were in place, the headrest centered, the heavy cloth bag attached to the frame of the cot. Sam left the gurney behind the hearse, and gestured for Robbie Jo to follow him to the front door.

It was answered by a skinny middle-aged woman with wet, red eyes and a snotty nose. Sam put on his most sincere expression of sympathy. "I'm from the Sweet Hereafter Funeral Home, ma'am. I'm here to escort Mr. Bob Cameron on the beginning of his journey to his final rest."

Robbie Jo's eyes went wide, and her mouth did something funny. Sam realized that she had just suppressed a laugh. He was liking her more all the time.

"Cub id," said the woman, dabbing at her eyes with a thoroughly soaked handkerchief. "He's in the back bedroob." She blew her nose noisily.

Sam walked through the modest house, making sure the path of the stretcher would be clear. He encountered a clot of blubbering relatives in the kitchen, drowning their sorrow in chunks of sticky-looking coffee cake. He smiled sadly and sympathetically at them. Most looked at him with an expression of horror he had come to recognize and dismiss. He was the one who had come to take their loved one away forever.

Sam was proud of Robbie Jo. She walked behind him demurely, hands clasped, eyes sad and downcast. She could have been a professional mourner.

The scrawny woman opened the bedroom door and gestured, evidently unable to speak.

Sam could smell Bob Cameron well before he saw him. He wrinkled his nose in disgust. You could say what you wanted about the redneck rabble who lived in Possum Kingdom, but at least they had the sense to wash up their own dead. Town folks were just as likely to leave them in their own cold shit, which seemed to be the case here.

Bob was lying on his back in a four-poster queen bed, a well-worn blanket pulled up over his substantial gut to his chest. He looked to be in his early '60s, sun-creased skin, greasy gray hair sticking out all over his head. His eyes were half-closed and sticky looking. His mouth was hanging open, jaw slack and somehow sunken. It was an expression Sam had seen hundreds of times. Dead Bob was wearing blue pajamas with little red sailing ships on them.

Sam glanced over the death certificate signed early that morning by some local hick doctor (massive coronary) and gave the widow a release form to sign. All the while, he watched Robbie Jo in his peripheral vision, staring at the body. She had her hands still folded and her head down, but she was staring at it, all right. Her expression was totally unreadable.

Sam brought in the gurney and unzipped the transport bag. He locked the gurney down level with the bed and got ready to muscle the body onto it. To his absolute surprise, Robbie Jo grabbed Bob's legs. She didn't flinch at the cold that was creeping through the dead man's clothes, or the stiff, refrigerated-bread-dough texture of his flesh. In fact, if Sam was not mistaken, the girl actually squeezed Dead Bob's calf as if she were testing an orange for ripeness.

Together they lifted the corpse onto the gurney, and Sam zipped it up tight. He centered Bob's rocklike head on the pillow, and made a show of reverently draping him with the gleaming white sheet. The widow wordlessly gave Sam a scuffed little black suitcase. He knew what would be in there. Bob Cameron's Sunday best. He smiled reassuringly, squeezing the woman's cold, bony hand. "We'll take good care of him, ma'am." She nodded, fresh tears spilling down her hatchet face.

The wails of the bereaved followed him out the door like the ghosts of stray dogs.

Sam had had girls and corpses in the hearse at the same time before. It made the chicks nervous. They'd squirm around on the seat, leaning forward, as if to get as far away from the thing lying cold and still behind them as they possibly could. They giggled a lot, talked a lot, made stupid jokes. Filled the air with noise, so the silence wouldn't remind them of the silence that would one day be their whole world. If Sam touched one of them unexpectedly, she'd jump like a cat.

Not Robbie Jo. She was leaning back on the soft leather seat, hands behind her head, eyes closed. She hummed along with the tape he'd popped into the deck; dirty old blues songs full of heartbreak and fornication. When he patted her knee, she turned a lazy smile on him.

"You okay there, honey?" Sam asked her.

"Mm-hmm. A lot better than old Bob back there, anyway."

Sam laughed. Against his will, he was really starting to like the girl. He glanced over at her again and slowed the hearse down, pulling off on a wide spot by the road.

Robbie Jo rubbed the back of her slender neck and yawned. "What are you up to, Sam Dunwiddie?"

"Why, I believe we've run out of gas." He grinned at her slyly. "Would you care to go take a walk in the woods?"

She laughed, a musical giggle with a little edge to it. "Good lord. Does that really work on other girls?"

Sam felt his grin slip, just a little bit. "More than once, sugar."

"I see. Well, I don't think I wanna walk in the woods with you, Sam."

He scowled. Had she been teasing him, after all? He felt his face start to flush with anger. Robbie Jo patted his hand.

"Oh, don't get pissy. I want the same thing you want. I just don't wanna do it out in the woods where a weasel might bite my ass. Why don't you slide on over here and sit next to me?" She patted the seat with her little hand.

Sam blinked. "You—you wanna stay in the hearse? With Bob?"

"It's okay, Sam, honey. He promised not to tell." She winked at him.

You didn't have to ask Sam Dunwiddie twice. He was on that girl like a duck on a June bug.

It was obvious from her awkwardness that she didn't have much experience. Hell, maybe she'd never even been kissed before. But it was also clear that she was eager enough. Her hands were all over him; in his hair, gripping his shoulders, running over the lean muscles of his back. She nibbled at his lips as he kissed her mouth open wider and wider. Her tongue met his like a wrestling partner.

She didn't resist when he touched her peach-sized breasts through her thin cotton dress. She didn't resist when he unbuttoned it and reached inside, squeezing and stroking. She let out a tiny little moan when he nibbled her neck. A little bit louder when he started on her nipples.

It was hot in the hearse with the engine off and the windows rolled up. There was a pretty sheen of sweat on Robbie Jo's near-perfect skin that made her glow like a saint in the grip of revelation. Sam licked it from her neck; salty-sweet. He wanted to taste every inch of her. He wanted to own her.

She was breathing fast by the time he reached into her panties. His fingers felt silky hair, then her sweet little cleft, and wet wet wet. He rolled his finger around the bitty button he found there, just to make sure she was good and ready. Her gasps turned into little whimpers, which just about made his hard-on leap out of his pants and do a dance on the dashboard.

Sam slid Robbie Jo's panties down over her butt and pulled them off. Little cheap cotton things with tiny blue flowers along the elastic. He pressed them to his face for a moment, inhaling her musky, gingery smell. Then he grabbed her ass and pulled her onto his lap. His hard-on pressed against the inside of her thigh, agonizingly close to the Promised Land. Sam reached for his zipper.

"No," said Robbie Jo, and she started to pull away.

Sam grabbed her around the waist and pushed her down on the seat. He pressed his pelvis against hers. "It's okay, honey," he whispered in her ear. Again, he went for his zipper.

"Stop it, Sam," said Robbie Jo. She tried to wriggle out from under him.

He was starting to get very irritated, but of course, he couldn't let it show. "Don't worry, Robbie Jo," he breathed, giving her his sexiest smile. "I'm not gonna hurt you. You'll love it, I promise."

Robbie Jo shoved Sam away with a strength he never would have guessed she had. "I'm not ascairt of you, you eedjit." She sat up and started buttoning her dress. "I just decided I don't wanna fuck you in the car. Let's go someplace where we got a little more room."

It wasn't a request. It was an order. Sam grinned. This was one strange young lady. "Well, okay, then. Where do you wanna go?"

"Your house."

"My—I think my folks are there, Robbie Jo."

She wrinkled her nose, as if he were a little kid who said something embarrassing at a church picnic. "It's a big house, Sam. They won't even know I'm there."

He thought about it. Why the hell not? "Whatever you want, pretty girl." He started the engine and hit the gas so hard that Bob bounced off the back door.

Robbie Jo had her eyes closed, head leaned back on the cushy seat, when Sam pulled the hearse around behind the Sweet Hereafter and put on the brake.

"I gotta get old Bob here inside, honey, before he starts to stink even worse. Wait here, I'll come out and get you when I'm done."

"I wanna go in with you." Robbie Jo gave his crotch a little squeeze, so he wouldn't say no.

"You... You wanna go into the embalming room?"

"Sure do." Another squeeze, and a stroke or two.

Sam shrugged. "Suit yourself, sugar."

They took the gurney through the back door and down a long, tiled corridor. Robbie Jo could smell the formaldehyde before Sam ever opened the embalming room door.

It was just beautiful. The steel table in the middle of the room like an altar, channels for fluids leading to drains in the floor. Strange electric pump devices, hoses everywhere, dials and knobs and pressure gauges. Gleaming instruments; sharp scissors, long surgical clamps, scalpels, hooks, needles; big metal syringes from a 1950s horror movie. Shelves full of strange chemicals, jars of unknown glop with weird names. Abdo-seal. Edema Eliminator. Viscerock. Close-A-Wound. Cavity Wax. Robbie Jo started to giggle. Cavity Wax, indeed.

"What's so funny?" Sam grunted, wrestling Dead Bob onto the embalming table. Robbie Jo paused to admire the way his biceps bulged under his thin cotton shirt.

"Everything. All of it. All this stuff just to pretty up dead meat."

Sam grinned. "Don't you have any respect for the deceased, honey?"

"Shit, no. Like the Cramps say, 'there's nothin' on the radio when you're dead.'" She leaned over to examine a piece of equipment on the counter. An electric aspirator, according to its label. Designed by a company called Necro-Tech.

"You're a strange one, Robbie Jo." Sam, washing his hands in a steel sink, grinned over his shoulder at her.

"You have no idea, Sam."

He crossed the room in a flash and took her in his arms.

"So is it true?" Robbie Jo asked. "About the sin eater?"

Sam winced, as if she'd smacked him upside the head. "Oh, for God's sake."

"Then it is true."

"Yeah, it is. My folks insist on lettin' him in. I think it's fuckin' sick."

Robbie Jo laughed. "Sicker than drainin' the blood out of a dead body and fillin' it with chemicals?"

A sly smile from Sam. "We do a lot sicker stuff than that to 'em, baby. But yeah, what that boy does is just plain horrible. He eats food right off the croaker's chest."

"Boy? I thought the sineater was an old man."

"He was, but Jeremiah died. It's his boy Simon who does it now." Sam growled, low in his throat, and pulled Robbie Jo close. "Now let's get on up to my bedroom."

She kissed him hard, then pulled away. She snatched a foot-long hollow needle as thick as her forefinger off the counter. "What's this?"

Sam rubbed his forehead, looking a little irritated. "It's called a trocar."

"What's it for?"

"You really wanna know?"

"I wouldn't ask if I didn't."

"You use it to drain the fluids out of the body cavity and hollow organs, then again to inject 'em with embalmin' fluid."

"Tell me how it works." She rubbed her body against his.

"All right, honey. Don't blame me if it makes you sick." He leered at her, waiting for a reaction he never got. After a moment, he told her.

"You hook it up to that thing, the electric aspirator. Then you ram it into the abdomen, right about here." He touched her belly, a few inches up from her belly button, a little to the left. "You turn on the pump, and you start rammin' it into anythin' you can find. You gotta be sure to get all the juice out of ever'thin'—the stomach, the intestines, the heart and liver, all of it. It's not a pretty thing to see, and hear, all that nasty stuff gurglin' through the tubes. When you've drained ever'thin' you possibly can out of there, you hook the trocar up to the embalmin' machine, and fill the body cavity with a really strong preservative." He cocked his head, seeming to study her face. "Satisfied?"

Robbie Jo purred and licked his neck. "Not even close. What keeps all that fluid from leakin' out? I thought dead folks couldn't even hold their own water, much less all that stuff you fill 'em with."

"Jesus, Robbie Jo!"

"Tell me," she whispered.

He sighed. "Back in the old days, we used to pack 'em with cotton and wound sealer. But now we have these." He opened a cupboard and pulled something out of a little cardboard box.

It was a sort of white plastic rocketship, long and smooth on one end, and a cone with plastic threading on the other, like a giant screw.

"What the fuck is that?" Robbie Jo thought it looked like one of the sex toys she'd seen on the Internet.

"It's called an A/V Closure."

"A/V—as in anal and vaginal?" Robbie Jo started to laugh.

"Well, it sure don't mean audio/visual."

"A butt plug for the dead!"

"It's worse than you think. You have to screw it in."

Robbie Jo was howling with laughter now. "A butt plug for the dead!"

"You twisted little bitch." Sam had a nasty grin on his face, and a light in his eyes that would have made most people turn tail and run. He lifted Robbie Jo up on the counter, stepped between her legs, and kissed her.

"Tell me about it," she breathed. "Tell me everything."

So he did, in between the kisses and the bites and the squeezes. He told her about dissecting up the major arteries and putting in the draining needles. Pumping out the blood, pumping in the embalming fluid. Too much formaldehyde and the body's hard as a frozen turkey. Too little and it starts to stink. "Fluid distribution's an art form," he told her while unbuttoning her dress. "You gotta get the pressure juuuust right," while rubbing her between the legs. He told her about the staples in the gums to wire the jaws shut, the heat spatula on the inside of the eyelids if they're swollen, like cooking the blood out of a hamburger. She moaned. Plastic caps to keep the eyes nice and round under super-glued lids. Cotton up the nose. Wax and putty, rouge and powder. He sank down and buried his face between her legs.

Robbie Jo cried out, hands clutching his hair. She was right about Sam; the boy was good. He was doing things to her with his tongue that made it hard to breathe. And she felt something building inside her, something that made her pant and moan and wrap her legs around his head. She was close. So close—

And then he stood up and tried to plant his sticky mouth over hers. Robbie Jo snarled and tried to shove him back down.

"Uh-uh-uh, baby. It's time we made you a woman." She heard his zipper, and then he was pressing against the inside of her thigh, homing in like a smart bomb.

She grabbed his cock. She liked the feel of it; smooth and silky on the outside, hard as a chair leg underneath. "Hold it right there, Sam. You put on a rubber. I just ain't the teenage mother type."

"Oh, I dunno," Sam leered. "I can see you with my little ol' black-haired baby pressed to your titty."

Robbie Jo glared at him. "I'd prob'ly eat it. Put on a rubber or put on your pants."

He had one out of his wallet and onto his dick faster than you could say "rubber baby buggy bumpers."

He went back down and Robbie Jo tried to keep him there, but once again he popped up like a cork. Sam Dunwiddie wriggled himself between her thighs and in one practiced bump he was suddenly inside her.

It hurt. Holy fuckin' shit, it hurt a *lot*. Robbie Jo pitched herself sideways and reached for the trocar.

She could see it there on the counter, just waiting for her. If she could ram it into Sam's throat, she was sure his blood would shoot thirty feet. She leaned, hand outstretched. Her fingers brushed the gleaming steel.

Sam slid his hands down to her ass and moved in closer. He started rolling his hips in a fluid motion, ever so slowly. It felt pretty good. No, it felt pretty *damn* good.

"You like that?" he whispered.

"Mmmmmm," said Robbie Jo. Her hand dropped to the countertop.

Sam slid his hand in between them and rubbed her clit with his thumb, still rocking between her legs. Robbie Jo's hands slid up his back and her short nails dug into his shoulders.

"Oooooh," and then she couldn't think anymore, because the world was turning colors and she couldn't believe how good it felt and her legs locked around his waist all by themselves and her chest hitched and her hips pumped and Robbie Jo threw back her head and howled.

Sam dropped the used condom into the "Hazardous Waste" can and watched the door shut behind Robbie Jo Ridgemont.

She was some piece of work, that girl. Stranger than a moon-crazy roof rat. Sam had never before in his life met a girl who was turned on by embalming. For that matter, he had never met a virgin who popped her cork like that. The scream she let out was loud enough to make ol' Dead Bob sit up and sport wood.

But virgin she was. The smears of blood on his white Fruit of the Looms told him so. Maybe he'd just keep those underwear, blood and all, like a trophy. Pure pussy was hard to come by, so to speak.

Sam sighed. It was dangerous to fuck a virgin, of course. They get attached. They fall in love. And what a pain in the ass *that* was! Oh well, just one of the risks a man's gotta take in life...

It was worth it. He rewound his brain and ran through the whole act again. It was pretty goddam fine. It did bother Sam a little bit, though, that she never said his name, not even once. Most of the girls he'd fucked sang it like grand opera. And it bothered him that she left right afterwards. She'd patted him on the ass and said "Thanks, Sam, honey. That was fun. I'll definitely be lookin' you up again." Then she buttoned her dress and walked out the door. She didn't even bother to put on her panties.

But she couldn't have, Sam remembered, because they were still in the hearse. Her little white panties with the blue flowers, and her musky-sweet scent and her girlie juices all over them...

Maybe he'd just keep those panties. Maybe he'd tie them in a knot with his bloody briefs and keep them in the bottom drawer of his dresser, under his white t-shirts. The idea was starting to give him another hard-on.

That Robbie Jo, she sure was somethin' else, all right. Sam just hoped she didn't get too hooked on him.

ROBBIE JO

Sex. Fornication. Fuckin'. Makin' love. Screwin' bangin', knockin' boots, humpin', grindin', bumpin' uglies.

Sure, I knew what it looked like. I've seen every possible thing two or more people can do to each other on the Internet. I studied the pictures carefully; all those swollen cocks and shiny wet pussies, open mouths, slimy pink tongues and lots and lots of sweat. I was pretty sure I got it.

But you know what? I just found out that you *can't* get it, not really, until you get your own ashes hauled for the first time. Now, brothers and sisters, I have seen the light!

I guess I understand, now, how some poor stupid girlies could mistake fuckin' for love. An orgasm is a pretty powerful thing, 'specially if you've never had anythin' much nice happen to you before. But you gotta take a step back and look at what's really goin' on. An orgasm ain't love. It's just body parts rubbin' together. A gal could get the same effect with a pickle, a co-cola bottle, her own hand, a well-trained mule, or a bump on a log.

The truth is, you don't even have to like a body to fuck 'im. I know it seems like you should, or at least trust him a little before you let him ram that little meat-sword up your ya-ya and start stabbin' away. But that just isn't the case. Now listen close, girlies, because here it comes. The only reason to fuck a guy is to take control of him. Pussy is power, my little sisters!

From the time they're old enough to have wet dreams, guys are slaves to their peckers. You think I'm exaggeratin', do ya? Look at President Bill Bentdick, who put himself through a whole impeachment trial because he couldn't keep his wee-wee out of some chubby little chicky's pie-hole. Or Jimmy Swaggart, who didn't quite have the balls to stick it in the whores he hired, but couldn't stay away from 'em anyway. Or all the other "great" men like Kennedy and Churchill and Martin Luther King, who shoulda known better but followed their dicks around like dowsing rods anyhow.

And if you think their pee-pees get 'em in trouble when they're fully functional, you should see what happens to 'em when they don't work right. You end up with somebody like Andrei Chikatilo, who killed fifty-two people because he could only come on corpses. Or Jeffrey Dahmer, a guy so pitiful he could only get it up for dead boys who couldn't say no. Or Albert Fish, who had to be eatin' little-kidmeat stew with extra onions before his gnarly old unit would stand up and salute.

A man's sexuality is a whole dynamo's worth of energy. Energy isn't good and it isn't bad. It just is. A gal can take a man's sex drive and shape it into anythin' she wants, if she knows what she's doin' and she doesn't soften up and go all sweet on him. You'll run into gals who think they're feminists, and they'll tell you that women shouldn't use sex to get what they want. They'll tell ya it's backwards and demeanin'. Well, that's just plain ridiculous. To us smart girlies, sex is just another weapon, not much different from a knife or a gun, a college degree, a friend on the inside at the I.R.S.. Tellin' us not to use our sex is like tellin' Rambo he can use the Uzi and the hand grenades but not the rocket launcher. It's just plain silly.

Let's look at it this way. A penis is just a rudder. I put a pretty good grip on Sam's today. All I gotta do now is decide where I'm gonna steer him.

ROBBIE JO, ROSE, AND THE REVEREND PRIMUS REYLARK

So it's still Saturday, late afternoon, and Rose has been working in the general store since nine this morning. She's decided it's fun.

Yesterday Owen and Naomi showed her how to work the cash register (she couldn't believe anyone could trust her so much), how to measure out flour by the pound, where to find the deer repellent, and other such important things. After ringing up customers all day, Rose was starting to feel like a pro.

It was kind of flattering, really. The buzz had gone around town that a stranger was working for the Tanners, and just about everybody in Possum Kingdom had come up with a reason to drop by and see her. But it wasn't like a freakshow; everyone seemed to like Rose, from the ladies who patted her hands and commented on her pretty face, to the blushing young men who mumbled greetings and good wishes, to the little kids who giggled and asked her to tell about her narrow escape from the hearse over and over again. Rose felt like a debutante. She felt like a bride in the reception line. She felt wanted.

People in Possum Kingdom weren't so weird, Rose decided. They were just people, like anybody else. Maybe better, for their simplicity and their friendliness. She was surprised and delighted at the mix of races who came through the General Store. The white folks outnumbered the black by only a slight margin, with a liberal sprinkling of Native Americans mixed in. Not the redneck podunks she'd expected at all.

Rose smiled, wiping down the counter. Possum Kingdom was a pretty nice, pretty normal place.

"Time for supper!" Naomi called, peering around the canned vegetable aisle. "We're having black beans and cat heads!"

Rose blinked as her worldview shifted one more time.

But it turned out that cat heads were just soda biscuits ("See how the corners are, honey? Just like little pussycat ears!") and they tasted pretty good with black beans and collard greens. Rose leaned back in her chair, happy, full and satisfied.

There was a knock on the kitchen door.

"Well, hi there, Miss Robbie Jo! What brings you here?"

"Hi, Mrs. Tanner." An enormous grin. "I've come to take Rose to church!"

Rose and Robbie Jo walked through the late afternoon sunlight, heading for the far end of town. Robbie Jo seemed really happy, Rose noticed. She was smiling at nothing, humming under her breath, practically dancing as she walked. Rose thought of asking her about it, but somehow, it seemed a private thing.

Rose wondered about Owen and Naomi's reaction to Robbie Jo's entrance. They had seemed suddenly flustered, fussing over Rose, telling her to be careful, as though she had been invited to a wild party instead of church. How weird could Southern Baptists be?

But the Baptist church was dark and empty, and Robbie Jo was walking right past it.

"Uh...maybe you got your dates wrong? I don't see anybody in there..."

Robbie Jo looked at her, eyes sparkling. "There isn't, girlie. That's because we're not goin' to this church."

Rose stared at her for a moment. Then with a jolt, she remembered what Robbie Jo had said to her in the diner. About *her* church. About snake handlers.

Rose's brain filled with images of cold, scaly hide and dry rattles. Rose knew with absolute certainty that she wanted no part of this. Especially when Robbie Jo steered them off of Main Street and onto a narrow dirt road called Reaper's Row.

"Uh, listen, I'm really not a very religious person. Maybe I should just take a pass..."

Robbie Jo laughed. "It doesn't matter if you worship the devil, Rose, honey. You don't want to miss this. The Church of the Holy Blood is a part of Possum Kingdom history. Some folks say it's the very heartbeat of this little town."

"Um, okay, but I don't want to touch any snakes..."

"I'll keep 'em away from ya." Robbie Jo winked.

As they walked through the dense trees, the shadows lengthened, the light grew golden and soft. Squirrels jumped from tree to tree. Birds sang good-night songs to each other. The air went from sticky-hot to gently warm, like the soft breath of a lover. Rose wondered if Possum Kingdom wasn't the most beautiful place on Earth.

Then the trees parted, and the girls stood before the iron fence of a cemetery.

Rose loved cemeteries. When her father would get into one of his drunken rages, screaming incoherent curses and smashing anything within reach, Rose would go to the little Cuban cemetery six blocks from her apartment building. There, among the little square stones, she was safe. She'd take a book with her, and read sitting in the soft grass for hours. Her father never found her there, not once. It didn't even enter his rum-soaked brain to look for his daughter in the cemetery. It had been a pleasant place, with its well-kept lawn and willow trees. But this cemetery, this was something different. Something amazing.

"Wow..." Rose pushed the hair back from her forehead and took a step closer. It was beautiful. Tall angels, wings outspread, cast long shadows over the perfectly trimmed grass. Weeping cherubs clutched their fat cheeks and gazed up to the sky. Headstones, worn with time and rain, bore intricate carvings of skulls and harps and shroud-draped urns. A fantasy land. Dead-people Disneyland.

A raucous laugh startled Rose out of her enchanted reverie. Her head snapped up. She could hear people talking, but no one was in sight.

"The church is right there, behind that stand of trees." Robbie Jo was pointing. "C'mon, we don't wanna be late!"

The building was old, the unpainted wood silvered with age. It was a simple, old-fashioned, peak-roofed church, with a huge, rough, wooden cross rising up over the front doors in place of a steeple. Despite its age the church looked solid, almost immovable, as if it had grown up from the fertile Tennessee ground of its own volition.

People were coming out of the thick woods from all directions, some going into the church, others standing outside to chat. Rose recognized many of the people from town. Others she had never seen; hill people in overalls and work boots, faces lined with years spent outdoors, missing teeth, roughened hands, hard, unflinching eyes.

Rose was ashamed to find herself drawing away from these people. Unpleasant words flickered through her brain. Hillbillies. Rednecks. Inbred.

You don't know them, she told herself angrily. *And you're not exactly a fashion plate yourself.* Bigotry made her sick. She flinched, remembering words like "nigger" and "wetback" spewing from her father's wet, drunken lips.

"Don't worry, they won't eatcha," Robbie Jo whispered, nudging Rose in the ribs. "Country folk take their suppers early. They're full."

Rose flushed. Had her reaction been that visible? God, she hoped not.

Rose didn't see everybody in town, though. Robbie Jo explained that the Tanners and the Dunwiddies went to the Baptist church, along with Doc Poteet. Michael Yeats, the vet, and Jimmy Liggett never went to church and were suspected of being heathens.

Robbie Jo steered her through the open door of the Church of the Holy Blood. Inside it smelled faintly of old sweat. There was another, more subtle odor too, and it took Rose a moment to recognize the acrid smell of reptiles. She shuddered.

The pews were simple benches, low and shiny with years of usage. There was no altar to speak of, just a whitewashed podium. Two big jelly jars of some kind of milky-looking liquid sat on top of it. On the wall behind the podium was a simple, almost childlike painting, faded with age, of a white man in red robes, arms outstretched. Jesus? Rose had never seen Him depicted with short black hair and no beard. Below the painting, at the base of the wall, sat box after screen-topped box. *Yuch.*

"We got a few minutes. Let's look around." Robbie Jo pointed to the walls of the church. Between narrow, age-rippled windows were more paintings on what looked like large boards.

Weird. Rose had never seen anything like them in a church before. They were painted in some kind of bright-colored tempera which glowed even in the failing light. There was the red-robed man again, surrounded by tiny human figures with their arms raised in worship. Another showed him surrounded by forest creatures; possum, squirrels, bears, deer, birds. Was he some kind of backwoods St. Francis?

Rose looked at the other panels. Seven black dogs, racing through the woods, tongues lolling. A huge bear-like creature, yellow eyes blazing with rage. Two young girls, hands bloody to the elbows. Some kind of ugly possum-headed thing standing on its back legs.

"Not exactly the stained glass windows of Notre Dame, are they?" Robbie Jo grinned.

"What do they mean?" Rose narrowed her eyes, not really wanting to look at the paintings anymore, but unable to look away.

"Nobody's sure. We know that the guy in red is the Reverend Meshach Reddingale, who built this church. He painted all these himself. But he never told anybody what they were supposed to be."

"Huh." Rose heard a quiet rustling, a muffled hiss, and realized she was very close to the snake boxes. The screens were almost opaque, but she could make out something squirming in the nearest box, twisting, trying to get out. No, make that a lot of somethings.

"Can we sit in the back?" she asked Robbie Jo as she retreated rapidly.

"Sure. Every seat in the house is a good one. I suspect people can hear Reverent Primus's preaching all the way in Kentucky."

People were filling the church now, sitting side by side in the pews, grinning and laughing. Watching the hill families together, happy and excited, Rose was even more ashamed of her first reaction.

Something began a sputtering roar somewhere behind the building. Light bulbs on strings on the ceiling lit up, making the church almost unbearably bright.

"Gas generator," Robbie Jo said. "There's no power lines this far out into the woods."

To Rose's surprise, three men and a woman came in carrying electric guitars and amplifiers. Others had tambourines, and a young boy was setting up a kettle drum. A tall, stoop-shouldered scarecrow of a man with rattlesnakes and crosses embroidered on the arms of his denim shirt carried a beaten-up standing microphone.

"The Holy Spirit rocks," Robbie Jo grinned.

Rose was mildly surprised to see that the ethnic mix of Possum Kingdom was represented in the church. Back home in Miami, churches tended to have congregations of mostly one race or another. Rose remembered sitting under the window of the black church near her elementary school, listening to the singsong voice of the preacher, hearing the clapping and yelling and singing. Her father never thought to look for her there. Although she never once spoke to the skinny young preacher or even set foot in the church, she felt like he was her protector, her guardian angel.

"Penny for your thoughts?" said Robbie Jo.

Rose grimaced. "There're not worth a plugged nickel."

To her surprise, Robbie Jo hugged her around the shoulders. Rose felt the sting of tears in her eyes, and blinked them fiercely away.

A hush fell over the church. "Here comes the rev'rend and his wife!" Robbie Jo whispered.

Rose's breath caught in her throat. She had never in her life seen anyone quite like the Reverend Primus Reylark.

To start with, he was big. Maybe six-foot-six, with shoulders as wide as a doorway, arms as hard and thick as the limbs of a hundred-year-old oak. His skin was the near-black of bittersweet chocolate. Although he only looked to be in his forties, the reverend's short, curly hair was streaked on either side with pure white. His face was strong and square, his features even, stern but not unkind; the face of a legendary hero.

His wife, although she was tall for a woman, seemed tiny beside him. Even in her simple long blue dress, she seemed a queen; neck long, jaw firm, eyes a clear, walnut brown. A perfect match for Reverend Primus. Rose thought they looked like some kind of demigods, or fierce, proud angels deigning to visit the Earth for a while.

The reverend strode to the front of the church, giving faint smiles and little nods here and there. The congregation was silent as he rolled up the sleeves of his white cotton shirt. Rose blinked, and squinted her eyes. What did he have on his forearms?

Tattoos. White rattlesnakes twisting up the backs of the reverend's massive forearms. They were beautiful; sensuous and simple. Rose shook her head, bemused.

I don't think we're in Kansas anymore...

She found herself holding her breath, waiting for the big man at the front of the church to speak. Instead, he began to clap. The two electric guitars roared to life. Four women swayed and pounded tambourines. The boy hauled back his skinny arm and hammered the drum with what looked like a small tree branch. Rose could feel the deep bark of the drumbeats in her breastbone.

The scarecrow-man gripped the microphone and began to sing. His voice was piercing, nasal but true and strong. It reminded her of a famous old country singer; maybe George Jones? He danced in a jerky, storkish way, bony knees flying high. Rose squinted. She wasn't sure, but it looked like the guy was missing most of the fingers on his left hand.

The congregation began to sing along with him, loudly, joyously. She recognized the hymn; "Leaning," it was called. Leaning, leaning, safe and secure from all alarm. Leaning on the everlasting arm. What a fine thought that was.

And the music absolutely kicked ass. Rose had no idea that religious music could sound so much like rock and roll. She found herself swaying in her seat. Robbie Jo was singing loudly, her voice high and clear.

Rose felt the odd twist of alienation in her chest that always caught up with her in the company of true believers. Religion, it seemed, just wouldn't take on her.

It wasn't that she hadn't tried. Around the time of her thirteenth birthday, when waking up bruised and sore between the legs was just part of her day-to-day routine, Rose had passed a street preacher on her way to school. She listened to him talk of heaven and redemption and the perfect love of God, and oh, she had wanted it. She had suddenly wanted it more than anything. Rose bought a cheap little Bible, and read it cover to cover. She snuck out to church on Sunday mornings when her father was still passed out in a stinking cloud of alcohol and sweat and foul breath. Standing alone on the beach, she accepted Jesus Christ as her personal Lord and Savior.

She spoke the words, spoke them again and again. And each time she felt like she had put on someone else's clothes; fine clothes made of silk, but they just didn't fit her right.

Rose willed herself to believe. She could fool herself into thinking she did, from time to time. But then at some point, usually after her father left her for the night and right before she fell asleep, the thoughts would begin. *Why? Why does God let awful things happen? If God loves us, why does He let us suffer? Why should unbaptized babies and Bushmen and Buddhists fry in Hell? Why doesn't He strike my daddy dead?* Her brain would begin picking at the thin veneer of her faith, and it would flake away at the edges like bright, glittering nail polish. Then one day, it was gone, all gone, leaving Rose to stare into the howling darkness that was herself, alone, a tiny speck in an infinitely vast universe.

Sometimes she wondered if perhaps she were defective, blind to religion, simply handicapped in the way that some people are tone deaf or color blind. She hoped that if that were the case, God would cut her some slack. Surely He wouldn't toss her into the Lake of Fire for having a bad microchip somewhere.

Rose looked at the upturned, ecstatic singing faces, and felt desperately alone.

The song was over. The church rang with the echoes of the music for a moment, then fell silent. The Reverend Primus

Reylark stepped up to the whitewashed podium. He took a breath. His huge chest expanded like a bellows.

"Good evenin', brothers and sisters! And what a fine evenin' it is!"

His voice was like the roll of distant thunder; deep and reverberating. He swept the congregation with a fiery stare as they replied "Yeah!" and "Yes, sir!" and "Amen!"

"Summer has come to us, brothers and sisters, in all its glory. The sky is blue. The flowers are bloomin'. Possum Kingdom seems like paradise on Earth."

The congregation nodded and murmured. The reverend stepped out from behind the podium. He drew himself up to his full height, eyes flashing.

"Summer is God's gift to us. Life is God's gift to us. We are meant to appreciate it, to love it, to enjoy it. But remember somethin'. I said, remember somethin'! It will not last!"

"Amen!" agreed the crowd.

The reverend seemed to have taken on an inner rhythm. He swayed slightly as he spoke. Sweat beaded his forehead.

"The days of the Earth are numbered, my brothers. The end of this world is approachin', my sisters. It's comin'. It's comin'. You can't look away!"

"Excellent!" whispered Robbie Jo. "We're gonna get some good stuff tonight!"

Rose shifted in her seat, terribly uncomfortable.

"John! John had the sight, he had the vision, he saw the future through the eyes of our Lord Jesus Christ. And the future, the future, the future is fire! The future is war! The future is death! But only if you don't believe, brothers. Only if you aren't saved, sisters. Jesus is the way. Jesus is the light. Come to Jesus. Come to Jesus!"

"Amen!" The congregation was swaying with him, on the edge of their seats.

"Let me tell you now. Let me tell you. Let me tell you about the Book of Revelation."

"Yeah!" Robbie Jo was grinning ear to ear.

"Do you know what he saw? Do you know what John saw? He saw one like a Son of Man, dressed in a robe reaching down to his feet and a golden sash around his chest. His head and hair were white like wool, as white as snow, and his eyes were like blazin' fire. Blazin' fire!"

The congregation murmured and nodded.

"His feet were like bronze glowing in a furnace and his voice was like the sound of rushin' waters! In his right hand he held seven stars, and out of his mouth came a sharp, double-sword. His face was like the sun, shinin' in all its brilliance! And who was that, brothers and sisters? Who was that?"

"Jesus!" they roared.

"Yes! Jesus! Not the gentle lamb but the fearsome judge! The stern son of his Father who spares not the rod! And he told John, he told him, he told him what the fate of mankind was to be! Oh, the fate of unbelievers! Oh, it will be terrible!"

And the Reverend Primus spared none of the details. He told his people of the opening of the seven seals, the coming of the Four Horsemen, the raising of the righteous dead, the sky turning to soot, the moon turning to blood, the stars falling from the sky. He sang, he thundered, he roared of the seven angels and their trumpets, of fire mixed with blood scouring the Earth, of locusts like scorpions stinging and torturing the flesh of sinners.

Rose, against her will, began to tremble.

As he reached the Seven Bowls of God's Wrath, the preacher was on fire. His voice grew louder and louder, shaking the walls of the old church. His arms raised over his head, fists clenched, as he conjured the end of the world. As his eyes rolled back in his head, his wife rose from her seat in the front row, threw open one of the rattlesnake boxes, and plunged her hands in. She half-danced to the reverend, two fat, rough-scaled snakes held high over her head.

"Ohmigod!" Rose whispered.

The reverend took them, seemingly without seeing them, one in each of his massive hands. They twined around his tattooed arms as he held them high.

Rose gasped; another snake, a huge one, was poking its ugly, pug-faced head out of the still-open box. The reverend's lovely wife grabbed it and hauled it out, coils and coils of well-fed, wicked-looking serpent. She draped it around her husband's neck.

The band took up their instruments and began to play a pounding version of "Won't it be Wonderful There." The Reverend Primus spun like a dervish. The snakes clung tightly to him, but didn't seem to be too upset by all this. Rose thought that, in their position, she'd be scared shitless.

The congregation rose to their feet and began to dance. Some folks just swayed in place, hands held high, eyes heavenward. Others, like Robbie Jo, stomped and spun and shook like mad things. Rose raised an eyebrow; some of the dancing seemed less than holy. Pelvises thrusted, butts shimmied. A lumpy middle-aged woman in a dirt-colored dress, jerking and twitching like a palsy victim, let out a stream of shrill, jabbering nonsense. Rose guessed that she must be "speaking in tongues," something which she'd heard of but never thought she'd see.

Never wanted to see.

Rose stood up and eased to the rear of the church, pressing her back against the wall.

A young, lovely woman with pale skin and long, deep brown hair flung open a snakebox and came out with a nasty-looking rattler twined around her wrists. As her hair flew around her face, Rose saw that her right cheek was sunken and pitted, almost like the flesh beneath it had dissolved away. An old man, tanned and tough as shoe leather, wore a snake on his bald head like a scaly crown. His eyes rolled up in his head as he stomped and twirled. Twin boys, no more than eighteen, grabbed the jars of liquid and each took a big slug. Their faces twisted for a moment, and then they grinned and raised their fists in triumph.

What the hell was that about?

The reverend's wife danced in the center aisle, radiant as an angel. She wore two big rattlesnakes around her neck and waist. They clung to her tightly, as if they were creatures in love.

"Oh, no!" Rose said. Her words were lost in the roar of the music and the pounding feet of the dancers and the cries of those in the grip of the Holy Spirit. She couldn't believe her eyes. Robbie Jo was headed for the snakeboxes.

Rose watched, paralyzed with horror, as Robbie Jo held up a twisting snake that was bigger around than her bicep. She danced with the thing held over her head for a moment, then jumped up onto a pew and wrapped it around her body. Robbie Jo danced sensually, sure-footed and wild, up and down the bench. She caressed the snake, stroking its rough, patterned skin, touching its long, evil rattles.

The snake on Robbie Jo pulled its head back and stared into her face. Rose stopped breathing. There they stood, the girl and the serpent, faces not six inches apart. The snake flicked its forked tongue at her, moved a little closer.

Robbie Jo grinned.

Holy shit, Christ on a biscuit, Robbie Jo kissed that snake on the lips.

Then she was laughing maniacally, copper-colored hair flying, as she leapt from pew to pew, easily as a cat on the rooftops.

She landed on a pew just six feet from Rose and danced there, holding the snake close to her, like a lover. Rose could see its cold, beady eyes, its bulging jowls swollen with venom sacs. She started to shake.

Robbie Jo's face was a mask of pure ecstasy as she danced away again.

There was a scream from the front of the church, a hoarse, male shout of pain. Then a woman's high pitched shriek. Rose jumped up on a pew to see. A heavyset old white man with a long, white beard was staggering in a circle. The rattlesnake wrapped around his neck was chomping up and down his arm like an ear of corn. People stepped back in horror. The band stopped playing.

The Reverend Primus was wrenched from his joyous trance. He plunged his own serpents into the nearest box and grabbed the snake on the old man right behind its triangular head. It lashed its body angrily, rattling like mad. The dry, alien sound made the hairs on the back of Rose's neck stand up.

Robbie Jo stopped dancing and watched, stroking the big snake in her hands. It looked like it was about to fall asleep. After a moment, she got down from the pew and put the snake gently away. She hustled over to Rose.

"C'mere, girl. You've gotta see this."

Rose shook her head violently. "Robbie Jo, I don't want to—"

"Sure you do. Life experience, right? C'mon, you know you want a better look." She began hauling Rose to the front of the church. Rose, to her own disbelief, let herself be hauled.

Because part of her *did* want to see. Part of her wanted to see every last detail.

The reverend put the offending reptile in solitary confinement and knelt down next to the bitten man. The poor old guy was sitting on the wooden floor, holding his arm like it was a wounded puppy. The arm was already swollen to twice its normal girth, the skin blackening, tight and shiny, fingers like rotten sausages. Blood oozed steadily from dozens of fang-holes. The guy was having trouble breathing. The skin of his face was darkening like the sky before a storm, and it looked like it was beginning to swell, too. Abruptly the man let out a choking gurgle and pitched over backwards, convulsing.

"Stand back!" roared the reverend. He took the man's head in his massive hands, to keep him from pounding it on the floor. "Give him some air! Those of you who want to, stay and pray for Brother Alki. Mike Dobson, you run for the Doc. The rest of you, clear on out of here."

Robbie Jo watched Brother Alki for a moment longer, eyes narrowed, head slightly cocked. Then she grabbed Rose by the arm again and sprinted for the back of the church.

"Is he gonna be all right?" Rose asked as Robbie Jo dragged her out the door.

"Who knows? He's been bitten enough times before, he might have an immunity. On the other hand, that snake was really munching on him." Robbie Jo paused to lift her sweat-soaked hair off the back of her neck. Then she turned to Rose and grinned. "I'm not ready to go home yet, are you?"

"Well, uh, I guess not…"

"Good. Let's go."

"Where?"

"The cemetery. It's time you learned about the dark side of Possum Kingdom, honey."

The Reverend Primus Reylark, Taylor Alki's twitching head in his hands, watched the two girls leave the church. Robbie Jo and the other one, the new girl. He blinked, not quite believing what he saw.

The sound of his wife Jerianne's voice, deep and bell-like as she prayed for the life of Brother Alki, gave him comfort and strength. He looked down at Brother Alki, worried by the bruise-color of the man's bloated face, the foam flecking his yellowish beard, the wheezing whistle of his breathing. He was a tough old man, he'd been bitten many times before, but never this badly. Primus was worried most of all by the sickly gray light surrounding him. He feared the man was dying.

Primus Reylark had been able to see a body's light, what some folks called an aura, ever since he was a tiny boy. His mother's had been as cool and blue as the waters of Virgin Pond, as comforting as a kiss. Most folks had a pretty light about them; Primus believed that people were basically good. Oh, they had their black spikes and brown hazes from time to time, when their hearts were heavy with sin. But sin was forgivable.

The air in the church seemed somehow more breathable now that Robbie Jo was gone. It grieved and shamed him, but Primus didn't like that girl. He didn't like her from the very core of his being.

It wasn't that she'd ever done anything bad to him. As far as he knew, she'd never done anything bad to anyone. But there was something in her foxlike eyes, something as alien and unreachable as the stars, and it unnerved him. And then there was her light.

Or lack of it. Robbie Jo was surrounded by a black-purple glow that seemed to suck the radiance from the auras of those around her. It was a cold glow, black light the color of a bruise. It was unclean.

But Robbie Jo came to church every week. She attended the picnics, helped decorate, helped clean up. She did well in school, from what he'd heard. She smiled and her clothes were clean and she always said "please" and "thank you." And then there was her way with the snakes.

Almost every week, Robbie Jo was overcome by the holy spirit, and took up serpents. She took them up joyously, without fear. She danced like she had angel wings. But Primus had seen something on her face while she danced, more than once. A subtle expression, slightly smug, as if she were getting away with something.

In the back of his mind, The Reverend Primus didn't believe that Robbie Jo had ever been taken with the Holy Spirit. He believed that the snakes didn't bite her out of professional courtesy. They recognized one of their own.

Or maybe they were just plain scared of her.

Primus knew he certainly was.

He turned his eyes to the rough beams of the church ceiling and beyond, praying to his Lord God to be merciful, to spare the life of His faithful servant who lay fallen in His house. But even as he prayed, even as he felt that warm, electric channel open up between himself and the Divine, an image kept flickering at the edges of the reverend's consciousness. Something he had seen as Robbie Jo and her friend ran out the door. Something that didn't appear until Robbie Jo grabbed the other girl's arm.

When she stood alone and worried at the back of the church, the new girl's light had been a deep, shimmering violet. Oh, there had been a few dark streaks of pain and a jab or two of sin, but there wasn't a body alive who didn't have something or another to regret. The girl's light was normal, healthy, even. Until Robbie Jo touched her.

When the girls' skin met, their lights merged, becoming one. Not black. Not violet. Something new, something the Reverend had never seen before. A pulsing, darkly angry red. When he saw that red, like a mix of hellfire and clotted blood, just one word popped into his mind.

Murder.

A shiver wracked the Reverend Primus Reylark, from the base of his spine to the top of his neck and back down again.

With a choking shudder, Taylor Alki died in his arms.

GIRLIES IN THE BONEYARD

obbie Jo walked fast, holding tight to Rose's hand. Rose let herself be led.

This is all too goddam weird. I didn't just see that. Did I? Rose closed her eyes for a moment. The cool night air was like a caress on her sweaty face.

Rose glanced around at the weeping angels looming in the darkness, the gravestones rising up from the ground like monstrous teeth. Any normal person would be scared. But compared to the freakshow in the Church of the Holy Blood, the graveyard was a peaceful oasis.

"Here we are." Robbie Jo stopped beneath a massive monument and grinned up at it. In the cool blue light of the near-full moon, Rose could see that the statue was in the form of a woman. Her robes were full and flowing, her outspread arms like wings. Her face was slightly downturned. Rose could make out the fine angle of her jaw, the gleam of moonlight on her white stone hair, but nothing of her face. The back of Rose's neck prickled.

"Isn't she purty?" Robbie Jo stroked the statue's robes, touched the top of a sculpted foot. "Her name was Helena O'Riley. She was the wife of a logging baron. Helena died in eighteen-eighty-seven, just twenty-two years old."

"Geez. What'd she die of?"

Snakebite?

"Childbirth. Poppin' puppies used to kill a lotta women back then."

Rose stared up at the statue, thinking of how much the young woman's husband must have loved her. "That's really sad. You know a lot about the town's history, Robbie Jo?"

The other girl laughed. "Nah. It says all that stuff on the base of the stone. Here." She pressed Rose's hand against the carved letters.

"Oh, okay." Rose liked the feeling of Robbie Jo's hand over hers. For some reason, her friend made her feel safe, even in a cemetery at night.

Robbie Jo sat down in the grass, leaning her back against the monument. Rose sat down next to her, shivering at the chill of the stone creeping through her t-shirt. "How you feelin', gal?" Robbie Jo asked.

"Okay, I guess. That was pretty intense."

"Yup."

Silence, for a little while. Then the questions burst out.

"Robbie Jo, what was that about? Why do you guys pick up snakes? What does it mean?"

A soft little noise from Robbie Jo. A chortle? "Well, y'see, there's this quote in the Bible, from Mark. 'And these signs shall follow them that believe; In my name shall they cast out devils; they shall speak with new tongues; They shall take up serpents; and if they drink any deadly thing, it shall not hurt them; they shall lay hands on the sick, and they shall recover.'" Robbie Jo spoke in a stilted, singsong voice, as if reciting before a Sunday school class.

"Yeah?"

"Yeah. And there was this old guy right here in East Tennessee, back in nineteen-twelve, he decided that righteous folks should take those words lit'rally. He's the first preacher who taught folks to follow the Signs. To take up serpents, drink poison, stick their hands in blazin' furnaces, all of it."

Rose's mouth dropped open. "Poison? That stuff in the jars—"

"Strychnine. A little bit diluted, but still nasty stuff."

"Holy shit."

Robbie Jo laughed. "You're right, it's very holy shit. That's the whole idea. Through all the dancin' and prayin' and preachin', you get in touch with the Holy Spirit. The Holy Ghost, some folks call it. When you got the Holy Ghost in you, you can pick up those snakes, drink that poison, heal the sick, even raise the dead, some folks say. It's like grabbin' the power of divinity by the bare electric wires."

"Oh. Wow." Rose shook her head, not sure of what to say. It was all so alien. She turned to look at Robbie Jo. She could see the curve of the other girl's cheek in the moonlight, the pale glint on her hair, in her eyes. "Your faith must be so strong. I can't imagine—I—I envy you. What you did with that snake—it was like a miracle."

Rose was startled by Robbie Jo's piercing yip of laughter. "Faith? The only thing I've got faith in is my own bad self, Rose, honey. I don't believe a word of that silly bullshit!"

For the first time in her life, Rose understood the true meaning of the word "thunderstruck."

"But… but you believe in God?"

"Shit no. You?"

"I… no. No, I don't." She'd never told anyone before. No one had ever asked her.

"Ha! I knew it! You're a godless little heathen, just like me!" Robbie Jo shoved Rose's shoulder, starting her giggling.

"I guess I am. But shit, Robbie Jo, how did you do that? With the snake? God, you kissed the fucking thing!"

A flash of teeth; Robbie Jo's wide grin. "I just have a way with animals, that's all. Critters like me."

"I'd say that one was about ready to marry you."

"Ol' Wigglestick? Yeah, he's my fav'rite timber rat'ler. Big sucker, id'n he? I like some of the copperheads, too. They're kinda purty."

Rose was taken with another fit of the giggles. "Don't take this wrong, 'cause I really like you, but you're one weird little chick, girlfriend."

Robbie Jo leaned toward her, until their foreheads were almost touching. "Yes. I am. And you are too, you just don't know it yet."

For some reason, Rose liked that idea. She liked it an awful lot. And in that moment, she wanted to put her arms around Robbie Jo, to hug her, to hold her like a sister.

Rose didn't. She leaned against the cold stone again. "Why do you go then? If you don't believe any of it?"

"Ain't it obvious? Entertainment value. It's the best damn show in Tennessee!"

Rose snorted. "I guess you could say that." She grimaced, remembering Brother Alki's fat purple arm, blood flowing in trickling fits and starts like raindrops on a windowpane. She scowled. "Hey, if they believe that you won't get hurt by snakes if you've got the Holy Ghost, how do they explain what happened to that old guy tonight?"

Robbie Jo leaned back, too. "It depends on who you talk to. Some folks take the hardline. They say that if you get bit, it's 'cause your faith wavered. Others say that gettin' chomped on is just a test of faith. And if you die, well, it's just 'cause God's called you home. Rev'rend Primus, he's more of the 'test of faith' school."

"Do people get bitten a lot?"

"All the fuckin' time. Did you get a look at Jeremiah? The singer? He got bit on the hand a couple years back. Bad bite. His fingers swole up, and the flesh on 'em just died. He lost most of his fingers. And Ruby, the gal with the long hair, she got bit in the face by a copperhead. Damn, if that wasn't ugly!"

"Yuch!"

"You said it. They die, too. About five years ago, a guy named Abe Treadwell got bit and died—at the funeral service for another snakebit brother!"

"Oh, you're makin' that up!"

"Not atall. These folks just don't know when to quit. Ol' Taylor, the guy who got bit tonight, he gets chomped more than a turkey's ass on Thanksgivin' day. The snakes just seem to hate him. But the stubborn shithead keeps on pickin' 'em up. I think he's done for this time."

"How come?"

"Sometimes if a body gets bit once too often, he gets a kind of allergic reaction to the snake venom. There's a big-ass word for it."

"Anaphylactic shock."

"Well, don't you just have brains of steel, Rosie! That's right. Anyway, did you see the way Taylor was swellin' up? That was way too fast. I'll bet he's dead as a veal cutlet right this minute." Robbie Jo stood up, stretched. "My legs are gettin stiff. Walk with me."

"It's too dark…"

"Take my hand. There you go. I see in the dark real well."

Robbie Jo pulled Rose to her feet, and together they walked, slowly, aimlessly. A thin mist had risen up from the grass, and it felt cool on Rose's bare arms. She wrapped them around herself.

"Feelin' the chill? Good. Perfect for scary stories. Booooo!" Robbie Jo wiggled her fingers in Rose's face.

Rose grinned. "Ghosts and stuff?"

"Nothin' that tame. Possum Kingdom's haints and boogers are pretty special."

Rose cracked up. "Haints and boogers?"

"Oh, you wouldn't be laughin' if you ran into the Wampus Cat or the Creek Devil."

"You sure?"

"Oh, yeah. The Wampus Cat, he's a Cherokee demon with the power to drive people crazy with one look of his blazin' eyes. He appears as a huge cat, big as a man, that walks on its hind legs."

"Puss in boots," said Rose.

"Okay, then. The Creek Devil is an evil little monster, older than mankind. It's only a foot-and-a-half tall, with wrinkled, gray skin, little horns, and huge eyes that never blink. If it catches you alone, it'll hex you and paralyze you, a part at a time, then drag you into the creek and drown you. Then it eats your body, little by little, 'til there's nothin' left but your skeleton."

"I'd drop-kick the little shit," said Rose.

"Well, you are bad, ain't ya? But Possum Woman could wipe that sassy smile off your face, missy!"

Rose howled with laughter. "Possum Woman!"

"Yes, ma'am. Half human, half possum. Lives in the woods not too far from here, some folks tell it. Sleeps all day, hangin' by her tail. Prowls for food at night. If she catches a little kid, she can just open her great ol' big jaws and swallow it whole. A big girl like you, she'd have to take bites."

Rose had to bend over. Her sides were starting to hurt.

"You just better hope you never meet the Mingit Toad, Rose Heron! His hide looks just like tree bark, so you can't see him lurkin', just waitin' in the shadows to steal your soul. He freezes ya with a look of his evil eyes, then grabs ya up with his loooong, black tongue and eats ya! Slurp!"

Another tide of laughter. Rose finally caught her breath with a gulp. "Shee-it, Robbie Jo, possum people? Giant toads? If that's all I have to worry about in Possum Kingdom, I think I'll just live here forever. Forgive me, but I'm a little more worried about humans than Creek devils and Wampum cats."

"Wampus," said Robbie Jo, feigning offense. "And we've had our share a' nasty humans. Some folks say the Rev'rend Meshach was a bad one."

"Well, he sure wasn't much of a painter. Why'd people say he was bad?"

"Nobody's sure. That was a long time ago. Maybe he was just bangin' the local widows. Maybe he was workin' up to bein' a backwoods snake-jugglin' Jim Jones. We'll never know, 'cause he just up and disappeared one day, I guess. People 'round here speak his name cautiously, though. Like he might just pop up out of the ground and get 'em if they're not too careful."

"Maybe Possum Woman ate him."

"That's the spirit, girlie! Then there's Miss Reenie Rackham. She's pretty spooky. She's an ol' root woman. Lives just outside the Kingdom. The old folks around here go to her for love potions and spring tonics and the like. But the weird thing is, she won't set foot in Possum Kingdom. She says it's cursed. Unholy ground."

"Huh. I know people who feel that way about West Palm Beach."

Robbie Jo grabbed Rose's hands in both of hers and spun her around, faster and faster.

Heart pounding, hair flying, Rose threw back her head and laughed and laughed.

White headlights pierced the night, flashing over angels and ivy, lighting Robbie Jo's pale face and sparking fire in her eyes.

The hearse.

"See?" said Robbie Jo. "Didn't I tell you? Another dipshit bites the dust!"

Rose knew she should feel something. She should feel sorry for the old man. She should be upset by what she'd seen. She should cry.

A slow smile crossed her face. "Uncle Darwin strikes again!"

Laughing, the two girls ran through the graveyard to the gate, and into the dark woods beyond.

THE DEFLOWERED DAWG AND JOE REECHUR MEET AGAIN

The black dog opened her eyes a little bit and licked her lips. She had been awakened by the sound of people screaming. For a moment, she thought she was home with the Man and Woman. Then she felt the cool grass under her belly, the damp air on her nose, and remembered.

She stood up, stiff and slow. Her back end felt strange, where the not-dog had done whatever he did to her. She thought briefly of his moon-colored eyes, and wondered what that had been all about.

After taking a deep, long drink, she realized she was hungry. Beyond hungry. She felt as if she had never eaten in her whole life. She had to find something, and soon.

The black dog stretched, wincing at the pain it caused her, then walked into the blackness of the woods.

She sniffed the air, hoping to catch a whiff of the dry, greasy kibble the Woman used to put in her dish. The night was filled with amazing smells. Night-blooming flowers, dark, pungent earthworms, the sharp, warm scent of bats, the underlying smell of decaying plantlife. The dog realized that there were many other animals in the woods with her. She whined softly, tucking her tail against her body.

The dog trotted on the spongy forest floor, head hanging down. There just didn't seem to be any kibble. She spotted a mouse perched on a rock, cleaning its whiskers, and it smelled fat and juicy and spicy with urine. She crouched down and gauged the distance, then pounced. But she was sore and slow and the mouse was long gone before she ever hit the ground.

The dog walked on. She smelled something enticing nearby, like ripe fruit, rich earth, and warm flesh. Sniffing, she followed its trail.

She found the thing in a hollow log. It looked like a rat or a mouse, only much, much bigger. She could eat for two days on a thing like that. The dog was already drooling when she stuck her head into the log to drag the animal out.

But the critter was having none of it. Its entire head seemed to open up, exposing endless sharp and jagged teeth. It let out a weird snarling roar and jumped at the dog.

Yelping, she turned and ran.

She smelled the pile of guts from a long way off. She remembered the rich, delicious, overwhelming flavor, and started to drool uncontrollably. Then she remembered the old man pointing a thing at her, and the terrible noise it made. She had never seen a rifle fired before, but somehow, she knew it was meant to hurt her.

But her paws didn't slow down. Her hungry belly had taken over completely, bypassing her fear and her better judgment.

The house was dark when she crept up to the luscious pile of entrails. Maybe the old man was asleep. Maybe not. The dog was intoxicated with the smell of food, and nothing else mattered. She let out a tiny groan of satisfaction as her teeth sank into the first chewy loop.

Joe Reechur woke up with a start. There was a critter outside, eating on the bait. He grinned in the darkness.

He sat up on his narrow cot and took the rifle out from under it. Standing up, cursing under his breath at the shrieks and groans from his old, swollen joints, he took the big Maglight from the table. Joe padded to the door, stark naked.

He eased the door open and pointed the unlit flashlight at the dark shadow that was wolfing up raccoon guts like they were going out of style. He zeroed in on the smacking, chewing, gulping noises, and switched the flashlight on.

The animal's head snapped up and its eyes locked with the flashlight beam. It froze. Jacklighted. Joe wheezed a chuckle and raised the gun.

It was that scrawny old dog again. The one that dumbass city girl had made him miss. Well, he wouldn't miss this time.

He started to slowly squeeze the trigger. The dog lowered its head and let out a low, piteous whine. Its eyes weren't on the light anymore; it could have run away. But it didn't. Almost like it expected Joe to shoot it. Almost like it thought it didn't deserve any better.

That's when Joe noticed just how ratty the damn thing really was. Half the skin was missing from its side. Instead of fur, it had a thick, steak-red scab. What fur it did have wasn't so great, either. The dog had scrapes over one eye, on its cheek, on its forelegs. Its tail was ratty, uneven, like an old, worn-out bottlebrush.

"Sheee-it. That thang ain't worth shootin'. It ain't even worth blowin' up," Joe muttered as he lowered the gun. The dog whined again and wagged its tail hopefully.

Joe decided he'd just let the dog be. He'd never shot a dog before, and the idea kind of bothered him. He'd had a dog, at least he thought he did, when he was a young boy, running through the green velvet hills as free and fast as a deer. Dogs had never done anything bad to him. Not like the woods critters who whispered his name on moonless nights. Dogs were man's best friend.

Besides, if he let the thing live, if he let it eat from his bottomless pile of animal insides, it might just heal up and grow a pelt worth hanging on his wall someday.

He scratched his skinny old ass and went back to bed.

.

DEAD BOB, JIMMY LIGGETT, AND THE SINEATER

Still Saturday night; Sunday morning, really. Jimmy Liggett was working late. That was his preference, Jimmy was a night owl. Besides, he was less likely to run into Sam at this hour. Just thinking about Sam made Jimmy's lip twist into an Elvisy sneer.

He'd finished embalming a guy named Bob-something about an hour ago. The hard part was over. After making himself a cup of coffee, Jimmy cleaned the dried blood and crusty fluids from Bob's pallid skin, washed his thin, brittle hair and combed it, dressed Bob in the worn black suit his wife had packed for him.

Jimmy peered down at Bob's cold, still face. He'd done a nice job, if he did say so himself. Bob's eyes were closed and peaceful, not squinted or uneven. No trace of the superglue holding the lids together. He had wired the jaw just right; the mouth was closed, but not compressed. Bob looked relaxed, laid back.

Okay, he didn't look "just like he was sleeping." They never did. The face was just a little too flaccid. The tiny muscles around the mouth and the eyes that gave a person character and expression were stilled forever. With no brain to power it, no force of will, the dead body looked more like a wax dummy than a human being. But at least it was a nice-looking wax dummy, one that Bob's relatives would recognize as their dearly departed.

Jimmy took the foundation make-up from the cupboard. He patted Bob gently on the cheek. "Lookin' good there, ol' boy. We'll have you ready for company in no time."

Jimmy began to apply the make-up to Bob's face with a sponge, making sure it was even and smooth and not too obvious. The last thing the bereaved wanted was to see their lost loved one gussied up like a five-dollar streetwalker.

He was adding the tiniest hint of color to Bob's lips when someone knocked, ever so softly, on the back door.

"Just a sec," Jimmy called. He quickly washed his hands, then hurried to the door. "That you, Simon?"

"Sure is," came the quiet young voice.

Jimmy opened the door. Simon stood there, head down, arms wrapped around himself. The kid always seemed to be cold, even on the most sultry summer night. Probably because he was so damn skinny, Jimmy thought.

"C'mon in," said Jimmy, with a smile. Simon McCray, the sineater, smiled back at him and blinked his big dark eyes. The poor little guy always seemed to be so grateful if you were nice to him. Most of the town shunned him, thought it was bad luck to even look at him. Ignorant asswipes.

"Who is it?" asked Simon, stepping into the embalming room. He tugged at the long sleeves of his tattered blue cotton shirt.

"Nobody from town. A guy from Jonesborough, name of Bob."

Simon nodded. He approached the corpse on the table, inspected it carefully. "Nice job, Jimmy. He looks just as good as he can."

"Thanks." Jimmy tried not to let his glow of pride show too much.

"Bob's folks—they asked for me?" Simon scratched his arm, rubbed his nose. A nervous kid, Jimmy thought. And who wouldn't be, in his position? What a shitty job.

"Nope. Mrs. Dunwiddie sent for you. You know how she is."

"Yep. Can't let a body get out of her house uncleansed. She's a good woman. Don't you think, Jimmy?"

"Sure do. She left you a basket of goodies to take home with you. I'm pretty sure one of her cherry pies is in there."

Simon's face split into a wide grin, unselfconscious as a little kid. Of course, at sixteen, he wasn't that far removed from being a little kid. Jimmy felt a stinging tug; a jab of sympathy for a soul trapped as surely as a rat in a washbucket. He frowned, not wanting the boy to see what was in his eyes.

Jimmy went to the small refrigerator in the corner of the room and took out a covered tray. He set it carefully on Bob's polyester-suited chest, and lifted off the cover.

Simple food. Thickly sliced homemade bread, little apple tarts, sliced peaches, a boiled egg.

"Looks good," said Simon, with a sardonic little smile.

"Only the best for you, partner." Jimmy patted the boy's shoulder and felt him cringe almost imperceptibly, like he was expecting a blow.

There was an awkward moment, where neither knew quite what to say. Then Jimmy cleared his throat. "Well, I'd best be going. If I stay up too late I'll have to drink too much coffee in the morning, and that always makes me feel bad. My stomach. You know…"

"Sure." Simon smiled at him. Jimmy smiled back. He'd put a twenty dollar bill and a Ray Bradbury collection in the basket Mrs. Dunwiddie had prepared. It was the only way he knew of to help the kid, just a little.

Jimmy grabbed his book club space opera from an overhead cupboard, along with his threadbare denim jacket, and headed out the back door a little bit too quickly.

It wasn't that he found what Simon did to be disgusting. A confirmed atheist, Jimmy hadn't wanted to believe the boy was doing anything at all, other than acting out a superstitious backwoods version of a silly Medieval custom. Watching the Sineating a few times had changed his mind about that. Changed it entirely. Still, he didn't think Simon was corrupted, contagious, unclean, the way most of Possum Kingdom did.

He just couldn't stand to hear the kid screaming.

Simon sighed deeply, looking into Bob's powdered face. Jimmy was a real artist. The man looked peaceful, innocent, like a dead saint. But Simon knew full well that he wasn't. Everybody had something for him to eat. Everybody.

He stared at the food for a moment, steeling himself. He chewed his chapped lips, scratched his bony arms. Then he grabbed the bread from the dead man's chest and began to devour it, quickly, like ripping off a band-aid. It was mere seconds before the sins began to kick in, as juicy and dark and bitter in his mouth as rotten fruit.

Little-boy Bob, stealing money from his mother's purse. Lying. Lying. Lying. Pushing his sister off the swings. Teenage Bob and his friends, beating up a skinny, fey kid named Maurice. Swiping a bottle of whiskey from the drug store. With a girl in the backseat of his father's car, pretending he doesn't hear her say 'no,' pushing her down, pushing her apart, pushing into her.

Simon ripped into the apple tarts, unaware of his own howls and sobbing. Sweet apple and pastry in his mouth, then other things; pedestrian evil, the banality of suburban sin. Grown-up Bob had nothing spectacular under his belt; no murders, no robberies, but what he had was so ugly. Bob cheating on his wife, lying to his family, ignoring his children. Stealing from work. Leaving his mother to rot in a "rest home." And so on. And so on. And so on.

Sometime later, Simon came to, squatting on the floor by the embalming table. He hadn't been asleep, not really, but in a torpid, trancelike state while Bob's sins permeated the membrane of his soul and became his very own.

Bob. Bob's sins. More than some, but less than most. Simon struggled to his feet and looked at the man on the table, a man who had been reduced, in Simon's mind, to only his evil deeds. Bob's face no longer looked innocent to him. He just looked like meat, dead and rotting, shot through with corruption.

The boy's stomach was filled with lead. The sins were gone from the food, taken into his system like a potent drug. What was in his belly now was just a lump of chewed-up, inert glop.

Simon threw open the door and breathed in the clean night air, trying to fight off the nausea. Of course, he couldn't. He bent over and emptied the contents of his stomach at the base of a big castor bean plant. He was wiping his lips on the back of his hand when he saw the lights of the hearse come swinging onto the driveway.

He ducked back into the embalming room and grabbed his basket. It was heavy; he needed two hands to hold it. Simon slipped into the trees and the shadows before the hearse came to a full stop.

The walk home was long and tiring. Simon was always exhausted after a Sineating. A little older. A little more weighed down. The basket seemed like it would pull his arms out of their sockets. His feet were like lead.

He walked through the darkness, relying on the thin streams of moonlight through the trees to guide him home. Although the night was dark and filled with sound, he was unafraid. No one would dare hurt the sineater. No one dared touch him. Even animals seemed to avoid his company.

He was starting to hurt by the time he reached his old, impossibly tiny house. Muscle cramps, nausea, headache, the beginnings of a twitch under his eye.

Simon stumbled through the front door and set the basket down heavily. He crossed the cramped living room, where he had slept when his father was alive, to the bedroom where he now spent his nights. He pulled a battered metal box from under the narrow bed and set it down on the mattress.

He took out the World War II injection kit he'd bought at the flea market in Jonesborough, and the little silver spoon he'd found at the city dump. He took out a plastic Bic lighter, and one of the tiny glassine packets that were scattered around the bottom of the box.

This packet had a crude little drawing of a face with spiky hair and X's over the eyes, and the words "DEAD BOY" underneath it. That made Simon smile.

He shook the powder out into the spoon. There was still some water in his washbowl, thank God. He didn't have to go staggering out to the creek tonight. He sucked some up in the syringe and added it to the powder in the spoon.

Simon held the Bic's little flame under the mix. It bubbled fast. Good news. Probably pretty good stuff.

His hands were starting to shake, so he didn't bother to filter. He drew the stuff up in the syringe and dropped his pants.

The veins in Simon's arms were starting to get trashed, and he was a hurry, he didn't want to spend twenty minutes jabbing around for a good one. He stuck the needle into a vein in his inner thigh instead. The heavy glass syringe bloomed with a curling ribbon of blood as he drew back a little. Simon pushed in the plunger.

Ooooh. Yes. The warm rush started at the base of his spine, spreading down to his groin and legs, up through his skinny chest and into his brain. Simon fell back on the bed with his eyes closed. The needle hung embedded his leg for a moment, then dropped to the bed.

Breathing deeply, Simon was content, even happy. The heroin had shoved all the bad things from his brain; all the sins, all the guilt, all the horror. He was floating on soft, skin-warm clouds. Even his soul felt clean; shiny and new.

Simon wondered, as he started to nod off, if the drug really did have the power to cleanse him. If he overdosed, would he float to heaven like a feather on a breeze, or would the weight of the sins he had swallowed drag him down to the blazing depths of Hell?

Either way, Simon thought he'd be better off than he was in Possum Kingdom.

SLUMBER PARTY

Rose couldn't believe how quickly, how confidently, Robbie Jo moved through the darkness. She was as sure-footed as a deer, stepping over fallen branches and stones like they were illuminated with spotlights. Rose, on the other hand, couldn't see shit.

Well, that wasn't quite true. If she looked up, she could see the tree branches silhouetted against the bluish moonlight. She could see that it was darker in the woods than it was on the path, an inky blackness that made her feel short of breath. Every now and then, she caught the yellow glint of some little animal's eyes, watching from a tree or the underbrush. She could hear the animals, too. The soft hoot of an owl, little things scuttling through the bushes, the delicate flutter of bats' wings.

Rose never would have admitted it, but she was more than a little freaked out. Night in the woods was darker than any dark that existed in Miami. Anything could have been out there, watching, waiting for the perfect chance to reach out and grab her. Every stupid slasher film that featured inbred freaks or hockey-masked dead guys began playing on the bigscreen in her head. She remembered one about a giant, mutant, inside-out bear. The flesh on the back of her neck began to crawl.

Then Rose began to wonder about real bears. Her stomach cramped, thinking of what else might be out there.

Like her father, maybe, because he'd found out where she was, and he'd been following her for days, and he would step out from behind a tree with that big, shit-eating grin of his, long ape arms held wide to pull her back in...

No. No. No. He wasn't there. Of course he wasn't. That was just stupid.

But maybe a puma was. Or a pack of rabid dogs. Or a pissed-off wolverine.

Robbie Jo didn't seem concerned about these possibilities at all. The other girl glanced around as she walked, alert as a hawk, but not scared. Not even worried.

Rose held onto Robbie Jo's hand tightly. She didn't need to see, as long as she had Robbie Jo.

Something crossed the path ahead of them. Something big. Something on two legs. It had a weird, shambling gait, and there was something all wrong about the shape.

Rose let out a little yelp and backpedaled as her heart squeezed down to the size of a walnut. "What the hell was that?" she squeaked. "Oh, fuck!"

Robbie Jo laughed. "You've got the nightvision of a nearsighted chicken. That was just a kid. Some scrawny boy with a big ol' basket in his hands." She paused seeming to consider something.

"Holy shit!" said Robbie Jo.

"What?"

"I'll bet that was the sineater. He was comin' from the direction of the Sweet Hereafter."

"Oh, for shit's sake. What's a sineater?"

Rose saw the flash of Robbie Jo's teeth. "'Round here folks believe that a dead person can't get into heaven all weighted down with sins. The sineater's a guy who comes over and eats a plate of food off the corpse, symbolically consuming his sins so the croaker's soul is nice and clean when he gets to heaven."

"You're making that up." Rose giggled.

"Nope. The ignorance of Possum Kingdom knows no bounds."

Rose thought about this for a minute. "But…isn't Jesus supposed to forgive all your sins? Isn't that kind of the point of being Christian?"

"Well, sure. But Catholics still need to confess and do penance, don't they?" Robbie Jo was swinging their clasped hands like a little girl might.

"Yeah, that's true…now that I think about it, that doesn't make much sense, either, if Jesus really forgives everything."

"Don't ask me, honey, I ain't no theologist. Maybe they just don't want to take up J.C.'s time, forgivin' all those sins, when they could just get wiped clean beforehand. Like the Paperwork Reduction act."

Rose snorted. "Or maybe you get a nicer condo in heaven if you show up with no sins."

"Prob'ly! And if you're really bad, you end up in a trailer park in Purgatory!" The girls dissolved into laughter.

They were walking again.

"Robbie Jo?"

"Yeah?"

"What happens when the sineater dies? Who eats his sins?"

"The next sineater. His son, maybe. Or some poor worthless sumbitch the town puts pressure on to do it."

"Oh. Um, what happens if no on eats the sineater's sins?"

Robbie Jo grinned, eyes glittering. "Burn, baby, burn. Express elevator to the bottom circle of Hell!"

And just like that, they were out of the woods, back in town. Robbie Jo had guided them through the darkness.

Walking down Main Street in the middle of the night was weird. It was a ghost town. People in Possum Kingdom went to bed early, even on Saturday night.

Robbie Jo pointed out the lights on in the Sweet Hereafter. "Jimmy and Sam are gonna have a challenge with ol' Taylor Alki. He wasn't that much to look at before, and now he's all swole up with rattlesnake venom!"

"Ugh," said Rose. "They'll have to close the casket."

"Nope, prob'ly not. A little ice, a little Edema Eliminator, and a whole lotta make-up, and Taylor'll be presentable."

Rose grimaced. "I could have gone my whole life without knowing that."

Robbie Jo pointed to a faint light through the trees. "That's Jimmy Ligget's house. He's prob'ly up reading. A real night owl, that one."

"Are you guys friends?"

"Acquaintances. That Jimmy's a sharp guy, though." Rose wondered, briefly, about the way Robbie Jo's eyes narrowed when she said the embalmer's name.

They turned down the path to the Tanner's house. Rose saw that they had left the porch light on for her.

"Well, here you go, Rosie. I'd best be headin' home." Robbie Jo let go of Rose's hand and started to turn away.

"Uh—wait a second, Robbie Jo! It's really late!"

She turned around. "Yeah? So what?"

"You shouldn't be walking home in the middle of the night, all by yourself. It's not safe!"

Robbie Jo chuckled. "This isn't Miami, honey. No muggers in Possum Kingdom."

"What about wild animals? Bears and mountain lions and things?"

"Lions and tigers and bears, oh shit!" Robbie Jo whispered. "Listen, Rose, I've been walkin' around Possum Kingdom at night since I was knee-high to a milk goat. I'll be fine."

Rose shifted from foot to foot. "I'm sure you would be...but why don't you come inside with me? You could stay over, the Tanners wouldn't mind. That way I won't worry about you all night."

Robbie Jo seemed to consider this for a moment. Then she smiled. "Well, okay, then!"

The two girls in Rose's big wooden bed, propped up on pillows, chatting and giggling. Robbie Jo braiding Rose's hair. Rose painting Robbie Jo's nails electric purple. Rose was suddenly certain that she'd never before in her life been as happy, felt as secure.

Then Robbie Jo had to rock the boat. Shit, she capsized it.

She rolled over onto her stomach, propped her chin up on her hand, and fixed Rose with those amazing copper eyes. "Listen," she said, with the slightest smile. "I know the story you told the Tanners is complete bullshit. What are you really doin' here, Rosie? What are you runnin' from? That drunken daddy of yours?"

All the air seemed to suck out of the room. Rose's eyes actually went out of focus for a moment. Her heart pounded. Her mouth went dry. She had never talked about it before. Never.

But why shouldn't I? Why not? For the first time in my life, I have a friend. A real friend.

"You're right." The words came out in a whisper. "I ran away from my dad. He…" She swallowed, coughed, trying to dislodge the words stuck in her throat. "He molested me."

Robbie Jo nodded, eyes not wavering from Rose's. "I see. Was he fuckin' you?"

A hot spike of anger flashed through Rose's brain. "Why would you even ask a thing like that? Jesus!"

Robbie Jo's face remained placid. "My daddy molested me from the time I was a baby. He never got around to fuckin' me. Oh, he tried when I was ten, but I ran from him and the dumb sumbitch tripped and cracked his skull on a rock. Killed him deader'n a slaughterhouse cow."

Rose blinked. Her brain went blank for a flickering moment. "I—oh my God, Robbie Jo. I'm sorry."

"Don't be. I got over it. Seein' my daddy's brains washin' down the creek helped me some." The corner of her mouth quirked up.

Rose chewed her lower lip. "Yeah, he fucked me. All the time. From the time I was about eleven." Tears began to slip down her cheeks. She let out a harsh, barking laugh. "Thank God the bastard had a vasectomy by then. I think I'd have blown my brains out if he'd knocked me up."

Robbie Jo reached out and stroked Rose's hair. "Where was your mama durin' all this?"

Rose's eyes narrowed. "Dead. She died when I was three. Of a fucking brain tumor, of all the stupid things. I don't really remember her much. I remember the color of her eyes, they were green as mint leaves. I remember how good she smelled. I remember her arms around me, her kissing my forehead." Rose sniffed noisily. "I remember her voice, singing The Itsy Bitsy Spider."

"Your dad started drinkin' after she died?"

"Well…I think he drank before that, but my mom kept him in line. He didn't start—he didn't start with me until after she was gone."

Robbie Jo wriggled closer on the bed, resting her forehead against Rose's. "Did your mom know?" Rose asked softly. Robbie Jo took in a ragged, uneven breath.

"She...she didn't know. But she did. She knew somethin' was wrong. She had to. But she's a drunk, a fuckin' drunk, and when she drinks ever'thin' looks nice and purty, and that's how she likes it. I think she just decided not to see it. Y'know?"

"I think so. Robbie Jo, how do you live with her? Don't you resent her?"

Robbie Jo dropped her face to the bed. "Yeah. You could say that. You could also say I hate her mis'rable guts. You could also say I hope she chokes to death on her own vomit."

Robbie Jo peeked up at Rose, her eyes red and wet. Rose held out her arms. Robbie Jo's face shimmered through a number of almost-emotions. Then she lay down next to Rose, and rested her head on her shoulder.

Rose closed her eyes and listened to her friend's breathing. In a little while, it grew deep and even. Robbie Jo's eyes were closed, her long coppery lashes bright against her white cheeks. Her lips were slightly parted. She looked like an angel.

Rose rested her cheek against Robbie Jo's soft hair. A feeling of peace, of sweet, cool calm, began to flow through Rose's brain like honey.

Robbie Jo, for all her weird little quirks, despite her morbid bent...Robbie Jo may well have been the best thing that ever happened to Rose.

Robbie Jo, and Possum Kingdom.

ROBBIE JO

*R*eligion. Faith. The opiate of the masses, right? Well, I think it's more like the crack-pipe of the masses, a cheap high for very little effort, but the drug analogy works just fine. After all, religion and drugs are two things that some people need, absolutely can't live without. They're two things that people will mindlessly kill for.

I don't want anythin' to do with either one, personally. Both will fuck up your thinkin' and take your free will. But if I had to pick one, I reckon I'd take drugs. At least gettin drugs into your system doesn't involve swallowin' a gigantic lump of horseshit.

Let's just think about Christianity for a minute. The first thing you gotta believe is there's this big ol' man up in the sky who sees and hears ever'thin', who knows ever'thin' you do or say or think. He's s'posed to be a good guy. He's s'posed to be Love Incarnate. But He lets pedophiles ass-fuck and murder three-year-olds. He lets babies get AIDS. He lets men beat their wives to death, wives beat their kids to death, kids walk into their schools and hose down their little friends with automatic weapons.

That's 'cause he lets us have free will, right? He lets us make our own choices. But what about the innocent folks who get in the way of our choices? People tell their kids to pray and God'll keep 'em safe. But where is He when the guy with the candy bar and no handles on the back doors of his car comes around? Where is He when the little kids in Bangkok brothels are gettin' drilled by one old fat white sumbitch after another, until they die of some loathsome disease or internal bleedin' or just plain broken-hearted misery?

Where is He when some drunken redneck peckerwood bitch decides it's a good idea to put her baby in a coffin on stilts?

Some folks will tell you that the people who die untimely deaths, the little kids and the babies and the young men shot in ridiculous street wars, are the ones God loves most, the ones He wants to call home. If that's the case, why the hell does He have to torture 'em first? If He liked 'em so goddam much, why'd he put 'em on Earth in the first place?

If you ask me, the whole thing's a pretty sick little fuckin' game. God sets people on the Earth like some zit-faced kid with his ant farm, just so He can fuck with us? Just so He can make some of us blindly obey him, praise Him endlessly, kiss His divine ass? So He can throw the rest into the burnin' depths of Hell for havin' a different opinion? And hey, if you really irritate Him, God might kill you outright, pull out His holy magnifyin' glass and fry your pathetic little insect ass. What fun.

Then there's Jesus, the Lamb of God. He died for our sins, to clean us all up so we're decent enough to get into heaven. But it doesn't really work that way, does it? There's a little extortion goin' on here. You've gotta pledge your undyin' love to JC first, declare Him your Lord and Savior, before you get the membership card to the Pearly Gates. And He wants you to do it, 'cause He loves us all. Well, if He's so fuckin' sweet, why'd He let the Crusaders slaughter thousands of folks in His name? Why'd He let the ever-lovin' Spanish Inquisition do what they did under His banner? I mean, wouldn't you be just a little bit pissed if some serial killer wasted a passel of men, women and children, and when the cops picked him up, he said he did it just for YOU?

Sorry, I just don't buy it. None of it.

And shee-it, Christians can't even agree which version of their bullshit story is right. Protestants and Catholics slaughterin' each other, Baptists sayin' you'll go to Hell if you dance, Calvinists sayin' you'll go to Hell if you so much as crack a smile.

Even a bunch of fuckin' freaks like the snake handlers can't settle on a story. They're divided into two camps; Trinity and Jesus Name. The Trinity folks believe the Godhead's divided up into three critters, so they're baptized in the name of the Father, the Son, and the Holy Ghost. The Jesus Name crew think that God's just one guy, and Jesus and the Holy Ghost are just parts of Him, like multiple personalities or Halloween masks or some shit. So they're baptized "in the name of Jesus Christ."

If that's not enough, the snake handlin' churches quibble over whether footwashin' should be part of the service (now that's puttin' the fear back into religion—you should see these inbred motherfuckers' gnarly feet), if church members can get divorced and remarried, and whether JC should be called Jesus, Jesus Christ, or the Lord Jesus. (I prefer to call Him the Zombie of Zion, my ownself.)

I gotta admit, I just kinda stand back and gape at all this arguin' over the fine points. It's surreal, that's what it is. Like folks fightin' over whether flyin' dogs levitate, have propellers, or if they're jet-powered.

Then there are those folks who decide the Christian God is too male-oriented, too brutal, too pushy. So they turn to the Goddess instead. Oh, that makes a lot more sense, doesn't it? Instead of a giant ol' man in the sky, it's a giant chick. Or three giant chicks. Or three giant chicks and their deer boyfriend. Now, I like the idea of sacrificin' boys to make the corn grow tall, but modern pagans just don't have the ovaries for that stuff. And you know what? I don't buy their line, either. It's just another bunch of superstitions and lies, cooked up to keep people from facin' up to the fact that they're gonna die and rot someday.

Jehovah, Gaia, Vishnu, Kali, Ra, Isis, Klingons, Bigfoot, the Loch Ness Fuckin' Monster. If I can't shove a cantaloupe up my right nostril, how the hell am I supposed to shove a honeydew up my left?

That Rosie, she feels just the same way. I'm sure of it. She wishes it were diff'rent, but she believes in God about as much as she believes in the Weekly World News Bat Child.

I'm startin' to really like that girl. It's a weird feelin'.

I'm not sure if I care for it or not.

TIME PASSES THROUGH POSSUM KINGDOM

The sun came up on Sunday morning, and the day after that, and Rose settled into the routine of life in Possum Kingdom. She worked in the General Store, getting to know the people who came in by their first names, then by their family names, then by their reputations and the miasma of gossip that surrounds every single resident in a tiny town.

Dr. Michael Yeats, the doggie doc, came in a few times as the summer wore on. He was always polite and friendly, making conversation, asking Rose how things were with her. She answered him haltingly, feeling that her tongue had swollen to three times its natural size. He didn't seem to mind.

Naomi began to teach her to cook. The brown, crispy "ears" on Rose's cat heads could stand up there with the best. Her corn pudding was downright succulent. Her gravy had a few lumps in it, but, as Robbie Jo put it, it didn't purely suck.

She bought a few new pieces of clothing; flowered sundresses and short overalls that Naomi sold to her for practically nothing. The Tanners paid her generously for her work in the General Store, and never would take a penny in rent from her. At first that made Rose uncomfortable. A little later, it made her feel like a member of the Tanners' household, not the stray boarder they'd picked up in the street.

Over time, Rose began to relax. She no longer thought she saw her father in every shadow. She no longer cringed when a short, muscular man walked through the doorway of the store. She knew it wasn't him. A day at a time, Rose convinced herself that he'd forgotten all about her. She liked to pretend she had been born in Possum Kingdom. She liked to pretend that Naomi and Owen were her parents. They made it easy for her; they seemed to love her like a daughter.

Rose was happy. Life was slow and easy. Life was good.

Robbie Jo wasn't exactly happy, but she was having a lot of fun. She and Sam had sex every chance they got, in every position and every weird place they could think of. She particularly enjoyed the top of the refrigerator, and the soft patch of grass in Sam's backyard, under the castor bean trees.

She just hung out at Sam's house a lot too, because he had cable, a VCR and DVD player, *and* a digital satellite dish, all hooked up in his room. Sam's parents didn't like her, that much was obvious by the narrow looks they gave her, cracking the façade of their Southern courtesy like thin ice on a shallow lake. Robbie Jo didn't give a rat's ass.

Nancy grew more and more irritating, sullen and resentful as Robbie Jo spent less and less time with her. Again, Robbie Jo didn't give a rat's ass. She had the copy of "Freeway" that she made Nancy tape, plus six HBO "Autopsy" specials, and a copy of "Silence of the Lambs" that Nancy had bought at the Wal-Mart in Jonesborough, just for her. She didn't need Nancy any more.

Whenever Robbie Jo wasn't fucking Sam senseless, she was with Rose. The two girls were so happy in each other's company that the town began to call them the "sunshine sisters." It made them both want to puke.

The black dog dug herself a den underneath a fallen log. She ate guts from Joe Reechur's bottomless supply, and she got fatter and fatter. The rounder her sides grew, the more she needed to eat. She supplemented the guts with grass and wild berries, and developed an insatiable craving for mice. She had grown so large and awkward that catching them wasn't easy, but still she managed it, pouncing after them like a black furry beach ball. A sense of contentment washed coolly through her days and nights. Although she missed the company of humans, the black dog was happy.

The sun grew hotter, the days grew longer, and Possum Kingdom hummed with the sweet vibration of summer. Tempers didn't grow short; instead, everybody grew languid and affable. The laughter of children rang through the narrow streets, and folks stayed up late sitting on their front porches and swapping stories. Life in Possum Kingdom was about as fine as it could be.

Then, of course, the shit hit the fan.

POOR OLD MISS LYNDON

Effie Granger boiled into the General Store like a bloated summer stormcloud, redfaced and thundering.

"She's daid!" Effie bellowed, looking almost pleased. "Doc found her at the base of the stairs, and her neck was busted so bad her haid was on backwards! It's awful! Just awful!"

Rose, who was wiping down the candy counter, blinked a couple of times. Naomi popped out from the dry goods aisle before she could say a word.

"Effie, what in God's name are you talkin' about? Who's dead? What happened?"

Effie took in a great, whooping gulp of air, and her face went from crimson to raspberry. "Miss Lyndon! Hazel Lyndon, Doc Yeats' receptionist!"

Naomi's sweet face fell. "Oh, the poor old dear."

Effie scowled. "It was her cat that done it, I'll bet! That damn ol' fat cat of hers!"

A giggle burst from Rose's lips. She clapped her hand over her mouth.

"Oh, good lord!" cried Naomi. "Are you tellin' me you think Miss Lyndon's cat murdered her? Are you out of your mind, Effie Granger?"

Effie snorted like a bull. "I'm sayin' I think it tripped her! She didn't come in to work this mornin'. When Doc Yeats went to her house to check on her, he found her at the bottom of the stairs, cold as a mackerel. Her neck was broke in seven places. Sam Dunwiddie is over there right now, pickin' up her poor ol' body. And I'll bet that ungrateful ol' cat of hers tripped her on purpose."

"Oh, her cat did nothin' of the sort, Effie. Old folks just lose their balance. It's a tragic accident, that's all." Naomi shook her head.

"And do you know what else? Do you *know* what *else*?"

Effie glared back and forth between Naomi and Rose, as if she were accusing them of being in on it with the cat.

Naomi's eyebrow shot up. "No, I don't know, but I'm sure you're gonna tell us." Rose shoved down a little grin. This was the closest she'd ever seen Naomi come to being rude.

"Doc Yeats took that horrible cat home with him! It oughta be put down, that's what, but he took it home and it's prob'ly sleepin' on a silk pilla right now! The vicious thang!"

Naomi feigned shock. "Is that so. Well, Doc had just better watch his back, that's all I have to say. I hope he hides the kitchen knives!"

Effie's mouth compressed itself smaller and smaller, until it was a tiny red slit. "Well!" She turned and stomped out of the store.

Rose burst out laughing, and immediately regretted it. "I'm—I'm sorry, Naomi. I think it's terrible about Miss Lyndon. But—"

Naomi chuckled. "I know. That Effie is just an eedjit sometimes. I'm sure that poor ol' kitty is simply brokenhearted. I'm glad Doc took him home."

"Me, too."

Naomi sighed, and crossed her plump arms. "Poor Miss Lyndon. She was a sweet ol' thing. And poor Doc! What's he gonna do without her?"

Rose didn't know what to say, so she kept her mouth shut.

"Well, listen, honey. I'm gonna go over and see if Doc Yeats needs anything. Would you watch the store for a little while?"

"Sure thing."

Naomi gathered up a sackful of food (canned soups, dried beans, macaroni and cheese, cookies and candy) and headed out the door.

It wasn't five minutes before Robbie Jo came in.

"Have you heard?" she asked, leaning across the counter with a bland expression.

"Yeah," said Rose. "Bummer."

"Poor Doc Yeats is pretty shaken up. I guess it wasn't such a pretty sight."

Rose shuddered. "Yikes. I sure as hell wouldn't like to find a body. Especially not somebody I knew."

"You get used to it," said Robbie Jo. "Makes you think, though, doesn't it?"

"What?"

"Death. Makes you think about what you wanna do with your life."

"Mm," said Rose. She wasn't sure she was comfortable with the subject.

Robbie Jo opened a big bell jar and helped herself to a blackberry taffy. "So tell me, Rosie," she said with her mouth full, "What are you gonna be when you grow up?"

Rose bit her lip. A weird, empty feeling passed through her as she realized she honestly had no idea.

She'd never thought that far ahead. In Miami, her life had been pain and degradation and wishing for death each night, and the blessed relief of school during the day. Nothing else. She was an excellent student. She threw herself into each subject, learning as much as she could, basking in the approval of her teachers. School was the place she felt valuable and special.

The guidance counselors loved her. They told her she could be anything—a doctor, a lawyer, a scientist, a writer. She gamely took Anatomy and Physiology and American Law and advanced chemistry classes. But just so they would smile at her.

Because she couldn't have a life of her own. There was no future for her. Although she dressed and entered the living world when the sun came up, every night she had to return to Hell. She was a citizen of the seventh circle, and the devil who had her eyes would never let her go.

Then she did what she had to, and she left Miami, and life pushed her down the river like the tiniest fallen leaf. She had just been existing in Possum Kingdom, hiding out, surviving, a frightened squirrel in the deep Tennessee woods. There was no tomorrow. Just today, this minute.

But her father hadn't found her. If she thought about it rationally, Rose realized he probably never would.

Ridiculously, her heart began pounding. She had been her class Valedictorian. Almost any college would accept her. She could work her way through. Or get a scholarship. The world suddenly cracked wide open and lay itself down in front of Rose Heron.

"Rose, honey? You okay? You're lookin' a little peaked."

"I—yeah, I'm fine. You first, okay?" Rose grinned. "You gonna be rich and famous, Robbie Jo?"

Robbie Jo nodded slowly. "I'm gonna be rich, all right. Obnoxiously rich. Obscenely rich."

"Famous too?"

"Oh, yes. My name's gonna be a household word. People are gonna write books about me. Make movies about my life." Robbie Jo lowered her eyelids. Her mouth bowed up in a sly little smile. "But only after I'm dead, Rosie."

Rose hesitated, then laughed. "It's always that way with true genius, huh? So how are you gonna make all that money, anyway? Find some rich old fart to marry?"

"Shit, no. I'll find a way to do it real fast, I don't wanna spend too much time on it. I'm thinkin' the stock market. Then, when I've got all the money I need, I can travel all over the country. Around the world, even!"

"Sounds great. Going anywhere you want to…seeing everything…are you gonna visit the Grand Canyon and the Eiffel Tower and all that stuff?"

Robbie Jo nodded. "Oh, prob'ly. Mostly I just wanna meet new people. All kinds of people."

"I didn't think you were that sociable, Robbie Jo."

"I'm not. So, have you figured out what you're gonna do with your life yet, ya slacker?" Robbie Jo reached across the counter and gently tugged a lock of Rose's hair.

Her brain flashed through a myriad of possibilities. Then, for some reason, she saw the black dog in her mind's eye. Lost and alone. Standing in the street, head hanging, hurt and afraid.

The answer popped into Rose's mind like a flashbulb. "I... I really like animals. I'm thinking about being a vet."

"Well, damn! That's a worthy occupation. You'd be good at it too, Rosie. You're such a sweet thang." Robbie Jo batted her eyes.

Rose laughed. "Fuck you."

"Such a mouth on you! Somebody should wash it out with soap so you learn some fuckin' respect."

"Here, I'll sweeten it up for you." Rose popped a taffy onto her tongue and waggled it at Robbie Jo.

"Ugh! I don't have to take this, y'know. See you later, you lil' heathen. I've got a date." Robbie Jo tossed her hair, spun around, and marched out the door.

Rose chewed the candy slowly, and watched her friend leave. She knew Robbie Jo was seeing Sam all the time. Although the other girl had never said anything, she was pretty sure Robbie Jo was sleeping with him. It worried Rose sick.

But what could she say? Love is blind, deaf, and stupid. If Robbie Jo couldn't see what a creep Sam was with her own eyes, Rose pointing it out wouldn't make her vision any clearer. It would probably just make Robbie Jo mad, Rose thought. Maybe so mad they wouldn't be friends anymore.

And I just couldn't live with that.

Rose sighed, and hoped with all her heart that Robbie Jo was being careful.

ROBBIE JO PLANTS A SEED

Sam stared up at the rust-eyed goddess impaled on his pecker and wished like crazy that he could touch the sweat on her breasts, cup the cheeks of her ass, wrap his hands around her tiny waist as she rode him like a bronco.

He couldn't, of course, because he was tied to the bed.

With the wickedest of winks, she'd taken some of his expensive silk Italian ties from his antique cherrywood dresser and lashed him down with unnerving efficiency.

At first he didn't like it. Sam liked to be in control. Period. He told Robbie Jo to untie him.

"Nope," she'd said, and gave his unit a sqeeze.

Sam started swearing and struggling. Then Robbie Jo was doing incredible things to him with her hands and her mouth, and his brain went away.

It was mere moments before Sam discovered how good it was to stretch and strain against his silk bonds as Robbie Jo nipped her way down his abdomen.

She tortured him, in the finest possible way. God, it was hard to believe the girl was only fifteen years old. She'd picked up moves that a professional would envy. By the time she slid down Sam's flagpole, he was crazy with need, whimpering and writhing like a submissive puppy. He realized that Robbie Jo was in complete control of him, that he was, at that moment, her creature. He didn't give a fuck.

Sam's breathing got fast and ragged as he pumped into her. He was vaguely aware of the fact that he was letting out little grunts and groans. Then the orgasm hit him and his spine bent like a bow and he threw back his head and cried out:

"Robbie Jo! Oh, God, I love you!"

Quiet, then. Tension ran from Sam's body and limbs like water. He felt like he was floating. Sam's eyes were closed. He breathed deeply, half drowsing, enjoying the weight of Robbie Jo on his groin and the cool feeling of sweat drying on his sides. He felt her tiny, amazing hands on his chest, stroking, toying with the silky hair around his nipples.

"Did you mean that, honey?" she whispered.

Then Sam remembered what he'd said to her. Slick evasions boiled up in his throat like vomit. He'd never said that to a girl, not ever, but he was sure he could come up with something to get out of it. Of course he could. Sam was a born talker.

But to his complete and utter amazement, he didn't want to.

Sam was paralyzed. For a moment, he couldn't even breathe.

I love Robbie Jo.

I love her.

I do.

"Yes," he said, smiling. "Yes, yes, yes." And he felt himself surrender to her, surrender completely.

Robbie Jo gripped the edges of the rubber and slid Sam out of her. She collapsed onto his finely muscled chest and buried her face in his neck so he wouldn't see her grin of triumph.

"I'm so glad, baby," she murmured. "Because I love you too. I was just afraid to tell you." She tenderly untied the knots that held Sam's wrists and ankles to his magnificent cherrywood four-poster.

He ran his hands up and down her back, and that was nice. Sam sure had his uses.

"Christ, Robbie Jo. I—I've never felt about a girl the way I feel about you." Sam's voice was hesitant, almost shaking, as if he were confessing to something deeply embarrassing.

She shoots, thought Robbie Jo. *She scores!*

"Me too. You're my first, Sam, and I want you to be my only."

Robbie Jo held her breath. A calculated risk, but he didn't flinch. Instead, he kissed her on the forehead and stroked her hair. She nestled in tighter, and they lay that way together, for awhile.

"I just wish your folks liked me better," she said in a voice as tiny and pathetic as she could muster.

Sam sighed deeply. "I know. Daddy at least tries to be polite, but Mama's downright rude to you. I can't stand it, sugar, but I don't know what to do about it."

"Don't you even think about tryin' to run off with me," Robbie Jo said bravely. "You've gotta stick it out. One day the Sweet Hereafter will be all yours."

"Don't I know it. That's the only reason I stick around. I fuckin' hate those old fossils." She felt Sam's body tense up as he thought of his parents, his jailers.

"Maybe they'll die soon," Robbie Jo whispered, stroking Sam's thigh.

He snorted. "No such luck. They're both healthy as pack horses. They'll prob'ly outlive me."

"I don't know how you can stand it. A man like you, havin' to tiptoe around his mama and daddy like a scared little kid. It must eat at your soul, Sam Dunwiddie. It must make you just plain sick." She heard the faint sound of Sam's molars grinding together.

"Sometimes, Robbie Jo, I think about killin' 'em."

Bingo! A direct hit! You win the kewpie doll, Sam honey! Somehow, Robbie Jo managed to not leap up and dance around the room.

"You...you could, Sam." She barely breathed the words, sounding frightened and a little shocked, as if she couldn't believe the words were coming out of her mouth. "You could do it. Get rid of 'em." A stellar performance, thought Robbie Jo, if she did say so herself.

Sam heaved another sigh. "Get serious, honey."

She raised herself up on her elbows and gazed into his deep green eyes. "I am serious. I can't stand to see you sufferin' like this, baby. You gotta get yourself free. Somehow."

He studied her face, tracing her lower lip with his finger. "How?" he said finally. "I just can't march into their bedroom and shoot 'em."

"'Course not. It shouldn't look like a murder at all."

A slow smile crept over Sam's perfect features. "Oh yeah? What, then? Ever'body who knows my folks also knows they'd never kill themselves."

"An accident, maybe. Or somethin' else. Let me think on it some, sugar."

He grinned. "Let you think on it? What does a lil' schoolgirl like you know about plottin' a murder?"

More than you ever will, she thought.

"You know what a good study I am. I'll go to the computer lab and poke around on the Internet."

"And just how are you gonna get into the computer lab at school in the middle of summer, little lady?" Sam lightly smacked her butt.

"I've got a key."

"Your teacher gave you a key?"

Robbie Jo grinned down at Sam. "Nobody gave me nothin'."

"Shee-it, girl, you're amazin'!" Sam kissed her fiercely, and rolled over with her until he was on top.

Robbie Jo kissed him back, fingers tangled in his thick black hair. She ran her hands over Sam's finely shaped skull. Wondering. Wondering exactly what was in there, and why it was so easy to manipulate, just like soft summer mud.

WHAT NAOMI SAW
(A PECK OF TROUBLE)

*N*aomi walked down the street, away from the vet's office, toward the Sweet Hereafter. She felt a lead weight in her chest, and wished she could have done more for Doc Yeats. Let's face it, a few groceries didn't amount to squat, in the face of Granddaddy Death. But that was the way you did it in the South. The way you told somebody you cared, that you were thinking of them in their hour of grief.

He was such a nice young man, and he was obviously so upset by Miss Lyndon's death. When Naomi called on him he had been scattered, unfocused, his eyes dry but rimmed with red. He held Miss Lyndon's big old cat, Pun'kin, cradled in his arms. A furry security blanket.

Miss Lyndon had worked for him since he took over the running of the vet's office almost four years ago. Before that, she'd worked for Doc Mitchell, the old vet, for so many years the town had lost count. Doc Yeats had never considered replacing her. He seemed to care for her as if she were his own grandma.

"Poor boy," murmured Naomi. She bustled up the walk of the Sweet Hereafter and rang the doorbell.

Ephram Dunwiddie answered, looming in the doorway like a long, dark shadow. Naomi had to put a crick in her neck to look him in the face. He was wearing his standard mask of sympathy, but when he saw it was Naomi, he smiled.

"Hello, Mrs. Tanner," he said, and Naomi found his voice as rich and pleasing as the rumble of distant thunder.

"Hello, Ephram. I've come about Miss Lyndon."

"Do come in, dear lady." He held the door for her, and escorted her to the parlor.

Naomi loved the Sweet Hereafter's parlor. She supposed she wouldn't find it quite so nice if she'd sat there before, discussing the final arrangements for someone she loved, but she'd been lucky in life and that had never happened. Her parents were gone, of course. But they'd died in Jonesborough. Her experience of the parlor consisted of afternoon tea, and lunches spent chatting and politely gossiping with Ruth.

"Now then," said Ephram, who sat down only after Naomi had, "how may I help you?"

Naomi shifted in the leather wingback chair, suddenly uncomfortable. "I know that Miss Lyndon didn't have any kinfolks in town. And she was such a fine lady."

"That she was," Ephram agreed.

"Owen and I…we'd like to pay for her final arrangements. She was important to this town, Ephram. She was a part of us." Naomi hadn't actually discussed this with Owen, but she knew he would agree. He had a heart bigger than the sun.

Ephram smiled. "Why, that's terribly kind of you both. But I'm pleased to tell you that Miss Lyndon had insurance. Not much, mind you, but enough to give her a decent funeral. A lovely funeral."

"My goodness." Naomi had no idea why she should be surprised. She knew next to nothing about Miss Lyndon's personal life. "Well."

She and Ephram stared at each other for a moment. Then Naomi had a wonderful idea.

"I'd like to hold the wake at my house."

A hint of a frown crossed Ephram's forehead. "Wouldn't that be a great deal of trouble for you and Owen? The chapel here is beautiful, don't you think? We'll do right by her. I promise."

Naomi smiled, slightly rankled. "I know you would. But it would mean a lot to us. Miss Lyndon was such a sweet, friendly soul. I think she'd like the idea of bein' in our parlor, surrounded by her friends."

Ephram opened his mouth, as if he were about to say something, and then closed it again. He locked eyes with Naomi. They both wore tight, polite smiles.

Come on, you stubborn old goat. Ephram was a good man, but he got mulish about the damndest things. Naomi wasn't about to give on this one. Why? She had no idea why. That made her smile grow a little wider.

Ephram let out a nearly inaudible sigh. "Certainly. We'll be happy to transport her earthly remains to your home. Of course, that won't be until tomorrow. She hasn't been…taken care of."

Naomi nodded, triumphant, wondering only briefly why Ephram never seemed to want to say the word "embalmed."

"Well, that's very kind of you. Spread the word, Ephram. We'll have the viewin' tomorrow afternoon, and the service in the evenin'."

There was the flicker of a frown again. "And who will be conducting the service, Naomi?"

She knew immediately what he meant. Would it be Reverend Thomas Rye, the Baptist preacher, or the Reverend Primus Reylark? That question had been buzzing around town since the news broke this morning. Miss Lyndon never went to either church, although rumor had it she used to attend the Holy Blood, many years before.

"Rev'rend Rye," said Naomi. "But please invite the Rev'rend Primus. He's a fine, holy gentleman." In truth, she thought Reverend Rye had the personality and presence of a skinned rabbit, but she couldn't stand snakes. And when push came to shove, she thought the whole idea behind snake handling was silly. Being a Baptist was interesting enough for her and Owen.

"I'll do that."

Naomi started to stand up and excuse herself, as she had plenty to do to prepare for Miss Lyndon's arrival.

A scream ripped through the house, echoing down the stairs, bouncing off the wood paneling and entering Naomi's ears in jagged shards. A woman's scream.

"Ruth!" cried Ephram. He leapt to his feet.

Another scream, and Ephram bounded up the stairs on his long black-clad legs, looking like some kind of funereal grasshopper. Naomi bustled after him. She knew some first aid, after all; maybe she could help.

They ran down a seemingly endless hallway, past doors and wall sconces and lush Victorian wallpaper. Naomi wondered how folks could ever feel at home in a house this big.

Ruth was standing in front of an open door, clutching the knob so hard her knuckles were white. Ephram gripped her elbow, touched her face, saying "What is it, Ruthie? What is it?" Shaking, lips compressed, she raised an accusing finger and pointed into the room. Ephram gasped and started coughing. Naomi peered around him to see.

Robbie Jo sat on a huge four-poster bed that looked like it would be at home in a New Orleans bordello. Her hair was tousled, her eyes wide and frightened. She had a sheet pulled up to her neck, but she was obviously naked. Sam was crouched on the floor on the far side of the bed with just his head sticking up, a red-faced, angry groundhog.

"What the hell is going on here?" Ephram rumbled, supporting his vibrating wife.

"For Christ's sake, Daddy, are you really so old you don't know?" Sam crept up onto the bed beside Robbie Jo. He had the sheet over his lap, but impudently left his lean, muscled chest bare.

Ruth was trembling, her face the color of red brick. Her eyes bulged. Her lips writhed. Naomi wouldn't have been a bit surprised if steam had started blasting from her ears. The woman looked like she was about to explode.

"Whore!" she spat. "Harlot! Jezebel! Get out of my house, you gutter-trash slut!"

Robbie Jo burst into tears and hid her face in her hands.

"Shut the fuck up, you dried-out old bitch!" Sam snarled.

"Don't you dare talk to your mother like that!" roared Ephram, taking a step forward.

"Come get me, old man!" Sam reared up on his knees, dropping the sheet.

"Hey!" yelled Naomi. They all paused to look at her.

"Sam, you don't talk to your mama and daddy like that. And for heaven's sake, put your little doodle away." Sam blushed from his hairline to his nipples. He sank back down and pulled up the sheet.

"And Ruth, don't you talk to Robbie Jo like that. She's just a poor little innocent girl."

"Innocent!" Ruth stomped her foot. "Look at her! Like the whore of Babylon!"

Robbie Jo's sobbing increased.

"Hush! Show a little Christian charity, Ruth. Are you okay, Robbie Jo, honey?" She pushed past the rigid Dunwiddies and patted Robbie Jo's hair.

Robbie Jo looked up at her with wet, weepy eyes. "I—yes, I think so, Miz Tanner."

Naomi glanced at the bed, and saw the ties lashed to the bedposts. "Dear God," she breathed. "Did he tie you up? Sam, did you do that? Robbie Jo, did he hurt you? Do you need a doctor? Honey, are you bleedin'?"

Robbie Jo threw her arms around Naomi's waist and buried her face in Naomi's belly. Naomi stroked her hair. *My lord God. The poor little angel.*

Ruth strode in. "Get out, devil-girl. Get out or I'll throw you out by the scruff of your neck."

Naomi was mad now. "Ruth Dunwiddie, you just shut your pie-hole. Your boy has been a girlie-hound since he was ten years old, and everybody knows it. Have you forgotten the time Mac Dupree found him in the woodshed with his daughter when he was twelve? Or the time Ralph Cutler caught Sam with his wife, and Sam just fourteen years old? Have you forgot the pumpkin patch incident? Vegetables, Ruth! The boy has no control!"

"That isn't true!" Sam bawled. "I tripped on a vine!"

"Shut up, boy!" from Naomi and Ephram.

Ruth swelled up like a helium balloon, ready to release a torrent of rage. Naomi held up a finger and waved it under her nose.

"Save it," she snapped. "Save it for Sam, who's ruined another young life." She gently pried Robbie Jo loose. "We're gonna leave this room. You get your clothes on, Robbie Jo. Sam, if she's not out here in five minutes, I'm comin' in after her. And I'm bringin' my hedge trimmers." Naomi was gratified to see a moment of serious fear cross Sam's perfect face.

She took the Dunwiddies by the arms and marched them out of their son's bedroom, slamming the door. The three of them stood in the hall in awkward silence. Ruth still looked like a teapot about to boil, but Ephram put his arm around her waist and gave her a good squeeze every time she seemed about to go off. From inside the bedroom, the creak of bedsprings, the whisper of clothing on skin, soft, urgent voices.

The door opened. Robbie Jo came out, head down, like a kicked puppy. Naomi's heart broke at her thin, homemade blue dress. She put her arm around Robbie Jo's narrow shoulders. "Come on, honey," Naomi whispered.

Holding her chin up high, Naomi walked with the girl down the long hallway. Without looking back, she called to Ephram: "I'll be expectin' Miss Lyndon tomorrow afternoon."

"You'll have her, Mrs. Tanner," came Ephram's stiff reply. Naomi nodded, and steered her charge down the stairs.

But what was she going to do with the little thing? If it had been anyone but Robbie Jo, it would have been easy. Go to the girl's daddy and set him on Sam like a charging bull. But, of course, Robbie Jo didn't have a daddy. And her mama...well, Naomi suspected that most of that woman's blood had turned to gin by now. She was useless as tits on a boar hog.

"You'll be okay, sugar," as Naomi opened the front door and bright sunlight washed Robbie Jo's tearstreaked face. "You're comin' home with me for awhile."

From upstairs, the screaming began in earnest.

Rose glanced up at the two people walking past the storefront, looked back down at her tattered copy of *Rose Madder*, then did a doubletake. Why on earth was Naomi walking with her arm around Robbie Jo? And was Robbie Jo crying? Rose ran out the front door as Naomi steered Rose down the path to the Tanners' home.

"What's going on?" Rose asked, trying to get a good look at Robbie Jo's face.

Naomi stopped, heaved a sigh. "Robbie Jo's had a bit of trouble. She'll be all right. I'm takin' her to the house to rest. Can you watch the store a little longer?"

"I want Rose to come with me," said Robbie Jo in a tiny voice.

Naomi frowned. "You don't mind if she knows...?"

Robbie Jo shook her head. "She's my best friend."

Rose's mouth filled with bitter fear. "What's wrong? Are you hurt?"

"Close up for a few minutes," said Naomi, her sweet voice sure and strong. "We'll talk in the house."

Naomi sat Robbie Jo down at the kitchen table and went to the fridge for some lemonade. Rose desperately wanted to talk to her friend, but Robbie Jo's face was in her hands.

"Now then." Naomi sat an icy glass of lemonade in front of Robbie Jo, and another in front of Rose. "Take a deep breath, honey. Are you hurt?"

Robbie Jo raised her head. Her eyelids were red and puffy. "I don't think so," she whispered.

"Did he force you?" Naomi took Robbie Jo's hand.

Rose literally saw red. "Who? Who, Robbie Jo?"

"Sam. Nuh—no. He didn't force me. Not really."

Okay, what the fuck is going on? Rose knew damn well that Robbie Jo had been sleeping with Sam for weeks. She wasn't exactly a blushing virgin. But still... *If that fucker hurt her, I'll kill him. I'll rip his goddam head off and go bowling with it.*

Naomi leaned across the table, dark eyes intent. "Listen close, honey. This is really important. Were you usin' some kind of protection?"

Robbie Jo stared at the table, then nodded. "He...he put a...on his..."

"Okay. All right. That's good. That's real good." Silence, for a few moments. A sniff from Robbie Jo. Then Naomi spoke again.

"Little girl, just because Sam talked you into it once doesn't mean it has to happen again. You're safe from him here. Okay?"

Robbie Jo bit her lip. "But me and Sam are in love. He said he's gonna marry me someday."

"Oh, Lord Jesus Christ on a biscuit!" Naomi rolled her eyes heavenward.

"It's true!" said Robbie Jo, a little defensively.

Naomi sighed, a sound that carried the weight of the world. "I believe you, sugar. Would you like to lie down for awhile?"

"I'd kind like a shower," Robbie Jo whispered.

"Sure thing, honey. You go right on upstairs."

Rose stared at Robbie Jo's back as she walked from the room, completely confused.

Then Robbie Jo glanced over her shoulder and winked at her. That's when Rose knew everything was just fine. She felt her whole body relax as she turned back to Naomi.

Naomi and Rose stared at each other across the table. Rose felt vaguely uneasy, a little bit wrong. Robbie Jo had put one over on Naomi. She obviously thought she had to, but it didn't make Rose feel any better.

Naomi smiled at her. "She'll be okay, honey. Don't you worry."

"I know." Guilt, guilt, and more guilt.

Owen, dressed in overalls and a workshirt, wandered into the kitchen. "Got that back bedroom all rewired," he said, kissing Naomi on the cheek, heading for the refrigerator. Then he spotted Rose. "What's up, Naomi?"

Naomi smiled at her handsome husband. "You're pretty handy for an old man. Come sit down, Owen. We need to talk." He did.

"I talked to Doc Yeats for a long time this mornin'. He's in a bad way. He really loved Miss Lyndon."

Owen nodded sadly.

"He needed her, too. You wouldn't think so at her age, but the poor old dear pretty much ran the office. He's lost without her."

"A shame," said Owen.

Naomi turned to Rose. "Honey, you've been such a help to me and Owen. And I'd never presume to try and run your life for you. But I suggested, just suggested mind you, that maybe you'd think about goin' to work for Doc Yeats. And I'm tellin' ya, Rose, he was just tickled with the idea. Just tickled."

Rose's newfound stable world tilted sideways and pitched her off the edge. The idea was wonderful. The idea was terrifying.

"Uh..." she said.

"Of course, I told him how smart you are, sugar. And what a quick study you are. Why, I don't think we had to show you anythin' more than once before you got it down cold. And poor Doc, he just doesn't know what to do without Miss Lyndon. Not to put pressure on ya, honey. It's totally up to you, of course. What do you think about it?"

Owen picked up his wife's hand and kissed it. "Well, Naomi, I'm not sure she can think at all, with that wall of sound batterin' her poor little ears."

Naomi grinned and swatted him. "You old pill."

"I...I could try..." The words slipped out of Rose's mouth, easily, like a silk sheet off a rumpled bed. *Oh, Jesus! Did I just say that? Did I really?*

Naomi beamed. "Wonderful, honey! Just wonderful! Oh, Doc Yeats is just gonna love you."

That made Rose's stomach dance the cha-cha.

"Of course, sugar, you're still gonna stay right here with us. Why, I think we'd just die of loneliness if you left us, wouldn't we, Owen?"

"Yep." He nodded, solemn.

"You're gonna be so good at this! You got a way with animals, I've seen it. I'll go tell Doc this afternoon. He's gonna be thrilled! Just thrilled!"

Rose managed a smile. "Thanks, Naomi. I mean, thank you for everything. You too, Owen. You've—you've just been so kind to me. Like family."

Like family should be, anyway. Fuck you, Daddy Dearest.

"Oh, stop it!" cried Naomi. "You're gonna make me cry. We just love you to death, Rose, honey. You've brought so much joy to our lives, little girl."

Rose felt her face go hot. "I'd better check on Robbie Jo..."

"You do that, honey. Oh, I'm gonna make molasses cookies to celebrate!"

Rose had to hold on to the satiny rosewood banister tightly, take slow steps, because her head was spinning. She couldn't seem to speak a coherent sentence to Michael Yeats. How was she supposed to work for him?

She wanted desperately to talk to Robbie Jo about it. But when she opened the door to her room, her best friend was curled up on the bed, wearing Rose's Cramps t-shirt, sleeping. With a sigh, Rose kicked off her shoes and lay down next to her.

Naomi leaned her head against her husband's belly as he stood behind her chair and rubbed her shoulders. She was delighted that Rose would help out poor Doc Yeats. She was still disturbed by the ugly scene at the Sweet Hereafter.

Sam Dunwiddie was no good. Everyone in town knew it. But he was as handsome as the devil, and evidently just as silver-tongued. Poor little Robbie Jo hadn't stood a chance.

But what could be done about it? Naomi would make sure that the story didn't get out, and that was about it. It would be easy. She wouldn't breathe a word, and she knew the Dunwiddies wouldn't want to tarnish their son's already blackened reputation any further. They'd keep quiet. But it wouldn't help, not in the long run, because Robbie Jo was in love, and there was no reasoning with a person in that state. Naomi knew that from personal experience. The girl would go creeping back to that scoundrel's bed the very next chance she got.

Naomi knew all about love. Sometimes it seemed like yesterday, the first time she laid eyes on Owen. She remembered the way her heart raced, the way she could think of nothing else from that moment on. The smell of his skin, unchanged in forty years. Their first trembling touches, and the raging fires of lust that followed.

Theirs had been a secret love, too.

Sweet God, it had been so hard. But her Owen was a good one. Not like Sam.

Sam would break Robbie Jo's heart. It was just a matter of time.

Naomi closed her eyes, loving her husband's touch. She hoped that Robbie Jo would someday find a man as kind, as simply good, as Owen Tanner. She deserved it. She was such a sweet little girl.

ROBBIE JO

So you're thinkin' I killed Miss Hazel Lyndon, are ya? Well, DUH! Of course I did. Sit tight and I'll tell you all about it.

I'd been plannin' it for awhile. I'd been watchin' Miss Lyndon at night, peekin' in through the windows. She had a routine like clockwork, that one. She'd get home from work and watch TV for awhile. Then she'd feed that fat ol' cat of hers, defrost a TV dinner in the oven, and read a crappy romance novel while she ate it. Then she'd go upstairs, take a bath, and go to bed. It was kinda sweet, really.

A couple days before I did her, I crept into the house at night and watched her, right up close. That was interestin'. For one thing, Miss Lyndon was quite a fine housekeeper, even at her advanced age, which I estimate at three years older than God. The house was clean and tidy and smelled a little bit like lemons. There were little knitted doilies all over the place, and great big ones on the couch and chairs. At some point, she'd been a demon with the needles. And she drank peppermint tea. When I bent down and stared at her face to make sure she was dead, I smelled it on her.

On the night I did it, I waited for her upstairs, in a hall closet. The cat knew I was there, the little bastard, but he didn't bother to tell Miss Lyndon. He sniffed under the door a few times, then turned away, like I was just too fuckin' borin' for him to bother with. I really like cats.

She came up the stairs at the usual time, slow as a trap-crippled rat, because she couldn't see for shit. She sure didn't see me when I stepped out of the closet, grinnin' like a possum. She walked right past me. I felt like a ghost. That was kinda cool. I coulda reached out and touched her right then, but I didn't.

I'm a little ashamed to admit that I wanted her to turn her back on me. It wasn't personal, see, Miss Lyndon had never done anythin' to me. I almost liked her. But I needed to do it, because I was desperate to kill someone, and because it was part of my plan. I just didn't wanna see her eyes, that's all. Besides, they were pretty goddam spooky, all milky and shiny, like opals. Yeah, yeah, I know. I was bein' a big chickenshit. I'll do better next time, and you better believe it.

So anyhow, I fished a marble out of my pocket and tossed it down the stairs.

She turned around. "Pun'kin?" she said. "Is that you, sweet boy?" It wasn't Pun'kin. The fat ol' reprobate was sittin' next to me. I reached out, and with one hand, I pushed on the center of her bony ol' back. Hard.

She didn't make a sound. She pitched forward and fell down the wooden stairs, head first. The thumpin' and bumpin' was somethin' else. You wouldn't think that someone that scrawny could make that much noise. Her thin ol' skull hit on the way down, and I heard her neck break. CRUNCH! Sounded just like when you wring a chicken's neck, only louder.

She hit the bottom, kinda bounced, and then she was totally still. Her neck was bent at a seriously gross angle. So was the rest of her, for that matter. She was all tangled up, arms and legs everywhere, like a cast-off spider skin caught in the blackberry bushes.

I went down the stairs to take a look at her. The cat followed me. I knelt down next to Miss Lyndon and looked her in the face.

Y'know, I don't really get why folks are so freaked out about gettin' old. Sure, it sucks to lose your eyesight and your hearin' and maybe have to wear a diaper and such, but it's got its own kinda beauty. Miss Lyndon's skin was thin and pale and translucent, like she was made of old silk. You could see the bones underneath her face like they were tryin' to push out and run away. Her hair was the whitest thing I'd ever seen, whiter than snow, fine as a spiderweb. It was thin but long, and she wore it in a braid that reached the middle of her back. I lifted the braid, rubbed it against my cheek. It was heavy, and that surprised me, for some reason.

Her eyes looked the same in death as they had in life, like two pools of bluish milk. It's a wonder she could see out of 'em at all. I remembered the crazy guy in that Edgar Allan Poe story who freaked out on an old man's blind eye and ended up killin' him and buryin' him under the floorboards. That made me smile.

Her face was weirdly calm, but no one would ever think she was just sleepin'. There were thin trickles of blood leakin' from her ears, bright red against her tracin'-paper skin. The bones in her neck weren't just broken, they were shattered, and they poked against the skin of her neck like shards of pottery under a Kleenex. The side of her head was a little flat, too, like a boiled egg you dropped on the kitchen floor.

I stood up and stepped over her. Pun'kin came down the stairs and sniffed at Miss Lyndon's lips. He lashed his tail a little, then ambled off to the kitchen.

"You useless furball!" I called after him, laughin'. "If you'd been a dog, you'da tried to defend her!" He ignored me. Of course, if he'd been a dog, he also would have started snackin' on her corpse if they didn't find her right away.

I stretched and yawned. Now that it was done, I felt all warm and relaxed. I decided to take a good look around Miss Lyndon's house. It wasn't exactly a reckless choice. It's not like anybody'd be looking for her until mornin'. Besides, she didn't strike me as the type of lady who had nocturnal visitors, if you catch my drift.

Just goes to show you how wrong you can be about a person.

I checked out the first floor, openin' closet doors, inspectin' the linen cupboard, admirin' the fine hardwood floors and the pretty wildflower wallpaper. Except for a conspicuous lack of family pictures on the walls, it was a hardcore Old Lady House, right down to the tea cozies in the pantry and the glass display case filled with thimbles and tiny ceramic animals. There was a big bookcase in the livin' room, that was a little different. It was filled with the worst, drippiest kind of romance novels. I was tickled to see that some of 'em were the softcore porn variety, with lots of heavin' boobs and throbbin' manhoods.

Upstairs was more of the same; the only unusual features bein' the massive old clawfoot bathtub, and the lavender silk sheets on the bed. Silk sheets, and gauzy lavender bedcurtains. I wasn't sure what to think of that.

But the cellar was somethin' else. All I expected to find down there was some canned fruit and veggies, maybe Miss Lyndon's hopeless hope chest. I'm tellin' ya, I got a good deal more than I bargained for.

I trotted down the basement stairs, pulled the chain on the lightbulb danglin' down over the landin'—and my jaw dropped so hard it bounced off my collarbone. The walls of the basement were hung with heavy black cloth curtains. All of 'em. The effect was weird, like bein' backstage in a theater that had no doors. I touched the curtains. They were some kind of heavy woven cotton, thick and fibrous, like the sacks dried beans come in. I peeked behind 'em. I was halfway expectin' a hidden room or a secret door or some kinda spooky bullshit, but there was nothin' but cold stone walls.

The only other things in the basement were a tall old wardrobe and a metal banded trunk. I thought maybe I'd found that hope chest after all.

I opened the wardrobe first, and got hit in the nose with the stuffy smell of lots and lots of mothballs. The wardrobe was filled with fancy, old-fashioned dresses; the long, traily kind from the 1930s or so. I touched 'em. Nice fabrics. Expensive cuts. Miss Lyndon had evidently been quite the fashion plate in her younger days. When I closed my eyes, I could see her; those fine cheekbones covered with pink, downy flesh instead of dry parchment. Her eyes jewel-blue, the clouds in them years and years away. Her knobby old body straight and slim. I wondered why she'd never gotten married. Maybe she just had too much sense.

I turned to the chest. The lid was heavy, dusty, and the hinges creaked like crickets when I opened it.

I was delighted to see that it wasn't filled with musty linen and a forlorn, unused wedding dress. Nope. It was jammed with papers. Right on top was an old, yellowed poster for a revival meetin'—by the reverend Meshach Reddingale. There was a drawin' of his face in the middle, and if it was anywhere

close to true, he was a fine-lookin' devil. Slicked-back dark
hair, a long, fine-boned face, and eyes hot and black as pitch.
Sorta reminded me of those old promo pictures of Harry
Houdini, where he looks like he's just darin' ya to fuck with
him. The poster promised "Two days of Singing, Praying,
Salvation and Miracles!" Sounded like a party to me.

Under the poster were bundles of letters, tied with velvet
hair ribbons. Love letters? Oboy, I thought, time for the juicy
stuff!

Well, you coulda knocked me over with a dust bunny
when I pulled one out of the bundle and started to read. It was a
love letter, all right. Or maybe it was the script for a porno
movie. Get a load of this:

Hazel, my heart,
I miss you. Every day we can't be together sears my soul
like the fires of Hell. Someday, I swear, we'll be together
forever. But until then, all we have is our stolen time together.
God forgive me, all I can think of is your soft, sweet skin, the
way you smell like the summer sun all the year round. And then
my mind leads me down the Devil's path, and I dream of your
luscious milky breasts, your nipples like gumdrops in my
mouth, my face between your thighs. My whole world becomes
the taste of you, and your silver cries of delight.
I have to have you. Come to me tonight.
Your lover, your slave,
Meshach

The thought of someone bangin' Miss Lyndon up, down
and sideways just gave me the grins. So much for her
reputation as a dried-up old maid, huh? And with a preacher!
Well hey, if you're gonna sin, you might as well sin big, right?
Of course, I wondered why he didn't just marry her. The
bundles of letters were thick; ol' Meshach was evidently as
quick with his pen as he was with his dick. I figured the answer
might be in there, somewhere.

I dug into the chest a little deeper. There were some legal
papers, the deed to the house, a Lyndon family genealogy—and
what I'd bet my left tittie was a witch's spellbook. Or

somethin' like that, anyway. It was a small book, bound in some kinda diseased-lookin' green leather. Inside was all this weird, half-illiterate shit about potions and glamours and curses. The thing looked older than dirt. What fun! And then I came up with the gold. Miss Hazel Lyndon's diary, for the years 1936 to 1939. I wanted to sit down and read it cover to cover, find out what she thought about fuckin' a man of God. But, of course, that would have been pretty stupid of me.

But I had to have it.

I went back upstairs and rooted around in the linen cabinet until I found a canvas laundry bag. Then I went to the basement and stuffed it with the letters, the diary, and the book. I left the poster, the genealogy, and the legal stuff. No one would ever know that anythin' else had ever been in there.

I'm gonna read it all. Every tasty bit. Nah, I'm not that desperate for a thrill. But I have the feelin' there was somethin' goin' on between Hazel and Meshach, somethin' other than just garden-variety fuckin'. Somethin' strange.

Then again, maybe it's just my fucked-up brain playin' tricks on me.

So how do I feel about killin' Miss Lyndon? Mostly happy. I proved to myself that Daddy wasn't just a fluke; I really am what I was born to be. Happy, too, because it had just the result I was hopin' for. Naomi Tanner got Rose a job with Doc Yeats. She'll be workin' for him tomorrow. Odds are, she'll be bangin' him by next week. See, I like that girl. She deserves to find out that fuckin' can be fun, when it doesn't involve immediate family members.

Watchin' it fall into place, that was all pretty damn tasty. I'm wonderin', is this why folks get hooked on power? Just one tiny move from backstage, and ever'body's doin' just what I wanted 'em to. Like they were sock puppets with my hands up their woven cotton asses, makin' their mouths work with my fingers. I wonder what else I could get folks to do for me?

But I have to admit, I'm a little disappointed. The killin' part was so damn quiet. Just a little shove, not even as hard a push as you'd give a little kid in a playground swing, and Hazel Lyndon was bouncin' down the stairs like tantrum-tossed

Barbie doll. There was no terror involved. No screams. Less blood than your average monthly curse.

I need somethin' with a little more meat to it.

Somethin' messy.

Somethin' downright ugly.

Soon.

Not right this minute, though. I've gotta help Rose and Miz Tanner make cookies for Miss Lyndon's visitation.

MISS LYNDON IN THE PARLOR
(DEATH SOUTHERN STYLE)

*R*ose woke up with her back pressed to Robbie Jo's. She stretched and yawned, warm and happy.

The smell of Naomi's fantastic blackberry cake wafted up the stairs and into her room. Rose, Robbie Jo and Naomi had cooked and baked late into the night, and Naomi was evidently at it again. All for Miss Lyndon.

Rose sat on the edge of the bed contemplating a shower when she remembered that she was due to start working for Doctor Michael Yeats, DVM, on the day after tomorrow. Her heart thudded like the hooves of a panicked filly. She took a few deep breaths, hung her head between her legs. Laughed at herself for being such an idiot.

"What's ticklin' your ribs?" came Robbie Jo's sleepy voice.

"Oh, nothin'. Just my silly brain."

Robbie Jo chortled. "Well, put a cork in it and show some respect, girlie. There's a corpse on the way here, or didja forget?"

An hour later, the girls up and showered, working with Naomi and Owen Tanner to prepare for Miss Hazel Lyndon's visitation and service. There were shelves to be dusted, sofa cushions to be fluffed, floors to be swept, flowers to be cut from the garden and placed around the house. And there was the food, of course. All that food. Did death make Southerners hungry, Rose wondered?

It was about ten-thirty when the doorbell rang. Owen let in Sam, Ephram Dunwiddie, and Jimmy Ligget, all wearing their most solemn black suits. Sam looked gorgeous, the utter asshole. Rose could see why Robbie Jo would want to boff him, even if he was a champion dickweed. She thought Ephram looked like the undertaker from every episode of Night Gallery and Thriller that had a mortuary in it. Or maybe the Tall Man from Phantasm. Feeling ridiculous, she shuddered.

Jimmy, now. Jimmy was something else. Rose smiled. With his gently round body, his narrow-cut Southern suit just didn't sit quite right. He looked uncomfortable, hot and sweaty, wiping his wire-framed glasses on his crisp white shirt when he thought no one was looking. There was something about his dreamy eyes and earnest expression that reminded Rose of some of the boys she had known in high school, the unpopular boys who read Tolkein and ran A/V equipment and played Dungeons and Dragons. She decided she liked Jimmy Liggett.

Sam and his father were looking at the parlor together, measuring the space between the doorway and one oak endtable, eyeing the rug in the hallway like it might rear up and bite them. Rose realized they were making way for Miss Lyndon's coffin.

A few minutes later, the three men went outside. When they came back through the front door, they were rolling a glossy maplewood coffin on some kind of brass and steel gurney.

There's a corpse in there. A dead person.

The thought was amazing. The thought was appalling.

Like most Americans, Rose had never had much of anything to do with death. It was all over the television, of course, in the movie theaters and in the news, but none of it was real. And on the rare occasions that it was real, Death happened in the hospital, never in your house. Then it was whisked away to the funeral parlor, where it was cleaned up, sanitized, sterilized, and sometimes burned away to almost nothing. Rose remembered her grandfather's ashes, which her father kept in a coffee tin in his closet. A whole man, who lead a whole life, cooked and reduced down to seven pounds of bone chips that looked more like dry laundry detergent than anything that ever supported human flesh.

Rose remembered how her father would open the tin and shove her face down close to it. How he'd tell her that her grandfather's blazing spirit would rise up out of the Folger's can and burn her up if she didn't do what he wanted her to. Sometimes he'd shake the can and she could taste the bone dust, chalky and bitter.

Of course, that only scared her when she was very small. Later, she was too afraid of her father to worry about ghosts.

Jimmy locked the wheels of the gurney in place. Sam draped it with a black velvet curtain like a bedskirt, which hung from the bottom of the coffin all the way to the floor. Ephram solemnly opened the lid.

Robbie Jo walked right up to the coffin and looked in. She didn't say a thing, and her face was as calm as the surface of a quiet pond. "Poor old thing," she said. Sam gave her a look so hot Rose thought it might actually sizzle the air between them. Robbie Jo raised an eyebrow and went into the kitchen.

They had talked yesterday, after Robbie Jo had awakened from her nap as fresh and cheerful as a preschooler. Robbie Jo told Rose all about how Ruth Dunwiddie had walked in on her and Sam, and how she'd had to play the innocent maiden wronged, to preserve her reputation in Possum Kingdom. Of course, Robbie Jo went on, she hated to fool with the Tanners, but once the fib got started, she didn't know how to stop it without looking like a liar and a slut.

Rose completely understood. She had quickly come to see the carnivorous nature of a small town. If Robbie Jo had been branded a tramp, the reputation would have stuck to her for life, even if she married a preacher and had six perfect kids and sang in the church choir.

But damn, she sure had done a convincing job of it. Rose wondered if Robbie Jo had ever considered a career in acting.

Rose looked at Sam's deepening frown and smiled. She was pretty goddam proud of the way Robbie Jo had just given him the cold shoulder. Maybe she wasn't as besotted as she'd seemed. Even if she was, maybe she'd learned how to play the game; how to string a guy along to make him appreciate her a little bit. Of course, that was a game alien to Rose; she'd never even been on the playing field. But if Robbie Jo could do it, more power to her. Sam could use a little jerking around.

"Oh!" cried Naomi, looking into Miss Lyndon's powdered face. "You did a lovely job, Jimmy. She's as pretty as a picture."

"Thank you, Miz Tanner." He looked at the floor and smiled.

Rose realized she was walking, her treacherous feet taking her to the open coffin. To see.

But it wasn't horrible. It wasn't scary. Miss Lyndon was dressed in a pretty, old-fashioned dress of peach silk. Her white hair was shimmering and clean, the single braid of it draped girlishly over one shoulder. Her skin was oddly opaque, a little too matte, like a cloth blind over a darkened window. Her cheeks had been rouged, but ever so slightly. There was a pale and delicate pink tint on her lips. Her eyes were closed, of course, the lashes a white, silky fringe against her cheek.

She didn't exactly look dead, but she didn't look alive, either. Like Snow White, if her prince had never come to wake her.

"We brought you a wreath," Ephram said to Naomi. "Shall we hang it on the door for you?"

"Yes, please! Mighty kind of you, Ephram."

"We'll be back this evenin' for the funeral, if you don't mind, Naomi. To show our respects to Miss Lyndon."

"Of course."

Ephram cleared his throat, looking a little uncomfortable. "Will you want us to remove the—Miss Lyndon after the service?"

Naomi's brow furrowed. "No, you don't need to do that. You can pick her up in the mornin'. The wake might run late."

"Certainly. Come on, Jimmy. Sam. Sam? Sam!"

Sam was staring at the kitchen door like a dog waiting for his supper. Naomi gave him a look that, had he seen it, might have caused Sam's balls to crawl up his abdominal cavity and hide behind his ears.

"Sam! Have you gone deaf, boy?" Sam turned to look at his father, his eyes venomous. Jimmy stuck his hands in his pockets and looked embarrassed.

Then they were gone, and it was just Rose, Robbie Jo, the Tanners, and Hazel Lyndon's earthly remains, lying in the parlor on white, white silk.

The visitation began at two o'clock. The girls helped Naomi set out just a little of the food; some fresh fruit and cookies, some lemonade, and gumdrops from the store. First there was a trickle of visitors, then a stream, then a flood. They'd come in one after another, curiosity shining behind their somber mourner's eyes, and line up to take a peek at Hazel Lyndon's mortal shell. They brought flowers, hundreds of them. Soon the Tanners' parlor looked like the inside of a greenhouse, and smelled like heaven. Rose was glad of all those flowers; she didn't want to smell anything else as the meltingly hot day wore on. She glanced at the coffin mistrustfully.

Rose smoothed down her dress. It was dark purple, not black, but Naomi said it was just fine. She'd lent Robbie Jo a smock of navy blue cotton from the store. The Tanners had both the girls playing hostess, and Rose liked it just fine. It made her feel like she belonged here.

Despite the numbers of people who trooped through the parlor, the viewing was quiet, sedate. Nobody cried; Rose had the impression that no one in Possum Kingdom knew Miss Lyndon well enough to cry for her. Nobody but Michael Yeats, maybe, and he didn't come to the viewing. Instead they looked at her with sympathy, talked in hushed voices about how sweet she had been, complimented the Dunwiddies on the fine job they'd done in "preparing" her.

Rose was amazed, not to mention appalled, at the number of people who patted Miss Lyndon's hands, touched her hair, kissed her powdered cheek. People just weren't quite that friendly with the Grim Reaper back in Miami.

The last of the visitors had said their personal farewells by five o'clock. By six, folks were showing up for the funeral service, although it wasn't due to start until seven. And by God, everybody had changed their clothes. It was a human ocean of black. Black suits, black dresses, little kids in black t-shirts and black shorts.

And they brought food. Lots of it. One after another they carried their casserole dishes and Tupperware and plates and cake pans into the kitchen, worshippers bearing offerings to the kitchen of Death's hostess. The smells of food and flowers slugged it out for supremacy. Which won depended on where you stood.

The Dunwiddies were there, of course, all of them, and Jimmy Liggett as well. They brought a box of black paper fans, each imprinted in gold with "The Sweet Hereafter."

"We would normally have printed Miss Lyndon's name on them," she heard Ephram say to Naomi in his deep, sonorous voice, "but there simply wasn't time."

Naomi smiled up at him, ever gracious. "I realize I didn't give you much time, Ephram. You've done a lovely job in spite of me." His face softened, and he patted her shoulder.

The Baptist preacher, Reverend Thomas Rye, arrived at about the same time as the Reverend Primus Reylark and his elegant wife, Jerianne. They all exchanged pleasant nods and greetings. Rose thought she caught a green glint of jealousy in Reverend Rye's pale eyes.

By seven, the house was packed. People were spilling out of the parlor into the halls and the kitchen. Rose wondered how many of the mourners were there because they cared about Hazel Lyndon, and how many were there because it was the hot ticket in town that night.

She heard Effie Granger's loud, braying voice, telling some poor victim trapped in the crowd about how Miss Lyndon's cat had murdered her. Rose had a fleeting, unpleasant wish that some household pet would decide to do the same for Effie one of these days.

It was hot. Too hot. Too many bodies in one enclosed space, and the smell of armpits began to give the flowers and food a run for their money. Owen brought out four big standing fans and a box fan and turned them all on full blast. Black clothing fluttered like the wings of a thousand bats. The flowers, whipped in the breeze, seemed to take on a life of their own, dancing and impudent in the face of the Reaper.

The Reverend Thomas stepped to the side of the coffin and cleared his throat. No one heard him but Owen, who went out and got him an orange crate to stand on. Towering above the crowd, Reverend Thomas pushed back his sweat-slick blond hair and called out "Excuse me." His voice was high-pitched and gravelly, as if he had trouble forcing it out over his vocal cords.

People began to take notice then, and soon he had the crowd's attention.

He's not going to say "Dearly Beloved," is he?

"Dearly beloved," began the Reverend Thomas. "We are gathered here today to celebrate the life of Miss Hazel Lyndon, and to celebrate her passing into the glorious Kingdom of Heaven."

Robbie Jo had made her way through the crowd and stood elbow to elbow with Rose. The girls exchanged a smile.

"When you thought of Miss Lyndon," Reverend Thomas continued, "You thought first of her smile. Her beautiful smile, undimmed by her many years of life. A life spent selflessly, in the service of her fellow man, and of God."

He's not that bad, thought Rose. *But compared to Reverend Primus, he sounds like a pious chipmunk.*

The eulogy went on for awhile, maybe just a little too long. Reverend Thomas talked about Miss Lyndon's cheerfulness, her gentleness with the animals, her industrious nature and her generous heart while the townspeople nodded and murmured that it was so. And this time, a few of them did shed a tear here and there.

As she glanced restlessly around the room, Rose caught sight of Michael Yeats in the far corner. She hadn't seen him come in. His face was white and drawn, his eyes narrowed in pain. His mouth was pressed tight, turned down a little. Rose imagined brushing his lips with hers and blushed.

Reverend Thomas ended the eulogy with a prayer. Then there were shouts of "Amen!" which almost startled him off his orange crate. He asked the crowd if anyone would care to say a few words about Miss Lyndon. There was a moment of silence, then Michael Yeats' hoarse voice saying "I would."

The crowd made way for him as he approached the coffin. He looked in at Miss Lyndon's face, and for a moment, it looked like his own face would crumple. Then the look passed.

Reverend Thomas stepped down from the orange crate and offered it to Michael, but he declined with a shake of his head. The room was silent, except for the roar of the fans.

"Miss Hazel Lyndon... Miss Lyndon was my friend." He looked up at the ceiling, as if asking for help. "When I first came to Possum Kingdom looking for a place to hang my shingle, she treated me like I belonged here. She ran my office so well, so smoothly, I thought there must be two or three of her."

A few sad little laughs and nods.

"We'd talk, Miss Lyndon and I, when it was quiet in the office. She—she was a delightful person. A good, decent person. I'll miss her. I'll miss her until the day I die."

He bent and kissed Miss Lyndon's cheek, then walked silently out of the room.

"Ah... anyone else?" asked Reverend Thomas, wiping his high, pink forehead with a handkerchief.

There were no takers, so the food came out.

The dining room table, the credenza, and two folding card tables were creaking with overfilled dishes. Naomi had set out Chinet plates and napkins and plastic utensils, buffet-style. People attacked the food like ants. They stood in the corners, sat on the stairs, lined the hallways, and ate like they'd never seen food before, talking and laughing all the while.

Rose was amazed. *What is it about death that makes Southerners want to pig out?* She decided it was one of the great mysteries of life, and better off unsolved.

Rose and Robbie Jo wove through the crowd to Naomi. "What can we be doing now?" Rose asked.

"Eat!" said Naomi, shoving a plate into her hands. The girls obliged, loading their plates with everything from beans and cornbread to double-chocolate brownies. They wandered through the crowd as they ate, watching and listening.

Sam Dunwiddie to Owen Tanner: "Don't worry about Miss Lyndon, she'll stay fresh as a daisy overnight. I had Jimmy embalm her extra-firm."

Effie Granger to Primus Reylark: "You didn't bring any rat'lers with you, didja? Because Miss Lyndon didn't go to your church."

Primus Reylark to Effie Granger: "No, ma'am, but Jerianne did bring some corn fritters."

Doctor Vanguard Poteet to Fayelynn Plum: "Yes'm, it was me signed the death certificate. I know you're supposed'ta when an old person dies of a fall, but I didn't see a need to send her to the county coroner. It was pretty clear how she died, her neck broke and all. I don't like to bring in outsiders to Possum Kingdom's bidness."

A strange look on Robbie Jo's face, wide-eyed, and then a grin that was almost maniacal. Rose was about to ask her what was so funny when Nancy Plum descended on Robbie Jo like a purposeful limpet. Robbie Jo scowled and pulled her to one side, but Rose could still hear part of the conversation.

"But you *said* you'd come over yesterday, Robbie Jo, and you *said* you'd come over last week, and you *didn't*. You never come over anymore. Are you mad at me or somethin'?"

Robbie Jo, smiling: "No, of course not, sugar. I've just been—well, kinda busy. Hella busy. We'll get together real soon, okay?"

But Nancy stayed narrow-eyed and mistrustful. "Uh-huh. Sure." Nancy turned to walk away from Robbie Jo, and by God if she wasn't mad. It was the strongest emotion Rose had ever seen come out of her.

Poor Robbie Jo, thought Rose. *That's what you get for being nice to the socially challenged.* This was another arena where Rose had never done combat. She'd never had a friend close enough to be jealous of her. Rose decided that wasn't such a bad thing, after all.

Nancy looked over her shoulder. "I've heard a few people guessin' about what you been busy with, Robbie Jo. You just better be careful."

A little electric shiver passed through Robbie Jo. Rose briefly thought that deathrays might shoot out of her eyes. Then it was gone, and Robbie Jo was next to her again, talking her into going back for seconds on the corn pudding.

The wake went on late into the night, and when the last of the stragglers left, the clean-up lasted into the wee hours of the morning. By the time Rose slogged up the stairs behind Robbie

Jo, she was too tired to even worry about the fact that she was going to be spending the night in the same house with a corpse.

Almost.

Her sleep was heavy, but the overpowering scent of flowers in the house intruded on her dreams, making her walk through an endless, wild, orchid garden filled with orange tomcats and the occasional rattlesnake.

Rose opened her eyes for a moment when Robbie Jo got quietly out of bed, but her eyelids sank and she drifted back toward her garden.

She thought Robbie Jo was only going to the bathroom.

ROBBIE JO AND THE SINEATER

*N*aomi couldn't sleep. Partly it was due to all the day's excitement. Partly, she felt sorry for poor old Miss Lyndon, and thought she could use some company. So she sat on the sofa, sipping lemonade and reading "Jane Eyre" for the fifth time. The scent of the flowers had settled in the parlor, filling the room with a luscious perfume that was right on the edge of overpowering. Naomi breathed in deeply. It was a warm summer smell that made a body want to do crazy things, like dancing naked in the rain, or howling at the moon.

"Doesn't it smell like heaven, Miss Lyndon?" Naomi murmured.

Tap. Tap. Tap. Three small knocks. Naomi jumped out of her skin.

Tap. Tap. Tap. "Miss Lyndon?" she whispered. "That you?"

The knocks came again, louder this time, and of course they didn't come from the coffin, they came from the kitchen door. Scowling, Naomi gathered her robe around her and went to see who it was.

She peered through the curtain and saw a slight figure standing there, arms wrapped around himself. It took her a moment, and then she realized who it had to be. Naomi opened the door.

"Hello," said the boy in a soft voice. "I'm sorry if I woke you."

"You didn't, honey, I couldn't sleep. Is that you, Simon McCray? I haven't seen you since you were no bigger than a butterbean."

"Yes ma'am." Simon stepped in as Naomi held the door for him. They looked at each other for a moment. Good Lord, but the child was scrawny.

"Now don't you usually do...do your work at the Sweet Hereafter, Simon?"

He nodded. "I went there last night, ma'am, and I was gonna do it then. But...but they were...there was a lot of yellin', Miz Tanner. A whole lot of yellin' inside the house, and things breakin', and I got scared and ran away."

Naomi reached out to pat his cheek. He blinked hard, like he thought she might hit him. His skin was as soft as a baby's. "I don't blame you one bit, honey. You're welcome to do it right here. Now, what do you need? Anythin' special?"

"Nothin' special, ma'am. Jus' a little bit of food on a plate. It don't have to be nothin' fancy. A little bit of bread and cheese will do it."

"Well, we've got that, plus about a million pounds of other food. Simon, before you leave, why don't you pack yourself up a big basket of it? We couldn't eat this many leftovers if we lived to be two hundred."

"Thank you," said Simon, smiling at the floor.

Rage boiled up in Naomi as she prepared Simon's plate. No child as young as Simon should be on his own. No child should have to do the things he did. She knew it was the way things worked here. She knew Possum Kingdom had never been without a sineater. But she wanted to gather him in her arms and save him.

She handed him the plate. "Here you go, sugar."

"Thanks Miz Tanner." A pause. Simon shifted from foot to foot, chewed his lip. "I—I hate to ask you in your own house, ma'am, but I, um, I like to do the sineatin' alone. Sometimes it's not real purty..."

"Of course, Simon. I'll just toddle off to bed. Honey, it's so late, you can stay the night here if you want to..."

He smiled. "No thanks, Miz Tanner. But you're awful nice. And you got a purty house."

"Thank you. Goodnight, Simon."

"Goodnight, ma'am."

Tears stung Naomi's eyes as she climbed the stairs to her bedroom, and to Owen's arms, where she could safely weep.

Robbie Jo willed herself to be invisible as Naomi passed by. She closed her eyes, afraid their reddish glint would give her away in the darkness. When the Tanners' bedroom door closed, she crept down the stairs and stopped halfway down, peering into the parlor between the carved wooden railings. *Shit, it's really him, the fuckin' sineater. And he's gonna do it right here.*

She studied the face of the boy who was setting a plate of food on Hazel Lyndon's cold, sunken chest. He was pretty, in a funny sort of way. Silky hair, a little long, so blond it was nearly white. Dark, dark eyes, maybe even black. From up on the stairs, his eyes looked like holes in his pale, narrow face. Sweet lips, though. Finely curved and just a little pink.

Scrawny little guy. You'd never guess he ate for a livin'. Robbie Jo's mouth quirked up.

The kid took a deep breath, like he was about to dive into deep, cold water. Then he tore into a hunk of bread.

The effect was immediate. His body stiffened, and he groaned, still chewing. He stuffed some cheese into his mouth, and then some more. His legs went out from under him and he collapsed.

Robbie Jo cocked her head as Simon McCray thrashed on the floor next to Hazel Lyndon's coffin. He was making weird little noises; half grunt, half moan. His black eyes were rolled all the way up into his head, leaving only slivers of white.

It occurred to her that maybe he was just crazy, or maybe he had some other kind of problem, like epilepsy or something. Or maybe it was real. Maybe he was devouring Miss Lyndon's earthly sins, consuming them, digesting them, right before her eyes.

Simon had stopped writhing like a buckshot snake, and now he was sitting on the floor, breathing hard. His eyes were open, but he wasn't seeing anything. He was somewhere else entirely.

Is it real?

Robbie Jo decided that she would find out. Tonight. She crept down the stairs and sat on the floor in front of Simon. Waiting.

Simon woke up staring at the holes in the knees of his thin blue jeans. He was sitting crosslegged on the Tanners' parlor floor. His mouth was bitter with the taste of Hazel Lyndon's sins. He raised his head, rubbing the back of his neck, and stared into the face of a girl. A beautiful girl, with eyes and hair the color of a fox's coat in the summer sun. Looking at him. He let out a hoarse cry of surprise and staggered to his feet.

"Wait!" the girl whispered. "Don't go, Simon." But the nausea hit him and he ran for the kitchen, threw open the door, and ran out into the night.

Robbie Jo let the kid finish barfing, then gave him a little lead and followed him through the woods. He was quick and sure-footed, but so was she. Keeping up was easy.

There was something wrong with him. His footsteps grew uneven. He ran half bent over, like his stomach hurt him. She caught the sound of a little whimper, filtered through the trees.

They were in a part of the woods where children never played. It always seemed darker here, even on the sunniest summer days. It was the part of the woods where the sineater lived, and you were a damn fool if you didn't know it was cursed.

Yeah, right. Double leapin' bullshit. Robbie Jo wasn't the least bit afraid of the skinny kid she was tracking like a spring hare. *I shall fear no evil, for I'm the deadliest little bitch in the valley.*

Simon McCray lived in a tiny wooden house, old and decrepit, much like Robbie Jo's. She felt a pang of empathy for him, which she squashed like a bug.

He threw open the warped front door and dashed inside. She heard fumbling, a match striking, and then the glow of a kerosene lantern. Robbie Jo strolled through the open door and into the house.

It had only two rooms, plus the kitchen. Gray wooden floors, faded, threadbare rugs. The furniture was simple and rustic. Rough wooden chairs, a heavy, scarred table, a sunken, colorless, herniated thing that might have once been a couch. And shelves.

Little narrow shelves, all over the walls, filled with tiny carvings of animals. Raccoons, rats, bears, squirrels, possums. Robbie Jo picked up a miniature dog and looked it over.

It was rough and spiky, full of motion and life. Not what you'd call realistic, but wonderful anyway. From its curved, happy tail to its long inquisitive nose, it was Essence of Dog. Robbie Jo smiled and set it down.

The boy, Simon, was in the back room. He was sitting on the bed, fumbling with a little metal box, panting, nearly sobbing. He'd torn off his holey white t-shirt, and his whippet body was covered in a sheen of sweat.

Robbie Jo stepped forward. "Hi," she said.

"Oh God," Simon hissed, eyes bugging.

"Not exactly. I'm Robbie Jo. What are you doing, Simon McCray?"

"I—I'm sick." He clutched the metal box to his chest.

"I can see that. And you have medicine in there?"

He dry-swallowed, eyes squeezing shut. "Yeah."

She sat down on the worn-out sheets next to him. "Let me help you."

"No! No, I—" Simon bent convulsively and cried out. The box hit the floor. Robbie Jo picked it up and opened it. Saw the spoon, saw the lighter. Saw the little glassine packets. She picked one up and looked at it. It had a crude little drawing of some kind of rodent, big round ears and long scaly tail. "RAT FUCK," it said under the picture. Inside the packet was a tiny amount of white powder.

"This isn't medicine," said Robbie Jo. "It's heroin." Simon started to cry.

Robbie Jo put her hands on his sweaty shoulders, rubbed the bowstring-tight muscles. "It's okay, honey. I don't mind. Let me watch you."

Simon stared at her, like he wanted to say something. Then he started to shake all over. When his hands were still again, he grabbed a small hinged box from the larger box and opened it. Robbie Jo had never seen a glass syringe before.

He got the water from an old ceramic basin, and she sat behind him on the bed and steadied his arms as he fixed the shot. He gave it to himself in the belly.

Robbie Jo hooked her chin over his shoulder and smiled down at the plume of blood in the syringe. Simon's whole body relaxed as he pushed in the plunger. He gave a deep sigh and sagged against her, eyelids fluttering.

She pulled the needle from the skin of his pale, flat stomach and examined it with narrowed eyes. She unscrewed the needle from the syringe and rinsed it in the washbasin, then set them carefully in their velvet cradles in the injection kit. Then she crawled back up onto the bed and put Simon's head in her lap, studying his slack face, stroking the track marks on his wiry arms with her fingertips.

"Are you an angel?" Simon whispered.

"Not exactly, honey." Robbie Jo stroked his damp forehead, his moonlight-colored hair, and smiled.

When Simon awakened in the early afternoon, his angel was gone. He decided that he had dreamed her. He smiled, thinking of her milky skin and her eyes like autumn leaves, and drifted back to sleep.

ROSE TOUCHES DEATH; SAM PAYS A CALL

ose woke up in the late morning when a ray of sun crept over her face. Robbie Jo was gone. Rose wasn't surprised; Robbie Jo did that a lot. Sometimes when she stayed over, she'd vanish before dawn. Sometimes she stayed for days at a time. Once in awhile, Robbie Jo would appear in Rose's bed in the middle of the night. And that was fine. Weird, but fine.

She could smell breakfast cooking. Rose quickly brushed her hair and pulled on a brown cotton dress, then trotted downstairs to see if she could help Naomi.

The sight of Hazel Lyndon's corpse was a dip in cold water. Rose had put the old woman right out of her mind.

The flowers had all started to wilt and droop, their smell turning the corner from sweet to overripe. Miss Lyndon, on the other hand, still looked as fresh as the dew. She hadn't changed at all, overnight.

Rose crept up close to the coffin and took a long look inside. It was strange to see Miss Lyndon with her milky eyes closed. It made Rose uncomfortable, like she was spying on someone in her sleep.

But she's not asleep, is she, and she doesn't give a rat's ass whether you look at her or not.

Rose's hand came up from her side and reached into the coffin. She was quite amazed to see it hovering over Miss Lyndon's cheek.

You're not really gonna touch a corpse, are you girl? You're not, are you?

But she did. Hazel Lyndon's cheek was cold—how could it be so cold when the room was so warm? And it was hard. Not hard, exactly, but stiff, like a partially thawed turkey, or bread dough that you left in the refrigerator too long. Rose pressed, ever so gently.

The doorbell rang. Rose let out a little scream and jumped backwards. She was horrified to see that her fingers had left two little depressions in Miss Lyndon's cheek.

Owen came out of the kitchen to answer the door. "Good morning, Rose," he smiled, as he turned the knob.

"Good morning," she said, feeling like she'd just done something dirty.

It was Ephram Dunwiddie and Jimmy Liggett. No Sam this time. The two men efficiently and quickly got Miss Hazel Lyndon out of the Tanner's house and into the big black hearse. Both Owen and Naomi thanked them profusely. Ephram was gracious, businesslike. Rose thought he also seemed a little worried.

"Where's she going?" asked Rose, as the hearse pulled out of the driveway. "I mean—where are they taking her?"

"Back to the Sweet Hereafter. They'll powder poor Hazel's nose one last time, then seal the coffin. Get her ready for graveside services. Now come on in and eat. Your beans and bacon are gettin cold."

Rose ate, but only after scrubbing her hands and arms to the elbows. Even under the hot water, she could still feel Miss Lyndon's cold skin on her fingertips.

Robbie Jo was sound asleep, face mashed against the mattress, arm hanging off the battered single bed her father had found for her at the Jonesborough dump when she was five, when somebody started pounding on the front door.

She opened her sticky eyes and blinked at the late morning sunlight. It took her a moment to realize what she was hearing; no one ever knocked on Robbie Jo's door. No one ever came to visit her. She wouldn't permit it. And no one sure as hell came to visit her gin-soaked mother.

Speaking of her mother, where was the rummy bitch, anyway? "Get the door, Ma," Robbie Jo yelled, not getting up. No answer. Just more knocking, louder this time.

"Fuck off," Robbie Jo muttered. She rolled over and closed her eyes.

Someone pounded on the window. Robbie Jo sat up, fast as a striking snake. It was Sam, peering in at her like a puppy in a pet store window.

A hot flush of shame. Sam was looking in her grimy little window, at her grimy little bedroom, in her cheap, piece-of-shit little crackerbox house. She toyed with the thought of killing him, and maybe taking his eyes.

"Robbie Jo! Let me in, honey, I have to see you!"

She stared at him. It really would be a waste to kill him now. She hadn't gotten half of what she wanted from him. Robbie Jo stood up, pulled down her thin white t-shirt so it mostly covered her butt, and headed for the front door.

She shut the door of her tiny bedroom behind her, feeling protective of the letters and the book she had hidden under her bed. She opened the front door, which didn't even have a lock, and glared at Sam.

"What the hell do you want?"

He looked at her like she was a T-bone and he was a hungry dog. "Can I come in?"

What the hell. He knows what a fuckin' cesspool this place is now. It can't get much worse, can it? Robbie Jo stepped back and opened the door wider.

Sam rushed in and gathered her in his arms. "Oh baby...what are we gonna do? My folks told me I can't see you anymore or they'll cut me out of their fuckin' will. Oh Robbie Jo..."

He buried his face in her neck as she tried not to laugh. *Oh, Bob! Oh, Marsha! Oh, motherfuckin' Melrose Place!*

His hand was on her thigh, sliding up under her t-shirt. She grabbed it. "Hold it—hold it, Sam, honey. First we gotta talk about this. We gotta figure out what to do."

He started to protest. His mouth shut like a leghold trap as the door to Robbie Jo's mother's room (added on by Robbie Jo's father when she was two years old, so he could molest her more privately) swung open with a creak.

Mrs. Lureen Ridgemont stood in the doorway, swaying like a cornstalk in a gentle breeze. She kind of looked like a cornstalk, too; skinny (except for her face, which was as puffy and pasty as a dumpling), with a long, unkempt mess of blond and gray hair. The stink of cheap alcohol rolled into the living room. Sam yanked his hand out from under Robbie Jo's shirt.

Mrs. Ridgemont blinked her swollen pink eyelids. She rubbed her shapeless nose. A little belch, and her rough hand flew to her mouth. Robbie Jo wanted to die.

"Whass' goin' on, honey?" More reptilian blinks, slow and gluey.

"Nothin," Robbie Jo said to the floor. "Go back to bed, Ma."

Robbie Jo's mother licked her cracked lips with a fat red tongue. "Who's your friend?"

"Uh…Hi, Mrs. Ridgemont, I'm—"

Robbie Jo closed the distance between her and her mother in a single breath. She grabbed the woman's spongy upper arms and hissed in her face. "Go back in your room. Now. Before I fuckin' kill you."

She didn't wait for an answer. She backed her mother into her eternally darkened den, and slammed the door in her face.

Robbie Jo rested her forehead on the door, shaking with rage. Burning with embarrassment.

"Robbie Jo—"

She spun around. Sam wasn't laughing at her. He wasn't even smiling.

"Come on," said Robbie Jo, grabbing his hand. "Let's go for a walk in the woods."

Sam stared at her. "You're not dressed."

She ran into her room and grabbed a frayed denim skirt and her battered tennis shoes. "I'll put 'em on outside." Before he could say a word, Robbie Jo dragged Sam out the door and into the sunshine.

She didn't bother to close the door behind her. She imagined throwing a firebomb into the house as they walked away. She wouldn't even bother to watch it burn. She'd just listen for the screams.

Lureen Ridgemont sat on the filthy floor of her bedroom, crying silently. Mouth open, tears and snot running down her face and onto the front of her gray, baggy dress.

Robbie Jo hated her. Of course she did. It was never a surprise when she acted like this, but it hurt. Oh Jesus, how it hurt.

Which was good. Because Lureen deserved it.

She wallowed in the pain. There was nothing Robbie Jo could do to her that would be enough hurt. Nothing in the world. Because Lureen had let it happen to her.

She had refused to see it when it was happening. She drank back then to put up a wall between herself and the ugly things her husband was doing to her daughter. It had been there all along, stinking like a dead rat in the wall, but Lureen had made it invisible. When Otis had died, Lureen had thought it would go away.

But it didn't, of course. It just rotted more, stank more, until it was as much a part of the house as the walls and the floor. And over the years, it had trickled through the wall toward Lureen's consciousness, polluted groundwater through layers of granite, until the day it burst through into her brain in a venomous, icy flood. Robbie Jo's fear of being alone in the house with her father. The muffled sounds at night. Robbie Jo's funny, bowlegged walk. The stiff spots on her sheets. Her little underwear, stretched out of shape. Lureen had fallen to the floor and screamed, sobbed, vomited until she felt inside-out.

Robbie Jo wasn't there to see it, of course. She was hardly ever home.

Lureen didn't know her child at all. She never had, really. Robbie Jo had always been a strange little thing, smart and quietly thoughtful in a way that none of Lureen's family had ever been. Lureen loved her; of course she did. Robbie Jo was her little girl. But she never knew what Robbie Jo was thinking, and she knew she never would. Except, of course, when Robbie Jo made it this obvious.

Lureen stood up and wiped her face with her hands. She'd clean up, that's what, and fix Robbie Jo some biscuits. It wouldn't make Robbie Jo like her any better. Lureen wasn't stupid enough to think that. But while she was cooking, she could pretend that she was a regular mother, a happy mother with a loving husband and a pretty, popular daughter. Not a betrayer. Not a bone-deep failure. Not a drunk and a belly-crawling coward.

And when the ugly little house filled with the warm, buttery smell of the biscuits, Lureen could close her eyes and pretend that she was sixteen again, laughing in her mother's kitchen, and that she'd never laid eyes on Otis Ridgemont.

Or better yet, she could dream of the day that her sweet Lord Jesus would come and take her home.

Sam watched Robbie Jo pull on her skirt with a mixture of lust and anguish. If he never saw her again, he was sure that he'd die. She was his angel.

"What the fuck are you lookin' at?" Robbie Jo yelled at the scrawny chickens in the tiny side yard. She threw a stick into their pen, making them squawk and flap. She sat down on a treestump to put on her ratty, colorless tennis shoes.

Sam came around behind her and massaged her shoulders. "I know it's awful, baby. What are we goin' to do?"

She glanced up at him, and for just a moment, he thought she might be mad at him. Her eyes flashed hard rusty sparks, her mouth a twist of contempt. But then she smiled, and it was okay.

"Tell me what they said, Sam honey. Exactly."

He frowned and rubbed his chin. "Well, my mama said that you were a sneaky little lowlife whore. My daddy said we should hear your side of things. Then my mama said you were a slut and a piece of white trash and that you oughta be on the bottom of a compost heap somewhere."

A snort from Robbie Jo. "You sure have a good memory, sugar."

"Thanks! Then my daddy told her to calm down. She screamed a whole lot then, and I didn't understand some of it. But she ended up sayin' that if I ever saw you again, she'd call our lawyer right then and there and cut me out of their will. And I said 'C'mon, Daddy, talk some sense into her,' and then she yelled even more and threw a Franklin Mint plate at his head. Then he said 'You heard your mama, boy,' and that was pretty much that."

Robbie Jo stood up and took Sam's hand. He loved the feel of her fingers; tiny, soft and cool. "Come on," she said. "Let's walk."

For awhile, they walked in silence. Sam started to speak a few times, to tell Robbie Jo how much she meant to him. How he worshipped her. How he wanted her to be his wife. But it all seemed so fragile right now. He was afraid that the wrong word might shatter the glittering bond that tied him to this strange, beautiful creature. So he squeezed her hand instead, and smiled at her from time to time.

They reached a pretty grove, a ring of oaks with thick, twisting roots like rough sea serpents rising up from the soft moss around them. Robbie Jo sat on a root and looked up at Sam, smiling.

He narrowed his eyes and checked the root for slugs, spiders, slimy leaves, and any of the other disgusting things that infected the woods. Sam wasn't big on nature. It was too messy. You always ended up with something or another stuck to your clothes, or worse yet, in your hair.

"You gonna stand there all day, Sam? I'm gettin a crick in my neck."

Reluctantly, he sat, putting as little of his butt on the root as he possibly could without falling off. He grabbed Robbie Jo's hands in both of hers, gazed into her beautiful eyes. "What are we gonna do, baby?"

Her gaze was steady, cool. "I'll tell you what *you're* gonna do. You're gonna stay away from me. You can't throw away your inheritance, Sam."

"But I can't! I'm dyin' to touch you right now. If I can't have you, I'll die, Robbie Jo."

She kissed him, sweet and hot. He started getting hard and had to shift his butt.

"I don't mean forever, honey. Just until it's done."

"Until...you mean..."

"I mean until your parents are dead, Sam."

Hearing her say it made his heart pound, made his dick even harder. "You're really serious?"

"As a heart attack, handsome. I'll got to the school this afternoon and figure out how."

Sam looked at her, at her ivory face and her amazing eyes. There was a spark in those eyes, fierce, cold, hard as steel. He knew she could do it. He knew that, with her help, he could do it too. He went on his knees before her, in the leaves and the moss, his hands on her hips.

"You're perfect, Robbie Jo. Absolutely perfect." He pushed up her dress and licked the sweet curve of her inner thigh.

She ran her hands through his hair and sighed. "It won't be long, Sam. No more than a few weeks."

"I can't wait that long," nibbling at the waistband of her panties.

"I know. I can't either. But if you have to come to me, Sam, don't get caught. Sneak a little extra time on one of your pick-ups. Come to me in the middle of the night, when your folks are asleep. But don't you let 'em catch you."

"I won't." Kissing her breasts now, his hand in her underwear. "But what about your mama? What'll she do if she finds out?"

Robbie Jo stiffened. "She won't do a goddam thing. She doesn't control me. Don't worry about her. She doesn't exist. You just worry about yourself, okay?"

He rubbed her slowly, felt her clit rise up under his thumb like a little pearl. "Okay," he whispered. "I won't let 'em find out."

"You better not. 'Cause I've got no tolerance for fools, Sam. You understand me? Ohhhhh…" Her head fell back. Her breathing got faster.

"Perfectly. I'd do anything for you, sugar." Her pussy felt like wet silk under his fingertips.

"I'm countin' on it," she smiled, and he pulled her off the log and they rolled on the ground, her hair spread like fire on the leaves. He buried his face in her neck, inhaling her scent as deeply as it would go. In that moment, Robbie Jo was his entire world.

Robbie Jo wrapped he legs around Sam's waist, dug her fingers into his sculpted back as he pounded into her. She knew he'd do what he told her. It was in his eyes, like a well-trained hunting dog who'd die for you if he had to.

Robbie Jo moaned in Sam's ear. She'd go surf the Net, after she'd cleaned up in the stream and changed her clothes.

She'd find a way to take care of Sam's goddam pain-in-the-ass parents. Something painful. And maybe something else, something really special for her own mama. "Oh, yes," Robbie Jo breathed.

"C'mon, baby, c'mon," groaned Sam.

Robbie Jo licked his neck like an animal, tasted sweat and aftershave. She felt her orgasm building up like a pot simmering on the stove; first a warm tingle in her toes, then heat in her thighs and the base of her spine. She thrashed, she cried out, and in a single blinding moment of pleasure, her mother winked out of reality like a soap bubble popping on the point of a blade of grass.

HAZEL, SIX FEET UNDER

The funeral procession left at noon. Rose sat between Owen and Naomi, in their ancient Chevy pickup truck. The bed of the truck was filled with flowers; they spilled out on every side. The hearse was behind them. It made Rose nervous, glancing at its chrome leer in Owen's rear view mirror. At least Ephram was behind the wheel. Rose thought she might just have had to climb over Naomi and jump out the window if Sam had been piloting the big black deathmobile.

Reverend Rye was next in line, driving his little blue Pontiac. Behind him were a few more vehicles, the battered farm trucks and late-sixties sedans of Possum Kingdom's dedicated mourners. It seemed terribly sad to Rose that Hazel Lyndon had no living relatives to miss her.

The procession rolled through the gates of Angel's Rest, the lovely cemetery behind the Holy Blood, and came to a stop. Rose followed Owen and Naomi like a puppy, lost and uneasy.

Among the pallbearers were Owen Tanner, Sam Dunwiddie, and Dr. Michael Yeats. The other three were local farmboys who could have been Hazel Lyndon's grandsons, but weren't. They carried the casket with ease. Hazel's frail little body couldn't weigh more than a hundred pounds. Rose imagined her, sealed inside her satin-lined, lacquered box, preserved like a jar of peaches.

Formaldehyde-filled peaches.

With a cramp of guilt, Rose wondered if the Dunwiddies had found her fingermark in Hazel's powdered cheek, and if they had been able to fix it.

How would they do that? A little spackle?

Rose shuddered, swallowed a nervous giggle.

They followed the coffin and the preacher to Hazel Lyndon's waiting open grave. No gravestone; just a whitewashed wooden cross with Hazel's name carefully painted in black.

Naomi caught her staring. "We ordered a little stone from Jonesborough, but it won't get here 'til next week." Rose nodded. What would Hazel's stone say? Not "Beloved Wife" or "Our Precious Mother." *A Nice Lady that Nobody Really Knew?* And what would her own marker say, if she were to drop dead where she stood?

Here Lies Rose Heron, Drifter.

Runaway.

Liar.

Nobody.

Rose felt tears sting her eyes, but she wasn't sure if they were for Hazel, or for herself.

Suck it up, honey. This isn't about you. You aren't the one who's dead here, are ya.

And how presumptuous, to think that nobody really cared about Hazel. As he lowered the coffin, Rose could see that Michael Yeats' jaw was set, tears streaming down his face and into the starched white collar of his shirt.

There was no motorized casket lift for Possum Kingdom. The coffin rested on boards set across the grave. Ropes were strung beneath it, waiting for strong hands to lower the box and its pathetic contents into the rich Tennessee earth.

The turnout was nowhere near as strong at the graveside as it had been at the wake. Rose supposed that most folks figured they had done their duty by Miss Lyndon, paid their share of respects, ate their share of ham and cornbread. They had other things to do, things more important than watching Miss Lyndon's mortal remains get planted like a tulip bulb. Things were different here. You didn't call in sick when you worked for yourself. You didn't take a personal day from a blueberry field.

A movement in the woods caught Rose's eye. It was Robbie Jo, slipping through the trees in a simple black sleeveless dress. She stayed behind the small circle of mourners surrounding the grave, as if she felt she didn't really belong.

Rose caught Robbie Jo's eye, gave her a rueful smile. Robbie Jo nodded, face still and solemn. Rose gestured for Robbie Jo to join her.

But the preacher started talking, and Robbie Jo melted away, slender form invisible behind the wall of black-clad townsfolk.

Reverend Rye said all the things Rose would have expected him to. He spoke of Miss Lyndon's kindness, her friendliness, her generosity and willingness to help. As Rose stood there, in between Owen and Naomi like she was their daughter, it occurred to her that the Reverend could have been talking about anyone. He hadn't known her at all. As she sweated in the sauna-like heat of the afternoon, as she brushed gnats away from her sticky forehead and tried not to feel quite so sleepy, Rose wondered how a woman who had lived in the same town all her life could be such an enigma. It had to be, she decided, by choice.

At last Reverend Rye's doleful droning stopped, and the casket was lowered into the earth. Michael Yeats made no effort to stop the tears from rolling down his face as the rough rope passed through his slender surgeon's hands. Rose had the sudden urge to go to him, hug him, let him cry and cry and cry. Instead she leaned against Naomi, who slipped a plump, warm arm around her shoulders.

Folks began to file past the casket, dropping in single flowers and handfuls of dirt. Rose scooped up a mound of the black soil, squeezed it in her hand. She had never liked being dirty, always a fastidious little girl. But this stuff didn't seem unclean. As she crumbled the earth through her fingers and onto Hazel Lyndon's casket, Rose could smell it, rich and fertile and sweet. She had the ridiculous impulse to rub it on her skin, to drop to the ground and roll in it. Rose knew, then, why some people never left the little towns where they were born, why some farmers died rather than sell their fathers' land. It was powerful. It was magical.

She glanced up and Owen caught her eye. She blushed and dropped the rest of the dirt from her hand. He smiled at her, and nodded.

It was over then. A couple of strapping young fellows from the Holy Blood shoveled dirt into the grave by hand; old-fashioned sexton's spades, bulging biceps, sweat-stained white cotton shirts. People carried flowers from the Tanners' pickup truck and took them to the graveside, where they'd cover the raw wound in the earth when the church boys were done with their job.

And that's that, thought Rose. *The end. Curtains. Thuh-thuh-thuh-that's all, folks.* She imagined what it would be like, lying in the coffin, hearing the hollow rattle of dirt raining down, the voices above growing fainter and fainter...

She shivered, and felt foolish. *Nobody's hearin' a thing, brainiac. Hazel Lyndon's dead. Cold as clay. Stiff and deaf and dead. Just like we'll all be. Just like I'll be, someday.*

Michael Yeats stood under an oak tree, watching the boys fill Hazel's grave with dirt. He was oddly still, like the stone angels around him. Rose had the feeling that he'd be there an hour from now, two hours, maybe more.

Naomi touched Rose's elbow, whispered that it was time to go.

Not yet, Rose thought, climbing into the truck. *Not today, anyway.*

ROSE FUSSES, ROBBIE JO DIGS UP THE PAST

By late afternoon, Rose was getting nervous. Getting, hell, she was already there and checked into the spaz-out hotel. The graveyard dirt was washed from her hands, and the funeral was gone from her mind. Something else had pushed it out; something looming in the future, not buried in the past. Just the thought of working side by side with Michael Yeats made her stomach twist like a worm on a hot sidewalk.

She bustled around her room, trying on every outfit in her modest wardrobe, taking them off, trying them on again. Would jeans be too casual? No t-shirts, definitely not. She had two blouses Naomi had given her. Or a dress? She wanted to look nice. More than nice, she wanted to look pretty. The pale blue sleeveless one with the dropped waist, maybe. But what if she had to help Dr. Yeats hold down an animal? What if some big-ass dog bit her? What if it barfed or peed or crapped or bled on her?

What if she fainted at the sight of blood?

What if she cried when they lost a patient?

What if Michael thought she was an idiot?

Oh, shit fire and save matches.

Rose grabbed her head with both hands and sat down on the edge of her bed. She threw her arms out and fell back on the tangle of clothes, laughing at herself.

Robbie Jo stayed in the woods for a long while after Sam left. Naked, she wriggled down into the soft leaves and lay very still, pretending to be a dead thing. She imagined herself decaying; her eyes withering like grapes and falling back into her head, her body bloating, blackening and splitting, organs sinking liquid into the forest floor, lips drawing back from her teeth to leave her with a great big bony grin. She didn't move when a black, shiny beetle crawled over her arm. She didn't move when a daddy long-legs strutted importantly over her cheek. It just felt too good to be rotting.

When the sun was directly overhead, Robbie Jo got up. She stretched, brushed herself off, feeling lighter than air. She washed Sam's sweat off her body in Two Fox creek, put on her clothes, and went home.

Robbie Jo peered in through her mother's bedroom window. Lureen was lying on her back in bed, mouth wide open, in a drunk's soggy sleep. *Good.* If she'd been awake, Robbie Jo was fairly certain that she would have killed her.

She studied her mother's doughy face and imagined pouring Clorox down the stinking, wet hole of her mouth. She imagined plunging a fork into her throat. She imagined pounding a tenpenny nail through her mother's greasy forehead. Robbie Jo's hands crept up the dusty glass, clawing spiders hungry for blood.

Then Robbie Jo smelled biscuits. Her stomach rumbled; a more ordinary hunger. She smiled, and the rage drained out of her like dirty bathwater.

Robbie Jo ate six biscuits thick with butter and honey. Then she went into her room and took the cardboard box out from under her bed.

She turned a bundle of letters over and over in her hands. Smelled it. Old paper, old ink, cedar and tears. Flipping through them, Robbie Jo saw that they were in chronological order. She opened the first one.

May 9th, 1937
My Dear Miss Lyndon,
I hope you will forgive my boldness, but I cannot remain silent. Your beauty gives me the voice of a lark. I saw you at the revival, radiant as an angel. Pure as sunlight. Sweet as the first spring flowers. When you left you took my heart along with you. Please, dear girl. Meet me at the pond tonight, when the moon is high. I am your willing servant.
Meshach Reddingale

"You sly old fucker," Robbie Jo chuckled. Then she remembered the drawing; Reddingale hadn't been old. She pictured his dark, sexy eyes, and wondered what Hazel might have thought of his attentions.

"I'da banged him," she muttered, flipping through the stiff leather diary. There it was; the entry for May 9th.

Oh. Oh. I don't know how to tell you what happened tonight. It was so wonderful. So thrilling! The Reverend Meshach slipped a note in my handbag as I left the church. He asked me to go to him! Did he know how long I have loved him? How I have looked into his face and dreamed that we were alone, not as pastor and parishioner, but as lovers? He must have. He looked into my heart.

He stood by the pond waiting for me, the moon silver in his black eyes. My heart pounded so that I could hardly hear what he said to me. He took me in his arms and whispered such things to me; so passionate! So sincere! I dare not write them here, for fear that I will break the spell. But I am his. His kisses claimed me, body and soul, now and forever. When at last he left me, I was nearly delirious with passion for him.

We didn't make love, but I know we will soon. I want to. I know it's wrong, but I want to so badly.

"Naughty girl." Robbie Jo smiled, trying to imagine a blushing, nineteen-year-old Miss Lyndon. She flipped through the letters, following the secret romance. Meshach laid it on with a trowel, that was for sure. And Hazel ate it up like candy.

July 17th, 1937
I must see you tonight, my dearest Hazel. I must taste your skin or I will starve. I must feel your lips on mine as sweet as sugar, your legs wrapped around my waist, your body swallowing me whole. Come to me tonight. Come to me, my love.

"Yeah, yeah, yeah." Robbie Jo flipped through the diary, read Hazel's breathless, coy description of her deflowering, and her ongoing fuckfest with the good Reverend. Pretty boring stuff. Back to the letters. Aha, here was an interesting one:

November 2ⁿᵈ, 1937

Please, please forgive me. It meant nothing. Reenie Rackham brought me a rhubarb pie, to thank me for healing her father. When I told her it was the Almighty, and not I, who took the cancer from his face, she threw her arms around me and began to sob for joy. That was what you saw, my love. Nothing more. You must believe me.

Reenie Rackham? The crazy old rootwoman who lived outside of town? That was too bizarre. Grinning, she consulted the diary.

How could he? How could he do this to me? God in heaven, men are heartless creatures. I went to Meshach's cabin with a sweater I had knitted for him. The door was open, so I went in, thinking to surprise him. My heart stopped, no, froze, when I saw them. My Meshach and Reenie Rackham, locked in a passionate embrace. His arms around her waist. Her hand on his cheek, black as a charcoal smudge. I threw the sweater at them and ran, ran through the woods crying so hard I couldn't see.

He has betrayed me. I think I might die.

"Well, you evidently didn't, because you lived another hundred and fifty years." Robbie Jo went through a number of cajoling letters from Reddingale; read Miss Lyndon's anger, her softening, and finally her forgiveness. The sneaky SOB talked himself right back into her bloomers.

December 10ᵗʰ, 1937

It is such joy to have you back in my arms. I'll never, never let you go. I'll never hurt you again, I swear. You are my heart, Hazel.

"Yeah-fucking-right." This wasn't as interesting as she had hoped it would be, at least not yet. Broken hearts and fractured love affairs were a dime a dozen. Jerry Springer shit. Robbie Jo had long held the belief that anyone who appears as a guest on Jerry Springer should be electrocuted on the way out, just to tidy up the gene pool. She pulled out another letter from Meshach, and grunted. Of course, he hadn't kept it in his pants.

January 13ᵗʰ, 1938
I cannot bear your silence. I know that I promised never to see Miss Reenie again, but she came to me with a spiritual dilemma. I was holding her hand merely to comfort her. You are all I want, Hazel. All I want in the world. Please, talk to me.

Robbie Jo was about ready to give up. She flipped through the diary, skimming through Hazel's emotional roller coaster as Reddingale jerked her around. She began to wish he were alive, just so she could kill his lying ass. Then something caught her eye.

I know I cannot trust Meshach, but still I love him. I wish I didn't. I know he is still seeing Reenie Rackham. But I'm afraid it might be even worse than I imagined. I think she's polluting him with her evil, witchy magic. His kindness toward animals was always one of the things I loved about him, but now it has become strange. He talks to horses and birds and squirrels, not like you'd talk to your dog, but like he expects them to answer him. He talks about their purity, about how they are innocent but humans are corrupt. He is rude to the parishioners, treats them as if they're unclean. I don't know what to make of it.
Even when he's with me, he isn't really there. Is he with Reenie? Maybe. Dear lord, is he going mad?
Maybe. Maybe.
I can't be there to watch it. I am telling him good-bye tonight.

"Well, good for you, girlie, you finally stopped taking his shit." Robbie Jo dug out a letter from the same time frame.

February 19ᵗʰ, 1938
Everything is hollow. Everything is black. Without you I cannot see the beauty of this mortal world; just the ugliness, the sin, the hatred. It is unbearable. Please, Hazel, come back to me. I'm begging you. Please.

Back to the diary. "Make him suffer, honey," Robbie Jo grinned.

Meshach will not give up. He follows me around town. I know people are talking about it. And I fear, oh, I fear he has truly lost his mind. Whenever he can catch me alone, he tells me wild stories of talking with the animals and the spirits of the forest. His sermons have grown more and more bizarre, mostly berating the congregation for their sin and imperfection. A few people have stopped going to church altogether. Strangest of all, when he handles the serpents, they seem to dance for him. They twist around his body in patterns; they rear up on either side of his head and sway with the music, they slither around him in circles on the floor. I swear it is true! It frightens me. I want nothing to do with it. I want nothing to do with him.

Robbie Jo blinked. "I think we've just entered the Twilight Zone, Hazel old girl." At least this was more fun than infidelity.

Had Hazel and Meshach gone crazy together? There was a word for that; she searched her brain for the term she'd read on one of her serial killer websites. *Folie a' deux.* Madness of two. Leopold and Loeb, Lucas and Toole, Homolka and Bernardo.

Heron and Ridgemont? Robbie Jo grinned, imagined standing shoulder to shoulder with Rose, both of them bloody to the elbows, savaged corpse at their feet. Girlish laughter. A red wet kiss. Sweet, sweet. Robbie Jo had to lean back for awhile, lie on the floor, stare at the water-stained ceiling and dream.

At last, with a sigh, she came back to her room, the box on the floor before her.

"Okay," she whispered. "Let's see what you have to say about all this, Dr. Doolittle." She took out another letter.

March 5th, 1938
This world has come to its end. God has turned his face from us. We are ugly in his sight. Ugly and imperfect and unworthy. The human race must be cleansed. Renewed. Born again fresh and scrubbed and screaming. You must help me, Hazel. I know you hate me. But you must help me save the world from damnation.

"Well, that's a new line." Robbie Jo rolled her eyes. "'Help me save the world, baby!' Fuckola, guys will say anything." A check of the diary showed that Hazel wasn't impressed either.

Meshach has painted strange and terrible images on the walls of the Holy Blood. Many of his congregation have decided that he is insane, or maybe possessed by a demon. He has stopped begging me to be his lover; now he wants me to help him with some outrageous, blasphemous scheme. He has whispered a little of it to me, and I wish he hadn't. It's madness. I'm afraid he's going to hurt me.

Robbie Jo pulled the last letter from the bundle.

May 22nd, 1938
I've found the way. You must come to the pond tonight, Hazel. You must. Please, do this for me. It is the last time you will ever have to see me. I love you, Hazel. I will never forgive myself for breaking your virgin heart.

And Hazel's entry for May 22nd:

He's dead. He's dead. Oh my sweet Jesus, he's dead and we buried him. No one must ever find him. Not like that. Not looking like that. I can't stop shaking. Will the sun ever come up? It has to. Oh please, it has to.

Robbie Jo raised an eyebrow. There were a number of pages torn out after that entry. Then nothing until June 30th, where Hazel was prattling on about a church picnic and how much chicken she had to fry and whether she should wear yellow or pink. No mention of Meshach Reddingale. No mention of anything unusual, not to mention interesting.

Robbie Jo flipped through the diary, finding nothing of interest. Just the ramblings of an innocent, pious young lady whose whole life was her mama and daddy and her church. The young lady Hazel had been before she met Meshach. It seemed that she had just wiped him from her life like a splattered moth from a windshield.

The diary ended on December 31, 1938. Hazel had gotten a quilt and two new dresses for Christmas. She wished the world peace and love in 1939.

Robbie Jo turned the book over in her hands. She smelled it, picking up the faint scents of cedar, mulberries, and chamomile. Had Hazel stopped journaling after 1938? More likely her other diaries were in another part of the house. So what. Robbie Jo had the good stuff right here.

But what did it mean? Had Hazel killed Meshach in a jealous rage? Not likely; her journal entries sounded more like she was ready to slap a restraining order on the guy. Had Reenie Rackham killed him, then? Or had he killed himself in some form of religious frenzy, martyred himself to the God who had forsaken his world?

And what had Hazel meant, about Meshach's body "looking like that?" His death must have been ugly. Robbie Jo chewed her lower lip. She was betting on self-immolation. That was a good, solid, religious-wacko way to go.

She pulled out some of the loose sheets of paper and looked them over. A smile tugged at her lips. They were spells, no doubt about it. There was one for "Love and Pashin," one for "Welth," and one for "Power over Anamals."

Robbie Jo's eyebrow shot up. Maybe Meshach really had been dancing with snakes. Because he had Power over

Anamals. "Oh bullshit," she grinned, and picked up another page.

Resurecshun

Said the shaky letters at the top of the page. Like the others, it was a strange mix of near-illiterate language and weirdly kinetic drawings, all in blobby black ink. But for some reason, this one was unsettling to look at. There was something wrong about it; something that made Robbie Jo want to close her eyes and wash her hands.

Furst take a ded cat and fill its mouth with blak mud...

Robbie Jo shivered from the base of her spine to the back of her neck, and was immediately angry about it. She dropped the paper back into the box, kicked the box under her bed. "What a bunch of fucking horseshit," she said.

Robbie Jo stood up and stretched. It was time to go to school, and do a little surfing.

As she walked to town, leaving her mother still passed out and snoring, a thought was rolling around Robbie Jo's mind like a heavy marble.

Maybe she'd go pay Miss Reenie Rackham a visit. Maybe sometime soon.

THE BLACK DAWG GETS READY; ROBBIE JO GOES SURFING

The black dog woke up, blinked her eyes at the mottled sunlight. She stretched out long and wallowed out of the den she had dug beneath a hollow log. She plodded through the trees, heavy and tired, toward the familiar scent of other animals' guts. Her huge belly swayed beneath her. She could feel the squirming inside.

She knew she carried pups. One day, she had simply awakened knowing, and had begun digging her den.

Her steps were noisy, splayed paws breaking twigs and crunching leaves. The dog winced, tried to walk lightly. She had scented a bear the day before. Not close, but not far, either. She lowered her head and watched all around.

She reached the pile of guts and began immediately to eat. Her hunger was urgent these days, not to be denied. It wouldn't be long before the pups were here.

Her ears stood up as the door of the shack opened. There was the old Man, looking at her.

The dog wagged her tail. She knew better than to approach the old Man, to try to get him to pet her. Whenever she tried, he either shut the door in her face, or shoved her away with his foot. Still, she liked him. He didn't kick her, he didn't yell at her, and he let her eat in peace.

The old Man shut the door. The dog ate some more, then drank from the rusty water pan the old Man left out for her. She wagged her tail in gratitude, although the water tasted of metal and mildew.

The dog's head hung down as she plodded back to her den. She was tired most of the time these days. She sighed, and wished that she had the Woman to pet her head and stroke her ears. She remembered the woman's arms around her, the warm smell of her hair and the bitter scent of tears.

The dog slid her bulk into her cozy den, closed her eyes, and slept. She dreamed of resting with her head in the lap of a young girl, who smoothed her fur and called her a good dog.

Robbie Jo wove through the lush jungle of the Internet, looking to meet Death. Not just any death, of course not, but the perfect Death; the one that would be effective, irreversible, and vicious. The vicious part was important, Robbie Jo decided. She'd taken quite a dislike to Sam Dunwiddie's parents.

Robbie Jo took her time; she wasn't afraid of discovery. She had picked the lock of the library quickly and quietly. No one saw her. The custodian only came on the weekends in the summer, and no one in Possum Kingdom would even entertain the ridiculous idea of a school security guard. So, she wandered from the path, taking dark and shadowed sidetrips through the squelchy underbrush of the Internet.

She looked at pictures of abortions and suicides, deformities and sodomy and self-mutilation. Giggled over video of a train accident. Lingered over death camp victims bulldozed into mass graves.

The school was too stupid to put in a filter to protect the young and innocent. Hell, after a week and a half, Robbie Jo knew more about the workings of the Web than any of the staff members.

If anyone ever found out about her snorkeling through the Web's most foully polluted waterways, it wouldn't be good. She might get expelled. She might get stuck into counseling. Worst of all, it might mess up her chances to get a full scholarship to some college that was far, far away from Possum Kingdom. But that would never happen, of course, because Robbie Jo was logged on as Richie Brazil. Good old Richie. Foul-mouthed baseball player with a carrot-colored flattop and the shiny face of a boiled pig, who called her an egghead freak to his buddies and grabbed at her boobies when his pals weren't looking. She made sure to check out a few hardcore gay porn sites, just in case ol' Richie's website history was ever discovered.

She rocked out while she surfed. Robbie Jo found a website with a catalog of millions of songs she could play, and dove in with glee. The Cramps, The Damned, Deadbolt, Nekromantiks, Nine Inch Nails. She found that she could search for tracks by keyword. Typing in "death" and "murder" and "zombie" revealed delicious results. Robbie Jo found bands she'd never heard of before. Ghoultown. Those Poor Bastards. Sons of Perdition. Searching for "funeral" found her E.J. Wells, who sang (in Robbie Jo's opinion) the greatest song in the world, "Downstairs at the Funeral Home." She played it over and over again.

Robbie Jo belted out the chorus one last time: "DOWNstairs at the funeral HOME, by myself but I am not ALONE, I see spirits dancin', bodies movin', good God, now the aspirator's pointing at MEEEEE!" She laughed, spun in her chair, and got back to the task at hand.

She'd pretty much settled on poison, but there were so many to choose from. She needed something that would mimic an ordinary illness, something that wasn't easy to detect.

"Arsenic is for idiots," she murmured, scrolling through a PH.D candidate's thesis on toxicology. Botulism would be fun, but it wasn't a sure thing. It would be a crack-up to slip a few rattlesnakes into the Dunwiddies' bathtub, but that was hardly practical. It sure as hell wouldn't look like an accident. Besides, any self-respecting snake wouldn't lay a fang on a bitter old bitch like Mrs. D. *If he did, it'd prob'ly kill him outright.*

Robbie Jo's chuckle caught in her throat. She breathed in sharply. There it was. It was perfect. It was ugly, incredibly painful, and very fatal. And when Robbie Jo realized it was as close as the Sweet Hereafter's back yard, she laughed and laughed and laughed.

Robbie Jo stood up and did a little twirling dance around the computer stations. This called for a celebration. A special treat. Something hands-on. Robbie Jo quickly shut down the computer. She was already planning the evening's festivities.

Oh, it was gonna be good.

As Robbie Jo strolled through one of the school's back doors, pausing to lock it up tight with a bobby pin, clouds were forming over Possum Kingdom. The air took on a silky, sultry quality and a breeze quickened, stroking her cheeks like delicate fingers in kidskin gloves, lifting her hair, fluttering her thin yellow dress. Fat raindrops warm as blood began to fall, soaking into the sidewalk, making the blades of grass dance. Lightning lit the sky, far to the east. A distant growl of thunder made her close her eyes with pleasure.

Robbie Jo breathed in the rich smell of rain. Lightning flashed again, closer this time. Laughing, she threw her head back, arms reaching for the sky, daring God to strike her down.

The black dog shivered, tried to wriggle deeper into her den. It wasn't from cold; the air was nearly as warm as her breath. She was terrified of the thunder. It was still faint, far away, but each time it rumbled, she flattened her ears against her skull and whined. Big raindrops began to rattle through the trees. The dog tucked her muzzle under her front leg and squeezed her eyes shut.

JOE REECHUR'S GHASTLY DEMISE

*I*t was pouring by nightfall. Sheets of rain whipped through town on an angry wind that changed directions as quickly as a madman's thoughts. It rattled windows, banged shutters, made tree limbs scratch on rooftops like claws. Naomi and Owen closed the general store early. Rose, kneading bread dough in the warm sanctuary of the Tanners' kitchen, looked out the window and wondered what Robbie Jo might be doing. She thought of her friend, in her tiny house with no electricity, probably reading a book by the light of a kerosene lantern. Thin walls shaking with the thunder. Roof leaking.

She wished Robbie Jo were with her, helping her make the bread. Rose hit the dough with her fist and sighed. She hoped Robbie Jo wasn't scared of thunderstorms.

Joe Reechur sank his knife into the soft belly of a muskrat as a monstrous crack of thunder shook the ground. His kerosene lamp rattled, his old, blood-soaked table shuddered. The tip of the knife poked through the muskrat's ribs and out through its back.

"Shee-it," muttered Joe. Now the skin would have a hole in it, unless he stitched it up. Either way, it wouldn't look right. "Well, shee-it."

He jerked out the muskrat's insides and, clutching the slimy lumps and loops in his gnarled fingers, started for the door to toss them into the neverending gutpile.

Light as bright as day blasted in through the windows. Joe flinched, closed his eyes. A blast of thunder hit, almost simultaneously. A tremendous crack, not far away, and the sudden smell of ozone and smoke. Lightning had hit a tree. Close enough to worry about. Joe dropped the guts on the table and wiped his fingers on his stiff, crusty pants.

"Do it later, he grumbled." "Don't wanna get my goddam ass blown off." He set in to skinning the fat rodent.

The door rattled. Joe's head snapped up. It rattled again.

Joe Reechur's ill-worn heart began to pound. Could it be? Could it be that the beasts of the forest had finally come for him? "Who's there?" he screeched. The door rattled again, more faintly.

Joe let out a long, slow breath. It was just the wind. That's all. If it had been the beasts, they would have spoken his name. But they were cowards, and they only whispered it to him late at night. They wouldn't dare walk right up to his home. He grunted and started peeling the muskrat again.

Something began to scratch at the door. He heard a whine, low and miserable.

"Dawg?" he asked. "That you?" Joe Reechur opened his door.

Stared into the rust-colored eyes of a naked young girl clutching a kitchen knife, grinning like a moon-mad possum. Then she was on him.

The girl jumped like a striking snake and hit Joe in the chest, knocking him to the hard dirt floor. His breath was expelled from his lungs in a whoosh, and for a moment, he couldn't breathe. Hot pain as he felt the knife bite into his chest and scrape along his breastbone. He tried to bring the big skinning knife up, to stick it into the thing that sat on his chest (not a girl, not really, surely no real girl would do this to him).

Lightning flashed, lighting the girl's eyes in a hellish Halloween orange. She brought her knife down in a gleaming blur and Joe howled as his wrist was pierced, pinned to the floor. She grabbed the skinning knife from his spasming fingers. He felt steel punch through his rib cage and into his right lung. Thunder, loud as a curse from God.

Her arm was pistoning now, up and down, the knife ripping into him again and again. Joe couldn't breathe, he could just bubble blood. He wanted to move, but all his limbs would do was tremble, like an animal with its neck in a steel trap.

The girl was laughing, shrieking with glee, his blood was spurting red as Christmas. It hurt so much it didn't hurt any more. His vision started to swim. He noticed her little breasts bouncing as she stabbed him, remembered a girl sitting on his hips and bouncing once, so long ago he couldn't remember her face. His bladder let go, but he couldn't really feel it.

She stopped stabbing him. Her head cocked, she studied Joe's face, alert as a hunting dog. His blood covered her naked skin; she was more red than white. A stripe of crimson crossed her eyes like the mask of a raccoon.

The girl gripped Joe's head in her hands, stared into his face. He wanted to ask her why she'd killed him, but of course, he had no breath to speak with. He opened his mouth, and let out a gush of bloody froth.

This seemed to strike the girl as funny. She giggled, looked at him like he had made a silly face. Then she brought the knife up high.

Joe was sinking into blackness. It was nice there, warm and comfortable. Joe closed his eyes.

The girl's fingers, prying his eyelids open. Then she had the knife again, up over her head, and it flashed down across Joe's throat. He saw the feeble spurt from his neck, what little blood he had left jumping up to greet his killer before sinking into dirt soaked with the blood of a thousand animals. Then the blackness, gentle as a mother's kiss, pulled him under. He didn't manage to close his eyes again.

She sat on the old man's belly for awhile, looking into his dead face. She rubbed his blood all over her, reveling in its slickness, its sharp smell, its metallic taste. Massaged it into her hair like cream rinse.

Her groin throbbed pleasantly. She'd had two orgasms while she was stabbing the old man. Maybe more; it was hard to keep track when she was that excited.

It was all she had hoped it would be, and more. Oh, yes.

A flash of lightning, a roll of thunder. The storm had passed over Possum Kingdom. It was on its way out of town. Robbie Jo sighed, as deeply satisfied as a girl could be. She stretched extravagantly. Smiled. A few minutes more, and she got off of the old man's flaccid body.

She grabbed his ankles, wrinkled her nose at his bare feet, toenails like thick yellow soap, and tried to pull him out of the shack. Her hands were slick with blood and slipped over his anklebones.

"Shit." She went to wipe her hands on his clothes, but they were too soaked in blood. She stepped outside and scrubbed her hands on the spongy moss growing beneath a tree. It did the trick. She put a grip on Joe's scrawny ankles and hauled him out through his own front door.

Panting, grinning, dragging him through the woods, he wasn't very heavy, just a bony old rooster carcass in filthy overalls. Dragging him to the hole in the ground she had dug, just a hundred yards from Joe Reechur's shack. In a shaded clearing she had spent the afternoon digging in the rain, digging, digging down through the leaves and the mulch and the rich, black earth like a thing possessed, blisters on her fingers but who gave a shit about that. Not a shallow grave, no not at all. The hole was five feet if it was an inch. She'd had to grab a tree root to haul herself out. Not a perfect rectangular grave but a pit, round and gaping like a scream. Water had filled the bottom; Joe made a pitiful little splash when he went in, and a nasty wet smack like a rotten melon hitting a hard floor.

She cocked her head and stared at him. Poked him with a long branch to get him curled up just so, a sorry little ball of bony arms and legs. She thought he looked like a stillborn baby, caught in a dead mother's womb. *A stillborn baby wearin' overalls.* That made her laugh.

She covered him with thick branches to keep him still, then pushed the dirt back into the hole with her hands. Every now and then she'd jump in and stomp it down good and hard. Then she replaced the spongy moss, the mulch, the dead leaves, spreading them around until it seemed that the ground had never been disturbed at all.

No one would find him. No one would even miss him. She stretched, then smiled at her filthy arms, streaked now with black dirt as well as blood so that she looked like a zebra from Hell. She took a pee behind a bush, took the croker sack from the tree branch where she'd hidden it. Walked on bare feet as hard as hooves, feet that had run unshod through the woods of Possum Kingdom since they could hold her up, and went back to Joe's shack.

There was nothing worth taking, other than the skinning knife she already had. Oh wait, there was his shotgun. A girl never knew when she'd need one of those. She stuffed it into the sack, though the barrel stuck out the top a good six inches. She closed Joe Reechur's door, and walked through the dark, dripping forest.

Naked. Fearless. And what would someone think, seeing a naked young girl as red as a juicy watermelon coming toward them in the darkness? He wouldn't have time to think much, because she'd kill him. She had the skinning knife in one hand, a hungry fang waiting for a taste of meat. She had no fear of bears or puma or any other wild things, although she smelled like a slaughterhouse. They wouldn't dare come near her. Not tonight. Tonight she was Death.

Robbie Jo wasn't right about everything. Joe was eventually missed, but not until fall, almost winter. A cop from Jonesborough came out to his shack and looked around. He found nothing unusual. Joe's shotgun was gone. He must've gone into the woods to hunt and gotten lost. Probably dead of exposure. Possibly et by a bear. End of story.

The people of Possum Kingdom didn't quite believe that. Everybody knew Joe was crazy. Some folks said that he wandered away, either running from or following the voices that he said he heard in the night. Some folks said that he met up with the Wampus cat in the darkness. A few suggested that Possum Woman got him. And then there was the perplexing little mystery of why he had gone off and left his boots under his bed. Maybe he was just nutty enough to walk around the woods barefoot. Or maybe something dragged him out of his bed in the night.

But no one even came close to guessing the truth. That he'd been butchered on his own bloodsoaked dirt floor. That it was done by a little girl, just two days before her sixteenth birthday. That he was buried under the spot where the cop from Jonesborough paused to smoke a butt.

Joe Reechur's body was never found. A handsome young poplar tree has sprouted up on top of his grave. Its roots are threaded through his rib cage. An underground fungus grows in his skull, giving him eyes black and wet. Joe Reechur is woven into the black, fertile heart of Possum Kingdom, and there he will stay.

STORM SUITE: YOUNG LOVE AND PUPPIES

Rewind: the height of the storm. The black dog is paralyzed with terror. Her den is filling with water. Her insides are cramping. The puppies inside her seem to feel her fear, and they wriggle and roll. She pants, eyes bulging, drooling, shaking.

The water is up to her chest, and she starts to pull herself out of the den, but the ground is slippery and she can't get a grip on it. More water, up to her neck. In a blind panic now, scrabbling, clawing. She pushes hard with her back legs; one sinks into mud, the other touches a sunken snag on the tree above her den. She braces against it, digging, wiggling, and suddenly she's out, sprawled on the ground in the pouring rain.

She gets to her feet, awkward and heavy, but she has to run. She can't see anything but the blinding flash of lightning. Can't hear anything but the deafening roar of thunder, the voice of a monstrous beast that is hunting her like a rabbit. She runs. Pain in her sides, ache in her legs, but she runs, because the beast is right behind her. Right behind her.

She reaches the home of the Old Man, races past the slimy pile of guts and heads for the door, but there's something horribly wrong. She hears his screams. She smells his blood. She smells the musky, savage scent of a predator in the act of killing.

The dog skids to a stop. She stands still, trembling, for a few brief seconds. Raindrops pound her like tiny, angry fists. Eyes rolling, claws scrambling on wet leaves, she spins and runs the other way.

———

Robbie Jo, floating in the pond on her back, arms spread, hair streaming, a contented, murderous Ophelia.

She stared up at the sky, patches of deep black shimmering with stars in between the thinning clouds. Ran her hands lazily through her hair one more time, just to make sure all the blood was out. Did a somersault in the water like a frisky otter pup. Finally, with a deep, happy sigh, she got out of the pond.

She took a thin gray towel from her croker sack and dried off. Slid a cornflower blue dress on over her head. She fished around in the bottom of the sack for a couple of square plastic packets, then slipped them into the pocket of her dress. A girl could never be too careful.

Other than the fact that she was carrying a wet towel, a skinning knife and a shotgun in a bag and was wearing no shoes, Robbie Jo decided she was fairly presentable. It was time for dessert. A little after-dinner mint, anyway. She heaved the sack over her shoulder and started walking into the deep woods, toward Simon McCray's house.

But it's still storming, thunder blasting, pouring down rain, and the black dog is running in a blind panic. Her sides hurt like they did when the Man used to kick her, and her back legs feel like they're pulling off of her body at the hips. But she can't stop, for fear that the Thing who killed the Old Man will get her, too.

She stumbles, staggers. She can't run much farther. She probably can't walk much farther. Her breath comes in whining gasps. Her eyes are slitted against the rain, against the knifing agony in her flanks.

Suddenly she's not in the woods anymore. She's running on a graveled path. There's a light ahead, warm, promising safety and food.

Or maybe the Thing is in there, waiting to splash her blood around, too.

It doesn't matter. It doesn't matter. Because she's collapsing on the doorstep, breath wheezing. She barely has the strength to scratch at the door once, twice, and then her eyes go shut, all by themselves.

Simon couldn't sleep. He sat on the floor of his shabby living room, carving a rat from a block of wood. He'd just finished the sinuous, scaly tail when something told him to look up, heads up, somethin's watching you, boy.

Simon's heart kick-started. He gasped, his head snapped up to look at the doorway, three-inch pocketknife blade held out in front of him. The rat rolled across the floor.

The girl in the open door grinned at him and shook her head. "You thinkin' of carvin' me up, Simon? And I thought you liked me."

It was her. His angel. He blinked. With his mind clear of fresh sin and heroin, he recognized her; he'd seen her before. Through the eyes of a sinner.

"Robbie Jo Ridgemont," he said, and felt a scarlet flush creep up his neck and face.

"That's right." She cocked her head. "Why you blushin', boy?"

He opened his mouth, but nothing came out. Simon stared at the floor.

She chuckled. "You ate my daddy's sins, didn't you. You know what he did to me. Isn't that right?"

"I—" Simon got a tickle in his throat and started coughing, coughing, until tears rolled down his face. Robbie Jo got him tepid water from the tin pitcher in the kitchen. Still an angel. He drank it gratefully.

She sat down on the floor next to him. He glanced at her, afraid to look her in the face, but she wasn't embarrassed, or ashamed, or even angry. Her face was smooth and cool as a marble statue's, her russet eyes like autumn leaves. She smiled at him, and touched his cheek. "You okay?"

He nodded. Swallowed hard, gathered his courage, and met her gaze full-on. "It wasn't your fault," he whispered. "You were just a little girl."

She laughed and kissed his forehead. "You're so sweet. I just can't believe you're real."

Simon gasped, closed his eyes. He could feel the brush of Robbie Jo's lips on his skin long after she pulled back. He blinked back tears. "I wasn't sure you were real either, after…after we met the last time."

He immediately regretted saying it, as his stomach tied itself in knots. She'd seen him at his worst, crying, desperate, scrambling for the needle like a starving dog for table scraps.

It was like she'd read his mind. "Tell me about it," she said. "Tell me about the heroin."

His face got hot again. "Wha—what do you want to know? Why I do it?"

"Nah. I figure it's 'cause you're the sineater. That's gotta be a shitty job." She stroked his hair lightly, and he shivered.

"Yeah, that's one way to put it. It's…it's just about the worst thing there is."

She nodded, then smiled, a wry little twist. "You've gotta tell me, Simon. Where do you get it? Not in Possum Kingdom, surely?"

"Nope. In Jonesborough. From a guy who runs an antique store."

She laughed. "How'd you ever hook up with him?"

He was nervous; there was something wrong with talking about sineating. But Simon couldn't say no to her, not to his angel. "I, um, ate the sins of one of his, uh, customers. I saw him buyin' the stuff, even saw the name of the shop." A sad little smile, which felt more like a grimace to him. "Eatin' sins is kinda like watchin' a movie, 'cept you're right <u>there</u>, seein', smellin', ever'thin'."

"Virtual reality, backwoods style." Robbie Jo giggled.

Simon narrowed his eyes, wondering if she were laughing at him. "What's virtual reality?"

"Aw, nothin'." She toyed with one of his curls. "How do you pay for that stuff, Simon? It's s'posed to be really pricey. Nothin' personal, but it looks like you ain't got a pot to piss in."

He let out a little laugh. "I don't pay. The guy gives it to me. Once he realized who I was, he was scared. Even city folk know they shouldn't mess around with a sineater. He gives it to me so I'll go away." Simon tried to laugh again, but it stuck in his throat, and his eyes started to sting. He bit his lower lip, blinked like an owl. He glanced at Robbie Jo, eyes narrow.

She was looking at him with sympathy, not pity, and he loved her for it. "It's gotta be so hard for you, Simon. How can you stand it?"

He hung his head. Picked up the half-carved rat from the floor, and turned it over and over in his hands. "I can't, Robbie Jo. I really can't."

And then her hands were on his face, and when he looked up at her, she kissed him. Heaven, oh, heaven.

"Oh my God, you poor little doggie!" Rose stood in the doorway of the Tanners' kitchen, half-eaten chunk of buttered cornbread in her hand, rain blowing in and spattering her t-shirt. She knelt down next to the wet, muddy creature who lay on its side, breath heaving in and out.

Lay on *her* side. It didn't take a rocket scientist, or even a vet, to see that the dog was pregnant.

"About to pop, aren't you," Rose murmured, stroking the wet, black fur. The dog rolled its eyes at her and whined. Rose held the cornbread under her nose. "Here you go, sweetie." The dog closed her eyes, didn't even sniff it.

"This isn't good. Not good at all." Rose tossed the cornbread down the path and wrapped both arms around the dog's chest. Planting her feet apart like a power lifter, she tried to heft the dog. She seemed to be filled with lead instead of puppies. Rose changed her strategy, and attempted to drag the dog over the threshold. It worked; she managed to pull her into the kitchen. Shutting and relocking the door, Rose wondered what she should do next. "I don't know nothin' 'bout birthin' no puppies," she muttered.

"What's goin' on?" A sleepy eyed Owen, standing in the doorway. He blinked a couple of times, then saw the dog and the puddle of water in the middle of the floor. "Oh. My."

"She came to the door. I couldn't leave her there…"

"Of course you couldn't, poor girl." Owen knelt down next to the dog and put his hand on her side. "It's her time. Stay with her, I'll get some blankets."

Rose stroked the dog's head and ears, murmuring softly to her, telling her she was a good dog, a sweet dog, a pretty dog. The dog whined, and licked her hand.

A sudden flash of recognition. She remembered the hearse bearing down on her like a Valkyrie, the dust, the fear, and the dog. The black dog in the middle of the road.

"It was you, wasn't it. Sure it was." Rose touched the short, plushy fur on the dog's shoulder; fur that had grown in since she was tossed by the deathwagon.

"Here we go." Owen had two thick, faded blankets in his arms. He put them in the corner of the kitchen, arranged them into a nest, then crouched down by the dog. He lifted her gently, and set her down on her birthing bed. The dog whimpered, and tried to stand up. She was staring right at Rose.

"She wants you with her," Owen said.

"You think?" She sat down by the panting animal and rested her hand on her bulging side. The dog immediately calmed. "How long will it take? Having the puppies, I mean?"

Owen grinned. "Oh, not long, I'd say." Rose followed his gaze, and her mouth dropped open. There was a tiny paw sticking out of the dog's back end.

"Oh, God... God... " Robbie Jo held Simon's wiry body close as he came. He twisted against her, every muscle tense, like one of the snakes at the Holy Blood. It was their second try; the first time he'd come on her belly, before she could even get the rubber on him. But this time wasn't bad. He not only made it in, he lasted close to ten minutes. The kid had potential.

His head was resting on her breast, body shaking. He was crying.

"What is it, baby," she whispered.

"I can't believe—no one's ever even touched me before. Except my mama and daddy. I never thought..."

"You're a beautiful boy, Simon. Beautiful and kind."

He buried his face in her shoulder. "No 'm not."

"'Course you are."

"Even if I was, it wouldn't matter. 'Cause I'm the sineater. I'm unclean, Robbie Jo. I hope to God I didn't infect you with it."

"That's bullshit, honey. You just got a hard job, that's all." She helped him hold onto the condom while he pulled out.

"It's just too much, Robbie Jo. All those sins in my head. I never forget 'em, you know. Not any of 'em." He rolled off of her, but put his arms around her like a child with a teddy bear.

"Maybe it would help if you talked about 'em."

He shook his head. "No, I don't—I don't think I can."

Robbie Jo smiled and brushed the hair off his forehead. "Tell ya what, why don't you start with somebody easy. Tell me about Hazel Lyndon. Tell me about her sins, Simon."

The storm was leaving Possum Kingdom, and four newborn puppies lay squeaking and wiggling against their mother's belly. The first had been born backwards, one tiny rear paw and then the other. The rest came out head first. The black dog quickly cleaned each pup and ate the afterbirth, but not before Owen noticed that there were only two cauls.

"Two sets of twins!" he'd said. "That doesn't happen too often, Rosie."

Rose didn't actually know that dogs could have twins, but it sounded reasonable to her. And oh, the pups were so cute! Tiny black things, silky and shiny as could be, eyes closed, little fat ears buttoned down tight. The black dog didn't seem to mind Rose handling her babies. So far, the puppies were all girls.

Rose was downright proud of herself. She'd never seen anything born before, except on TV. The real thing was much more intense, in full color, blood on the towels and the smell of meat and dog breath and wet fur.

But Rose didn't look away, she didn't even flinch. There had been a brief moment of horror when she thought the black dog was trying to eat her firstborn; when she bent over the tiny pup and began licking and chewing. Owen had laughed, told her that the dog was just reclaiming what she lost in the birth process. Gross. But it didn't make her yak.

Rose was starting to think that maybe she'd be a halfway decent assistant for Dr. Yeats, after all. She stroked the dog's still-bulging side, and smiled.

The dog didn't move, didn't raise her head or lick Rose's hand. Her eyes were half open. Rose realized that the animal's breathing was no longer a steady pant; it had grown ragged and shallow. "Owen—"

He knelt down beside her, placed a work-hardened hand on the dog's silky ear. Small hands, but strong. "I think she's in trouble," he said. "She's too weak to push. She's got at least two more in there."

"Well, get Doc Yeats on the phone, Einstein." Naomi stood in the doorway in her nightgown, sleepy eyes, her hair a gray puffball.

"I'm on my way, old woman."

Naomi lowered herself to the floor with an elaborate grunt. She felt the dog's belly, kneading and pressing gently. "Mm-hm."

The dog let out a barely audible whine. Naomi inserted a blunt finger into the animal's vagina. Rose winced.

"Can't feel anythin' 'cept for the caul. Damn thing's tough as a douchebag." Rose let out a little snort of laughter.

"There's prob'ly two pups in there," Owen said, peering into the kitchen. "The first four were twins. Doc's on his way."

"Well, I'll be. She doesn't have a chance of pushin' out two in a bag. The way she looks, I'm not sure she could push 'em out one at a time anymore."

"Could you break the caul? Cut it?" Rose stroked the back of one of the tiny puppies, who was already nursing with a slow, dreamy rhythm.

"Not me, sugar. I'd be afraid of hurtin' the little critter inside. Or the mama. We'd best wait for Doc."

An abrupt stab of pain, right through Rose's heart. It was suddenly very important that the dog and her pups not die. "What can we do to help her?" she asked Naomi. "What can I do?"

"Just be sweet to her, Rose. Let her know you're here."

Rose scooted across the cool Formica floor, until she could lift the dog's head and lay it in her lap. She stroked the black dog's velvety muzzle, smoothed the soft fur in the shallow crease on top of her skull. "Such a good dog," Rose murmured. "Such a sweet dog. Hang in there, girl. Stay with me, okay?"

The tip of the dog's tongue, dry and sticky, brushed the palm of Rose's hand.

"...I dunno, Robbie Jo...it just seems like there's somethin' wrong about it." Simon stared at the ceiling, desperately uncomfortable. The thing was, he wanted to tell her. He wanted to give Robbie Jo anything she wanted, anything in the world. But it seemed terrible in some way, a bone-deep betrayal of the now-innocent dead.

She cupped his face in her hands and kissed him, deep and long. Her tongue flicked the roof of his mouth, causing a direct reaction in his crotch.

"It's okay, honey. I mean, who am I gonna tell?"

He squirmed, feeling himself poking against her belly, which made him squirm some more. "It—it's not that, I know you wouldn't tell, Robbie Jo. It's just that I'm not supposed to..."

She laughed, low and throaty. "And who told you that, Simon? Did you learn it in Sineater School?"

"Well, no, nobody ever actually said—"

"Then it's okay. Trust me." Her tongue in his ear, and he got so hard he thought he might snap in two. "Besides," she whispered. "If you tell me, I'll do somethin' really, really special for you."

Robbie Jo reached down and squeezed his penis, and Simon's brain seemed to run out his ears. He groaned. Who would it hurt to tell, really? Hazel Lyndon was dead, her sins erased, digested. She was somewhere else now, far away from Possum Kingdom. Far, far away.

"What do you want to know," he asked, his hands wandering over her smooth little peach of an ass.

"What was the worst thing she did? The worst thing in her whole life."

"Uh...I guess it depends on what you call bad, Robbie Jo. She, um, did sex with a preacher...and they wasn't married..."

He felt her lips curve against his neck, a big toothy grin. "That ain't so bad, Simon. I don't think sex is sinful, do you?" She bit his earlobe.

"I'm beginnin' to think not," he gasped.

"She must've done somethin' worse. Tell me. Tell me."

Images boiled up in Simon's mind; darkness, dirt, sweat, shovels, dull, pounding fear. Horror. He shuddered.

"Come on, baby…"

"She—she was at a ritual with the preacher, one night. Her and Reenie Rackham. Somethin' bad happened. I couldn't tell what, it was confusin'…but it was really bad. And then the preacher died."

Robbie Jo reared up and looked into his face, a weird kind of smile on her lips. "Did Hazel kill him?"

"No…nobody killed him, I don't think. It was somethin' he done himself, but an accident. He was—he was messed up, Robbie Jo."

"Messed up how?"

"I'm not sure. What I get ain't always clear. But it was bad. And then Miss Hazel and Miss Reenie buried him."

Her eyes were sparkling. "They did? Where?"

"Why—why do you wanna know?"

"I just do, honey."

"Out behind the Holy Blood, out in the woods. Under a big ol' oak tree."

Robbie Jo scowled. "There's about a million oak trees in the woods, Simon. How do you know it was behind the church?"

He smiled. "'Cause they carved a snake on the tree. It's still there. I sometimes sit in that tree durin' services. Nobody can see me, but I can hear the singin' and such."

She grinned. "You sit in that tree, knowin' there's a dead preacher under it? Doesn't that scare you, Simon?"

"Nah. Dead folks never did nothin' bad to me. Just live ones."

"You ever eat his sins? Have yourself a little picnic?" She laughed and tossed her hair.

"Uh-uh. You can only eat sins for a day or two after a body dies. Makes me feel kinda bad, though. The poor fella down there with all his sins still inside him."

"Hmmmm. Let me show you a little somethin' about eatin'."

"What?" She was creeping backwards down his body, her hair making a delicious spiderweb tingle on his bare skin. And then she had him in her hand, and oh God, her mouth was on him, and her tongue, like his dick was a cherry popsicle. His eyes rolled back in his head. Simon McCray sank, sank deep down into warm clouds of nearly unbearable pleasure.

Rose was sure that the dog was dying. She was taking deep, slow breaths, hardly moving at all. She didn't seem to notice the four puppies nursing, their tiny paws swimming against her belly. She seemed far away, eyes half open, as if she could see whatever green, hilly heaven awaits good dogs when they die. Rose was wondering if she would have the strength to get a kitchen knife and save the puppies when Dr. Michael Yeats pounded on the door.

He was soaked to the skin, but that didn't slow him down. He wiped the water from his hair and face as he knelt down by the dog, checked her eyes, listened to her heart with a stethoscope. Rose tried not to stare at him. He looked impossibly beautiful, wet hair tousled like a little boy, mouth bowed down with worry.

He put one finger inside the dog, felt around for a moment, then nodded. "You were right, Owen. It's twins. Let's get 'em out." He went to the sink and began scrubbing his hands.

"Rose," he said over his shoulder, "Feel like helpin' me out?"

"Sure." *Don't blow it, don't blow it, don't make him think you're an idiot...*

He was next to her, and he smelled sweet and earthy, like he was made of the rain itself. He opened his black bag (he had a black bag, for chrissakes) and pulled out some long-handled forceps. "You wash your hands, then come back here, okay?"

"Sure."

Naomi bustled up with a clean towel, bleached as white as bone. "You can put your tools on here, Doc."

"Thank you kindly, Miz Tanner."

Rose scrubbed to her elbows, just like they did on "E.R.".
She hurried back and knelt down next to Doc Yeats. *Michael,*
she thought, *his name is Michael, what a beautiful name.*

"I'm gonna cut this membrane and get the first puppy out.
I need you to clean it off and put it by its mama, okay?" He
looked her in the eye, intent, serious. Her heart flopped, just
once.

"Sure." *Oh, great. He's gonna think I have a vocabulary
of one word.*

He slid the forceps inside the dog, who blinked, but didn't
move. He pulled out something red and veiny, like part of an
organic balloon.

So far so good. It was gross, but Rose wasn't in danger of
barfing or fainting.

She winced when Michael pulled out a pair of surgical
scissors, small and wickedly sharp. He snipped an incision into
the membrane, and widened it with his fingers.

Both Naomi and Owen were in the kitchen now, arms
around each other's waists. Owen chewed his lip. Naomi's
brow was knitted.

With one hand, Michael pushed on the dog's belly, gentle
but firm. With the other forefinger he reached inside the dog
and guided out a tiny black nose. Another shove, and the puppy
was out.

Michael quickly snipped the cord and handed the
squirming, wet pup to Rose. Naomi put a warm, wet washcloth
into her hand, and Rose began to clean the infant.

To her surprise, tears stung her eyes. It was possibly the
cutest thing she'd ever seen in her life, blunt and unfinished,
squeaking for milk. She cleaned it gently and set it down by the
black dog's belly. The puppy rooted around for a moment, tiny
head shaking like palsy, then latched on to a nipple.

Another squish, a dribble of bloody fluid, and the other
pup was out too. Doc set it into Rose's cupped hands, brushing
her fingers with his. *Did he do that on purpose? No, of course
not.*

She cleaned the pup while Naomi cleaned up the bloody
evidence of its birth. "It's too bad she's too weak to eat this

one, too," Naomi said, holding up the caul. "It's the way it's s'posed to be."

"Don't you be puttin' it in the freezer and fryin' it up for the pooch later, darlin'," said Owen, patting his wife on the shoulder. "I don't think my poor old nerves could stand it."

"Just for that, you old booger, I might just slip it into your chit'lins!" She spirited the gooey bundle away.

"Do you think the mama's gonna make it?" asked Rose, as the sixth puppy latched on like a tiny remora.

"Oh, I think so. She's just tired, is all. And dehydrated." Michael took out a syringe the size of a bicycle pump (or so it seemed to Rose) and a big needle sealed in plastic.

Oh lord, I hope this isn't gonna be something really gross...

But it wasn't that bad. He filled the syringe from a big bag of saline, and injected it under the dog's skin, between the shoulder blades. The dog didn't move, didn't even whine, as a great lump of fluid swelled from her back.

"There," said Michael. That should help her a lot."

"She looks like the God-forsaken Hunchback of Notre Dame," said Owen.

Naomi hip-checked him. "And you don't?"

Michael grinned; Rose basked in it like it was Jamaican sun. "Don't try to feed her tonight, but she'll likely be hungry in the morning. You might fix her some chicken broth, if you've a mind to."

"'Course I will," said Naomi, stroking the dog's ear.

Michael stood, stretched. Rose noticed how narrow his waist was, like a greyhound. "You did a fine job, Rose. You'll make a good assistant."

Rose's face grew hot, and she looked at her bare feet. With an overwhelming rush of embarrassment, she realized she was still wearing a t-shirt and panties. *Thank God it's a big t-shirt. Oh, Jesus.* "Thanks," she said.

"Considering the circumstances, I won't mind if you come in late tomorrow." He smiled, patted her shoulder. Rose let out a little gasp as a shiver whipped up her spine. She managed a smile back.

"Y'all call me if anything goes wrong, okay?" Michael washed the blood from his hands and packed up his instruments.

"We'll do that," said Naomi.

"I'll—I'll stay down here with her tonight, if that's okay," Rose said.

"Are you sure, Rosie?" asked Owen. "The floor's none too comfortable."

"I'd really like to, just to make sure she's all right."

"I'll get you some quilts, honey. I do believe you're the sweetest thing in creation!" Naomi patted her cheek.

"The last two pups were girls, too," Rose blurted, trying to shove down another tidal wave of embarrassment. "They're all girl dogs."

Michael shook his head. "Well, I'll be damned. Six girls, three sets of twins. That's more than a tad unusual. You have a special little mama dog here. Are you plannin' to keep her?"

"Oh, hell yes," said Owen, looking pained. "We'll call her Quasimodo."

"We'll do no such thing!" cried Naomi. "She's too pretty for that!"

"How about Onyx? Like—like the stone?" Rose was proud of herself; she managed to look Michael in the eye without turning lobster red.

Michael grinned. "That's a fine name. Poetic, even. I'm sure she'll like it." He stroked the dog's head, his long, artistic fingers caressing her soft ears and face.

Onyx passed from whatever in-between world she had occupied before into a deep, satisfied sleep. Her sides rose and fell evenly, her tongue protruded slightly from her black lips. "Sweet dreams, girl," Michael whispered. He stood up, smiled, and his eyes looked suddenly very tired. "And sweet dreams to all of you."

He was out the door, had almost shut it, when he peeked back into the kitchen. "I think it's wonderful that you want to stay with Onyx, Rose. Really wonderful."

Then he was gone, leaving Rose to glory in his approval.

Later that night, curled up on the floor on a heap of quilts and blankets, Rose drifted and dreamed. When the dog occasionally whined in her sleep, Rose's hand on her side would quiet her. More than once, she reached over and counted the puppies in the dark; a half-dozen sleek, soft bodies, wriggling with electric new life. Six girls, black as coal. And their mama. Seven black dogs. That meant something, Rose thought, but she couldn't remember what. Maybe she never knew.

"Goodnight, Girls," she whispered, voice slurred with sleep. "Welcome to Possum Kingdom."

ROBBIE JO

*H*allelujah, brothers and sisters, I have seen the LIGHT! Yes sirree Bob, I have found my true callin'. This must be how Picasso felt the first time he picked up a paintbrush. The way Charlotte Bronte felt when she escaped her shitty little world by puttin' pen to paper.

Okay, okay, I'm bein' kinda conceited here, I admit it. But I'm ridin' so high I can't even see the ground. How can I tell you how sweet it is? How beautiful, when steel slices into flesh? The joy, the heat, the overwhelmin' sense of power, when you punch so many holes in a body that he's just a wet, warm, water balloon? I've never felt so strong in my life. So in control. So sexy. I'm afraid that ever'thin' ol' Sam's done to me just pales by comparison.

Oh, Lordy, I want more!

This revelation makes my plan for the Dunwiddies tarnish in my eyes just a bit. To tell you the truth, I've always thought poisoners were pussies. And I'm not even doin' it myself! I've gotta trust that eedjit Sam to pull it off, and not fuck it up. I'm gonna miss all the fun. But then again, it's kinda fun to be the "evil mastermind," too. Push a little button, pull a little lever (like Sam's pecker, for instance), and people die! Yeehah! And what the hell, I've got plenty of time to slash and burn.

When I think of all the years ahead of me, all the bodies lined up as far as the eye can see, just stalks of bleedin' wheat before my scythe...Whoo! Gives me a sweet little chill.

This is me. My life. I was born to draw blood.

Oh, you may think I'm a sick fuck. In fact, you'd prob'ly be right. But at least I like who I am. Can you say the same thing?

ROSE STARTS WORK; ROBBIE JO BRINGS THE BEANS

T he black dog awoke with a jump, whimpering. She sniffed for her babies, and they were all there; six little warm bodies snuggled up against her. But there was something wrong. She felt a tearing in the center of her, like when the Man would kick her in the guts, only worse. Deeper. Something was being taken from her.

She stood on shaky legs and whined. She blinked her sticky eyes, looked around. The pups began to squeal, their tiny mouths seeking for her nipples.

The black dog began to cry; loud, miserable howls. She took a shaky step forward, tripping on the towels that were her bed, bowling over one of the fat, black pups. She knew that if the feeling inside her didn't stop, she would die.

And then she was there. The One who had taken her in. The One who had stroked her fur in the night as she gave birth, calming her like cool water in her mouth.

The dog sagged against the One's leg, letting out a deep sigh as the tearing anguish drained away. She closed her eyes and listened to the One's sweet voice, let it wash over her like a warm breeze. She sank back down onto her bed.

But the One patted her on the head, and turned her back. She was walking away. Out the door. The dog barked, then threw back her head and howled. When the One came close again, the dog grabbed her skirt in her teeth and held on, eyes closed. She expected a blow. She knew she deserved one. But she couldn't let the One get away from her.

Instead of hitting her, the One began to laugh. Not a bitter, angry laugh like the Man used to do, but a sound soft and warm. The dog gazed up into her face, and found her One smiling down at her.

The One said something to her, gentle words, and the dog knew it would be all right. In the deepest part of her, she knew. She sank back down to let her babies suckle.

Michael Yeats was surprised to realize that he was very nervous. He tidied his exam room, straightening bottles of vaccine in the cabinets, dusting the X-ray viewer, until he realized what he was doing and had to laugh.

He told himself that he was under a lot of stress; he was still grieving over Hazel, and training a new assistant was going to be a lot of work.

"But that's not what's wrong with you, is it, boy," he whispered. The fact of the matter was, Rose Heron was a beautiful young lady. Beautiful, intelligent, and capable. Michael couldn't believe how cool she had been last night as she had helped him bring the black dog's pups into the world. No squirming, no flinching, no girlish squeals of horror.

But she is a girl, isn't she, a very young girl. Too young for you. Don't even think about it.

Michael smiled, took off his glasses and wiped them on his lab coat.

"Um, hello?" Rose was peeking in through the front door.

"C'mon in," Michael smiled. "You don't have to knock."

Rose bit her lower lip, giving Michael time to note just what a red, juicy lip it really was. "Well, y'see, I'm not exactly alone..." She pushed the door open wide, revealing a child's big, red Radio Flyer wagon. Inside the wagon was the black dog, and all her pups.

Michael strode to the door, kneeling down to see. "Is she all right? She isn't hemorrhaging, is she?"

"Oh no, she's fine. She just wouldn't let me leave without her." Color flushed Rose's cheeks. "Oh God, that sounds stupid, doesn't it. But she started barking and howling when I tried to leave, and then she grabbed onto my dress and wouldn't let go..." She looked at the floor, an embarrassed smile playing over her lips.

Michael laughed. "I completely understand, Rose. I once had to keep a baby possum in my shirt for two weeks. Little thang decided I was his mama."

Rose chuckled. "That must've been inconvenient."

"Oh, it wasn't bad, except when the little critter would latch onto my ni—" Michael cut himself off, blushing furiously. *Lord, what an eedjit I am!*

Rose gaped at him for a moment, then cracked up. Laughing too, Michael helped her pull the wagon into the office.

"We'll make her a bed behind the counter. Hopefully, she won't scare Pun'kin too much." He scooped up one of the puppies, and brought it up to his face to inhale its brand-new sweetness. It wriggled against his cheek, tried to nurse on his earlobe.

Michael hefted the pup in his hands. "They're big girls, aren't they? No wonder she had trouble with 'em. If I didn't know better, I'd say they were even bigger than they were last night."

Rose fixed him with her sea-green eyes. "I wasn't gonna say anything, Doctor Yeats, but I thought that, too. I mean, I think they really are bigger."

Michael kept staring into her eyes, not wanting to look away. Inside the green there was gold, little flecks of gold around the pupil…He blinked. "Uh…Well, anythin's possible! I'm just glad they're such fine, fat pups. I think they'll do all right."

Rose nodded. "They're all the same size, too. No runts."

Pun'kin came in from the back and started to swirl around Michael's ankles. He spotted the wagonload of dogs and froze. Stiff-legged, he walked away, as if he smelled something bad.

"I think we've offended him," Rose said.

"He'll get over it. Nothin' could keep that critter from his food."

Rose stared after the cat. "I—I wanted to tell you how sorry I am, Doctor. About Miss Lyndon. She seemed like such a sweet lady."

Michael swallowed down the instant lump that appeared in his throat. "Thank you. She was very special to me." He blinked a few times, until the stinging left his eyes. "And call me Michael, okay?"

"Sure."

Michael looked at the empty reception desk, felt the cold, hollow thump of grief in his chest. He took a deep breath, pushing the pain down into an icy little ball in his stomach. "Well. Let me show you our filin' system. It's not exactly high-tech. But we did stop keepin' records on stone tablets a few years ago."

Rose laughed, eyes sparkling. Michael had the sudden, jarring thought that he'd like to hear that laugh for the rest of his life.

Peering through the trees, Sam watched Robbie Jo. She was sitting on a treestump, perfectly still. Face tilted heavenward, innocent as an angel's. It amazed him, how she could sit so still, lost in her own thoughts. Sam hated being alone. But that girl. That girl took his breath away.

At last, he stepped into the clearing, smiling. "Hi, baby."

She kept looking at the sky. "I was wonderin' when you'd talk to me. You been lurkin' in the bushes like a peepin' Tom for ages."

He knelt down beside her, took her hand. "You knew I was there. Of course you did. You're magic, Robbie Jo."

"Yeah, yeah, yeah." She turned the full force of her rusty gaze on him. "Tell me about your parents, Sam. Tell me how your mama makes breakfast."

"Whut?"

"Oh good God, you heard me. Tell me ever'thin', from the time she gets up and scares herself in the bathroom mirror to the time she sets food in front of your daddy." She looked at him sharply. "Your mama does the cookin', right? You don't have a cook or anythin'."

"No, no we don't. We've got a girl who comes in and cleans twice a week..." Sam was overcome, looking at the gentle curve of Robbie Jo's breasts under her thin summer dress. He slid his arms around her waist and started nibbling on her tummy.

She put her little hand in the middle of his forehead and shoved him. Sam went ass-over-teakettle onto the spongy forest floor.

"Listen to me, you eedjit. We can do that later. Now you tell me what I asked you."

"Okay," Sam said meekly. Her sudden aggression had given him a massive boner, and he had to arrange his pants carefully when he sat up. "Lessee…my mama and daddy get up about the same time, just before six. They wash their faces and brush their teeth. Then they put on their robes and slippers, and they come downstairs to the kitchen." He cocked his head at her. "Is this what you wanna know?"

"Exactly what I wanna know. Keep goin'."

"My mama starts breakfast while my daddy starts the coffee. We usually have eggs, sausage, and grits. Sometimes biscuits."

"Uh-huh. Your mama make her biscuits from scratch, or use a mix?"

"Scratch. Sometimes she uses pancake mix, though."

Robbie Jo ruffled Sam's hair. "Fascinatin'. Bestseller material. What kinda coffee do your folks drink?"

Sam made a face. "Well, a few years ago, my dad got hung up on these weird fuckin' French and Columbian beans. It's kind of a fetish with him. He gets the beans through the mail from some dumbass coffee club. Then he grinds 'em up in this little grinder, which is louder than hell and wakes me up whether I want woke up or not—"

Robbie Jo threw back her head and laughed, loud and long. "Perfect. Beautiful."

Sam stared at her. "You lost me, honey."

Robbie Jo reached into her pocket and pulled out a handful of little seeds, each no bigger than a nickel. "You know what these are?"

Sam took a closer look. They were shaped like lima beans, a smooth, creamy color with purplish spots. "Well sure I do, sugar. Those are castor beans."

"Good boy. You know what's inside 'em?"

"Uh…castor bean shit?"

"Ricin. One of the most toxic substances known to man, baby."

"Oh, yeah? I mean, I knew they were poison, when I was in school, some kid ate one and had to have his stomach pumped, but I didn't know—"

"Shut up. Here's what you're gonna do, Sam. You're gonna take these beans, and you're gonna put two or three of 'em in your daddy's coffee bean grinder. Then you're gonna stand back and watch." Her eyes sparkled, little red points glinting in the russet like rubies.

Sam wanted her so much.

"That's all?" he asked. "That's gonna kill 'em?"

"No, prob'ly not. But it's gonna make 'em real, real sick. We wanna make this look natural, right?"

"But I thought we were gonna kill 'em!"

Robbie Jo sighed. "We *are* gonna kill 'em, Captain Brain Cell! But first we're gonna make 'em sick. You come see me after you do it and tell me ever'thin', you hear?"

"I hear ya, sugar." Sam took the beans from her hand and slipped them into his pocket. Still kneeling, he gazed up at her. Perched on the stump so daintily, his goddess of the forest. "Are you sure this is gonna work, Robbie Jo?"

She took his face in her hands. "It will if you don't fuck it up, Sam."

He grabbed her by the shoulders and pulled her down on top of him. "There's only one kind of fuckin' I have in mind..."

She laughed softly in his ear, then nipped it. He breathed in the clean, sunshine smell of her hair, and knew he was the luckiest man in the world.

ROSE AND THE FLAT CAT; ROBBIE JO AND THE PREACHER

L ate afternoon, and Rose's workday had been smooth as glass. Other than her quadrupled blood pressure every time Michael Yeats got close to her, that was.

The paper filing system was simple and tidy. Miss Lyndon had kept it immaculate; not a misfile in sight. The appointment book was straightforward enough. Doctor Yeats kept his own books and payroll. Her only other duty was to assist him with his animal patients, when need be.

There had been just one that day; a sweet, overweight yellow lab with hot spots. The doc hadn't needed any help to lift her chubby doggishness onto the table and clean the raw sores on her shoulder and neck. He had let Rose pull the chart, though, and walked her through the billing process. The dog's owner, a plump tobacco farmer's wife, had seemed fascinated with Rose. Rose knew that the fact that Doc had a new receptionist would be all over town by nightfall. She didn't mind.

Now Rose was sitting dreamily behind the desk, stroking Onyx's smooth head, sleepy in the too-warm office, while Doc Yeats—*Michael, he told me to call him Michael*—inventoried his cattle vaccine.

The door burst open. A skinny woman with a pale, tear-streaked face, and something bloody in her arms.

Oh Lord, there was a lot of blood. All over the front of the woman's dress. All over the thing in her arms. Dripping on the floor.

"Doctor!" Rose screamed. Michael was there in moments.

"Oh, Mrs. Ryan. Oh dear. What happened here?" He had the sobbing woman by the elbow, leading her into the exam room. Rose followed.

"Jeepers—Jeepers was gone a couple a' days, and we been lookin' for him, and then I found him on Big Jesse's Walk and he'd been hit by a cuh—cuh—" The woman's voice dissolved.

Michael laid a towel on the steel table and gently took the animal from the woman's arms. A cat, Rose saw, a big old gray tom. At least the parts of him that weren't red were gray. He lay still on the table, barely breathing. When he did take a breath, there was a nasty rattling sound from somewhere inside him. Bloody bubbles on his nose. His back legs were broken, and there was a huge gash on his head.

Michael gently probed the cat's head wound while the woman, Mrs. Ryan, wrung her bloodied hands. He felt the cat's ribs, and grimaced. Didn't even touch the horrible angles of Jeepers' back legs.

"It doesn't look good, Mrs. Ryan. I can try to operate, but he's lost a lot of blood..."

"Please," she sobbed. "Please try. I cain't pay you all at once—"

"Don't worry about that. You go on home now, I'll call you when I know anything. Rose, would you come with me please?" He scooped the big cat up in the towel and headed back to the operating room.

Mrs. Ryan grabbed Rose's hand and squeezed. "You—you'll stay with him, won't you, missy? He—Jeepers likes ladies. He always liked me best. My husband says that cat's always tryin' to steal me away from him..." Her face crumpled, and she squeezed Rose's hand even tighter, slick blood over bony fingers.

"Yes," said Rose. "Of course I will." She managed a smile at Mrs. Ryan, then slipped her hand free. She started down the hallway after Michael.

Rose glanced down at her bloody hand, fingermarks curled around it like the scarlet petals of an orchid, and she saw something strange.

More blood. Blood on her other hand, on both hands up to the wrists, up to the elbows. Blood on her naked chest, on her legs, blood spatter slashing across her face like warm tropical rain. In her mouth, sweet and salty. In her eyes, and the world was red.

Rose's breath caught in her throat and she choked. She brought her hands up to her face, and of course, one was bloody and one was not. Her jeans and cotton blouse were clean, and Michael Yeats needed her to help him cut open a mangled cat.

"Get a grip, girl," Rose whispered. "Jeezus Christ. Keep it together." Holding her red, sticky right hand well away from her body, she strode into the battle zone.

Robbie Jo was strolling down the street with a smile on her face. The sun was out, the air bright blue, scrubbed clean by the rain. The thought that she had maybe come up with a perfect murder plot put a sweet little smile on her face. Life was just fine, at the moment. Life was beautiful.

"Robbie Jo? Robbie Jo Ridgemont? May I have a word with you?"

The voice brought her up short. She turned her head slowly to look.

"Reverend Rye." Yep, there he was, the washed-out, pasty ol' thing, smiling at her in a tight, uncomfortable way. Robbie Jo beamed at him. "What can I do for ya, Rev?"

"Please. Come into the church and set awhile." He really did look nervous, pink, shiny skin beaded with sweat.

"Why, certainly." Robbie Jo followed him in, wondering just what the fuck was going on.

He didn't take her back to his office; instead, he gestured for Robbie Jo to sit in one of the empty pews. She did, and the Reverend chose one two rows ahead of her. At first he just sat there, smiling nervously.

"What's this about, Rev?" Robbie Jo asked brightly, hoping to move things along.

"Well. A, um, a concerned friend of yours spoke with me this mornin'."

Robbie Jo fought to keep the smile from freezing on her face. "And what friend was that?"

The Reverend cleared his throat. "Just never you mind. Someone who cares about you a lot, is all. She, uh, your friend told me she thinks you may be in a spot of trouble."

Robbie Jo blinked innocently. "Trouble? I don't think so, sir." Her heart thumped hard a few times. *Relax, girl. He doesn't think you killed anybody, or he'd have called the cops by now.*

"Trouble...with a boy. Or, I should say, a man."

Robbie Jo stared at him.

"Sam Dunwiddie," Reverend Rye said, looking dyspeptic.

It was Nancy, thought Robbie Jo. *That miserable little bitch.*

"I, uh," she said, starting to fidget. *Better play it dumb and see what he knows.*

"Do you, um, do you have a relationship with Sam, Robbie Jo?" Reverend Rye's face was the color of a boiled shrimp. Robbie Jo wondered if he was going to have a heart attack.

"I—I think he's sweet on me," she stammered, willing herself to blush.

"I'm gonna ask you straight out, now. Do you have a sek-shul relationship with Sam Dunwiddie?"

Robbie Jo's eyes snapped up to meet Rye's. His slid away. "Nuh, no sir! Gosh no! I mean, he kisses me and stuff, and sometimes he tries...but I never..." Robbie Jo looked at her hands, folded in her lap.

"You're tellin' me the truth, aren't you, Robbie Jo?"

"Yes sir."

Reverend Rye let out a great sigh. "Good. I'm so glad. I thought you were a good girl, Robbie Jo."

She smiled. "I try, Rev'rend."

"Now you listen to me, little girl. Don't let that Sam take advantage of you! I know he's a sweet talker, but some things are reserved just for the sacrament of marriage. Do you understand?"

She nodded vigorously.

"All right then. I'll tell you what, Robbie Jo. You have a good friend out there. She'll be so relieved to know you're on the straight and narrow."

Robbie Jo beamed. "Yes indeed, Rev'rend!"

Walking out of the church and into the afternoon sun, she had just one thought in her head: *I'm gonna kill Nancy Plum. Before the week is over, she'll be dead as a gutted catfish.*

SAM'S SPECIAL COFFEE; THE BLACK DAWG'S BIG SURPRISES

Sam felt like he'd swallowed a nest of baby rattlesnakes. He was sure his heart was crawling up the inside of his throat as he stared at his father's coffee bean grinder.

It was still pitch dark outside. You had to get up pretty early to beat Ephram and Ruth Dunwiddie to the kitchen. He'd seldom seen this hour of the morning, except from the other end.

His hand was in the pocket of his pajama bottoms, rolling the castor beans around and around. They were so smooth they seemed to be alive, squirting through his fingers like quick little beetles.

He took them out of his pocket, but he didn't look at them. He knew what they looked like. Every kid in Possum Kingdom had played with them at one time or anther. You break them out of their spiny little shells, and then you have the slick little beans to use for checkers pieces, or poker chips, or pirate treasure. Everybody knew they were poison. Every summer or so, some dumbshit farmworker's kid had his stomach pumped at the hospital in Jonesborough from eating one. But they never killed anyone. Did they?

What if Robbie Jo is wrong? Sam bit his lower lip. *Oh well, if she's wrong, I guess they'll just get a little sick and we'll have to try somethin' else.*

He unscrewed the top of the grinder and dropped in three beans, plop plop plop. Was that an act of murder? It sure didn't feel like one. It didn't feel like much of anything.

What if Daddy sees the white shit in with his ground beans? Not fucking likely. His father seemed to perform the whole coffeemaking operation with his eyes mostly shut.

Besides, he'd just blame the coffee company for sending him a bad shipment, right?

"Right," Sam whispered. Feeling silly, he wiped his fingerprints off of the coffee grinder with a dishrag. Then he went back upstairs to bed.

"Sam, get yourself down here before the sausage turns to ice cubes!"

Sam opened his eyes. It seemed like he had just been downstairs moments ago.

"Sam!"

His mother certainly didn't sound sick. He rubbed his eyes and padded downstairs.

The table was full of food. Scrambled eggs, sausage patties, fried potatoes, biscuits. The air was rich with the greasy, luscious smells of breakfast, and the sharp, heady scent of fine coffee. *At least it doesn't smell weird or anything,* Sam thought, trying to clear his sleep-cottony brain.

Sam's father was wolfing down his food with his usual gusto. Sam's eyes slid to the cup of coffee by his father's right hand. The one at his mother's place setting.

"I thought you were never comin' down, slugabed," said Ruth, wiping down the frying pan. She always made a point of sitting down last, so everyone would be sure to notice how hard she was working.

"I was up late readin' 'bout a new kind of aspirator," Sam mumbled. He looked at his own empty coffee cup and froze. *Just pour yourself some, eedjit. You don't have to drink it.* Sam got his coffee and sat down. He helped himself to big servings of everything. His mother waited until he was a few bites in to take her place at the table.

"We don't need a new aspirator," said Ephram around a huge mouthful of sausage. "The one we got's plenty good enough. Damn thing could suck the guts out of a grizzly bear."

Sam tried to keep his eyebrows down as his father drained half his cup of coffee. Sam took another bite of eggs, but they had lost their flavor.

His mother was a hearty eater too, but she attacked her food with a military precision that was almost scary. Snap, snap, one bite of egg after another until it was all gone. The

sausage was the next to die. Quick sips of coffee, until the
whole cup was empty. Always the gentleman, Ephram got up
to pour everybody another round. Sam hoped neither of them
noticed that he was sweating.

Rose was up early, making breakfast for the Tanners. She
did that from time to time these days, and it gave her pleasure.

The black dog watched her with soulful brown eyes,
following Rose's every move. She was nestled deeply into her
blankets, and though none of the pups were visible, Rose could
hear them squeaking and smacking as they suckled.

"Don't worry, silly girl," Rose whispered. "I'll take you
with me again today. Doc says it's fine."

She could have been wrong, but Rose was sure that the
dog visibly relaxed.

Onyx had already proved herself to be a valuable member
of the staff. Mrs. Ryan had not gone home after bringing in
Jeepers, the pulverized cat. When Rose had emerged from the
operating room after three grueling hours, the woman had still
been there, waiting, on the narrow little bench. One hand was
twisting the tail of her bloody shirt, the other was wrapped
around Onyx. The dog had her head in Mrs. Ryan's lap, gazing
up at her adoringly. Giving her wave upon wave of innocent,
simple comfort.

Rose winced, remembering the raw, desperate look in
Mrs. Ryan's red eyes as Rose entered the room.

"He's alive," Rose had said, forcing a smile. "Jeepers
pulled through." The woman had started sobbing. She wrapped
her arms around Onyx's silky neck and cried into her fur for a
long, long time.

Rose still could hardly believe that the cat had survived. It
had looked like hamburger when it came in; she had been
certain it was minutes from death. Michael's work to save it
had been tireless, precise, almost artistic. Rose was afraid she'd
faint or puke when he opened Jeepers up, but instead had found
herself fascinated. She'd handed Michael clamps as he tied off
one shredded blood vessel after another, mopped up what
seemed like oceans of blood, even wiped his forehead with a
clean cloth like she'd seen nurses do on medical shows. He'd

smiled when she'd done that, smiled right at her for just a moment before he'd turned his formidable, electric attention back to the cat.

It almost like magic, what he'd done. His fingers were as nimble as a magician's. It hadn't seemed like three hours. Time had compressed as Michael wove the smashed cat back together into a complete creature. Rose almost felt that she had been in the presence of a miracle.

Not that Jeepers looked that good at the end of it all. His back legs were in big white casts, he was missing half his fur, and he had so many stitches he looked like Frankenstein's Cat. His flesh beneath the fur was a sick, milky white; Michael worried over how much blood the animal had lost. A resentful Pun'kin had donated some blood, but it was a drop in the bucket compared to what Jeepers had left in the dirt of Big Jesse's Walk.

But the tom held on. He held on by the tips of his claws, the tough old bastard. Rose could hardly believe what she was seeing, but the big cat's sides rose and fell evenly, his breath no longer bubbling over with blood.

"You did such a fine job, Rose" Michael had said, his smile warming her like the sun. "You go on home now. Naomi's bound to be worried. Your supper's probably cold."

And she knew what he'd done. He hadn't gone home at all. He'd stayed there in the clinic, with Jeepers, watching him through the night. The thought of someone caring so much about anything, much less an old tomcat, filled Rose with a kind of wonder.

Rose whisked eggs, smiling. Thinking of Michael Yeats. About his unguarded smile, and his mop of chestnut hair. About his scent, so subtle she could only smell it when she was right next to him; homemade soap, shaving cream, and a faintly spicy, clean undersmell which Rose was certain was just Michael. Standing next to him made her drunk on it.

Rose had no idea why she felt the way she did about Michael Yeats. He was an incredible vet, and he seemed like a really nice guy, but wasn't the world full of nice guys? Maybe not, but there had to be a few of them. Why did she find him so handsome? He was so skinny he looked like he might blow

over in a high wind, more young Anthony Perkins than Brad
Pitt. But when she thought of his gentle gray eyes, her insides
turned to marshmallow.

"Hormones," she told the dog. "Pheromones. That's all.
How can I be in love with the guy? I don't know him at all."

The dog licked her black lips worriedly.

Rose started to wonder what Michael thought of her, if he
really saw her at all. Was it possible he liked her too? But she
didn't want to think about that, she really didn't, so she set
down the bowl of thoroughly beaten eggs and pulled back the
blanket to tell the puppies good morning.

Rose gasped. She dropped the blanket and took a step
back. She wasn't looking at the puppies, she couldn't be. The
black lumps under the blanket were just too big. Far too big.

Rose crept closer. She saw a pink-padded paw, a black,
pointed tail. Fat little ears, no longer buttoned to the sides of
the puppies' heads, but sticking out in soft folds. Bright tiny
eyes, open, when they had been sealed just last night.

"No way," Rose breathed. "No friggin' way." She picked
up one of the pups and held it up to her face. It regarded her
back with sleepy eyes of yellowish gold, not spooky-milky
infant blue. It yawned, revealing swollen gums, a few teeth
starting to poke through. Breath like a new inner tube, sweet
and rubbery.

They were puppies, all right, and they had to be the black
dog's puppies (although it briefly and crazily occurred to Rose
that someone had switched them), but they seemed to have
grown a week and half overnight.

"Holy shit," said Rose, still holding the puppy.

"Why, Rosie. What on earth could make a sweet girl like
you say a thing like that?" Naomi stood in the doorway of the
kitchen, sleepy-eyed in her bathrobe. Then she saw the pup in
Rose's hands.

"Holy shit!" Naomi said.

The breakfast dishes were cleared away by seven-thirty.
Everybody was showered, shaved, sweet as a daisy. The
workday had begun, and no one was sick. Sam tugged at the
sleeves of his jacket and frowned. It certainly looked as if

nothing was going to happen. Nothing at all. Maybe castor beans were only poison to children. Or maybe they were just a little bit poison, like the bite of a house spider. *I guess it's back to the drawin' board*, he thought.

He actually liked the idea of Robbie Jo being wrong. The girl was unnaturally smart. She seemed so much older than fifteen. Maybe she'd cry when Sam told her that her plan hadn't worked. Maybe he'd have to make her feel better. Sam smiled.

He glanced out the kitchen window at his mother, getting in a little gardening before the day got brutally hot. His father was in the mortuary office, catching up on correspondence. Healthy as a couple of Tennessee farm horses.

If Sam had recognized the squishy feeling in his gut as relief, he would have been mortified.

"Holy shit," said Doctor Michael Yeats, holding up a fat black puppy, his exhausted eyes bright with interest. He promptly blushed scarlet. "Forgive me, Rose. But I've never seen anythin' like this before."

Rose laughed, trying to contain a lapful of puppies. "That was my exact reaction, Doc." She rubbed one of the puppies on her cheek. "You don't think they're sick, do you? You don't think they have that disease where you get old before you're even grown?"

"Progeria?" Michael smiled. "I don't think so. Children with progeria are tiny and wizened, not huge and healthy."

"But they're not...normal." She kissed the pup on the head, then pulled it away before it could chomp her nose.

"Well, no, they're not. There's clearly some kind of genetic anomaly here." He turned his pup over and over in his hands. It squeaked and waved its stubby legs indignantly.

Rose felt a little icy tickle at the back of her neck. "They're not gonna die, are they?" The idea was unthinkable. Rose wanted to gather the pups close to her, to protect them and their mother from the world. From whatever genetic time bomb might be growing inside them.

Michael's smile was gentle, maybe a little sad. "We'll just have to wait and see. Keep bringin' 'em in every day, that way

I can keep an eye on the little critters." He stroked silky fur, touched black rubber noses. "They sure look plenty strong so far."

"Maybe it's a miracle," Rose said.

Michael laughed. "You never know. It just may be."

Rose checked on the pups throughout the morning, wondering if they might grow before her very eyes. They didn't do that, but they did start toddling around the waiting room. She had to spread newspapers everywhere. "Two days old," Michael kept saying, shaking his head. "Two days old."

Mrs. Ryan came in to see Jeepers in the afternoon. She wept silently at the sight of him sleeping on his side, shaved and stitched, IV line running to white tape around his front paw.

"Is he in a coma?" she whispered, stroking one of the small remaining patches of fur on his side.

"No." Michael smiled at her. "He awakened once or twice this morning. He's just sedated, and on a lot of pain medicine."

"I can't believe he's alive," she breathed. "I thought for sure he was daid. Thank you. Thank you so much." She threw her arms around Michael in a fierce, quick hug. Rose felt a sudden, ludicrous thump of jealousy and killed it without mercy.

"It's unbelievable," Rose said after Mrs. Ryan left. "The way you saved this guy. I thought he was paste. It must be the most incredible feeling—" she cut herself off, realizing she was gushing.

Michael nodded, smiling faintly. "Oh, it is. That feelin' is why I became a vet. I saved a kitten from drownin' when I was eight..." He looked down, seeming a little embarrassed. "Anyway. I have to warn you, it's not always like this. A lot of 'em I can't save. Animals hit by cars because they're allowed to run loose all the time, dogs savaged by cougars that their redneck owners were tryin' to hunt, pets dyin' of parvo and distemper because they were never vaccinated...sometimes bein' a country vet really bites, so to speak."

"But it's worth it," Rose said. It wasn't a question.

"Yes."

"Hello, anybody—oh, my GAWD!"

Robbie Jo, standing by the reception desk, staring at the puppies gamboling around the floor. She looked up at Rose and Michael, eyes wide and bright.

"These aren't that black dawg's pups. They can't be."

"They are," Rose said. "Isn't it the damndest thing?"

Robbie Jo nodded slowly. "Never even heard of such a thang. You, Doc?"

"Nope."

Robbie Jo stared and stared. "Six pups. Seven black dogs."

"Yep," said Rose. "I call 'em the Girls. They're something special, aren't they?"

"Sure enough." Robbie Jo seemed to come out of her fugue. She wrinkled her slightly sunburnt nose. "They sure do poop a lot."

"Well, thanks for that brilliant observation, Miss Ridgemont. Since you're so astute, how 'bout if you help me clean up a little?" Rose grabbed a stack of fresh newspapers from under the desk and shoved them into Robbie Jo's hands.

"Sheezus. Me and my big mouth." Robbie Jo gave a rueful grin and started rolling up soiled newspaper. Rose knelt down to help, and as she did, noticed Onyx looking at Robbie Jo. Staring at her. The dog's body was trembling. Her golden-brown eyes held the oddest expression, like nothing Rose had ever seen on a dog before. It seemed to hold equal parts adoration and terror.

ATTACK OF THE CASTOR BEANS; ROBBIE JO AND REVEREND PRIMUS

Sam was in the Sweet Hereafter's business office, pretending to go over the books but really daydreaming about Robbie Jo's ass, when he heard his mother scream. He ran to the parlor and found her on her hands and knees, a rag in one hand, a can of lemon Pledge in the other. She screamed again, a high, reedy sound he wouldn't have believed she could ever make. She clutched her stomach, fell over on her side.

"Mama!" Sam yelled, his heart pounding. "Mama, what is it?"

"My stomach," she whined between clenched teeth. "It burns, oh God…" tears squirted from under closed lids.

"Mama…" Sam shifted from foot to foot. He started to reach for her. She opened her mouth as if to say something, and yellow vomit sprayed out. Her body bent convulsively and she vomited again, choked on it, gurgled, sobbed, puked some more.

I did this. I did this. I did this. Sam put his arms around his mother's body and lifted her to her feet. She was too heavy for him to carry, long and rawboned as an old horse. He wrapped her arm around his shoulder, gripped her around the waist, and started for the stairs. Her skin was so hot he thought her blood might be boiling in her veins.

His mother vomited again, covering the front of her dress, splattering Sam. To Sam's utter horror, there was a gurgling sound, an unspeakable stench, and a growing puddle of yellow-brown diarrhea. Ruth Dunwiddie hung her head and moaned in shame. Up until now, Sam hadn't believed his mother ever actually went to the bathroom.

This isn't happening, is it? Is it? Sam fought down his own urge to puke as he half-dragged her up to her bedroom.

Sam laid his mother down on her bed as gently as he could. She curled instantly into a miserable, clenched ball. He found it incredible that his parents slept in separate twin beds: why would anyone sleep alone if they had a choice about it? And Sam had never seen anyone looking more alone than his mother did right now.

She managed to haul herself over to the side of the bed before she let go again, puking miserably on the hardwood floor. Then that hideous gurgling again.

"I—I'll get you a pan, Mama." Sam trotted out of the bedroom, desperate to get away from the smell of vomit and shit, from the terrible thing he had done to his very own mama.

His father was crawling up the stairs, leaving a trail of puke and liquid diarrhea behind him. His skin was the color of ashes, eyes rimmed with scarlet. Ephram heaved so violently he hit his head on a step, then crawled through it, slow as a bellyshot possum.

Sam realized he was trembling. He hadn't known it would be this horrible. It sure as hell never looked like this on "Murder, She Wrote." It would have been better to have shot them in the head, thrown them down a cliff, cut their throats in their sleep. His father was dragging through his own puke like a drunk in a roadhouse.

Sam bit his own cheek until it bled just to make himself move. He helped his father up the stairs and into his narrow bed.

Ephram started to speak, choked and vomited instead. He clutched Sam's hand as he spewed what had to be pure bile on the nightstand. He spoke again, so softly Sam had to bend down to hear him.

"Help your mother," Ephram croaked. Tears sprang to Sam's eyes and he blinked them savagely away.

The next few hours were a blur of vomit-soaked hell. Sam cleaned up his parents as best he could, wiped the worst of the puke and shit up off the floor. He gave them cool washcloths for their burning faces, tiny sips of water which neither of them could keep down. Thick towels under their bottoms, as if they were incontinent infants. He told them it would be okay, and the words burned like acid in his mouth. Like poison.

At last they both slept; the hard, motionless sleep of the gravely ill. Mouths wide open, lips dry and peeling, breath stinking like death. His mother clutching the snow-white sheet in bony fists. His father's hair in sweat-soaked clumps and spikes.

Like a robot, Sam got a bucket and mop and cleaned the vile stuff from the wooden stairs. He rolled up the parlor rug and dragged it out the back door. Terror freezing his guts, he went back up to check on his parents.

They were still asleep, really sleeping, not dead. Sam stared at them, imagining their narrow beds to be coffins. He stared around the room, wondering what to do.

The rest of the house was undisputedly his mother's; all Victorian glass and linen doilies and dustless, shining wood. But the master bedroom was his father's.

Oh sure, there was fine furniture. There were pretty lamps. But the thing you saw, the only thing you noticed about the room, were the toasters. Shelves and shelves of antique toasters, all gleaming chrome and steel and weirdness.

They were all different; the sizes, the shapes, the mechanisms. Art deco, art nouveau, 50s spaceship chic. Springs to flip toast midair, robot arms to turn bread from one side to the other, slots and rollers and grills and levers. They had been there as long as Sam could remember.

It always struck him as incredible that people had spent that much time on something as frivolous as toast. So much energy and creativity, all those dead ends. Ridiculous machines, outdated, obsolete before they were even tarnished. Sam had always thought that the toasters were exactly like his father.

But they weren't, were they, because although they were old and outmoded, they were durable. Most of them would still work, if anyone was fool enough to fire them up. But Ephram Dunwiddie was breakable. Maybe already broken beyond repair.

Sam reached out to touch a shining clamshell-shaped contraption. His mind was caught in a ratwheel, and it spun and spun as his fingers brushed the steel.

Ephram let out a low, quavering moan. The halves of the clamshell sprang open like a Venus fly trap. Like a hungry mouth.

Sam ran from the bedroom, down the stairs, out the back door and into the woods.

Robbie Jo strode through the steaming, summertime woods, mind afire with curiosity. Seven black dogs. Two girls. She'd been seeing those images since she was a baby, since her parents first took her to church. She had to see the paintings again, right now.

"What does it mean?" she muttered to herself. Robbie Jo grinned. It was going to be something good, she knew it. Or something bad. Either way, it would be something new. Maybe something that would stir up the shit but good.

The Holy Blood was never locked. Reverend Primus wanted it to be open to his flock at any time of the day or night. Still, Robbie Jo felt like she was getting away with something when she eased open the door and slipped into the church.

It was empty, lit with buttery sunlight spilling through the plain square windows. Robbie Jo approached the wall with the paintings. Head cocked, she studied them. The seven black dogs racing through the woods, a wild hunt out for blood. The dog at the front had golden brown eyes, like the one Rose called Onyx. The other six had yellow eyes. Moon-colored eyes, like Onyx's pups.

"Well, I'll be damned," Robbie Jo breathed.

"Not if I can help it," rumbled a voice behind her; Reverend Primus Reylark's melodious baritone. Robbie Jo whirled around. The preacher was smiling down at her, big arms crossed over his chest.

"Hello, Robbie Jo. Can I help you with anythin'?" She looked up at him, mustering her most innocent expression. There was something about the Reverend that put her on guard. Something in the way he looked at her. He did his very best to hide it, but Robbie Jo knew she unsettled him. That made him dangerous.

"I...was wonderin' about the paintin's, Rev'rend."

He smiled. "You know the story. Rev'rend Reddingale painted them himself, not long before he up and vanished. They're s'posed to be some sort of prophecy."

Robbie Jo nodded. "Sure. Ever'body knows that. But Rev'rend Primus, what do they really mean? Do you know?"

His broad forehead wrinkled up. "I don't, not for sure."

"Are they somethin' from the Bible?"

"No. I'm certain of that."

Robbie Jo twisted a strand of her hair around her finger. "What do you know about Rev'rend Reddingale? What sort of man was he?"

Primus's scowl deepened. "Why do you ask?"

"Oh, I'm thinkin' that I might be an artist someday. I guess I find his work sorta inspirin'."

Primus smiled, a look which clearly could have been relief. "I see. That's nice, Robbie Jo. That's real nice. I'll tell ya, not a lot is known about Meshach Reddingale. He built the Holy Blood, you prob'ly know that. He was known to be the finest preacher in all of Tennessee. He was s'posed to be a handsome fella, very strong-willed. A lot of folks woulda died for him."

Robbie Jo weighed the risks, decided to roll the dice. "I've heard...I've heard a few other things about him. I've heard that he could make the snakes dance. And that he could talk to Indian gods."

"Where'd you hear that?" A rough edge in the Reverend's voice; maybe fear?

Robbie Jo grinned, looked sheepish. "Oh, just around. You know how people talk."

"Hmm. Well. Since you brought it up, Robbie Jo, I'll tell you. It's been said that Rev'rend Reddingale got himself involved in forces he shouldn't have ever gone near. Forces that destroyed him."

"Heathen forces?" Robbie Jo somehow managed to keep herself from giggling.

"Maybe. It's best we not even speak of it."

"I s'pose not. But if Rev'rend Reddingale did such bad things, why do you keep the paintin's up?"

Primus paused. "Because of what he was, before that. And because maybe these are important." He waved his big hand at the paintings. "Maybe they'll tell us somethin' we need to know one day."

Robbie Jo beamed. "'Magine that!"

"Well then. I'd love to see some of your work sometime."

"My—whut?" For an awful moment, Robbie Jo's mind went blank. *My work? Somethin' special for the Rev. Maybe he'd like to see me crucify somebody, live and uncensored! Or a decapitation, Herod style?*

"Your art."

"Oh! Oh, of course! I'll bring it by sometime." Robbie Jo giggled. "I'd best be on my way home now."

"Good afternoon, Robbie Jo. Always nice to see you."

"You too, Rev'rend Primus."

As she slowly walked home, Robbie Jo was more curious than ever. And there seemed to be only one way to get the goods, the real, no-bullshit answers.

Robbie Jo thought she'd just go home and take another look at that "resurecshun" spell.

Primus Reylark watched Robbie Jo leave the Holy Blood, her pretty hair shining in the late-afternoon sun. As usual, he felt a great surge of relief to see her walking away from him. As usual, he felt an awful stab of guilt for disliking a poor little girl so very much. There was something definitely off about Robbie Jo Ridgemont, but it wasn't her fault, he was sure of it. Everybody knew her father had been a worthless drunk and a wifebeater. Everybody knew her mother was drowning herself in cheap alcohol. They lived in the grimmest poverty. Folks out in Robbie Jo's neck of the woods didn't even have electricity or running water.

"Poor little thang," Primus muttered. Then he turned away. He didn't want to see Robbie Jo's black, thorny aura moving through the woods, trailing behind her in malignant tendrils like the arms of some venomous deep-sea creature.

SAM NEEDS A FRIEND

R obbie Jo was almost home when she heard someone crashing through the woods behind her, coming fast. She could hear his breath wheezing in and out. She whirled, teeth bared, halfway hoping it was some horny backwoods farmboy, looking to jump her and take a piece. *C'mon, honey. I'll have fun bitin' through your goddam fuckin' throat...*

But it was just Sam, hair sticking out like he'd been hit by lightning. Tears streaming down his face.

He threw his arms around Robbie Jo, sobbing.

"Calm down, baby! Calm down. Let's get off the path, now, before somebody sees us." *You godforsaken puddin' brained eedjit.*

Robbie Jo led Sam, docile as a sick child, to a shady place in the woods, where they sat together on a fallen log.

"What is it, sugar?" She stroked his hair, kissed his forehead. "What's the matter?"

"I did it," he said miserably.

"Did what? You mean you did your folks?"

He nodded, looking at his knees.

"Are they dead, Sam?" She kept her voice calm and gentle. Kept the tremor of excitement to a minimum.

"No! No, they're sick! They're so sick, Robbie Jo!"

"Tell me about it, baby. Tell me all about it."

It wasn't easy, it took a lot of coaxing and cajoling, but Robbie Jo got it out of him. Every last, drippy, vomit-soaked detail. She couldn't stop the slow smile from creeping over her face.

"That's good, Sam. That's real good. That's just how it's s'posed to happen."

"But they're not dead! What do I do now?" The edge of hysteria in his voice worried her.

"You do what you should have done in the first place. You go to Doc Poteet. You run there as fast as you can, and take him back to see your parents."

"Get the doctor? Robbie Jo, are you crazy? He'll know! He'll know, and then I'll fuckin' go to jail for the rest of my life! For nothin'!" He was practically shouting now.

Robbie Jo grabbed him by his white, starched collar, pulling his face inches from hers. "Listen to me, you dumb shit. The whole point is to make it look like they died of the fuckin' stomach flu. What are people gonna say if you just let your parents die without tellin' anybody? They'll say you killed 'em, you asshole. You shoulda called Doc Poteet as soon as you got 'em to sleep. Now you're gonna have to tell him your fuckin' phone didn't work or some shit. But Sam, you go get him, and you don't act like a cryin', blubberin' mess when you do it either. Don't you fuck this up, you hear me?" Robbie Jo's teeth ground together. *Don't kill him. Don't kill him. Don't kill him.*

Sam's face crumpled. "Please don't be mean to me, Robbie Jo." He put his arms around her, buried his face in her chest.

Holy mother of Christ. Maybe I just shoulda killed the whole family myself. With a chainsaw.

Robbie Jo stroked his hair, kissed his head. "I'm sorry, baby. It's just that this is so important. Important for us, Sam. If we do this right, we can be together for always."

He swallowed hard, nodded. "But what's the doctor gonna say? Isn't he gonna figure it out?"

She laughed. "I'd be surprised if Doc Poteet can find his dick to take a piss in the mornin'. He's two years older than God, and he's got the imagination of a constipated accountant. Don't worry about that. He's gonna say they've got a bad case of stomach flu, and he's gonna tell you to feed 'em clear liquids. Maybe he'll splurge and give you some Emetrol."

"But what if he sends 'em to the hospital?"

"Shee-it, Sam, you worry too much. He prob'ly won't. But if he does, all we've lost is a little time. They're not gonna figure it out, either."

He wiped his eyes. "It won't show up in blood tests?"

"Hell no. Ricin doesn't show up in the blood at all. They can test for antibodies, but they'd have to be lookin' for that, specifically. And why the fuck would anybody do that, Sam?"

"Okay." A sniffle. "So, what do I do after Doc leaves?"

"Dose 'em again, honey." The phrase "dumb as a box of hammers" rang in her brain like a fire alarm.

"Robbie Jo, I don't think they'll be up to drinkin' coffee."

She took in a deep, shuddering breath, and closed her eyes until the red went away. "Then you put it in their chicken soup. Or their tea. Got it?"

"Yeah." He slid from the log, rested his head in her lap. "Jeezus, Robbie Jo. I didn't think it was gonna be this awful. They just look so…"

"Hush. Hush, now. I know it's hard. But you just remember what they told you. 'Bout how they'd disown you if you went with me. Think of all the years of humiliation they've put you through, Sam. If you leave 'em alone, they could live another thirty years. Is that what you really want?"

"No," he whispered into her dress.

"Harden your heart, Sam. You gotta be strong. For me. For us. Okay?"

"Yeah. Okay."

Robbie Jo held him until his tears dried up and his breath didn't hitch anymore. Then she sent him off to find the doctor. After he was gone, she lay back on the log, looking up at the snips of blue sky between the lacework of deep green leaves. Wondering if Sam actually had the strength to go through with it, or if he had pale, weak tea running through his veins.

Thinking about slicing him open just to find out.

Sam shifted from foot to foot, twisted his handkerchief between his hands. Doctor Vanguard Poteet was taking his mother's pulse, listening to her heart with a stethoscope, shining a light in her eyes, moving as slowly as a lizard's blood on a chilly day.

Sam and Doc Poteet had returned to find Sam's parents still sleeping. Sam had been pierced with the sudden dread that they were in a coma, that Doc would send them to the hospital immediately, but they both roused up when Doc spoke their names.

Ephram had opened his gummy eyes, said "Whut?" then puked a thin stream of yellow over the side of the bed. Sam had thought he'd run screaming from the room, but somehow, he held it together.

Doc gave his parents tiny sips of water, so their throats weren't too dry to talk. They told the same story; getting suddenly, violently ill this morning. No, they hadn't felt funny last night. No, they hadn't eaten anything unusual. No, they hadn't been out of town.

Sam wiped his forehead, and his sweat felt greasy and foul to him. *Guilt sweat.*

Doc took two big plastic bags out of his case and hung them on the heavy Tiffany lamp between Ruth and Ephram's beds. "Well, you're both a bit dehydrated," he said. "We'll just take care of that, okay?"

"Okay," said Ephram.

"What's in that bag?" Ruth demanded, her red-rimmed eyes shiny.

"Just a glucose solution, Ruth. Sugar and water. You need the water, and ever'body could use a little sugar." The doctor winked at Ruth. She snorted and held out her arm. It suddenly occurred to Sam that his mother just might be too mean to die.

"They're gonna be okay, aren't they, Doc?" Sam asked.

"Oh, sure. They've just got a touch of the stomach flu."

"A touch? I collapsed like a wheat stalk, Doctor Poteet! I—I couldn't control my bodily functions!" Ruth's glare intensified.

"Okay then, you got a dog-kicker of a stomach flu. It happens, you know. You and Ephram ain't gettin any younger."

"Oh, and you are. Where'd you intern, the Civil War?"

Ephram groaned. "Ruthie, please."

Doc gave a genial laugh. "Now here's what you do, Sam. You make sure they get plenty of fluids. Give 'em 7-Up with the bubbles beat out of it. If they don't like that, try some peppermint tea. When they get hungry, give 'em some chicken broth. You know how to make chicken broth?"

"Boy can't boil water, but I s'pose he could open a can," said Ruth. Sam began to wish he had put a few more beans in the grinder.

Ephram raised up on one elbow. "Now Ruth, that boy took good care of us today. Who do you think cleaned you up and got you in bed?"

Doc Poteet smiled, which made his eyes disappear entirely. "You should be proud of Sam. This young fella took as good 'a care of you as I could have. And when he come to fetch me, why, I've never seen a boy so upset."

Ruth didn't say anything, but she looked at Sam, maybe just a little differently. Maybe a bit of the ice in her eyes melted away.

Later that night, as Sam stirred two fizzing glasses of 7-Up, he was horrified to feel tears prickling his eyes. He remembered sobbing in Robbie Jo's lap, and his face burned with shame.

"Robbie Jo. Robbie Jo. Robbie Jo." He whispered her name like a prayer. She was his shining goddess, and he prayed that she would give him strength. Give him the nerve to do what he had to do, in the morning, when he brewed his parents some peppermint tea.

THE SECRET BIRTHDAY PARTY

Rose was dreaming of snakes. Little green garden snakes, fat shiny pythons, writhing rattlesnakes in the hands of the faithful. A huge cobra, shimmering with dark iridescence, hood spread wide. Whispering in Rose's ear. Hissing.

"Psssst."

Rose murmured, rolled over.

"Pssssssst!"

She gasped and sat up in bed, heart pounding. Robbie Jo was perched on the windowsill like a girlfaced gargoyle.

"Hiya, sleepy," Robbie Jo grinned.

"Hey." Rose rubbed her eyes, ran her hands through her tangled hair. "Whassup?"

"It's my birthday, Rosie! I wanted to have it with you."

Rose blinked, processing the information through her sleep-soaked brain. "Geez, Robbie Jo, why didn't you tell me earlier today? We coulda done something…"

"Aw, you were busy. Besides, I didn't want to make a fuss. I just wanted to be with my best friend for awhile."

"Well come on in here, before you fall out the window and bust your silly head." Robbie Jo's grin widened. She hopped lightly from the sill and sat on the bed next to Rose.

Rose looked at her friend for a moment, her heart filling up with love. She threw her arms around Robbie Jo. "Happy birthday, girlfriend. Happy sweet sixteen."

Robbie Jo snorted. "That's me, sweet as a cream bun."

"I know," Rose said. "Naomi made this incredible blackberry cake with caramel frosting. Let's go down to the kitchen and have some!"

"Well damn, sounds good!"

The girls crept down the stairs, whispering and giggling. Onyx raised her head when they came into the kitchen, thumped the towels with her tail, and went back to sleep. The pups were clustered around her like plump black grapes.

"I still can't believe the size of those puppies," Robbie Jo whispered as Rose raided the fridge for cake.

"I know. It's weird, isn't it?"

Robbie Jo showed all of her gleaming white teeth. "Get used to it, honey. Possum Kingdom is full of weird."

"Y'know, I'm startin' to like weird," Rose grinned over her shoulder.

"Mm. Just don't get too comfortable, Rosie. Never let your guard down."

Rose's breath caught in her throat. "What's that supposed to mean?"

"Just what it sounds like. The world's a harsh place, girlfriend. I'm just sayin' you should never turn your back on anyone."

Rose felt the cold, familiar tickle of fear in the pit of her stomach, and willed it away. *You're never gonna find me, Daddy. Never.* She plunked two big pieces of cake down on the table and cracked a grin. "I'd turn my back on you anytime, Robbie Jo. I know you'd watch it for me."

"I'm always watchin' you, Rosie." Robbie Jo grabbed up her fork. "Yum yum!"

"Wait! Don't fork a single berry yet!" Rose rummaged around in a kitchen drawer, finally coming up with a fat white candle. "Here we go!"

She rammed the candle into Robbie Jo's piece of cake. Robbie Jo raised an eyebrow. "I feel violated."

Rose lit the candle. "Shut up and listen." She sat down, took Robbie Jo's hands in both of hers, and sang. "Happy birthday to you, happy birthday to you! Happy birthday Miss Robbie Jo Ridgemont…happy birthday to youuuuu!"

"Why, that was bee-yoo-tee-ful!" Robbie Jo laughed and tossed her hair. Rose thought she looked gorgeous in the candlelight, her hair like flames, her eyes a rich, autumnal orange.

"Why, thank you. I don't sing to just everyone, you know."

"I can see why. Can I eat my fuckin' cake now?"

"After you, madawm."

"Oh," said Robbie Jo, around a sticky mouthful. "Ohhh, man. That's incredible!"

"Isn't it?" Rose savored the fresh, plump blackberries, the smooth, sweet caramel. "You probably already had some cake today, huh?"

Robbie Jo let out a snort. "Well, I saw one, anyway. Right before it went up in flames."

"What?" Rose chuckled. "You're kidding." She got up to get two glasses of cold milk.

"I'm not." Robbie Jo started to giggle. "My mom...my fuckin' drunk mother made me this purty little chocolate cake while I was out today. She put it in the middle of our pissant little kitchen table, sat down, and got shitface drunk. At some point, she covered it with candles and lit 'em."

"Sixteen candles?"

"Nope. More like thirty or forty. The whole thing was lit up like a whorehouse on payday when I walked in. And there was my mom, passed out at the table with a bottle in her hand."

"Holy shit! What did you do?"

"I started yellin' 'Mom! Hey Mom, I'm home!' She musta been havin' some kinda gin junkie nightmare, cause she screamed and jumped up right outa that chair, and knocked the fuckin' table over!" Robbie Jo was laughing harder now.

Rose, giggling herself, put a finger to her lips. "Chocolate everywhere, huh?"

"Worse than that. All those candles didn't go out when the cake hit the floor. They lit the tablecloth on fire. Then the table started smokin'! My mama was screamin', and runnin' in circles just like a chicken with its head cut off."

"Oh my GAWD! What did you do?"

"I got the blanket off my bed and threw it over the fire. Then I threw a glass of water on my mom so she'd shut the hell up."

"Did she?"

"Oh, yeah. For a minute there, it was so quiet you coulda heard a rat tinklin' on a cotton ball. Then Mom pushes her drippin' hair out of her face, smiles, and says 'Happy birthday, Robbie Jo!'"

Rose heard herself still laughing, but suddenly she wanted to cry.

"I just turned and walked on out of there, Rosie. 'Cause if I didn't, I thought I just might pick up that gin bottle and beat my mama's head in." Robbie Jo's giggles had taken on a bright, bitter edge.

Rose grabbed her friend's hand and pressed it to her cheek. "I'm so sorry, baby," she whispered.

Robbie Jo abruptly stopped laughing. Her eyes grew bright and shiny with unspilled tears. "Don't be. 'Cause I'm here now, and everything's better." She poked at the thick candle, still standing in the center of her plate, now surrounded only by crumbs. "This is the best birthday I ever had."

"I'm so glad."

Robbie Jo grabbed the candle. With an impish smile, she held it over her right hand, and tipped it over. Wax began to drip into her palm.

"Jesus Christ, Robbie Jo, don't do that!"

"It doesn't hurt. Not much, anyway."

"Stop it! What are you doing?"

"I wish you were my sister, Rosie."

"I am your sister." Rose stared at the puddle of liquid white in Robbie Jo's hand.

"Then let's close the deal. Gimme your hand."

Rose swallowed, started to say something. Then she held out her right hand, palm up.

It didn't hurt that much. It was hot, but it wasn't taking off her hide or anything. There was something fascinating and sensual about the way the wax filled her hand with heat, hardening at the edges, pulling at her skin like a living thing.

"That's enough." Robbie Jo grabbed Rose's hand in a tight grip. Rose gasped. The wax in their palms squished together, gushed between their fingers, ran down their wrists.

It felt amazing. Painful, hot, weird, sexy.

"We are sisters," Robbie Jo whispered. "Sisters under the skin. Now and for all time."

"Sisters." Rose nodded. She tried to move her fingers, laced with Robbie Jo's, and found they were glued into place. For a strange moment, Rose couldn't tell where her own flesh ended and Robbie Jo's began.

They sat like that for a little while, not talking. Then Robbie Jo blew out the candle. She pulled her hand back abruptly, and their palms peeled apart.

"Yow," said Rose. It stung a little.

"Well that was kinda fun," Robbie Jo said. "Sorta like peelin' dried glue off your hand when you're a kid."

Rose grinned, and picked at the wax on her palm.

"Save that," Robbie Jo said. "Keep it somewhere safe. It's got power now."

Rose couldn't tell if her friend was kidding or not.

"I'd better go." Robbie Jo picked up the plates and carried them to the sink. "You need to get some sleep."

Rose slipped an arm around her narrow shoulders. "Stay here, okay? You can go home in the morning."

Robbie Jo planted a kiss on her cheek. "You don't have to twist my arm."

They crept up the stairs to Rose's bedroom, mouths sweet with cake, right hands still coated in wax. Rose's dreams were sweet too, flavored with the sunshine smell of Robbie Jo's silky hair.

DOC YEATS ROLLS THE DICE

*I*t was morning, and at the same time Sam Dunwiddie was watching the effects of the special peppermint tea he had prepared for his parents, fist pressed to his mouth and stomach roiling, Michael Yeats was fixing a huge picnic basket with hope shining in his heart.

Michael spent most of the morning mentally practicing what he would say to Rose. It was one sentence, but he thought of a hundred different ways to say it. After awhile it stopped making sense at all, it was just noise in his head. Finally, about ten o'clock, he just spat it out.

"Rose, would you like to have dinner with me?"

She seemed totally taken off guard. Her face flushed a pretty pink (Rose pink, he thought foolishly). "Why, uh, why sure!" she answered, with a shy little smile.

She's humoring me, he thought. *Humoring the dirty old man.* "Well, that's just swell." *Swell? Oh my God in heaven, I've never said that before in my life.*

"Um, are we goin' to Pete's?" She looked down and smoothed her blue flowered sundress. Her legs were long, smooth and tan. Dirty sneakers with no socks, like a little girl.

"Actually...I thought we might have a picnic."

"That'd be nice. I'm kinda hungry now, are you?"

He grinned hugely. "Why, yes! Just let me check on Jeepers, and we'll go on."

The old tom was awake today, eating and drinking on his own. He seemed perplexed and more than a little pissed off to have his back legs encased in Fiberglas. The pain meds made him drowsy. His inner eyelids were halfway across his yellow orbs, making him look wall-eyed. He gave a querulous meow when Michael reached in to pet him.

"I know, ol' boy. I know."

The puppies hadn't grown perceptibly overnight, but they were terrorizing the office just the same. Toddling underfoot, chewing furniture, and leaving little puppy bombs every few feet. Michael and Rose decided that Onyx and her brood would be happier in the clinic's fenced back yard. Onyx flopped down to bask in the sun while the pups took a terrible toll on the local grasshoppers.

"We could eat out here on the back porch," Michael suggested.

"We'd have fuzzy black piranhas hanging off of our sandwiches," Rose said. "Shall we go for a walk? There's a pretty place in the woods where I go to eat lunch sometimes."

Just the thought of walking in the woods with Rose made Michael's heart pound and his lower belly tingle. He hadn't suggested it himself, because he didn't want her to think he was a masher. "Sure," he said. *Hey there little Red Ridin' Hood, you sure are lookin' good...* Thoroughly ashamed of himself, Michael grinned. *Down boy. She probably thinks you're two years away from senility.*

They walked in silence. There was tension between them, but what kind Michael couldn't say.

"Here we are," Rose said. "Isn't it perfect?"

It was. A pretty little clearing where a huge old tree had been sawed down many years ago, making a wide, round table. Michael set the bulging basket down. Rose sat on the spongy leaves, legs folded prettily beneath her. "So what do you have in there?"

"Well, I didn't know what you liked, so I brought cheese sandwiches...and ham...and roast beef...and turkey..." He pulled one wrapped sandwich after another out of the basket. Rose began to giggle. Michael immediately felt like an idiot.

"What?" he said, hauling out ripe, red apples.

"Nothing," said Rose. "That's just so sweet."

The blush felt like it came from his toes.

Rose picked out a turkey sandwich and an apple while Michael poured fresh, cold milk from a thermos. Mrs. Ryan had brought the milk; it was from one of her own cows, and it had the faint, sweet taste of the wild onions that grew in the pastures all summer. Michael closed his eyes and savored it.

"Thank you," said Rose. "This is lovely."

"Thank you for joinin' me." *Don't mumble like a little boy, now.*

They ate quietly for awhile. "Rose," said Michael, looking up at the trees, "I think you're very special. You're smart, and kind, and competent, and—and I like you a lot." He winced. *Well. That was about as artful as any seventh-grader could have made it.*

She bit her soft, lovely lip and smiled at him. "I like you too, Michael. It almost scares me, how much I like you."

He tried to keep the huge, goofy grin off his face, but he didn't have a chance. He took a deep breath. "I'm twenty-eight, Rose. I'm a lot older than you are."

Her smile didn't slip. "You don't look that feeble to me."

"Tell me about yourself," he said. "How did you come to Possum Kingdom, of all places?"

It seemed like a simple enough question, but Rose's face went through a series of subtle changes, and then she had tears in her eyes.

"You don't have to," Michael said quickly.

"But I need to. If we're going to be—I have to tell you the truth."

"Okay." He wanted to take her hand, but didn't.

"I'm from Miami, just like Naomi told you. But I'm not taking a year off before college. I ran away from home." She smiled self-consciously, wiped her eyes. "That sounds so juvenile, doesn't it. But my father...my father...hurt me. Badly."

"Rose...I'm so sorry." This time he did reach for her hand. She slipped it into his, and held on tight.

"I got on a bus and left town. I got off at Possum Kingdom because, well, because that's where my two-day panic attack stopped, I guess. I just wandered into town." She grinned sadly. "I was brilliantly walking down the middle of the road when Sam Dunwiddie nearly made a Jeepers out of me."

"I saw you that day. I saw you with Owen and Naomi, right after Sam hit Onyx. You looked like an angel to me."

She laughed. "A sweaty, dust-covered angel with her hair stickin' up?"

"Yes ma'am."

"That's not all, Michael. I lied to you. I'm not eighteen. I'm seventeen." She ducked her head, looked up at him. "I really did finish high school, though." A wry little smile, worried and hopeful.

Christ amighty. It's not bad enough that I'm a decade older that she is. The girl's underage. He smiled weakly. "Thank you for tellin' me, Rose."

A little frown on her pretty forehead. "Does my age make that much of a difference? Do you still wanna, um, see me?"

Every day of my life, he thought. "Oh, I'd be lyin' if I didn't say it bothered me a bit. But I reckon I'll get over it."

"Good." She beamed. "Tell me about yourself, Michael. Were you born here?"

"Yep, right here in Possum Kingdom. My folks were blueberry farmers. I loved animals from the time I was a little boy, and they saw that. They knew I'd be a vet before I did. They scrimped and saved so that I could go to school in Memphis."

"That's wonderful."

"They were wonderful." He looked up into the cloudless sky.

"Oh Michael, what happened?" Her pretty face was pinched with sympathy.

"They were killed in a car accident. They were on their way to Memphis for my college graduation." The words didn't sound real to him. His parents' death didn't seem real to him, even after all these years. They had always been there, always so strong. How could they be dead? He swallowed down the lump of ice in his throat.

Rose's eyes sparkled with tears. "My God. I'm so sorry." Now she had his hand in both of hers.

"Thank you." He didn't speak for a moment, until he was sure his voice wouldn't shake. "I came back here after vet school. It was funny, I had never planned to. I was gonna move to the city and be a partner in some big vet'rinary practice...Anyhow, I sold my folks' blueberry farm, and I opened the clinic. It doesn't bring in much money, but I don't really need much. I spend a lot of time patchin' up hurt possums, fixin' stray cats, feedin' baby birds that fell out of their nests, and other such excitin' things."

Rose met his eyes, a little smile on her face. "I think I might want to be a vet someday."

"You'd be a fine one, Miss Heron." He looked at her pretty hands, fingers long and fine-boned. "You're good with critters. You don't get flustered in a crisis. And you've got surgeon's hands."

She laced her fingers through his. He raised her hand to his face and kissed it gently. She gave a little gasp, then grinned.

"Michael, would you think I was a total hussy if I came and sat down next to you?"

"Not in the least."

Then she was so close to him that he could scarcely breathe. They held hands. After awhile, he slipped his arm around her. She rested her head on his shoulder, and they watched the squirrels in a towering ash tree. Michael hadn't felt such peace since he was a little boy, picking blueberries with his folks on a warm, breezy summer day.

ROBBIE JO MAKES A DATE; WHAT NAOMI KNOWS; SAM AND HIS MAMA

As Rose and Michael were lost in their own bubble of bliss, Robbie Jo was strolling down Main Street with a smile on her face. She had just passed the Sweet Hereafter, and she wondered what horrors might be taking place behind the second-story window curtains. She wished she could be a fly on the wall, to watch the fun. Or maybe a fly on the ceiling, to avoid the flying barf. She was so lost in her reverie that she nearly bumped right into Nancy Plum, who was walking the other way.

"Oh, hi Nancy!" said Robbie Jo with a smile. "Forgive me, I didn't see you there."

Nancy glared at her. It was fascinating to see that level of emotion in those pale, watery eyes. It looked out of place, like a spiked collar on a toy poodle. "Oh, I'm invisible now, am I? You just think you're so great."

Robbie Jo sighed, and looked as contrite as she possibly could. "I'm so sorry I've been neglectin' you, Nancy. I never meant for that to happen. I really miss seein' you, y'know?"

Nancy crossed her bony arms and stuck her scrawny chest out belligerently. "Izzat right. Well. If you're so hot to see me, why don't you just come over for supper tonight? And no, Sam Dunwiddie is not invited."

She doesn't think I'll take her up on it. The corner of Robbie Jo's mouth quirked up. "Why, I'd be delighted, Nancy! Thank you so much. What time?"

Nancy's mouth dropped open, and her stance softened a bit. "Uh…how's seven? We could watch some TV…"

"That'd be great. I'm lookin' forward to it!" Robbie Jo thought about hugging her, but she didn't want to overdo it. She gave Nancy a big, warm smile instead.

"Okay then!" Nancy had done a complete one-eighty. She was now all smiles. Her pale eyes came close to sparkling. They lost their dull sheen, anyway.

Then her smile slipped, her eyes narrowed. "You will be there, won't you?"

"Of course, silly. I wouldn't dream of standin' you up." Robbie Jo touched a lock of Nancy's colorless hair.

"Good! See you tonight!" Nancy actually ran home.

Robbie Jo watched her go, sprinting on skinny legs like a startled water bird. She imagined Nancy asking her vast, spandex-coated mother to fix something extra-special tonight. She imagined Nancy dusting the TV screen and wiping down the popcorn bowl.

Robbie Jo stretched, reaching for the clear blue sky. She would have liked a little more time to plan things out, that was for sure. But this was kind of fun, too. She'd have the afternoon to think it over, but when seven o'clock came, she'd have to wing it.

The words had a magical ring to them. Just whispering them made Robbie Jo's tummy tingle.

"Spontaneous double homicide."

Naomi had no doubt that Rose was in love. The girl had come floating in from work about two feet off the ground, with a big, goofy grin on her face. Her love was rolling off of her in waves.

Naomi smiled a conspirator's grin. She had known this was a possibility when she had suggested that Rose become Doc Yeats' new receptionist. There was something in the way those two had looked at each other across the counter of the general store. Subtle, sure, but the sparks were there if you were paying attention. Naomi always paid attention.

There were some who would say that the age difference between Michael and Rose was too great. But probably not too many. Most folks got married young in Possum Kingdom, but matches between young girls and older men were quite acceptable. They wouldn't run into the troubles that Naomi and Owen had, when they were still in their teens and on fire with love.

Naomi remembered her mother's face, clear as a photograph after so very many years. Remembered her mother's anguished whisper: "Some things folks just won't put up with, child. Some things they won't allow to be."

But that was so far behind them now.

Naomi looked up the stairwell and grinned. Rose was in her room, singing. Soon she'd be down to help make dinner, and Naomi could bask in her glow.

Naomi went out to sit on the porch swing with Owen, who smiled at her and wordlessly slipped his arm around her shoulders. The sun was going down, and the whole town had turned to gold. Possum Kingdom was filled with magic.

Sam was a zombie. Sam was Night of the Living Dead. He went through the motions, cleaning up after his parents over and over again, wiping their burning faces with a cool, damp cloth. He whispered words of comfort and gave them sips of 7-Up and chicken broth, which came flying back out at him every few minutes. His hands did the work, his mouth said the words, his nose breathed in the ungodly stink, but Sam was somewhere else. He was in a gray limbo, where he wouldn't feel guilt or pity or crushing horror.

This isn't real was his mantra. *This isn't real. This isn't real.* His brain chanted the words, filling his skull with noise.

Sam wiped his mother's lips gently, cleaning the yellow crust from the corners of her mouth. He seemed to be looking at her face, but he wasn't. He was looking through her, right through the bed, right through the floor. He was looking into the future, where Robbie Jo waited for him.

Ruth Dunwiddie reached up and gripped her son's hand. Sam was unwillingly wrenched back to the stinking sickroom, and his mother's miserable, red-rimmed eyes. "You'll be okay, Mama," he murmured.

Unbelievably, she smiled at him. When she spoke, her voice was a grating rasp. "You're a good boy, Sam. I shouldn't be so hard on you."

A tsunami of guilt crashed over him, clutching his chest in an icy bear trap. His eyes stung, and he swallowed hard. "Hush, now. Save your strength." He held the glass of soda to her lips.

She took a tiny sip, still holding his hand. "I love you," she whispered.

It hurt so much that at first Sam thought he was having a heart attack. He couldn't breathe, and he started shaking. Two hot tears slid down his face and hit the pillow by his mother's head. "I love you too," he whispered. Sam didn't know if he meant it. He didn't dare think about it too much. He was scraped raw inside.

In that moment, Sam just wanted to close his eyes, lie down on the floor, and die.

ROBBIE JO AND NANCY'S RED-HOT SLUMBER PARTY

obbie Jo shrieked with laughter. Nancy glanced at her, and following her lead, started giggling too.

"Id'n this the funniest thing you ever saw?" Robbie Jo chuckled.

"Uh...yeah!" Nancy grinned at her. They were watching "Death Becomes Her" on cable. Meryl Streep had just noticed her head was on backwards.

It had been a lovely evening. Dinner was delicious. Fayelynn Plum had fixed fried chicken, turnip greens, corn on the cob, fresh biscuits, and fried potatoes, with Moon Pies for dessert. Of course, Robbie Jo hadn't eaten any chicken, which caused Fayelynn to go into paroxysms of worry. "You cain't not eat chicken!" she'd squealed. "You'll die of scurvy! Why, chicken ain't even really meat anyway. It's just a dumb ol' bird."

Robbie Jo had declined to point out that birds weren't actually members of the plant kingdom. Instead she'd changed the subject, talking with Nancy about American Idol and platform shoes and Leonardo DiCaprio and other subjects that bored the living shit out of her.

Now it was close to nine-thirty, and the three of them were watching TV, munching popcorn, and sucking down Cokes. The two girls sitting on the floor, Fayelynn draped over the couch.

Meryl Streep stretched her shattered neck like taffy, and Robbie Jo roared.

"I think this is kinda gross," said Fayelynn. "You girls want another Coke?"

"Sure!" said Nancy. Her mother started to heave herself upright.

"I'll get 'em, Miz Plum," said Robbie Jo. She lifted the Plums' cat, Goober, out of her lap and set him on his feet. He meowed crankily, stretched and scratched his claws along the rug.

"Why, thank you, honey." Fayelynn settled back down.

Robbie Jo went into the kitchen. She pulled three bottled Cokes out of the fridge, popped the tops. She took the bottle of Fayelynn's prescription sleeping pills, which she had snagged on an earlier trip to the bathroom, out of the pocket her dress.

Quickly, she opened the bottle. Thank God they were capsules. She could have found a way to grind up tablets, of course, but this made her life so much easier. Robbie Jo twisted one open and dumped the powder into one of the Cokes. A tiny fizz, and it was gone.

Six per soda. That oughta do it. She got the job done quickly, put the empty capsules back together and dropped them into the bottle, then shoved it back in her pocket. She swirled the two "special" Cokes around a little bit, and hurried back to the living room.

"I was startin' to think you got lost," Fayelynn said, taking her drink.

"I was just readin' your 'frigerator magnets," said Robbie Jo. The Plums' refrigerator was covered with lacy little magnets which said things like "Bless this Mess" and "Kiss the Cook."

"Didja see the new one?" asked Fayelynn. "It says 'God loves you, and I'm tryin'!'" She giggled, and Robbie Jo laughed along with her, then excused herself to the bathroom, where she put the bottle of sleeping pills back in the medicine cabinet.

They watched the movie. Robbie Jo held her breath when Nancy and Fayelynn took their first few drinks, but if the Cokes tasted any different, they didn't seem to notice. Robbie Jo suspected that years of Moon Pie consumption had killed off their taste buds.

Mrs. Plum sucked down her Coke in a few big gulps. By the time Meryl blew a hole in Goldie Hawn with a shotgun,

Fayelynn's head was nodding. "I think I'll toddle off to bed, girlies. I'm as tired as I can be."

"'Night, mama," said Nancy absently. She gave a big yawn.

"G'night, Miz Plum. Sleep tight. Thanks for a terrific dinner," Robbie Jo beamed up at her.

Fayelynn patted Robbie Jo's head with one red-clawed, meaty hand. "You sure are a nice girl, honey. I'm so glad you come over tonight. Nancy's been missin' you somethin' fierce."

Robbie Jo squeezed Nancy's hand. "I missed her too." Nancy smiled back at her, eyes more watery than usual.

Nancy took forever to drink her Coke. She took tiny little sips, few and far between, until Robbie Jo wanted to sit on her skinny chest and pour the bottle down her throat.

But it was happening. Nancy went from sitting to lying on the floor. Her yawns got more and more frequent. Robbie Jo was pretty sure Nancy was out, when her head suddenly popped up.

"Thanks for comin'," Nancy said. Her head was weaving back and forth, just a little. Her voice was thick and slurred.

"Sure thing, honey." Robbie Jo tucked a strand of lank hair behind Nancy's ear.

"'M so glad you didn't leave me. 'Cause ever'body leaves me." Nancy's eyes filled with tears.

"Now then—"

"My daddy left me, when I was jus' a little girl, y'know. An' my baby sister, that drowneded in the creek. She lef' me..."

Nancy's eyes were rolling. Robbie Jo stroked her hair until the other girl put her head down on her arms and sighed. "Don't worry, Nancy," Robbie Jo whispered. "No one will ever leave you again. I promise. I promise."

Robbie Jo leaned back against the couch and watched TV until Nancy's breathing grew deep and even. Then she set the bowl of popcorn on Nancy's back (she made a fine coffee table) and watched a little more.

It was horribly tempting to find out just how deep Nancy's sleep really was. It occurred to Robbie Jo to cut off her hair, sew her fingers together, carve a little poem in her back. But that would be silly. If everything didn't work out the way she planned it, her experiments might be discovered. "And that would suck, wouldn't it," Robbie Jo said to Nancy's sleeping form.

Goober watched with wide golden eyes as Robbie Jo wrestled Nancy onto the couch, then lifted the skinny girl onto her back in a fireman's carry. Robbie Jo hauled Nancy into her bedroom and dumped her onto her narrow bed. She arranged Nancy's arms and legs into what she figured was a natural-looking position to sleep in, then stepped back and took a deep breath.

Robbie Jo glanced around Nancy's bedroom. It usually made her want to barf, with its pink lacy bedclothes, horsie pictures on the wall, and shelf full of teddy bears. But tonight she drank it in. It was, after all, the last time she'd ever have to see it. The last time anyone would see it. "Bye-bye, now," she said to the sappy, crying harlequin poster on the inside of the door as she walked out. Robbie Jo thought looking at something like that every day might just kill brain cells.

She went into the bathroom, took the empty sleeping pill capsules out of the bottle and flushed them. Next she padded into Fayelynn's room. The woman was on her back, mouth open wide, snoring softly. Robbie Jo wiped her own fingerprints from the pill bottle with her skirt, then wrapped Fayelynn's thick paw around it and squeezed. She opened the woman's hand over the nightstand and let the bottle drop. She patted Fayelynn's sprayed-stiff hair, and went back out to the living room.

After pausing to pet Goober's sleek black sides, Robbie Jo took Nancy's and Fayelynn's Coke bottles to the sink, where she rinsed them out and wiped them off. *A girl can't be too careful.*

Robbie Jo yawned and stretched. She picked up a protesting Goober and set him on the front porch. She took her own half-full bottle of soda and peered around behind the TV set. Smiled at the overburdened plug, bristling with wires.

Slowly, Robbie Jo tipped the bottle. Watched the dark liquid getting closer to the glass lip. A splash of Coke on the plug, just a small one, but it was all she needed. Robbie Jo yelped and jumped backwards as the plug exploded with sparks. The lights went out with a pop. But Robbie Jo didn't need lights to see, because the sparks had caught the ugly yellow curtains on fire.

It happened so fast. Flame shot up, licked the ceiling. Burning bits of curtain floated down like slow-mo napalm. Laughing, Robbie Jo pressed herself against the front door, covering her head with one hand. Smoke was filling the room.

One of the flaming pieces of fabric landed on the couch. It smoldered for a moment, and then there was a deep, loud 'whump' and the couch was engulfed in a flash of fire.

Still holding her Coke, Robbie Jo high-tailed it out the front door. She nearly tripped over Goober. He meowed at her plaintively. "Beat it, buddy," she whispered, "or you'll be kitty flambe'!" Robbie Jo shoved him off the porch with her sneaker. He glared at her, then ran into the darkness.

She went into the edge of the woods and watched for awhile, sipping her soda. It wasn't long before the windows were glowing orange. Not long after that they exploded, sending raging tongues of fire up into the night.

Robbie Jo smiled, picturing what was happening in the house. She imagined the harlequin poster curling at the edges, the insipid, tear-streaked face turning to black. The teddy bears igniting one after another. The pink bedclothes flashing over, wrapping up Nancy nice and warm. Did Nancy have enough fat on her to catch fire, or would she just curl up like a piece of beef jerky?

Mrs. Plum would burn, that was for sure. Her hairspray alone was enough to cause a small explosion. Her slick polyester clothes were a wick waiting to happen. The woman might burn for hours, leaving a pool of drippings under the bed like an overdone pot roast.

The roof was catching fire. Black smoke rolled out the windows and gathered over the house like an evil spirit. Robbie Jo was just starting to smell bacon when she heard the siren coming. With a twinge of regret, she slipped away into the woods.

Robbie Jo had a long, leisurely swim in Virgin Pond, rinsing the smell of smoke from her hair and skin. She let the Coke bottle go, let it sink to the bottom, and wondered what small, biting things might make it their home.

It was nice to float on her back in the darkness, looking up at the stars. Like drifting through space. Like she was the only person on the planet, and wouldn't that be fine?

At last she came out of the water, her thin dress dripping wet and clinging to her body. Robbie Jo thought she'd go visit Simon for a little while.

FALSE DAWN; HELL ON EARTH

Rose awakened with a gasp, knowing something was wrong. She blinked, trying to focus on what she was hearing.

It was Onyx, downstairs in the kitchen, whining and crying. Rose stumbled down the stairs, dread starting to replace the sleep in her head. Was it the pups? *Don't let them be dead...*

They were far from it. The puppies were milling sleepily around the kitchen like a herd of miniature black sheep. But Onyx was scratching frantically at the door and crying.

"What's wrong, girl, are you sick?" Rose opened the door to let the dog out. Instead, Onyx cowered behind Rose's legs. Rose yawned, and something tickled at the back of her throat. She thought she could faintly smell smoke on the breeze.

"What in the world's goin' on?" Naomi bustled in, with Owen right behind her.

"I don't know, Onyx is freaking over something." Rose knelt down next to the dog and hugged her. Onyx was trembling.

"Dear God." Owen was looking out the kitchen window. Rose and Naomi came to see. There was a flickering orange glow across town. "Somebody's house is burning."

"Oh no. Get dressed quick, old man. We've gotta go." Naomi headed for the stairs.

Rose pushed the hair back from her face. "Go? But doesn't Possum Kingdom have a fire department...?"

Naomi looked over her shoulder. "A volunteer fire department, honey. They do their best. But we'd better go see if we can help out. You don't have to come if you don't want to."

"I'll be dressed in a minute!" Rose was right behind her.

Ruth Dunwiddie slowly drifted toward consciousness. She opened her sticky eyes, licked her cracked and bloody lips with a dry tongue. Her whole body ached as if she had been beaten. Her head burned with a hot, heavy agony, as if her brain had been replaced with a volcanic stone. Her stomach was a pit of flames.

She thought of calling for Sam, asking him for a glass of water and a cool washcloth for her head. But she couldn't seem to summon the energy. She closed her eyes again, praying for sleep.

"Ruth." Ephram's voice was a metallic rasp in the darkness.

"Yes, Ephram." She didn't recognize the harsh whisper as her own voice.

"The window."

She waited for him to say more, but he was silent. With a massive effort, Ruth managed to raise her head up, turn it, look toward the bedroom window which was open in the sweltering summer night.

A deep orange glow rose up over the trees, flickering and pulsing like a live thing. Ruth thought she saw tongues of flame reaching up to taste the sky.

"What is it?" came her husband's ghastly, disembodied voice.

Ruth's brittle neck screamed in pain, and her head dropped back down to the pillow. The agony in her stomach flared to a white-hot supernova.

"It's the fires of Hell," Ruth whispered, tears spilling from the corners of her eyes. "It won't be long now, Ephram."

THE KINGDOM FIGHTS THE FIRE
(AND THE FIRE WINS)

There was already quite a crowd by the time Rose and the Tanners got there. Rose clutched a canvas bag containing blankets, a jug of water, and a thermos of strong sun tea that Naomi had insisted they bring "just in case."

Rose had never seen anything like it, except on TV. The whole house was engulfed in fire. Flames roared from the shattered windows, shot up the chimney and into the night like raging demons. The volunteer fire department was there, battling away, but it was like squirting a water pistol into the fireplace. The stench of smoke was overpowering. There was another smell too, a sweetish, pungent smell like burning pork chops. It didn't occur to Rose, at the time, what it had to be.

"Dear Lord in heaven," said Naomi. Her face was wet with tears. Owen had his arm around her, holding her tight.

"Whose house is it?" Rose asked, stomach clenched with dread.

"The Plums'. Fayelynn and her daughter Nancy."

"Oh my God." Rose stared at the hellish scene. "Did they get out?"

A stout woman in a faded blue bathrobe turned around to look at Rose with stricken eyes. "No. No one got out."

Rose knew things like this happened. Of course she did. But it had never before happened to someone she knew. Not that she liked Nancy; she'd thought the other girl was a hopeless drip. But she didn't deserve this. No one deserved this. Her eyes, already stinging with smoke, began to fill with tears.

She wrapped her arms around herself and watched the firemen. They were doing their best, it was clear. A half-dozen men in yellow coats, fire helmets and face shields were spraying the hose in through the front doorway. The door was gone, either knocked down or burned away. It wasn't nearly enough, of course. The flames would retreat for a moment, then burst back through the door like an angry animal.

Rose thought they would leave, then. It was all over but the cryin', as Naomi would say. But they didn't. Owen and Naomi held their ground, arms around each other. At first Rose was shocked. She didn't think the Tanners were the kind to stop and stare at a tragedy. Even in Miami, a city filled with voyeurs of one kind or another, that kind of thing had always made Rose sick. But they weren't watching with shiny-eyed interest, or even the kind of repulsed fascination that made so many people slow down and stare at car accidents. In fact, they weren't watching at all. Naomi had her face buried in Owen's shoulder. He was turned toward her, stroking her hair. Rose realized they were waiting it out. Seeing it through to the end, because that's what neighbors did for each other.

So she waited too. Over the next hour, the firefighters pushed the flames back a few feet, before the living room roof collapsed. The crowd gasped when it happened, a few screamed. But luckily none of the firemen had been foolish enough to step inside the doorway. No one was hurt. *Except for Nancy and her mom, whatever's left of them.* Rose shuddered, and pushed the horrible thought away.

They could hear the big truck from Jonesborough coming when it was still miles away. It howled like a banshee in the smoke-filled night. It was brand-new, red and shiny, like a child's toy at Christmas. Possum Kingdom's truck, an ancient escapee from the 1950s with rounded fenders and a faded orange paint job, rumbled to life and lumbered down the block to give the sleek red engine room to work. The local firemen stepped aside as the Jonesborough boys took over.

As the volunteer firefighters took off their helmets, Rose was surprised to see Tab Sasso, the high school principal, was among them. Her first impression of him had been that he wouldn't get his hands dirty if he stuck them in mud. Tobias Thurber, the town manager, was there too. Her jaw dropped when one tall fireman turned out to be Dr. Michael Yeats.

Michael met her eyes, and his face was pale and tired, drawn with sorrow.

After shedding his fire gear, Michael came and stood beside Rose. Not so close the people would talk, but close enough, she hoped, that he could draw a little comfort from her. She suddenly realized how horrible it had to be, fighting a battle where nothing, no one, could really be saved.

The Jonesborough team made short work of it. To be fair, the fire had run its course and was beginning to die back by the time they blasted it with all they had. It became apparent that the fire had devoured everything it could. The house was nothing but a thin, black shell, dripping with dirty water.

The crowd stepped back as the hearse rolled up. A grim-faced Sam Dunwiddie, along with Jimmy Ligget, got out and began to unload the gurney. One of the Jonesborough firemen approached them, and they had what appeared to be a brief but heated argument. A ripple of murmurs went through the crowd.

"What are they saying?" Rose asked the woman in front of her.

"The fireman thinks Sam oughta wait to take out the— take out Nancy and Fayelynn. He says the roof might collapse, and besides, there'll prob'ly be a police investigation." She puffed up with pride. "Sam told him that folks in Possum Kingdom attend to their dead. They don't let 'em lie like roadkill."

People were nodding and muttering their agreement.

Clearly not pleased, the firemen stood and watched as Jimmy and Sam went around to the back of the house. *Probably waiting to pull them out if a beam falls on their heads,* Rose thought. She didn't think she'd mind seeing Sam get squashed like a cockroach, but she liked Jimmy. She held her breath along with the rest of the crowd. "Come on out, come on out," Naomi whispered under her breath.

They did come out. It had to be Fayelynn on the gurney first, because the body bag was bulging and lumpy. Way too much in there to be Nancy. Rose swallowed down bile. She noticed that Jimmy looked like he was about to barf, too; face pinched and sick, mouth turned down. Sam's expression stayed the same, a mask of solemn professionalism. For some reason it made Rose want to punch him.

After loading Fayelynn into the back of the hearse, they went back for her daughter. It took longer this time. When they finally came out, a horrified ripple went through the crowd. This time the body bag was covered with a sheet. The bag itself didn't seem to have much inside it; it could have been a spindly bundle of sticks. But something stuck straight out from the gurney, draped in clean white linen.

It's Nancy's arm, Rose thought, before she could stop herself. *Nancy's arm was sticking out when they found her, and they couldn't get it into the bag without...breaking it off.* Her skin started to fill clammy, her mouth filled with water. *Don't puke. Don't puke.*

They were almost to the hearse when Rose heard a muffled, brittle snap. Nancy Plum's twisted, blackened claw bounced into the gutter.

As Sam took out his handkerchief and bent to retrieve Nancy's right hand, Rose fell to her knees and was violently sick. She was dimly aware of Michael Yeats holding her hair back away from her face, his cool, strong hand on her forehead.

A STRANGE PHONE CALL

Jimmy Liggett was barely holding it together. Embalming a heart attack victim was one thing. Dragging around human barbecue was another. This stuff was just plain sickening.

Sam was strangely quiet as they unloaded the bodies into the embalming room. He was usually full of tasteless and ill-natured jokes about the deceased, but not tonight. Of course, he had a lot on his mind, with his parents sick and all. Jimmy didn't think Sam really cared if they lived or died, but not having Ephram around did leave the whole workload on his shoulders.

Sam noticed Jimmy looking at him. His lip curled. "What?"

"I was just wonderin' how your folks are doin'. It's not like them to take to their beds for this long."

"They got a nasty case of the stomach flu, but they'll get over it." Jimmy thought it was strange that Sam didn't meet his eyes. He usually had a politician's talent for staring you down.

Jimmy nodded. "Should we put these two in cold storage? They don't smell any too good, even through the bags."

Sam started to answer him, but the embalming room phone rang. "Son of a bitch, not another one," Sam muttered as he picked up. "Sweet Hereafter."

Jimmy shook his head, grimly amused. Sam had picked up Ephram's sonorous intonation of the funeral home's name.

Sam spoke a very little, and listened a lot. Jimmy watched in fascination as Sam's eyebrows crawled up his forehead. His boss seemed to be working very hard to keep his expression under control, but a deep scowl settled in on his handsome face and wouldn't budge. Sam said "Okay," and "I understand" a few times. Then he hung up.

"Another pickup?" Jimmy asked.

Sam seemed to hesitate just a beat too long. "No, just the Jonesborough fire department. They have some paperwork for me to fill out tomorrow."

Jimmy nodded. For no good reason, he didn't believe Sam at all.

Abruptly, Sam turned and looked Jimmy in the face. "You're right, Jimbo, those bodies stink to high heaven. Let's cremate 'em tonight."

Jimmy's jaw dropped. "Cremate 'em? Are we sure that's what they wanted?"

Sam raised his eyebrow. Jimmy knew that meant he was seriously irritated. "We'll never know what they wanted, Jimmy. Their house is ashes. They're nine-tenths cremated as it is. If some relative shows up later and wants to buy a coffin for 'em, fine. We'll just sprinkle 'em in like grass seed."

"Sure," Jimmy said. He felt there was something terribly wrong with this. It was possibly illegal. It was definitely unethical. But he wasn't about to argue with Sam. He knew from experience that no one could argue with Sam and win, and besides, he wanted to keep his job. But as he helped Sam load the body bags back onto the gurney, Jimmy Liggett felt a vague, creeping sense of guilt. He felt like he had just become an accomplice in something dark and ugly.

THE MORNING AFTER
(AN UNUSUAL SUSPECT)

Rose went to work in the morning, eyes red from smoke and tears. She had spent some of the night crying for Nancy Plum; why, exactly, she wasn't sure. She hadn't known the girl much at all. What she saw of her she didn't like. But Nancy had seemed so lonely, so clueless, so desperate to please. She had deserved to have a quiet, boring, pleasant life, a mundane happy-ever-after with a chubby, kindhearted accountant husband. Not to be burned to a blackened crisp like a chicken forgotten in the oven. The whole thing was just so utterly wrong.

Michael was subdued and quiet. He had sweet, gentle smiles for Rose from time to time, but he was deep within himself.

A pall hung over Possum Kingdom; both a haze of smoke and a cloud of sorrow. The little town was in shock. Rose supposed she was too. The serenity she had found since coming here was teetering precariously.

It hadn't helped much that the puppies were bigger again. They had grown a ridiculous amount overnight, and greeted Rose with squeaks, licks and nibbles as she helped Naomi with breakfast. They looked impossibly healthy. Owen commented on the downright scary amount of kibble they had begun putting away, along with their poor overworked mother's milk. The pups weren't creepy or anything. They were incredibly cute, in fact. When Rose looked at them, her heart filled with love. But let's face it, their growth spurts were weird. It wasn't normal. The whole thing added to Rose's growing sense of unease.

She jumped when the door swung open. *Effie Granger. Oh great. Just what I needed, a ray of fuckin' sunshine.* It took a maximum effort for Rose to smile.

"May I help you, Miz Granger?"

"Oh Lord. Isn't it terrible? Isn't it just terrible?" Effie glared at Rose, as if she blamed her for the whole thing.

"Yes, yes it is," Rose replied, wondering what the ill-natured old bitch really wanted.

Michael walked in and smiled politely. "What's up, Miz Granger? I trust Petey is well and healthy?"

Usually just the mention of Effie's beloved parakeet would unleash a tsunami of words, in which she would describe everything from the size of his bowel movements to the length of his claws, but not today.

She scowled. "Petey? Oh sure, he's fine. Isn't it awful, Doc? About the Plums? You do know they died in the fire last night, don't you?"

He sighed, face tightening. "Yes, Effie, I know."

"Well, it's just too bad our firemen couldn'ta done better. The whole place was an inferno by the time they even got there, that's what I heard. I heard the Plums were burnt to cinders. Nothin' left but their teeth."

Rose was surprised to see Michael's eyes narrow. She thought that he might just be about to say something rude to Effie Granger. *Go for it, Michael. Let her have it with both barrels.*

But he didn't, of course. "The volunteer fire department did their best. It was already too late by the time we got the call."

Effie's blue-shaded eyes popped open in shock. "We?"

Michael crossed his long arms over his chest. "Is there something I can do for you, Miz Granger? Because we're very busy here."

It wasn't true. Jeepers was the only patient in the back today, and he was recovering quite nicely. This was the closest Rose had ever heard Michael come to being sharp with someone, and it was suddenly hard for her to keep a grin off of her face. Effie Granger seemed to bring the worst out in people. Rose wondered if her parakeet liked her much.

Unbelievably, Effie seemed at a loss for words. "I, uh, I just—"

There was a plaintive meow from the front door. Everyone turned around to see. A plump black cat slunk in, ears and tail held low.

"Goober!" Michael scooped the cat up into his arms, scratched it behind the ears. The cat purred loudly and butted its big head against Michael's cheek.

"Someone you know?" Rose smiled.

Michael's expression was strange; mouth turned down, face drawn. "It's—this is the Plums' cat. I thought for sure he died in the fire. But you didn't, did you, sweet old boy." He stroked the cat's smooth side, eyes far away.

Effie Granger started gasping like a grounded fish. She pointed at Goober, mouth open, like one of the pod people from "Invasion of the Body Snatchers." Suddenly she cut loose with an earsplitting shriek.

Goober launched off of Michael's chest, ripping his shirt and leaving bloody lines on his skin. The cat hit the wall, landed scrambling, and dived behind the counter.

"What in God's name?" Michael actually looked like he wanted to do damage to Effie, for just a moment there.

"That CAT!" she screeched. "That cat prob'ly started the fire! It prob'ly knocked over a candle or somethin' and burned those poor gals to death! Just look at the black, evil thang!"

Michael took in a deep breath. "Now Miz Granger, nobody knows what caused that fire yet. It coulda been anything…"

Goober poked his head around the corner and blinked. Then he sidled into the room with Pun'kin companionably at his side.

The color drained from Effie's painted face. "Oh my gawd, they're in it TOGETHER!" she bellowed. She backed out the door, not taking her eyes from the cats. Pun'kin was washing Goober's ears for him. Goober had his eyes closed in lascivious languor.

Effie turned and ran.

Rose and Michael looked at each other. They had identical jaw-dropped, bug-eyed expressions. Rose began to laugh.

Michael held it together for a moment or two, then started to chuckle. Then they were roaring, holding each other up, tears rolling down their faces. The cats retreated to the back of the clinic.

"Is she...completely...insane?" Rose gasped, when she could breathe again.

"I've always thought as much. Now I'm certain!" He looked at Rose, blinked, and they started laughing all over again. Rose rested her forehead on Michael's chest, giggling helplessly. When she looked up again, Robbie Jo was standing in the doorway, with the strangest look on her face.

Rose gulped in air, hiccuped. There was suddenly a sick little cold spot in the middle of her stomach, like she'd been caught doing something terribly wrong. "Ruh—Robbie Jo. How are you doin', girl?" Rose took a step away from Michael, feeling like she'd been caught necking at a funeral.

Robbie Jo still had that tight, strange expression on her face, as if her emotions were in a pitched battle just beneath the surface. Her mouth twitched, then turned abruptly down. "I— oh, Rosie. I just, I just wish I'd spent more time with her..." Robbie Jo's face crumpled, and she began to cry. Rose took her in her arms. Michael retreated tactfully to the back of the clinic.

"It's okay," Rose murmured. "Nancy knew you cared about her." She had no idea if that were true or not, but she had to say something.

"Oh God, I hope so." Robbie Jo pulled back and wiped her eyes. "I've been so wrapped up in, in other things, you know, and I hadn't seen her in awhile, and I think she was mad at me..." Her eyes teared up, and she began to cry again. Rose stroked her hair, kissed her smooth forehead.

Michael cleared his throat quietly from the back of the room. "Um, if you ladies want to go out for a little walk or somethin', that's okay with me."

Rose gave him a quick, grateful smile, then took Robbie Jo's hand. "Walk with me?"

Robbie Jo nodded. "'Kay."

They walked along quietly for a little while, hand in hand. When Robbie Jo finally spoke, it was barely above a whisper. "He's in love with you, y'know."

"What?"

"Doc Yeats. He's in love with you." She gave Rose a wan smile.

Rose snorted. "Why d'you say that?" Her heart sped up just thinking about it, which made her feel like a fool.

"The way he looks at you. Like you were the holy grail or somethin'."

"Shee-it," Rose muttered, burning with embarrassment.

"The way he touches you. His hands in your hair, when you were laughin' on his chest—he's yours, Rosie, if you want him."

Rose's throat closed up for a moment. She couldn't think about that now, about whether that were true, or it would consume her like the fire consumed Nancy and her mother. "I'm sorry about that, Robbie Jo. The laughin', I mean. We didn't mean any disrespect. It's just that Effie Granger came in and said something totally weird, and we just lost it for some reason…"

Robbie Jo smiled and squeezed her hand. "I wasn't offended, girlfriend. Life goes on, right?"

"Sure…but I really am sick about Nancy and her mom. I—we were there last night, but I still can't believe it."

"You saw the fire?" There was a sudden, sharp urgency in Robbie Jo's voice. Rose wished with all her heart that she hadn't brought it up. *Oh, baby, don't dwell on it.*

"Yeah. I saw it." She hoped that would be the end of it.

"It was terrible, wasn't it. Like the mouth of Hell opened up." Robbie Jo's face was down, as if there were something fascinating on the sidewalk.

"Yes."

"Did you see them? See the bodies?"

"Jesus, Robbie Jo, you don't want to hear about that." Rose's stomach lurched, remembering.

"I saw a rabbit that got caught in a brushfire once. It looked like old black sticks of charcoal. Did they look like that?"

Rose's mouth went dry. "I don't think you—"

"Did they?" Robbie Jo's voice was a fearsome hiss.

"Yeah." *Why is she acting like this? God, she must be so fucked up right now...*

Robbie Jo made a choked little sound. Rose opened her mouth, and words poured out. "But you know, everybody says that it was smoke inhalation...they didn't feel anything. I think they just went to sleep."

Robbie Jo nodded. "I'm sure you're right."

Rose caught a whiff of something like wet charcoal and realized where their walk was taking them. "Uh, listen, I think we should go back now."

"No." Robbie Jo's voice was quiet steel. "I have to see, Rosie. I just have to."

WATCHING THE DETECTIVES

R obbie Jo had to work hard to keep the excitement off her face as they got close to the Plums' house. She hadn't been by to look yet; she didn't think it was prudent. But she was dying to see.

The blackened hull wasn't the first thing to catch her eye. It was the three white sedans parked in front of it. Official state plates, clean and shiny, as conspicuous on the street as a drowned rat in the lemonade.

There were people clustered around the house, keeping a respectful distance, but buzzing with curiosity. Robbie Jo's stomach twisted with excitement, and just enough fear to make it fun.

"What do you think's going on?" she asked Rose.

"I dunno." Rose looked terribly uneasy. Robbie Jo knew that the other girl wanted to protect her, and against her will, it touched her.

"Let's go see." Still holding Rose's hand, Robbie Jo slipped through the crowd.

She was impressed with the damage the fire had done. There wasn't much left of the house. Daylight showed through the walls. The living room ceiling was mostly collapsed. The charred beams looked like the ribs of some great animal, long dead and rotted away. The whole thing was soaked from the efforts of the firefighting teams. There was a wet, acrid smell in the air, so strong Robbie Jo could taste it on the roof of her mouth.

There were people inside. Two men and a woman in rubber boots, gloves, and hard hats were in and around the house, taking pictures, putting samples in little plastic bottles. A big, grinning German Shepherd sniffed intently around the floor.

"A fire investigation team," Robbie Jo said. "They're prob'ly tryin' to find the point of origin. Where the fire started." Her heart pounded pleasantly. *Let's see you figure this one out, boys and girls.*

"What's up with the dog?" Rose asked.

"He's looking for accelerants."

"What?"

"Things to make a fire burn faster. Gasoline, turpentine, kerosene, stuff like that."

"My God! They think someone did this on purpose?" Rose turned a delicate shade of green.

"Most likely not. I think they just investigate anytime there's a fatal house fire." Robbie Jo scrutinized the crowd. She spotted a plainclothes detective, taking a statement from Tab Sasso.

"How do you know this stuff?" Rose was looking at her with a kind of curious concern.

"Oh, I read a lot of true crime stuff. And I like to watch the forensic detective shows on cable."

Rose frowned, bit her lip.

"What?" asked Robbie Jo.

"Don't they...wouldn't they usually investigate a fatal fire with, uh, with the bodies still there?"

What a smart girl you are, Rosie. Robbie Jo nodded. "I'd think so. Sam took 'em last night?"

"Yeah." Rose looked like she had a bad taste in her mouth.

"Hmm. I hope the boy hasn't got himself in a peck of trouble." Robbie Jo suppressed a smile, thinking of just how much trouble Sam was probably in. *Hope you can handle it, honey. Just keep your cool.*

SAM ON THE SPOT;
ROSE MAKES A DATE

"Don't you talk to me like that! Don't you dare!" Sam roared.

"Do you have any idea what you've done? Any clue?" The short, pasty-faced detective bellowed back. His red hair, greased into an unflattering DA, bobbed when he screamed.

"Yes! I did my job! I honored those poor folks' last wishes! Do you have a problem with that?" Sam's heart was pounding so hard he thought it would leap out of his chest. He hoped his anger was masking the bone-deep fear he felt.

"You're goddam right I do! You should have known there'd be an investigation. And what did you do? You burned the fuckin' bodies!" The little man's voice was going up in pitch as he got angrier.

"What does it matter? They were mostly burned up already! You can't autopsy a charcoal briquette, detective." Sam spat out the last word, wishing he had the man's neck between his hands.

"You don't know what we can or can't do, you ignorant backwoods asshole!"

Sam felt his blood pressure rising. He thought his eyes were going to pop out and stick to the nasty little man's nice white shirt. "You can't talk to me this way. I could sue you for harassment."

"And I could arrest you for interferin' with my investigation!"

"Then why don't you just go and do it!" The two men glared at each other. Sam's head was buzzing with white noise. The detective's eyes were narrowed, his lips compressed to a thin white line. Sam was beginning to regret his last comment.

Why did I say that? This little shit-stain is gonna do it, he's gonna arrest me—

The sound of a bell, faint but urgent, broke the silence. A beat went by and it rang again.

"I have to go," Sam snapped.

"I'm not done with you yet!" The detective's fists were clenched at his sides. He looked like a nasty little dog that was just about ready to bite.

"You listen to me, Detective Woodcork-—"

"Woodcock."

"Whatever. My mama and daddy—both of 'em—they're sick. Terribly sick. And I'm the only one takin' care of 'em. And I'm the only one to run the business. So goddamit, I have to go and I have to do it now. If you're gonna arrest me, you can goddam wait until I get my mama a drink of water!" Sam was horrified to hear his voice crack, to feel the sting of tears in his eyes. He blinked them angrily away.

To his utter surprise, the detective's expression softened. "You—I'm sorry," he said. Sam nodded, not trusting himself to speak.

The detective shoved his hands in his pockets and sighed like a steam engine. "What's done is done, I guess."

"Yeah," Sam muttered. He saw his opportunity, and dove in. "I shouldn't have—you're right. I shouldn't have done what I did. It was stupid." The words were bitter as bile in his mouth.

The detective sighed again. "It's clear you're under a lot of stress, Mr. Dunwiddie. People make mistakes under stress. But please, if this ever happens again, don't cremate the bodies. Don't even move them. Okay?"

"I won't," Sam said, putting on his daddy's patented sorrowful expression. "But God forbid it should ever happen again."

"God forbid," agreed the detective.

The bell rang again, more feebly this time.

"I'd best let you go," said Detective Woodcock. By now he was looking a little embarrassed. "I hope your parents feel better real soon."

"Me too." Sam held out his hand, and the detective shook it. Leaving the man to find his own way out, he headed up the stairs, feeling like he'd just dodged an eighty-caliber bullet.

Rose walked back to the animal clinic, lost in a fog of worry. She'd finally left Robbie Jo by the ruin of the Plums' house, still watching the investigators. The girl had seemed to be in a fugue, utterly fascinated by what she was seeing. *At least she wasn't crying anymore,* Rose thought, *or beating herself up over it.* But the whole thing hadn't seemed healthy, somehow.

Rose knew that Robbie Jo had a morbid streak. It was in everything from her sense of humor to her taste in movies. It was one of the things Rose liked about her. But she hoped it wouldn't cause Robbie Jo to dwell endlessly on the Plums' deaths. And then there was her affectionate mention of Sam Dunwiddie. Robbie Jo was smart. Why couldn't she figure out that the guy was a waste of skin?

Rose heaved a deep sigh as she walked through the door of the clinic. But when she saw Michael, she had to smile. He was sitting behind the reception desk, tinkering with a weird little wheeled contraption of some kind. His forehead was knotted with concentration as he turned it over in his hands.

"New toy?" she asked.

He looked up at her and smiled, then held the thing up for her to see. It had two three-inch wheels attached to what looked like half of a cylindrical Tupperware container. Leather buckled straps hung from the sides of the thing.

"Bondage device for twisted poodles?"

Michael grinned, spots of color in his cheeks. "Closer. It's for Jeepers. He won't be able to walk with casts on both his back legs. If he drags himself around, he'll get dirty and he might reinjure the bones. So—"

"So you played the mad scientist and cooked this up in your basement lab?"

"You got it."

"Let's try it out!"

Rose cradled the big tom gently in her arms and carried him to the waiting room. He was as scrawny as a string bean;

he'd lost weight since his accident. "At least you still have all your kitty body parts," she whispered to him. He butted his big head against her chest and purred; a deep rumble like a distant truck engine.

Rose held Jeepers up while Michael strapped the wheeled device onto the cat's shaved belly.

At first Jeepers stood perfectly still, with a stunned look on his face. Then he took a step forward, and the wheels rolled with him. He whipped his head around to stare at them accusingly. Rose put her hand over her mouth to keep from laughing.

Jeepers trotted a few steps, and seemed appalled when the wheels went with him. He tried turning in circles, but the horrible thing attached to his stomach held fast. He let out a meow of outrage and tried to bite it.

Rose couldn't help it. She started giggling. It only got worse when Pun'kin and Goober took one look at Jeepers and fled to the corner, cowering under the waiting bench together as if they had seen a monster.

Jeepers lashed his tail, clearly offended. He stalked down the hall, stiff as a wind-up toy.

"Poor guy," Rose gasped, still chuckling. "His dignity's been wounded."

"He'll get over it," Michael said, smiling. "Once it comes off and he realizes he can't even stand up without it, the wheels won't seem so awful to him."

"Do you think he'll really figure that out?"

"Sure. Animals are a lot smarter than people give 'em credit for. Besides, cats are pragmatic things."

Rose realized she was standing right next to Michael; their arms were nearly touching. She looked up at his face, to see if he were kidding or not. He was looking back at her.

Time slowed down to sweet molasses. Michael's face bent down to Rose's, and their lips touched, pressed together. It was a gentle kiss, sweet and tender. Rose's breath caught in her throat and her head went light. The whole world was the warmth of his body and his sweet, heady scent.

"What do you think of that?" Michael whispered.

Rose brushed his face with her fingers. "I think I like it just fine."

"Would you join me for supper tonight? I make great corn puddin'."

A hitch of fear, then a rush of warmth in her chest. "I'd love to."

SAM AND HIS DADDY

As evening fell and Michael Yeats fretted over meatloaf with mushroom gravy, Sam Dunwiddie was busy slipping ice chips into his parents' dry, stinking mouths.

They were both desperately sick, he knew. So sick they would never get well, even if he stopped dosing them. He could see it in their dull and sunken eyes, their brittle hair, their papery skin. And that smell.

It wasn't just the vomit and the diarrhea. In self-defense, Sam's nose had pretty much stopped registering those. It was the smell under that, coming from his parents' flesh, from deep inside of them. The smell of death.

It was strongest on Sam's father. Funny, how such a big, healthy man could fall apart so completely. Ephram would die first, Sam was certain.

He passed a cool cloth over the old man's face, wishing it was all over and done with.

"Sam?" Ephram's voice was reedy and weak. It didn't sound like him at all.

"Yes, Daddy. I'm here."

"Is the doctor comin' back? I don't feel so good, son."

"He—he was here, Daddy. He gave you a shot and said you'd be fine. You and Mama were sleepin'." A blatant lie, of course, and it burned in Sam's mouth like acid.

"Good."

"Don't talk, now. Save your strength."

"I need to tell you somethin'." Ephram's hand came up, wavering, like a blind and seeking cave creature. Sam took it gently in his.

"I know we've had our diff'rences. But you're a good boy. You've been so very good to your mother and me. I'll be proud to pass the Sweet Hereafter on to you, Sam." He attempted a smile. It was horrible to see.

Bingo! There it was, the brass ring, the gold medal. Everything Sam had been working for had just been handed to him on a plate. He knew he should be happy, or at least relieved. Instead he had to fight down the urge to run to the bathroom and puke.

Maybe I'm sick, he thought. *Maybe I got some of that castor bean shit on my fingers.*

But he knew better. Sam Dunwiddie was sick, all right, as sure as his mother had pushed him screaming from her womb, as sure as he had his father's eyes and broad shoulders. Sick in the soul. He had poisoned it, little by little, each time he poisoned his parents. Each time he took their trust and gave them lies and peppermint tea.

It can't be fixed, you know. Time to finish it.

"Be still now, Daddy. Let me get you some more 7-Up." Sam managed to smile back at his father, and he felt his blackened soul shrivel up and die.

ROSE AND MICHAEL

"Everything was delicious. Where'd you learn to cook like that?" Rose couldn't believe how much she'd just eaten.

"My mama taught me. She thought ever'body should know how. Drove my dad crazy."

"Why?"

"He thought she was gonna turn me into a sissy."

Rose laughed. "Well, I think men who can cook are very macho."

"Oh yeah? You should just see me garden. You can practically smell the testosterone."

Rose helped Michael clear the table and put away the leftovers. He seemed to have made enough to feed half of Possum Kingdom. His mashed potatoes and gravy were almost as good as Naomi's.

"Would you like to sit and talk awhile?" Michael seemed a little nervous, which made Rose smile.

"Sure." They headed for the living room.

She glanced around his small house, which was tidy without being fussy. The furniture was practical and the décor simple; basic Sears-catalog country. There was a framed print of a dog sleeping blissfully on a sun-dappled bed over the sofa.

"I'm surprised you don't have any pets," Rose commented, sitting down. The sofa was soft and comfy.

"I'm, uh, between dogs. I just lost my yellow lab, Daisy, a few months ago."

"I'm so sorry, Michael."

"Well, she was old. Almost fifteen. And it was peaceful; she just went in her sleep." He looked at the ceiling, face pinched. "But that didn't make it any easier."

He paused, seeming lost in thought. "Have you ever had any pets, Rose?"

"No. I lived in an apartment all my life." *Not to mention the fact that my father wouldn't let me have anything that might have made me happy.* She blinked the ugly thought away.

"Well, you've got a few now, don'tcha."

Rose laughed. "I have a few to spare. You wanna dog or three, cheap?"

Michael grinned. "They're gorgeous pups, but somethin' tells me they may be a set."

It was true, in some weird way. The pups and their mother hung together, and they stayed close to Rose. When she was ready to take them back to Owen and Naomi's after work, the pups climbed into the wagon themselves, jammed in like furry sardines. There they sat, quiet as statues as Rose pulled them down the street with Onyx at her side. It plainly wasn't normal, but not much about the black dogs was.

"Mm," Rose said. "Naomi says they're witchy."

"She just may be right. But a little magic isn't such a bad thing, is it?" Michael touched Rose's hair, making her shiver.

"Not at all."

"Would you mind if I kissed you?"

In answer, she leaned in close as he slipped his arm around her.

They kissed for a long time. Rose tangled her fingers in his silky brown hair, ran her hands over his slim, muscled back. Her heart pounded. As Michael kissed her throat, as she felt his tongue flick against the tender hollow behind her ear, Rose's belly grew warm. The heat crept down, and farther down still, and she was suddenly wet between the legs.

Rose caught her breath in a shuddering gasp. She had never wanted anything so much in her life. And she had never been so afraid in her life. Images, squirming and ugly, pressed into the edges of her consciousness. Her father. All her father. Rose fought them with every ounce of will she had. If they got through, even one of them, she knew she would shatter like glass.

Michael's lips against her forehead, cool and sweet.

"It's gettin late. Why don't I walk you home, okay?"

She opened her eyes and looked into his. He knew. Not the specifics of course, but he'd felt her freeze up.

A flush of humiliation. "Michael—you don't have to—"

"Rose." He smiled at her, stroked her hair. "We don't even know each other yet, not really. I'll wait for you. I think I'd wait for you forever."

She opened her mouth to speak, eyes filling with tears.

He brushed her lips with his thumb. "Hush. We've got oceans of time."

ANGER, ASHES, AND SUDDEN DEATH

The funeral service for Nancy and Fayelynn Plum should have been a quiet, sorrowful affair. Instead it was alive with gossip, buzzing like a sewing circle on espresso.

"Can you BELIEVE it? I can't BELIEVE it!" Effie Granger clutched the skinny arm of Tab Sasso as she stared at the two ivory-colored urns.

They were pretty, Rose thought, smooth and creamy as carved vanilla fudge. She still couldn't quite convince herself that the two little jars held the earthly remains of two human beings.

Perched on a podium like pagan idols, the urns had been objects of horror throughout the service. "People just don't cremate in Possum Kingdom," Robbie Jo had whispered to Rose as she looked at the jars with dark disapproval. "I just can't imagine what Sam was thinkin'."

Rose was amazed to realize that she had been in Possum Kingdom long enough to see the point. You couldn't kiss an alabaster urn on the cheek. You couldn't pat its cold hand, smooth its hair and declare that it looked ever so lifelike. Not that you could have done that with Nancy and her mama, anyway. But she suspected that Possum Kingdom would have been more comfortable with closed caskets instead of "jelly jars," as one observer had uncharitably put it.

Rose herself was grateful for the urns. She knew that, if the Plums' bodies had been present, she wouldn't have been able to stop staring at the coffins, to stop imagining the burned stick limbs and clawed fingers and glinting teeth within. Ashes she could deal with.

Sam went by, looking hang-dog and slightly guilty in his immaculate black suit. For the first time since he nearly flattened her, Rose didn't want to kick his ass. In fact, she felt a little sorry for him.

When the crowd wasn't nattering about the urns, they was whispering about Sam's parents. Evidently, the senior Dunwiddies were sick with some kind of terrible flu, and Sam had been forced to handle the entire Plum funeral himself. He had blown it by cremating the bodies, and he knew it. He looked awful. His sculpted face was drawn. Dark circles under the eyes. Mouth compressed between sympathetic smiles.

"They're recoverin'," she heard him say to Naomi, as she gripped his hand and patted it. "No, they're not well enough to see anyone, but I'll pass on your good wishes." Had his voice wavered, just the tiniest bit? *Maybe a little pain will boost his humanity quotient,* Rose thought. *We can hope, anyway.*

She wove through the black-draped, weepy, critical crowd, making her way to the parlor. She hoped to find Robbie Jo, but the girl was nowhere in sight. Rose slipped past a tight knot of whispering mourners and sat down on the couch. Rubbed her eyes. Fanned the back of her neck with her Sweet Hereafter commemorative fan, which bore the names of Nancy and Fayelynn Plum.

Rose caught a glimpse of Michael in the doorway, gorgeous and awkward in his slim-cut dark suit. She wondered if it was a sin to feel lust at a funeral.

Sam felt as though his guts had been replaced with writhing, biting worms. His skin burned and crawled under the disapproving stares of his friends and neighbors. Jesus Christ, you'd think he'd pissed on the bodies in the middle of Main Street instead of just cremating them.

The fuckin' things you do for love.

He was dying to ask Robbie Jo why, exactly, she had murdered Nancy and Fayelynn Plum. She hadn't been foolish enough to say as much on the phone, of course. Not his brilliant girl. But her hissing orders to cremate the Plums had been as serious as death itself.

It had caused him plenty of trouble. But remembering the steel in her voice made his cock stir like a sun-warm rattlesnake. He'd ask her why she did it, but he wouldn't question her. Robbie Jo was his whole world now. His reason for living. His reason for killing. He'd caught her eye a few times tonight, and her look was as cool as ice cream. Sam knew he had to keep his distance for now. But just the sight of her, perfect face bone white above her black cotton dress, made him feel like his skin was on fire beneath his clothes.

"Evenin', Sam."

Sam started. "Oh, good evenin', Doc. Sorry, I almost bumped into you. I'm a bit preoccupied."

Doc Poteet nodded. "I understand. You've got a lot on your mind, son. How are Ephram and Ruth?"

Sam swallowed, his throat suddenly dry. "Oh, I think they're gettin' better. I got a little chicken broth into 'em this afternoon. This sure is one nasty bug, though."

"Sure 'nuff. Would you mind if I just nipped upstairs and looked in on 'em?"

Sam's heart froze. His brain screamed no, gibbering like a madman in a cage, but of course, he couldn't say that. "I'd appreciate it greatly, Doc. In fact, I was gonna ask you if you'd mind, but you beat me to it."

Doc Poteet smiled. "Not atall. I'll just be a moment."

Sam walked him to the parlor, and watched him go up the stairs.

The game is up. He's gonna know what you've done, said his brain matter-of-factly.

"Of course he's not," Sam whispered. *The worst that's gonna happen is that he's gonna think you're a dipshit for not callin' him sooner. And maybe he'll send 'em to the hospital.*

Oh fuck. I'm screwed.

Rose was nearly drowsing in the warm, close air of the parlor. Many of the mourners had left, but she was waiting for Naomi and Owen. Naomi was in rare form, telling stories about Nancy and Fayelynn, making their memories live in more vibrant color than they ever had themselves. She showed no signs of slowing down just yet.

Rose stretched, shifted her weight. Wished Robbie Jo would sit down and talk to her, but she hadn't seen the other girl for awhile now. Surely she hadn't slipped out without saying goodbye? *Nah.* Rose was contemplating getting up for a drink of water when Doc Poteet came bustling down the stairs. The man's face was as pinched and tight as a fist.

"Sam!" he called. "Sam!" The younger man met him in the hallway. Doc P. grabbed Sam's elbow and pulled him aside. His voice was soft, but Rose could still hear him.

"Oh Sam, I'm so sorry, but your daddy's gone."

"What?" Sam's face was blank, maybe with shock? Doc Poteet gripped his shoulders.

"Ephram's dead, Sam. Your father's dead."

Sam stared at him for another moment before his face crumpled. He covered it with his hands and began to cry.

WHAT ROBBIE JO SPIED (SAM'S MAMA AND THE SWEET HEREAFTER)

There were footsteps on the stairs. Robbie Jo smiled, and stepped back deeper into the blackness of the closet.

The old man was already dead when she crept into the reeking bedroom. That was a disappointment. She'd stopped by the sleeping old woman's bed and watched her for awhile. The crust of vomit on her lips. Her sticky eyes, glued shut by thick yellow tears. Her gray, sunken face, collapsed in on itself like papier mache in the rain. She looked like a corpse, but breath still stubbornly leaked in and out of her lungs with a thin, reedy whistle. All in all, it looked like ricin poisoning was a pretty fuckin' horrible way to die. Robbie Jo had smiled a little, then moved on to the man.

At first she'd thought he was just sleeping deeply. But then she saw the jaw—the way it had dropped down and in, leaving the mouth in a vacant gape. The way the rib cage had sunken into utter stillness.

She'd touched his forehead. It was still warm, and a little damp with sweat.

"Dammit." The moment of death, the magical, inimitable rattle, had eluded her by moments. She stared at the old man, whose name had been Ephram Dunwiddie but who was now a bundle of dead meat and protruding bones. Robbie Jo's mouth quirked up. She'd never understand how anybody could fear the dead. There was nothing on earth more harmless than a corpse. Hell, the dead were the only folks on the planet guaranteed not to hurt you, or lie to you, or fuck you up in one way or another. Most people, she thought, were at their absolute best after they stopped breathing.

When she was done staring at Ephram's house-of-wax expression, Robbie Jo had taken a leisurely look at the toasters. She decided that she liked them, in all their useless, inventive glory. Then she'd slipped into the closet to wait for Sam.

But it wasn't Sam coming up the stairs, it was old Doc Poteet. Robbie Jo grinned as he muttered horrified exclamations over Ruth, taking her pulse and lifting her gummy eyelids. She didn't wake up, but let out a long, gut-deep groan. Maybe she was past waking up. Robbie Jo crossed her fingers.

Then he got to Ephram. "Dear God," breathed the doctor. "Oh dear sweet God. Poor Sam." Then he hurried back down the stairs on his bandy bird-legs.

Robbie Jo leaned against the back of the closet, making herself comfortable amidst the Dunwiddies' faintly musty-smelling clothes. Smiling, waiting silently for poor Sam. Excited to find out just what was going to happen next.

Sam watched, utterly numb, as Doc Poteet hooked up an IV to his unconscious mother. Watched as Doc pulled the white linen sheet over his father's face.

"I—I feel so stupid," Sam whispered. "I had no idea they were that sick." He was sure that his lie was as transparent as onion skin.

Doc came over and patted him firmly on the back. "I know, son. They were—they both seemed so tough. Don't go blamin' yourself. You did well by 'em."

Sam tasted bile in his mouth. "Is my mama gonna make it?"

Doc sighed. "Honestly, I don't know. The ambulance from Jonesborough is on its way. They'll take good care of her. Now all we can do is pray."

Sam nodded. "Doc, would you, um, would you go down and send everybody home? I'd like to be alone with Mama for a little while."

"Certainly. I can come back up and watch over her after that, if you'd like."

"No, Doc, you go on home. I'll call you if anythin'—if I need to." Sam's voice wavered a little.

"All right." Doc looked at Sam with his sorrowful, hound-dog eyes. "I'm awful sorry this happened, Sam. Ephram was a good man."

"Yes, he was." It came out a whisper. Doc patted Sam's shoulder and silently left the room.

Sam watched out the bedroom window as the last remaining mourners left the Sweet Hereafter. Obnoxious Effie Granger, talking and waving her hands excitedly. Happy as a pig over another death in Possum Kingdom, no doubt. That pretty little Rose and the Tanners, the girl looking over her shoulder with worry on her face. Tab Sasso. Jerry McGraw and his egg-shaped wife. Sam closed the curtains, and turned around to find his mother staring at him.

Sam's heart gave a painful whump. He felt something akin to fear. But he made himself smile as he sat down on the edge of the bed. "Hey, Mama."

"Sam." A thin whisper, not much like a human voice at all. More like the hiss of wind through a dead tree. Sam lifted her head, helped her take a few sips of water. She retched hard, but kept them down.

"Ephram," she breathed, a question.

Sam took his mother's hand in both of hers, rubbed the dry, slack skin over the bones. "Mama...the ambulance is comin'. It'll be here soon. You'll be okay."

Ruth pulled her son's hand up to her withered cheek. "I love you, Sam. I know I never said that enough."

Sam's chest hitched. He felt the horrible, raw, ripping sensation inside of him that he did when Doc Poteet told him that his father was dead. Pain. Confusion. Relief. He was afraid he would start sobbing again.

"I love you too, Mama." The thought that he might mean it made Sam's gut cramp. An ocean of guilt was waiting to crash down on him and sweep him utterly away.

"Daddy's dead, isn't he."

Sam bit his lip, stroked his mother's forehead. "Yes, Mama. But the ambulance—"

"Sssh. I can't go without him."

"But Mama..." A painful lump stopped the words in Sam's throat.

"Give me your father's hand, Sam. I can't see him."

Slowly, slowly, Sam pulled Ephram's cooling hand from under the sheet. Ruth's in his other hand. He pulled them across the gap between their narrow beds, and joined them. Ruth's fingers laced with Ephram's, and squeezed. Sam could never in his life remember his parents walking that way, hand in hand.

His mother let out a soul-deep sigh, releasing the perfume of death into the air. "Kiss me goodnight, Sammy." She hadn't called him Sammy since he was almost a baby.

Sam pressed his lips to his mother's forehead. She smiled, the tiniest bit. "You're such a good boy," she breathed. Then a strange little hiccup. Quiet. Then a long, deep rattle, like a snake in dry grass.

"Mama?" Sam said, knowing she wouldn't answer. "Mama? Mama! Mama!" He grabbed her bony shoulders and shook her gently. Nothing, of course. Her hand slipped from Ephram's, and dangled by the side of the bed.

"Doc!" Sam screamed. He ran down the stairs, still screaming.

Doc had not, in fact, left. He had been waiting in the parlor.

There was nothing he could do, of course. Ruth Dunwiddie was as dead as her husband. Doc unhooked the IV, and closed Ruth's eyes. Gave Sam his deepest condolences, and offered to stay with him until the ambulance arrived. Sam sent him home.

Alone now, alone with his dead parents. Trembling with relief, and guilt, and horror. Sam half expected them to sit up under their white sheets, to come for him with clawlike hands and chattering teeth. Because he deserved it. But the world wasn't like that. The dead were just dead. Just meat to be processed; embalmed, wired, painted, planted.

Dead.

You got what you wanted. You did it to them, because it was what you wanted.

No. Not what I wanted. What Robbie Jo wanted. That murderous little psychotic cunt. She did this.

"No!" Sam hissed, and rammed his knuckles into his mouth. He could never think things like that about her. Not about his Robbie Jo. His angel. His only reason for living.

Sam took his parents' hands and tried to join them again, but they slipped apart, fingers like softened rubber.

Sam sat on the foot of his mother's bed and covered his face with his hands.

When someone placed a hand on his shoulder, he screamed.

SAM ON THE EDGE; SIMON COMES TO CALL; ROBBIE JO MAKES A PROMISE

"Hush, Sam, hush. It's me, baby." Robbie Jo slid her arms around Sam's neck, hands on his chest. His shirt was soaked with sweat. He was trembling.

Sam leaned his head back against her. "You're here. I'm so glad." Tears slid from the corners of his puffy eyelids, down over his temples, into his ears.

"'Course I am. I snuck into your bedroom to surprise you later. Then I heard Doc…" She kissed his forehead, just as he had kissed his mother's. "It's over, Sam. It's all over with."

He pulled her around to face him. Looking at his ash-gray face, Robbie Jo knew he was riding the barb-wired edge of a total breakdown. Little twitches pulled at his mouth, his chin, his eyelids.

"It's all gonna be just fine. I know that was so hard, Sam. Even though they didn't give a damn about you, they were your folks. But they're gone now. And the Sweet Hereafter's all yours." A gamble, slamming his parents. But he was going all gobby-sentimental. He needed to snap out of it.

Sam's eyes narrowed. "They told me they loved me, before—they both did."

Robbie Jo kissed him gently on the lips. "I know. People say what they think they should, before they die. But if they really meant it, honey, they would have treated you better before they were sick. But none of that matters now. It's all over and done with. You're free, Sam."

He looked at her for another moment, then sagged against her, head pressed to her chest. Arms around her so tightly it hurt a little. He stayed that way for a long time. Robbie Jo had to smile. She knew surrender when she saw it.

"The ambulance is comin'," Sam murmured into Robbie Jo's dress. "What will we do?"

She ran her hands through his sweaty hair. "You tell 'em what happened, and you tell 'em that Doc Poteet has already pronounced 'em dead. They can examine the—your folks, but don't let 'em take 'em anywhere. If they say an autopsy is gonna be required, you say you'll keep 'em at the funeral home until the county coroner sends a hearse to pick 'em up."

A harsh gasp from Sam. "Autopsy! Oh my God, Robbie Jo if they—"

"Hush. If they do an autopsy on 'em, they won't find a fuckin' thing. You can't spot ricin by lookin' at someone's innards, remember?"

Sam winced. "Yeah..."

"Stop thinkin' about it, Sam. Just think about you and me." She pulled him to his feet. He swayed, and she steadied him, arms around his waist.

A three-tone chime rang throughout the house. "The ambulance already?" Robbie Jo asked.

Sam shook his head. "No. That's the back door. The embalmin' room door. Prob'ly the sineater."

Robbie Jo smiled into his shirt, where he couldn't see. "Best to let him in, Sam. Gotta keep things as normal as possible."

Robbie Jo hung back as Sam opened the door. Simon came in, staring at Sam as if he were a bug-eyed alien. "I—I'm here for the Plums," he said quietly.

"Sure. They're in the chapel." Sam's voice was flat and dead.

Simon shifted from foot to foot. "Um...I need some food...to eat the sins..."

Robbie Jo stepped out from behind Sam. "I'll get it." She smiled sweetly. *Oh boy. This should be amusin'.*

Simon's jaw dropped. The color drained from his face. "Ruh—Robbie Jo! What are you doin' here?"

Sam scowled. "You two know each other?"

"What's goin' on?" Simon demanded.

"How do you know him?" Sam growled at Robbie Jo. His spine was straight as a poker. Simon, skinny little guy, puffed himself up and clenched his fists.

Whoooee! Smell that testosterone! "Sam, I met Simon last summer, when I worked in the blueberry field. Simon, I'm here helpin' out because Sam's parents were sick. Now let's get on with it, okay? I'll bring the food into the chapel." *Bang! Bang! A one-two bullshit punch!*

The two guys glared at each other for another moment. Then Simon wordlessly stepped around Sam and headed for the chapel.

Sam followed Robbie Jo into the kitchen, watched her as she put together a tray of bread and cheese. She could tell that he wanted to ask her more questions. She totally ignored him.

Simon burst into the kitchen. "What have you done?" he hissed at Sam.

"What do you mean?"

"I can't eat sin from ashes! They're lost to me! They're goin' to judgment carryin' all their earthly evils!" Simon was practically screaming.

"There was nothin' left of 'em! Could you eat sin from somebody cooked away to charcoal and bone?" Sam's face was flushed with anger, and Robbie Jo was glad to see it. Maybe he wouldn't fall apart after all.

"My daddy did!" Simon growled. "On old Webber Moomjean."

"I remember him. Dumb sumbitch tried to weld his gas tank without fillin' it up with water first. All we could do was box him and spray around a whole lotta Glade." Sam made a face.

"But you didn't burn him! He still had a body! You may have damned those two!" Simon trembled all over.

Sam took a step toward him. "Listen, I've had about enough of you as I'm gonna take."

Simon, right in his face. "Do you even know what you've done?"

"Stop it!" Robbie Jo set the tray down with a bang. "Simon, you need to be kind to Sam. His mama and daddy just died."

Simon turned a sickly shade of gray. "Yuh—you mean tonight?"

Robbie Jo crossed her arms. "Yes, tonight. Not two hours ago."

Simon ducked his head like a kicked puppy. "Dear God. I, uh, I'm sorry, Sam. I'm so sorry."

"Yeah," Sam grumbled.

There was a silence, long and uncomfortable. Simon looked miserably guilty. "Do you want me to take their sins now?" he asked in a quiet voice.

Sam stared at him, long and hard. "I guess so."

Robbie Jo handed Simon the tray. "They're in their bedroom, upstairs. Sam'll show you the way." She watched them go, Simon trailing behind like a dog who'd wet the rug and chewed up his master's slippers. Somehow, she managed to keep the smile off her face.

Sam was back downstairs before the screaming began. It didn't last long. Robbie Jo thought sardonically that the Dunwiddies must have been good people, light on the mortal sins. Simon, hollow-eyed and sick, left without a word, taking the bundle of ham sandwiches and apples that Robbie Jo had put together for him. Sam watched his narrow back suspiciously, like he was a skinny little fox sneaking out of the henhouse.

He didn't have time to bug Robbie Jo about it, though, because the ambulance came howling up the street.

It happened just the way Robbie Jo said it would. She waited in Sam's bedroom while Sam talked with the paramedics. They were sympathetic and kind, even helping Sam get his folks down the stairs and into the cold room. Robbie Jo thought that was pretty funny.

When they were gone, Sam went into the shower and stayed there for nearly an hour. When he came out, scrubbed pink and naked, he collapsed onto the bed next to Robbie Jo. He gathered her into his arms, resting his cheek on the top of her head.

"I love you," he whispered.

"I love you too, baby." She wondered why anyone ever believed those words. They were impossibly easy to say.

Sam pulled back, tipping her chin up to meet her eyes. "Robbie Jo, I mean it. You—you're everything in the world to me. You're my life."

Damn straight, she thought, and kissed him.

"I want you to promise me something." His eyes were bright with little star-shells of mania, waiting to explode.

She stroked his hair, kissed his nose. "Anything."

"Stay with me, Robbie Jo. I want you with me for the rest of my life. Will you promise me?"

"Yes." She pulled him close, enjoying the feel of his warm, finely muscled body against hers. "I promise. I'll stay with you, Sam, as long as you live."

He sighed with relief and closed his eyes. She watched him as he sank into sleep, watched the sweet curve of his full mouth and the gentle pulse in his throat as he lay naked and vulnerable as a newborn baby.

ROBBIE JO

*W*ell, well, well. I reckon I've got plenty of material for "What I Did On My Summer Vacation." And how am I feelin' by now? I've gotta be honest. Pretty fuckin' good.

Let's start with the Plums. Okay, it wasn't as spectacular as ol' Joe Reechur. But it had its own kinda charm. There's somethin' just plain thrillin' about homicidal arson. It's an act of creation, settin' a fire. Like givin' birth to this huge, hungry beast. It's a beautiful thing, to stand back and let it do its work, knowin' that it's your baby.

Even more fun is pullin' one over on the cops. I haven't heard anythin' more about the fire investigation, but I'm not sheddin' a single drop of sweat over it. What they're gonna find, if they're real lucky, is an outlet so overloaded it burst into flames. No crime but stupidity there. And nothin' to tie it to little ol' me.

They prob'ly wouldn't have found the drugs in the bodies, even if I hadn't made Sam burn 'em up. The Plums were pretty much beef jerky. Hell, they prob'ly wouldn't have done tox screens at all. But now I'm sure, just like the tampon ad says. Besides, it was worth it to hear the surprise in Sam's voice when I called him up. It was even worth the fuckin' five-mile walk to the Texaco to use the pay phone.

Poor ol' Sam. There isn't much left of that boy's innards. He's nothin' but marshmallow and guilt right at the moment. Which is fine by me, of course. Makes him easy to handle.

I've got to admit I was wrong about somethin'. I know I said that poisoners were pussies, but I s'pose I was speakin' from ignorance. I hadn't thought about how goddam coldblooded you've gotta be to dose your own family members over and over again, watchin' 'em puke and cry and call to God for help, all the while pretendin' to take care of 'em. How fuckin' hard you have to be to carry it right on through to the end and not show any weakness.

Sam sure as hell couldn't keep it together. Lucky for him, ever'body took it for stress and sorrow. Besides, he's got me to help him. I'll make sure he doesn't crack, if I have to wrap him with duct tape and pop him in the freezer.

Frankly, I'm jealous of that boy. What I wouldn't have given to be a fly on Dunwiddies' bedroom wall! Sure, I was there for the end, but I missed all the good stuff. Maybe I'll just have to try it myself sometime.

There's a certain kind of power in makin' somebody do somethin' like kill his own parents, though. That was a major rush. I think I'm startin' to understand why people run for public office.

Is it wrong for me to take credit for Ephram and Ruth, even though I never laid a finger on 'em? Nah. It never would have occurred to Sam if I hadn't put the idea in his head and given him a massive shove and multiple blowjobs. I did it. He was just the trigger on my gun.

So now I've got nothin' but time to figure out what I'm gonna do with my marshmallow man and his family business. And I've got time to get back to my research on the pretty Rev'rend Meshach Reddingale.

I have so many questions about him, and what he tried to do that summer night sixty years ago. In fact, I've decided to ask him myself.

Yeah, yeah, go ahead and laugh your ass off. I've decided to try that "Resurecshun" spell from Miss Hazel Lyndon's weird little hope chest. The ingredients for it are like a scavenger hunt from Hell—at the very least, I'll have some fun with that. If it doesn't work, at least I'll have some cool souvenirs. The catch is, it's only s'posed to work in the fall, right around Halloween. Shee-it, what a cliché, huh? But I guess I can wait that long.

I just hope I can keep from killin' anybody until then. Four deaths in three days is just about as much as this little town can take, for the moment. I've gotta play it cool.

Maybe I'll take up knittin'. I love those big needles.

AUTUMN IN THE KINGDOM

So the summer passed. Possum Kingdom staggered through the long, hot days in a state of shock. Surely, some evil influence had come to the little town. Some folks speculated devil worship. Others aliens. A few, serial killers. Effie Granger swore it was a Gypsy curse, despite the fact that there wasn't a Gypsy within two hundred miles of Possum Kingdom. Either way, church attendance went way up. Even Reverend Thomas Rye at the Wounds of Christ Baptist church had a congregation these days.

Rose's pups grew into big, sleek dogs in just two months. They stayed healthy, with glossy fur, bright eyes, and perfect white teeth. Rose finally stopped worrying that they would reveal some horrible genetic by-product of their astonishing growth, and started just enjoying them.

The pups worshipped her. They followed her everywhere. They didn't trail her in the loose, packlike way that dogs often do, but in two straight lines, with Onyx at the head. It was surprising to Rose, of course it was. But she wasn't nearly as astonished as she thought she ought to be. After all, nothing about the dogs was normal.

Somehow, the six pups never got their own names. They were so alike, for one thing, it was difficult for even Rose to tell them apart. And they seemed less like single dogs and more like parts of a whole. They were the Girls. The name quickly spread throughout the whole town.

Oh yes, Possum Kingdom noticed the Girls, and their strange, un-doggy ways. For the most part, Possum Kingdom didn't like it, not one little bit. There were mutterings of witchcraft, and hellhounds, and other such nonsense. But most folks had grown to like Rose, and they figured such a sweet young lady couldn't possibly be in cahoots with Old Scratch.

The rest of them may have thought otherwise, but they weren't about to say it to Rose's face. Not with seven big, toothy hellhounds right behind her.

Robbie Jo loved The Girls. Her russet eyes were shiny-bright whenever she watched them silently trail Rose down the street. She took to calling her friend "Dawg Goddess."

Did The Girls love Robbie Jo? It was hard to say. Their greeting for her was always solemn, as if for a visiting dignitary. Their moon-colored eyes avoided hers, and when they inadvertently connected, Robbie Jo thought she could detect equal parts fear and adoration. Well, that was okay. And it was fun to be included in the gossip.

The wagging tongues slowed, after awhile. In the grand scheme of things, Rose and The Girls were a minor bit of weirdness. Much stranger things had happened in the Kingdom. And much stranger things were coming.

The days got shorter, and the leaves began to change. Rose and Michael's love blossomed. They spent long nights and sleepy afternoons kissing, talking, cuddling in each other's arms. They didn't make love, not quite. But it was all right. Rose knew that the day would come when she would want nothing between the two of them. And she knew that Michael would wait for her. For the fist time in her life, she felt that someone truly loved her.

Robbie Jo watched this with amusement, and maybe just a twinge of jealousy. But Rose, she felt, was still more hers than Michael's. They still spent many hours together, talking and laughing and roaming through the thick velvet woods. Rose confided in Robbie Jo, opened her heart wide and showed her the delicate inner clockwork of her love for Dr. Michael Yeats. Robbie Jo was ever so tempted to reach in, touch the gears and the springs, maybe bend them a little or slip a needle into the works. But she held back. It was enough to bathe in the warmth of Rose's innocent trust, for now.

Besides, Robbie Jo had other fish to fry. There was her continuing education of Simon, for one thing. He was becoming quite a fine lover, in his own, affection-starved way. He lived to please Robbie Jo, gloried in her every moan and sigh. She enjoyed their sex, and appreciated Simon as a fine pupil, but his love meant not a thing to her. It was too easily won.

And there was Sam, of course, sick in love with her. Still stealing time with Robbie Jo in the woods, at her insistence. "It wouldn't be seemly for you to be keepin' company with me so soon after your parents' tragic death, honey," she'd told him time and again. "We'll be together, in front of God and everyone, when the time is right."

Sam hated it, but he was too busy to argue much. Running the business all by himself was harder than he'd guessed, and more rewarding. He loved the power. He even loved the responsibility. And when he worked hard enough, he didn't see his father's dead, slack face, his mother's slitted, dying eyes.

Folks noticed. "That boy has changed," they said, and gave Sam the respect they had once reserved for his father. That was enough to put a thin, glossy varnish over the jagged crack in his soul. Sam looked shiny and new.

School started. Robbie Jo's junior year. Her teachers were delighted to have her back, this sweet girl as bright as she was lovely. She was special. It was such a shame about her homelife, her poverty, her alcoholic, useless mother. Sometimes Robbie Jo would find a sweater or a skirt or a new pair of shoes tucked into her desk in the morning. There were no thanks or explanations—no one wanted to embarrass such a dignified, honest young lady. Just warm-eyed smiles between Robbie Jo and her teachers. Sometimes Robbie Jo worked up a glistening tear with her brave smile, which always sent Mrs. Buckworth diving for the Kleenex.

It was amazing, Robbie Jo thought, how people only saw what they wanted to see.

ROBBIE JO PAYS A CALL ON THE ROOT WOMAN

*H*alloween was coming. Robbie Jo gazed out the window, listening to Mr. Price trying to teach calculus to the meatheaded rednecks and redneckettes around her. Fat orange pumpkins in the school's garden plot, thick green stems like grass snakes. "Resurecshun," Robbie Jo wrote at the top of her paper.

She left her books in her locker after school; something she never did. But she had a long way to walk, and didn't want to be weighed down. Without a word to anyone, Robbie Jo slipped into the woods, walking in the opposite direction of her pitiful little house.

Robbie Jo wasn't certain where Reenie Rackham lived, but she had a pretty good idea. Her instincts were those of a tracking dog. It was still a full hour before dark when Robbie Jo found the little blue house at the end of a long dirt road.

She ducked into the bushes to think. *Walk up to the door? Sneak in through the window? Nah, better to knock.* She knew the old lady was home—there was purplish smoke curling up from the narrow chimney. Robbie Jo strode up the driveway.

The door was opened before she could knock, by an old woman in a blue gingham dress. Bony knobs and angles poked out through the faded fabric, making Robbie Jo think of dust-covered furniture. Worn hiking boots; a glimpse of dark, bristly shin. The old woman's spine was bent, her head thrust forward like a turtle's. She had once been tall, much taller than Robbie Jo, but now they stood eye to eye. The woman's dark-chocolate, wrinkled face was still, but her eyes were narrowed.

"Hello," Robbie Jo said with a pleasant smile. She held out her hand to Reenie Rackham.

Reenie glared at it. "Whatchoo want, fox girl?"

Robbie Jo let out a surprised laugh. "Fox girl? Oh, you mean my colorin', right? My hair and my eyes? Nobody's ever called me fox girl before. I think I like it."

Reenie Rackham's black eyes flicked over her face. "Whatchoo want?"

Robbie Jo dimpled. "Well, you see, I'm doin' a report on the history of Possum Kingdom in school. Everyone says you just know ever'thin' about it, and you have the most wonderful stories, so I was hopin' I could talk with you for a little bit."

Reenie glanced Robbie Jo up and down. Deepset eyes, dark and glistening, like the scales of a blacksnake at the bottom of a gopher hole. "Where's y'notebook?"

Damn. Sharp old bitch. Robbie Jo looked sheepishly at her shoes. "I left it at school. But I was halfway here before I noticed it, and I didn't want to go all the way back. But I have a good memory. Please, may I come in?"

Reenie's expression was stone. There was a moment where Robbie Jo thought the old lady was going to slam the door in her face. But she didn't.

"Well, jes' for a little while. I'm busy."

"Thank you so much." Feeling like Little Red Riding Hood's wolf, Robbie Jo followed the root woman into her tiny house.

It was surprisingly pleasant inside. Old, to be sure, but clean. Simple furniture; unvarnished maple and a tired old green couch, but homey. Your standard nice-old-grandma place, minus the family pictures. Knick-knacks here and there. Robbie Jo spotted a carved rabbit on the endtable that had to be one of Simon's. *Interesting.* The curtains were pulled back and the windows were open, letting the fresh air and leaf-filtered, late-afternoon sunlight in. A far cry from the dark den of Voodoo Robbie Jo had been expecting. *A hell of a lot nicer than Simon's place. Or mine.*

Reenie gestured for Robbie Jo to sit on the couch. She did, and a spring poked her in the butt. Robbie Jo turned her grimace into a smile and demurely scooted to one side. Reenie herself sat in an uncushioned armchair, sat straight as a fireplace poker. "Ax me," she said.

Thanks, I just might.

"You have a lovely house," said Robbie Jo. She glanced at the kitchen. Bunches of herbs hung from the ceiling. Bottles large and small lined the walls. *That's more like it.*

"I know that. Don't waste my time."

Robbie Jo didn't let her smile slip a millimeter. "All right, Miz Rackham. Since we're not mincin' words, I'll ask you a question directly. Why don't you ever come into town?"

"Nunna your business, fox girl."

"I thought you might say that, ma'am. But y'see, it's important for me to know. I'd like my report to be about you, not just the town. I mean, after all, you *are* this town." She grinned. "Besides, ever'body wonders."

The old woman leaned forward in her chair. "Ever'body, huh? Well, you kin tell ever'body this. I ain't parta Possum Kingdom. Haven't been in a long time."

"Why not? Are you angry at the town for somethin'? Did they let you down?"

"I ain't angry. They's nobody like me in Possum Kingdom, thass all. Make me nervous to be around 'em." Reenie licked her lips. Her bony old hands twisted together.

"Oh, Miz Rackham, you should see! There are lots of black folks now—"

Quiet, almost a whisper. "That ain't what I'm talkin' about. Nobody born in Possum Kingdom is—well, they ain't really human. Not even you."

Oh, great. She's fuckin' bananas. What the hell, this could be fun. Robbie Jo raised her eyebrows. "What on earth do you mean?"

"Nothin'. I said 'nuff 'bout that. If thass all you want to ax me, git out."

"Well, what I really wanted to ask you about was the Reverend Meshach Reddingale."

Robbie Jo had expected a big reaction from the name. She was disappointed. "What about him?" asked Reenie.

Let's start out slow. "You were a member of his congregation, weren't you?"

"Yes I was."

She's not gonna give me anythin' without a struggle. Okay, then. Let's get out the butter. "Was he a good preacher, Miz Rackham? Cuz I heard he was the best."

Was it possible that the old woman's eyes softened, just a bit? "That he was. The very best. His sermons rocked this valley. He could show ya the love a' God, bright an' hot as the sun on ya face. He could make the pits a' hell seem so close you could feel the breath a' Satan on the back of ya neck." Was that the hint of a smile?

"I wish I could have met him," said Robbie Jo.

Miz Rackham's smile took a tiny, sardonic twist. "I'm sure he woulda loved ya, fox girl."

"I also heard some other stuff, about how he had a special way with the snakes. I even heard that, well, that he could make 'em dance. That's not true, is it, ma'am?" Robbie Jo widened her eyes.

Reenie's lips pursed, her eyes narrowed.

Robbie Jo did her best to radiate innocent wonder.

"Yeah, it's true. The snakes loved him. He'd take 'em out, all of 'em at once, and jes' put 'em on the floor of the church, but they wouldn't run off. Nope. They'd start movin' around with the music, an' then they'd start makin' patterns on the floor, all of 'em together, like they was a high school marchin' band or somethin'. An Mesha—the Rev'rend jes' standin' there with his arms spread, not sayin' a thing, jes' smilin' an' peaceful as Jesus hisself." A sigh. "He had a way with all the critters. Bears would come right up to him, like they was lost puppies." Reenie's hands were clasped together, as if in prayer.

"It musta been amazin'," Robbie Jo gushed.

"Ever'thin' about that man was amazin'."

Time to go for it...

"I—I know I shouldn't be askin' you this, but, well... Miz Rackham, I heard that you and the Rev'rend, well, that you had a, um, a love affair." She batted her eyes.

The muscles of the old woman's face seemed to be moving deep beneath her skin. Her black eyes flashed, and she stood up faster than Robbie Jo would have thought she could.

"Who the hell are you, fox girl? Wasn't nobody knowed that. I want you to git outta my house. Now."

"Miz Rackham, I'm sorry. I knew I shoulda kept my mouth shut. But nobody told me about it. I used to clean Miz Hazel Lyndon's house for her sometimes, and when she died, well, I found her diary…"

The old woman blinked. "I hadn't heard she was daid. I'm sorry to hear of it."

Robbie Jo hung her head. "It was a tragic accident. But she didn't suffer."

Reenie sank back down onto the chair, face slack. "Dear God. The only really bad thing I done in my whole life, an' you hafta come here, dig it up, an' throw it in my face."

"Oh, I didn't think you were—it just seemed so romantic—"

"It wasn't romantic. It was stupid. But I swear to sweet Jesus, I didn't know he was seein' her when we started—when I took up with him. I didn't find out 'til later." She rubbed her face with her hands. "But when I did find out, well…thass when I went wrong. I shoulda broke it off with him. But I didn't. I never meant to hurt that gal. I never meant to hurt nobody."

There was a hiss from the kitchen, the sharp, pungent tang of something burning.

"Damn." Reenie stood up fast and bustled to the kitchen. Robbie Jo followed her.

The kitchen was small, but clean and well-organized. Dried herbs in neat bunches, bound with cotton string. Pots and pans hanging from a rack above the iron woodstove. Dozens and dozens of bottles, labeled, neat as soldiers in rows on the shelves. Cinnamon. Fennel. Foxglove. Rat bone powder. Robbie Jo felt a grin creep across her face.

Reenie grabbed a potholder and took a black iron kettle from a hook over the fireplace. Thick whitish glop had boiled over and run lavalike down the sides. *A cauldron, for shit's sake.*

"Is that some kind of—of poultice, Miz Rackham? Or a medicine?"

"It's grits, you eedjit." She set the kettle down on the hearth. "Dammit. They's scorched."

"I'm sorry, ma'am. I didn't mean to spoil your supper." Robbie Jo glanced around the kitchen. Nice counters; leaf-green ceramic tile. Nice big kitchen knife by the stove. Robbie Jo edged closer to it.

Reenie sighed. "Ain't your fault. But shouldn't you be gettin' home? Your mama's bound to start missin' you."

She wouldn't miss her own ass if it fell off and rolled down the hill. "You're right, Miz Rackham. I just have a couple more questions, then I'll get outta your hair."

"Git on with it, then."

"What do the paintin's in the Holy Blood mean?"

Reenie stiffened. Her eyes hardened. "I got no idea."

"Was it true that the Rev'rend started losin' his mind?"

"Some folks saw it that way. Go on home, fox girl."

Robbie Jo's grin widened. "And what was he tryin' to do that night, Miz Rackham? The night he vanished? You were there, weren't you?"

"Git out. I ain't gonna talk about it."

"What happened, Reenie? Somethin' went wrong, didn't it? And it killed him?"

"Out!" Reenie shrieked.

Robbie Jo took a step closer to her. "What was he tryin' to do, Reenie?"

The old woman's mouth twisted down. "I'll never tell ya that."

Robbie Jo's hand shot out, her fingers closed over the rosewood handle of the kitchen knife. Just like that, the point was under Reenie Rackham's chin. "Oh, I think you will."

Reenie didn't flinch. Her lips skinned back in a humorless grin, revealing teeth as yellow and strong as a rat's. Her eyes were locked with Robbie Jo's. "I thought you was all fox, but now I see you half rattlesnake, too."

Robbie Jo let out a giggle. "That I am. Thanks for noticin'."

"Well, don't be stupid, rat'ler girl. You don't want no part a' this. What Meshach did was unnatural. It was unholy."

"Unholy? Was he a devil worshipper or somethin'?" The idea tickled Robbie Jo.

"No. He jes'—he wasn't content. He had the Holy Spirit like no one else, but it wasn't enough. He was always lookin' for more. Thass why he came to me."

"I thought he came to you for sex."

The old woman glared. "That come later. He wanted to learn my ways. I's a Christian, a' course I am. But my family's from bayou country. My mama was a root woman, an' her mama before her. I know healin' herbs, an' potions, an' a spell or two. Nothin' harmful."

"What's so unholy, then?" said Robbie Jo, mildly disappointed.

"Meshach started combinin' my ways with his. That wasn't never meant to be."

"Like oil and water?"

"Nuh-uh. They mixed, all right. But they made somethin' that shoulda never come into this world."

"I see." Robbie Jo couldn't decide if Reenie were delusional or not. "And what does it have to do with the paintin's in the Holy Blood? You know what they mean, old lady. I can see that in your crinkly ol' face as plain as day."

Reenie licked her lips. "Meshach—he'd go out into the woods for days at a time, fastin' an' prayin' an' such. He tole me one time that he talked with Indian gods an' Christian saints out there."

"Did you believe him?"

"I believed ever'thin' he tole me, at first."

"Keep talkin'."

"He'd have visions out in them woods. He had one about his own death. I remember him at my door, eyes wild, body shakin'. He said them spirits had showed him his doom, but that some other haints had showed him how to come back from the dead. Them paintin's is supposed to show the way how. But I never could figger 'em out."

"So you worked up your own resurrection spell."

"Damn you, girl!"

"Didja try it? Didja dig him up, Reenie? Didja smell that death-stink on your lover's mouth? Look into his sunken eyes?" She brought the knife slowly down Reenie's crepey neck, resting the point in the deep hollow above her breastbone.

Reenie's eyes brightened; a glitter of tears. "No. I never did, thank God."

"Why? Doesn't the spell work?"

"Oh, it work sometimes. But things don't come back— well, they don't come back right."

"What, are they zombies or somethin'?" Robbie Jo laughed.

"No. They's jes' wrong. Sometimes missin' parts, sometimes with the wrong parts. I tried it on this ol' tomcat who got hisself kilt by a coyote. He—I couldn't look at him after. His haid…no. No, I ain't gonna talk about it."

Robbie Jo traced her breastbone with the knife. "Maybe I'll just try it myself sometime."

"You'd hafta be crazy, rat'ler girl. But you is crazy, isn't ya. Well, do whatcher gonna do. I'm tired a' standin' here." Reenie's eyes glittered hot with anger.

"It isn't what I'm gonna do, old lady. It's what you're gonna do. You're gonna tell me what Rev'rend Reddingale was tryin' to accomplish the night he died. I'll kill you if you don't." Robbie Jo pressed the blade in, until a ruby of blood appeared on the dark, soft skin.

"You gonna have to, then, cuz I ain't never tellin' nobody." A tear spilled down onto Reenie's cheek, zig-zagging through the wrinkles.

Robbie Jo thought about it. She thought about it hard, for a minute there.

I could just cut her up like a bony ol' chicken. It'd be easy. And fun.

But somebody mighta seen me comin' here.

Nah. Nobody saw me. There's nobody for miles around.

But I might need to talk to her later on.

It sure would be fun, though—damn! I almost forgot! I'm gonna be late! Well, I'll just hafta gut her another time.

"Well, git on with it," Reenie hissed. "Ima die of old age b'fore you git aroun' to killin' me."

Robbie Jo laughed. "You're fulla piss and vinegar, Reenie Rackham. I think I like you. But I just remembered, if I don't get goin', I'm up shit creek without a paddle." She lowered the knife, set it down on the counter, and walked away.

Reenie watched the snake girl go. She knew she was lucky to be alive. "You like me, do ya? I sure don't like you any," the old lady whispered. She looked at her pot of grits, and her stomach clenched.

Reenie hoped she would never see the snake girl again. But she knew she would.

ROBBIE JO'S GREAT BIG SURPRISE

Rose Heron, walking down Main Street, Onyx and the Girls behind her. She glanced over her shoulder, admired the gold of the setting sun on her dogs' jet-black fur. Silent, grinning, they trotted along behind her. "We'll follow you anywhere," said their eyes.

People stepped out of her way as she walked. Rose let them. She felt powerful, for the first time in her life. *Pitiful, girl. Feeling like the Queen of Siam because you've got a bunch of silly dogs who like to trail around after you.*

But it was more than that, and she knew it. There was a little smile on her face.

Rose thought about Michael. The warmth of his skin, his breath on her face. She had never felt as close to anyone, except maybe Robbie Jo. She knew she would be ready to be his lover soon. She wanted to be.

She breathed in deeply through her nose, savoring the crisp air, the scent of autumn coming, the promise of baking pies and burning pumpkin shells.

"Whatchoo smell, Dawg Goddess?" Robbie Jo, stepping out of the shadows of a big old maple tree.

"Holy shit, you scared me!" Rose laughed.

"Come with me, then, and I'll show you somethin' really scary." Robbie Jo's teeth sparkled white.

"Isn't that what Dan Ackroyd said to John Lithgow, right before he turned into a monster and ate him?"

Robbie Jo laughed. "You bet Vic Morrow's head, baby. C'mon." Humming the Twilight Zone theme, she started walking. Rose shrugged, and followed.

"You gotta be kidding," she said, as Robbie Jo strolled right up to the front doors of the Baptist church.

"Am I?" She threw the doors open and strode in. A knot of uneasiness formed in Rose's belly as she crossed the threshold.

The church was lit with candles. Reverend Rye stood at the altar. Sam Dunwiddie was up there too, wearing a tuxedo, grinning like a coyote.

"What's going on?" Rose looked at Robbie Jo. The other girl's eyes were lit like copper lanterns.

"A weddin'," she said. "My weddin'. You're my best friend, Rosie. I want you to be my witness."

The world turned to jello. Rose took a deep breath, then another. For a moment, she thought she might have to sit down.

"Um, young lady, I wonder if you might leave your, eh, beasts outside." The reverend was looking past Rose's shoulder with a slightly horrified smile.

Rose looked behind her. The Girls. She hadn't even realized they'd followed her in, but there they were, sitting like a group of well-behaved schoolchildren. She giggled, then clapped a hand over her mouth.

"No," said Robbie Jo. "I want 'em here. They can be witnesses, too."

The reverend's doughy face twisted down. "But—"

"Whatever my little bride wants," Sam gushed. "They're good dawgs. They won't do anythin' untoward. And I'll leave a big donation in the collection plate." He beamed at Robbie Jo. She dimpled back.

Reverend Rye's brow puckered, but he didn't have a chance to answer. "I brought you a dress," Sam crowed. "It's in the robe room."

"I'd best go change, then." Robbie Jo looked down at her faded yellow cotton dress. "No peekin'!" She slipped away.

Rose was faced with several incredibly uncomfortable minutes alone with Sam and the reverend. Her brain seemed to have stalled out, spinning slowly in place like a hamster wheel under water.

She licked her lips, shifted her weight.

Sam grinned.

The reverend smiled serenely.

Sam grinned some more.

One of the Girls groaned under her breath. Another one farted.

Just when Rose thought she might run screaming from the church, Robbie Jo emerged.

"Holy sh—" Rose bit off the word before it could escape, pressing her lips together so nothing else could make a break for it. There was Robbie Jo, in yards and yards of white. Shimmering, snowblinding, white satin. Delicate, frothy white lace. White crinoline like seafoam on a sparkling white beach. Puffed sleeves. Plunging neckline. Train a mile long. Robbie Jo twirled around, grinning.

"You look like an angel," Sam breathed.

Robbie Jo rushed to Rose, kissed her on the cheek, whispered "I look like a fuckin' whipped cream can exploded all over me." Nimble as a deer, she bounded up to the altar. Sam whipped a huge bouquet of pink roses out from behind a pew and pressed it into her hands.

"We're ready!" he said, looking at Robbie Jo like she was a prime rib dinner.

So Sam and Robbie Jo got married. The Reverend Rye pontificated awhile on love and family and responsibility, and then asked them the question. "I do," said Sam, puffing up like a rooster. "I do," said Robbie Jo, gazing sweetly into Sam's eyes.

Then they kissed, long and juicy. The reverend looked down at the altar, a slight pink flush in his pale cheeks. Sam picked Robbie Jo up and whirled her around, laughing. Rose saw a flash of grubby red Keds under mountains of white. Tears stung her eyes, and she blinked them away.

Numb, she signed the marriage license. Robbie Jo threw her arms around Rose's neck, kissed her cheeks, promised to call her later. Then she and her new husband were gone. The reverend thanked Rose's back as she walked slowly from the church.

The Sweet Hereafter's shark-finned funeral coach roared out from the church parking lot, windows soaped with "Just Married," cans and ribbons trailing from the back bumper. Robbie Jo waved from the front seat, grinning ear to ear. Rose willed her hand to rise up and wave back, but it hung at her side, limp as a dead bird.

Rose walked home, escorted by the silent, worried Girls. She took the dogs out back and fed them their supper, feeling the pressure inside of her building higher and higher. Rose slipped in through the kitchen door, where the delicious smells of dinner made her icy stomach clench into a knot of pain. She mumbled something about cramps to Naomi, ran up to her room, and flung herself face-down onto her bed. Rose began to sob.

Robbie Jo and Sam spent their wedding night in the coffin showroom. Sam balked at first, thinking of how horrified his father would be. But the sight of Robbie Jo naked in the twelve-thousand dollar mahogany Angel Rest, her russet hair a fiery cloud on the creamy satin pillow, her strong young legs spread wide and draped on either side of the casket, took all of his doubts away.

They tried them all. Sam liked the Angel Rest most of all. Robbie Jo's favorite was the brushed-steel Eternal Valor, because, she said, she liked the cold metal under her hands while Sam was inside her. As the sun came up, they fell asleep in the beautiful cherrywood Celestial Dreams, nine thousand dollars before taxes. Sam drifted off on his back, Robbie Jo sleeping deeply on top of him, wrapped in his arms. He was as happy as a man in a casket could be.

As Rose was washing her puffy face, pressing cold washcloths to her swollen eyes, as Naomi and Owen worried and fussed downstairs, as the Girls stretched and yawned and began to contemplate breakfast, Sam awakened, cold and alone. Robbie Jo was gone.

He heaved himself up on one elbow. "Sweetheart?" he called, voice rough with sleep.

She peeked around the showroom door and beamed at him. "Good mornin', baby." She was dressed and looked remarkably awake.

"What time is it?" Sam sat up in the coffin, ran his hand through his hair.

"Seven forty-five. I gotta go, I'm gonna be late!"

He licked his lips. "Late for what? C'mon back to bed, angel. We've only been asleep a couple hours."

"No, no, darlin', I can't miss school today. I've got a math test. Bye-bye!" She turned away.

"Wait!" Sam called.

"What?" Was that a hint of irritation in her voice?

"You don't have to go back to school, baby. You're my wife now. I'll take care of ya."

Her brow knit. "Are you outta your mind, Sam? Do I look like a high school dropout to you?"

Sam blinked, rubbed his face. He didn't like this any. Not at all. But he didn't want to argue with his bride on their first day as man and wife. Besides, he was too goddam tired to do much of anything at the moment.

"Well…well okay, sugar. But you're gonna come right back home after school, aren't ya? Baby?"

She was already gone.

A FEAST OF SIN (POOR OL' SIMON)

They were already whispering about it at school.

Did Robbie Jo Ridgemont really marry Sam Dunwiddie last night?

No, of course not.

Sure she did, I saw 'em.

Did not.

Did so.

Robbie Jo refused to say a word. She just grinned a coyote grin and enjoyed the ruckus.

After school, Robbie Jo did not go back to Sam at the Sweet Hereafter. She didn't go back to her poverty-stinking shack and her gin-soaked mother, who had no idea her only child had just been married. Instead, she went deep into the woods, to the little cabin of Simon the sineater.

She found him shirtless and sleeping, late afternoon sunlight making his long blond eyelashes sparkle like gold. *Such a beautiful boy.* Robbie Jo slipped her wedding ring off her finger and put it into the pocket of her dress. She knelt down beside Simon and rested her head on his flat, hairless belly. Simon awoke with a gasp, then smiled at her with the pure, worshipful love of a child, or a good hunting dog. His hands slipped into her hair. She licked his neck, salty and warm as springtime. Slowly, lazily, they made love.

Later, lying together as the sun went down, Simon turned his face to Robbie Jo's cheek and whispered, "I love you."

Oh, Christ on a biscuit. She sighed. "Do you, sugar?"

"You know I do."

"Mmmm." An idea crept ratlike into Robbie Jo's mind. "Do you love me enough to eat my sins, Simon?"

His mouth bowed down. "Well, if you was to die, of course I would, Robbie Jo. But you ain't gonna die. I won't let you." He wrapped his skinny arms around her, kissed her shoulder.

"I don't aim to die anytime soon, baby. And that isn't what I'm talkin' about. Would you eat my sins right now?"

He sat up. There was a spark of fear in his eyes, and more than a touch of horror. "I can't eat the sins of a livin' person. It just ain't done."

She smiled up at him, stretched like a cat. "Why not?"

"Well, I—I don't rightly know. But it just ain't right. Besides, a person don't need unburdened from his sins 'til he's ready to meet his maker. What'd be the point?"

She sat up and rested her head on his shoulder. "I just think it'd bring us together, Simon. It'd be a bond that nobody else in the world has. You could take my sins, and make me clean and new. There'd be nothin' between us." She rubbed her naked belly against his back.

Simon rubbed the back of his neck. "Can't we just get married instead?"

Robbie Jo worked up some tears. Her lower lip trembled. "You don't love me enough to do it."

"No! No, that ain't it at all. I love you more than anythin', Robbie Jo. I'm just—well, I'm afraid of what might happen."

She smoothed his brow, sprinkled little kisses all over his face. "You silly. What could happen? The way I see it, there're just two possibilities. Either it works, you eat my sins, and we're bonded together forever. Or it doesn't work, and things stay the same between us. Which isn't so bad, if you ask me." She nuzzled his chest, nibbled a nipple. "Please, baby. Please?"

"Oh God…all right, Robbie Jo. All right. I'll do it."

She kissed his nose. "I knew you would."

"I don't have much, just some crackers. But they oughta work as good as anythin'."

"I'll just wait here, then." Robbie Jo lay back down, smiling in her triumph.

Simon knew it was wrong. He felt it in his bones as he lay the stale crackers on Robbie Jo's perfect belly and chest. But he couldn't refuse her. He could no more do that than he could sprout wings and fly.

He closed his eyes a moment to clear his head. What was he so worried about, anyway? Robbie Jo was an angel. Her sins couldn't be anything worse than fidgeting in church, or fibbing to her mama about who ate the last cookie in the jar. This would be easy. Then she'd be his forever.

But still, his heart was fluttering like a hummingbird caught in a spider's web. His hand was shaking as he raised the first saltine to his mouth.

It hit him like a freight train. His ears filled with insane shrieking. His eyes with blinding white light. And there, in the center of the light, was Robbie Jo, his angel.

But why was she covered in blood?

Simon plunged into the black, tarry waters of Robbie Jo's sins. They filled his eyes and his ears. Poured into his mouth, his nose, down his throat, into his soul. Simon was drowning. He sank like a stone as the horrorshow began.

Robbie Jo, seven years old, grinning as she carves up a screaming, twitching squirrel. Robbie Jo, a little older now, sitting on her father's head as he slowly drowns.

Robbie Jo *(no, that couldn't be her)* shoving Miss Hazel Lyndon between her bony shoulder blades, sending her plunging down the stairs.

Robbie Jo with Sam, on top of Sam, under Sam, in every position imaginable *(no no no no no)*

Robbie Jo lying-- Stealing--

Robbie Jo naked, plunging a hunting knife into Joe Reechur over and over again until he looks like a splat of strawberry jam on a dirty kitchen floor—Robbie Jo laughing, howling, crying out in orgasmic rapture as Joe's blood sprays into her face, licking it from her lips, rubbing it into her breasts in a hellish sexual frenzy—

And it was that moment, that exact moment in time, that Simon McCray's mind shattered into a thousand razored, glittering shards.

It seemed to go all right at first. Simon was munching away on a saltine, eyes rolled back, as he entered the Sin Zone, as Robbie Jo liked to think of it. Then things started happening really fast. Simon pitched over backwards, spine bending like he'd been electrocuted. His body convulsed, twitched, his heels drumming on the dirt floor. Spit and foam leaked from his mouth. It occurred to Robbie Jo that he was having a full-on, four-alarm seizure. She watched with interest, eyebrows raised. She hoped he wouldn't bite his tongue off. He'd become very good with it lately.

Simon went limp. It was like somebody had pulled the plug on him, hit his off switch. His head rolled to one side, and then he was perfectly still. A thin line of drool slipped between his lips. His eyes were half open. He didn't twitch. He didn't even breathe.

"Shit," Robbie Jo murmured. She knelt down beside Simon and tilted his head back, preparing to start CPR.

Simon's eyes popped open. He took in a huge, whooping gasp of air, and he screamed.

Later, Robbie Jo would think that souls in Hell would sound like that, as they were boiled alive and their intestines drawn out on a spool. At the time it happened, though, all she could do was clap her hands over her ears and fall over backwards. The scream rose higher and higher; frantic, desperate, horrified, hopeless. It didn't seem like a human should be able to make a noise like that. Robbie Jo wondered if vocal cords could rip, or snap like guitar strings. The sound was hurting her ears, even though the heels of her hands were pressed tight against them.

"Simon!" she yelled, but her voice was lost like a shout across a river. Simon's eyes bulged, his hands clawed the floor. His mouth was open impossibly wide, like a snake about to swallow something bigger than its head. His face was purple. Robbie Jo wondered if a sixteen-year-old boy could die from a stroke.

His scream ended in a choking sob. Simon flipped over onto his belly, crouching like a kicked dog, crazy eyes looking at nothing. Robbie Jo reached for him. He let out a harsh, yelping cry and shoved her away. He leapt to his feet and ran, naked and howling into the night.

"Well, damn," Robbie Jo grumbled. She'd thought something interesting might come of having her sins eaten, but she didn't expect Simon to go utterly bugfuck. To her surprise, she felt a little bit bad about it.

And how else did she feel, exactly? Robbie Jo crossed her arms over her chest, closed her eyes, and examined herself for purity. *Am I innocent now? Washed clean?* She didn't feel very clean, at least on the outside. She was still slick with Simon's sweat, and dirt from the floor covered her butt and legs. *And on the inside?* She didn't feel clean, or pure, or innocent. If anything, she felt a little hollow. Like something important was missing. There was an uncomfortable emptiness in her chest and belly.

Oh well. Guess I gotta fill up on sins again.

She sighed, and slipped on her dress. Robbie Jo walked out into the night, not bothering to shut Simon's front door. She washed herself in the cold water of Two Fox Creek, and went to see her mother.

LUREEN'S EMPTY NEST; SAM LEARNS WHAT'S WHAT

L ureen Ridgemont smiled as her daughter walked in. Sure, she'd been gone a few days, but Lureen had learned long ago not to worry too much about her little girl. She could take care of herself. She was just glad to see her face. "Hi, sugar," she slurred, trying to stand without swaying.

Robbie Jo sneered at her. She went into her room without a word.

Lureen blinked back a few stinging tears, and followed her daughter.

Robbie Jo was grabbing things from her closet. A few dresses she shoved into her threadbare duffel bag; most she threw on the floor.

"Goin' somewhere, honey? Kin I fix you some biscuits first?"

Robbie Jo threw a handful of cassette tapes into the bag. "I don't want any fuckin' biscuits, mama. I'm movin' out. Sam Dunwiddie and I got married last night."

Lureen blinked. "You, uh, what did you say, baby?"

A disgusted sigh. "I. Said. I. Got. Married. To. Sam. Didja get it this time?"

"Oh," said Lureen, her alcohol-soaked heart sinking in her chest. "Oh, oh, oh. You're not in the family way, are ya, sweetheart?"

Robbie Jo barked a bitter laugh as she pulled a cardboard box out from under her bed. "Shit no, mama. I'm not an idiot like you are. I'd never let that happen." She zipped up the bag like it had offended her personally, and headed for the front door.

"Robbie Jo, wait! Cain't you stay awhile?"

Her daughter froze in the doorway, then spun around to face her. Her teeth were bared. Her eyes blazed a hatred so deep and hot that it nearly incinerated Lureen on the spot. "I could stay awhile, but I don't want to. Why should I? You're nothin' but a repulsive ol' drunk, Mama. You should be dead. What good are you? You couldn't even protect me from my own daddy."

"Robbie Jo—"

"Fuck you. Go drink yourself to death." And then she was gone. Lureen collapsed, sobbing.

Lureen Ridgemont did, in fact, drink herself to death that night. She sat on the floor and cried and poured cheap, fiery gin down her throat until she passed out, and then she choked to death on her own vomit. No one found her until three weeks had passed, and by then, of course, it was all over.

Robbie Jo hadn't even set her bag down before Sam started screaming at her. "Where the hell were you? I told you to come straight home after school, goddamit!" He was so angry he was shaking. It was the first day of the marriage, for chrissakes, and she was showing him no respect at all. Certainly not the respect a wife should have for her husband.

Robbie Jo cocked her head and eyed him coolly. She dropped her ratty duffel bag on the ground with a thud. "Chill out, Sam. What's your fuckin' problem?"

He closed the distance between them in a heartbeat. "What's my problem? I'll tell you what the problem is. I didn't know where you were. Your place is here, with me!" He grabbed her by the arms and shook her a little, just to make a point.

Robbie Jo snarled and twisted out of Sam's grip, quick as a water moccasin. "Don't you dare lay hands on me, Sam Dunwiddie. I'm not one of your dumbshit little backwoods pieces a' pussy. I won't put up with it."

Sam was on a roll, and he didn't feel like stopping. He took a step forward and thundered, "Well, I won't put up with my wife wanderin' around town all night, not tellin' me where she's goin'!"

Robbie Jo stayed right in his face. "Uh-huh. And if you weren't so fuckin' stupid, you'd see that I have a bag with me. Any numbskull fool should be able to figger out I'd been to my mama's house, packin' up my stuff. Any fool but you, that is!"

Sam's anger went flashover into rage. Before he knew it, he'd drawn his hand back to hit her.

The blow never landed. Robbie Jo coiled up and sprang at him, slamming into his chest with her forearms and knocking Sam down. The air was knocked from his chest in a whoosh, and he couldn't seem to make his lungs work for a minute there. His skull hit the hardwood and bounced. White sparks exploded behind his eyeballs.

Robbie Jo straddled him, hands holding his head down painfully by the hair. Her face was just inches from his.

"You listen close, Sam," she hissed. Her russet eyes glittered. Sam felt a little spike of fear in his gut. She banged his head on the floor, just once. "You listenin'?"

"Yeah," he said.

"Good. If you ever hit me, Sam, or if you even try to again, I'll kill you. And I don't mean that metaphorically. You understand?"

"Whut?"

She banged his head on the floor again. "Okay, you don't understand, so I'll make it plain and simple. I've killed people before. I'm not talkin' about fryin' the Plums. I'm not talkin' pussy-ass poison, Sam, I've murdered people with my own two hands. I got no problem with it. In fact, I enjoy it. Therefore, sugar, if you so much as think about hittin' me again, I'll paint the fuckin' parlor walls with your blood. I'll hang your intestines from the rafters. I'll use your bones for garden stakes, I'll eat your eyes, and I'll feed your goddam brain to a stray dog. Do you understand me now?"

She was breathing hard, lips skinned back, white teeth gleaming. Sam couldn't look away from her eyes, partly because she still had him by the hair, but mostly because he was paralyzed by what he saw in them. The truth. The cold, razored-steel glint of truth. This girl on his chest, this beautiful, vicious, unknowable creature, meant every word she said. She would kill him in a heartbeat.

Sam realized he was very afraid of her. He also realized he had a raging hard-on. "I understand," he whispered. "Oh baby, I'm sorry. I'm so sorry."

"That's better." She let go of his hair and sat on his pelvis. A slow grin spread over her face. "Well. I guess we understand each other, sugar." She reached down and rubbed him through his brushed cotton trousers.

She unzipped his fly and mounted him right there on the floor. Sam's fear remained as he thrust up into her. His fear grew as he squeezed her breasts, clutched her hips. His fear grew still more as his orgasm rushed toward him, unstoppable as a freight train.

Sam came harder than he'd ever come before in his life.

ROSE HAS A BONE TO PICK
(THE BLACK DAWG DOES TOO)

Saturday morning, two days after Robbie Jo's wedding, and things were mighty quiet around the Tanners' breakfast table. Rose was silent, picking at her food, red-rimmed eyes cast down at the table.

Naomi sighed. She knew about Robbie Jo's wedding, of course. Everyone did. The news had whipped through Possum Kingdom like a summer wildfire. Some folks were shocked, others horrified. A few cock-eyed optimists were delighted, but they were pretty rare. Effie Granger was going around saying that Sam's parents must be spinning in their graves, until Naomi rudely pointed out that they'd been cremated.

Not that she approved of the marriage. Naomi thought it was pretty foolish of the Ridgemont girl to have done such a thing, but at the moment, her concern was all for Rose. The poor little thing had spent most of the past two nights crying. She hadn't eaten enough to keep a muskrat alive.

Naomi understood how it was. She had been a young girl once. She vividly recalled the powerful friendships forged between teenage girls; intense, immediate, passionate as love affairs. So much intimacy, maybe more than a girl would ever have again in her life. So much potential for hurt. She glanced at Owen, who was smiling ruefully back at her. Naomi squeezed his hand.

"Rose, honey," Naomi said gently, "you need to eat somethin'. You're gonna waste away."

Rose raised her head and gave a strained smile. "Sorry, Naomi. Everything's delicious, as always. It's just..." Her voice trailed off, and her face contorted.

"I know, sweetheart. Robbie Jo marryin' Sam was a big shock to ever'one. I'm sure it was much worse for you. But don't worry about that girl too much. I think she'll do just fine." Naomi patted Rose's hand.

Tears spilled down Rose's cheeks, but her eyes were hot and fierce. "She won't do just fine! She's just married the biggest ass—the biggest jerk on the planet. She threw her life away, just like that."

"Oh, honey..." Naomi didn't really know what to say to that, because she thought it was pretty much true. There was a soft knock on the kitchen door. Owen got up and opened it.

"Hi, Mr. Tanner. Is Rose in?" Robbie Jo's voice, light and happy.

"Sure is. C'mon in." Owen shot a look at Naomi as he opened the door wide.

"Hi, Miz Tanner. Hey, Rosie. Can you come for a walk with me?" Robbie Jo was all sunshine, in faded overalls and a denim jacket with a smile-face flower patch on the shoulder.

"I have to work," Rose muttered.

"Nonsense. You go for a walk with your friend, honey. I'll call Doc Yeats for ya, and let him know you'll be a little late. Run along, now." Naomi smiled at Rose. Was that a dirty look the girl shot back? Well, almost. Naomi swallowed back a chortle. A little piss and vinegar never hurt anybody's disposition, and it was important that the girls talk to each other now, before the hurt grew into something unfixable.

"Thank you," said Rose, as she got up from the table. Without another word, she walked out the door.

"Bye!" chirped Robbie Jo to Owen and Naomi, and followed Rose through the back yard and into the woods.

The Girls started to follow. "Go home!" Rose barked. The dogs slunk back to the kitchen to beg for leftovers; all but Onyx, who slipped after her mistress like a shadow.

"Poor little Rose," said Owen, as he took Naomi into his arms for a big, long hug. "Guess it's hard to be a girl sometimes."

"That's the truth, my love." Naomi burrowed her face into the warmth of her husband's neck.

Rose stomped through the woods, looking straight ahead. If Robbie Jo felt her friend's steam-pressurized anger, she didn't show it. She was chattering away, pointing out birds, squirrels, flaming autumn leaves. "Look at that fat ol' muskrat, Rosie," she crowed. "He's as big as a basketball."

The pressure reached critical mass, and the valves blew out. Rose whirled on Robbie Jo. "Why?" she screamed. "Why did you do such a goddam stupid fucking thing?"

The muskrat bolted into the woods like someone had set his little tail on fire. Robbie Jo watched him go. "Rose, it isn't like that. I—"

"You're so smart, Robbie Jo, and you just threw your life away! Why? Are you fucking pregnant?" The tears had started up again, and Rose fisted them angrily away.

"No, of course I'm not—"

"But you will be. You're gonna have a houseful of Sam's babies, and you're gonna get fat and stupid and slow, and you're gonna spend the rest of your life rotting here in Possum Kingdom, aren't you. With Sam Dunwiddie. You gave up your dreams for a stupid, narcissistic asshole who's about as deep as a rainpuddle! You—"

Robbie Jo clapped her hand over Rose's mouth. "Hush, now. It just isn't like that, Rosie. I ain't pregnant, and I don't aim to ever get that way. I married Sam because he can help me. He's gonna put me through college, did you know that?" She cautiously took her hand from Rose's mouth.

"You could have gotten a scholarship," Rose muttered sullenly. "You're smart enough. At least I thought you were."

Robbie Jo laughed. "Let's not get snotty, now. I know why you're mad, sugar. It's because I didn't tell you."

An arrow of pain as Robbie Jo touched the sore spot. "No, it's—yeah. That's part of it. I thought we were friends, Robbie Jo. I thought you trusted me."

Robbie Jo put her arms around Rose and held her close. She tried to pull back, but Robbie Jo's arms were strong. "I'm your friend, Rose," she whispered. "And you're mine. You're my best friend in the whole world. I trust you like I've never trusted anyone before in my life. I just didn't tell you because…well, because I knew you'd try to talk me out of it."

Rose gave in and rested her head on Robbie Jo's shoulder. "Damn straight I would have. You don't need him, Robbie Jo. You've got so much going for you."

"I know I do, Rosie. I've got no false modesty. But I've lived my whole life poor. So far below the poverty line I can't even see the goddam thing. Do you know what it's like to go to school in a dress made of a feed sack, Rose? Do you know what it's like to eat nothin' but fried dough for two weeks, because it's all there is to eat?"

"No," Rose whispered.

"You don't know what it does to a person, Rose. It makes you…anyway. Sam's gonna give me a good life. I won't want for anythin', ever again. And he may be a jackass, but he does love me. He'd never do a thing to hurt me, I know that for a fact."

"Good." A tear slipped from Rose's cheek onto Robbie Jo's neck.

Robbie Jo pulled her closer. "I'm so sorry I hurt you, Rosie. You mean more to me than anythin' in the world. More than Sam ever will."

"That isn't right." A weak protest into Robbie Jo's sweet-smelling hair.

"Maybe not, but it's the way I feel. Do you forgive me, Rose?"

Rose sighed. It still stung, but the scalding anger and the worst of the pain was fading. "Of course I do. I love you, Robbie Jo."

"I love you, Rosie. Nothin' on earth could ever change that."

The girls held each other tight, and tighter still. Rose listened to the sound of her best friend's heart, and took comfort.

Onyx, the black dog, watched her mistress and the red girl from the shadows of the woods. She didn't know why she felt compelled to hide, or why she had disobeyed her special person. She loved Rose, the one who had saved her, who had loved her and her pups. She loved the red girl, too. But she feared her. She was more afraid of the red girl than of bears, or thunder, or the black, roaring monster that had run her down so long ago.

When the red girl was with Rose, Onyx feared for her mistress. Her mistress didn't seem to recognize that the red girl was a predator, smarter and more vicious than anything in the woods.

Onyx would defend her. The red girl seemed to love her mistress, but if that ever changed, if she should ever decide to sink her metal fang into Rose, Onyx would kill her. She would rip out the red girl's throat, or die trying.

RESURECSHUN; REVELATION

The morning had ripened to afternoon. The sky was clear blue, but a biting breeze rustled the flame-painted leaves and lifted Robbie Jo's hair around her face. She pushed it back; she was trying to read.

Robbie Jo sat at the base of Helena O'Riley's angelic gravestone, reading the Resurecshun spell. She could hear the singing from the services at the Holy Blood, just a few hundred feet away. But thick October fog swirled between the monuments, wrapped her in damp gossamer, hid the church from her view. She couldn't see it at all—it was as if the singing came from the fog itself, or the residents of the cemetery. And no one from the Holy Blood could see her. *I could do anything out here*, she mused, *and no one would know it*. That put a little smile on her face,

Robbie giggled at the list of ingredients needed to raise the dead. The skin of a rat. Graveyard dust. Seven drops of blood. The finger bones of a suicide. *Kind of clichéd*, she thought, *but fun*. It was going to be plenty of work to get it all, though. *May as well get started.*

She took the shovel from the ground beside her, and ambled over to Justin Raffkin's grave, born 1951, died 1989. According to his wife, Justin had fallen down the stairs and hit his head, but it was common knowledge that what had hit Justin's head was the slug of a '44, held in his own right hand.

Full dark. Outside the cemetery gates, Simon McCray kneeled on the unmarked grave of Reverend Meshach Reddingale, hands clasped in prayer. He was still mostly naked, but he had stolen a sheet from Wanda DuFree's clothesline, and wrapped it around his body like a shroud. He had been sitting on the reverend's grave for nearly three hours.

A line of drool, silver in the moonlight, ran from his lips to the grass between his knees. His fingers were blue from the cold, his knuckles white as bone. Simon was waiting.

At last, it happened. A voice began to whisper into his brain. A voice began to tell him what he must do next.

"Yes," Simon whispered through numb, cold lips. "Yes, it will be done. Thy will be done."

Midnight, six days before Halloween. Robbie Jo had all her ingredients. She had thought about waiting until Halloween itself, or at least All Hallows Eve, but the moon was full tonight. It was a special moon; orange as a pumpkin, bright as a cat's eye, round and ripe and ready to burst. A moon for witchcraft.

Robbie Jo knelt on Meshach Reddingale's grave. Thick candles surrounded her; a ring of flickering light. She took a paper-wrapped something from her pocket, and placed it on the grass. She began, very softly, to sing.

"Come back to me, come back to me. From dust to flesh. From dust to flesh."

She unwrapped her little package; revealed the ratskin, folded around the dirt and her blood and Justin Raffkin's finger bones, sealed with a spiderweb, sprinkled with powdered grave beetle. Robbie Jo dug a little hole and buried the gray, furry bundle.

"Meshach Reddingale, I call upon you. Awaken from your sleep. Arise, Meshach, arise." She was feeling dumber by the minute.

The incantation continued, written in tiny, scratchy letters on the parchment. "Life to death. Death to dust. Dust to life. Life to life. Life to death. Death to dust. Dust to life. Life to life…"

Nothing was happening. *Of course nothin's happenin', you dumbass. This ain't a Stephen King novel, and you ain't Buffy the Vampire Slayer.* But she finished the spell anyway, just because.

"Life to death! Death to dust! Dust to life! Life to life! ARISE! ARISE! ARISE!" She put a dramatic tremble into her voice, just like the Satanists in that old Christopher Lee movie. She threw her hands over her head, and laughed at herself.

The ground in front of her rippled, and exploded. Robbie Jo shrieked and jumped back, right over the candles behind her. She fell on her butt and stared into the circle, ready for a miracle.

But it wasn't the reverend's dirt-streaked zombie hand that blew out of the earth. It was the package she had placed there. The ratskin was split wide open, bones scattered around like spilled popcorn.

Robbie Jo snorted. "Well, that was fuckin' impressive. I coulda done the same thing with a cherry bomb." She sighed, and turned to walk away.

"What place is this?" whispered a voice, dry as the falling leaves.

Robbie Jo's heart kickstarted. *Hot damn, it worked!* Was Meshach Reddingale really there? Was he a strong young man, Reenie Rackham and Hazel Lyndon's handsome lover? Or was he a zombie, all leering teeth and wormy flesh and gravestench? Either possibility was utterly exciting.

She squinted into the darkness and the fog. The branches of the big old oak cast twisted shadows in the candlelight. Where was he? Behind the tree? "Meshach Reddingale? Is that you?" She couldn't keep the grin off her face.

"Yes. It is. Who are you?"

"Just a minute, rev'rend. I'll tell you who I am when you tell me where you are." *No goddam brain-eatin' zombie's gonna sneak up on this girl.*

"I—I seem to be in the branches of this tree."

He didn't sound much like a zombie. "Well, how the hell didja get up there? Show yourself," Robbie Jo hollered up.

The branches rustled. Robbie Jo's hand went to the big hunting knife she had taped to her leg, just in case. Something was moving down a thick, gnarled branch. Hunched. Eyes glittering. Too small to be human.

A long white face with eyes like wet, black stones stared down at her. A stringer of drool dangled from the thing's gaping, toothy mouth.

"Where are ya, rev'rend?" Robbie Jo called. "All's I see is a big ol' ugly possum."

"A possum? Where?" said the possum, looking around.

Robbie Jo started to laugh. "What's so funny?" asked the possum. She laughed harder and harder, until she fell to the grass and rolled around helplessly.

"You're a strange young lady," said the possum. Robbie Jo nearly peed her panties.

When she could breathe again, she sat up, holding her aching sides. "I'm strange? You've been reincarnated as a Virginia Opossum, rev'rend. I'd say that's a little more than strange. That falls under the 'pretty fuckin' bizarre' category."

"There's no need for that kind of language," huffed the possum, sending Robbie Jo into hysterics again. "I'm not an opossum. You're trying to trick me."

"Oh yeah? Take a look at your hands, then." The possum glared, then held its stubby paw in front of its eyes.

"My hand—what's wrong with it?" The possum's tail lashed. It drooled fountains in its agitation.

"Not a goddam thing, if you're a possum, which you are. Look at your tail!" The creature tried to look over its shoulder, which was impossible, because everyone knows possums have no necks and bodies like little whiskey barrels. Robbie Jo suffered another spasm of wild laughter.

"Stop laughing! I'm not a possum. Where's Reenie? I want to talk to her!"

"Well, you better hurry, 'cause she's so old she's got one foot and both titties in the grave, Rev'rend Possum." Robbie Jo's stomach was on fire, but she couldn't stop the giggles.

"You must help me, girl! Take me to Reenie! Now!" The possum sounded like a man who was used to being obeyed.

"I don't take orders from marsupials," said Robbie Jo. "Now shut the fuck up before I call a huntin' dawg to eat your possum ass." She turned to walk away.

"I AM NOT A POSSUM!" the possum roared.

"Oh yeah?" Robbie Jo walked slowly up to the base of the tree. "BOO!" she screamed.

The possum's body tightened. Its face contorted in a cyanide grimace. It pitched off the branch and landed in the spongy grass, stiff as a board, black legs and weird little pink people-paws extended in mock death.

"Ow, ow, ow," Robbie Jo groaned as she laughed and clutched her aching sides. "If you're not one, how come you're playin' possum, preacherman?" Giggling, limping, she walked into the blackness of the woods.

SIMON SAVES THE SINNERS

Effie Granger knew she was in trouble when she woke to find herself tied hand and foot to her bedframe, with a row of Hostess cupcakes perched on her quivering belly.

"What's goin' on," she tried to scream, but there was something stuffed in her mouth. A pair of her own pantyhose, she guessed, by the silky texture on her tongue. *Oh sweet Jesus. I've been captured by a killer rapist pervert.* Effie started to cry.

"Hush, now," said a quiet young voice. Her head whipped back and forth, trying to get a look at her attacker. A skinny blond boy, no more than a child, stood by her bed. He was wrapped in a muddy bedsheet. He had leaves and sticks in his wild, matted hair. And his eyes—

He's crazy. Boy's completely, totally crazy. Her hammering heart turned cold.

"Don't be afraid," said the boy, with a smile that could frighten a grown man. "I'm just here to eat your sins."

The sineater! She'd never actually laid eyes on him, but everyone knew he was there. *But I'm not dead! Am I?* She shook her head wildly, no, no, no.

"Oh, don't worry. It won't hurt you any. I can't say as much for what'll happen after, but I'll make it quick." He grinned. His eyes shone like lanterns. Effie squealed.

"Hush now, hush now." He stroked her sweaty forehead. "You'll go straight to heaven, you know. Your soul'll be as clean as a baby's. I know this ain't the way we used to do things, but I have in on good authority that it's the best way. 'Kay?" He patted her cheek.

"Mmm-mmm! Mmm-mmm" Effie screamed.

Simon folded his hands in prayer for a moment. Then he took a cupcake, peeled off the frosted top with the white wavy lines on it, and popped it in his mouth.

Simon awoke from a blackout a few minutes later, Effie Granger's greasy, venial sins coating the inside of his mouth. He wiped his lips with the back of his hand and stared at the dark stain left there? Blood? No, not yet, just chocolate.

Effie stared at him, eyes rolling like a spooked horse's. He smiled at her and went to the kitchen for a knife.

Killing a person was harder than Simon had guessed. First he tried to stab Effie in the chest, but the knife bounced off of her breastbone, making her squeal like a spring lamb. That made Simon feel bad. He didn't want to hurt anyone. He cut her throat instead.

There was a huge amount of blood. He couldn't have guessed how high it could spray. It gushed from Effie's throat in a pulsing red fountain. Simon watched, entranced. It was so red, so perfectly, beautifully red.

After Effie's wound stopped spurting, Simon went to investigate the fluttering noise in the next room. Beneath a velvet drape he found a cage, with a furious-looking bird inside.

The parakeet screamed and bit Simon as he wrapped it in electrical tape. He laid the bird carefully on its back, and lined up birdseed on its tiny, outraged body. The sins of a bird were interesting: spicy, alien, light as cotton candy. He was unable to interpret them, but he ate every morsel before he nailed the bird to the floor of its cage with a turkey-lacing needle.

THE DOGGIE DOC'S QUESTION; PRIMUS FRETS A BIT

*M*ichael and Rose lay on his bed in a tangle of arms and legs. Rose took a deep, shuddering breath and kissed Michael's shoulder. He rubbed his cheek on the top of her head. "I love you," he whispered.

"I love you too." It was so easy to say. And it was true.

It had started out as dinner; Michael and Rose had made the beef stew and cornbread together, laughing and joking, tossing far too many tidbits to Onyx and the Girls. The stew was finished, the cornbread cooling on the counter, when Michael took Rose in his arms and kissed her. And she had wanted him. Something ignited in her, and she had kissed him back with a ferocity she'd never felt before.

Then they were mostly naked, touching, kissing, rolling around the bed. *It's going to happen*, Rose had thought. And she wanted it to. But when she felt Michael's hardness pressing against her inner thigh, she'd had a flare of panic. Not that she said anything, or cried out, but he must have seen it in her eyes.

Michael had rolled off of her, still close, still holding her. He'd slipped his hand into her panties, and whispering sweet things which she only half remembered, he'd made her come. Her first orgasm, ever.

He hadn't asked for anything in return. She knew he wouldn't.

"What can I do for you?" Rose whispered.

Michael rolled over onto his side, brushed the hair from Rose's eyes. "Marry me," he said.

Rose's heart flopped, then started pounding. She sat up. "I, uh, Michael, I…"

He took her face in his hands. "You've gone white as a sheet, Rose. I'm sorry. I didn't mean—"

"No, no, it's fine. I mean, thank you for asking." *Stupid, stupid, stupid.* She shook her head, as if to clear it.

"Oh, God. I didn't mean to upset you. I don't want to put you under pressure. I just want to be with you." She looked at his face, at his stricken eyes, at his forced, sad little smile. *I should say yes,* she thought.

"I know, Michael. I want to be with you, too. I just—I need some time to think about it. Okay?" Tears stung her eyes. She kissed his hand.

"Okay. Take all the time you need."

She got up, started dressing. "Do you have to go now?" Michael asked. "We haven't even eaten yet."

Rose felt more like a jerk every moment. "Um, yes, I think I do. I have to go home and think. Save me some cornbread, okay? I'll come see you tomorrow."

"I'll do that," he smiled. The hurt in his eyes made her want crawl into a hole and die.

"I love you, Michael. I do." She kissed him on the lips, hard, and hurried out before he could say another word.

Rose walked home, deep in thought, tears slipping silently down her cheeks. The girls were unusually close behind her, their moongold eyes round and worried.

Reverend Primus Reylark strolled down the darkened Main Street, his purchases from the Tanners' store in a big, threadbare croker sack. The streetlights swirled with mist. It was early evening, but the streets were quiet. Jack-o-lanterns leered from porches and windows. Somewhere, a coyote yipped at the near-full moon.

Rose Heron and her pack of dogs appeared in the pool of light ahead of him. The girl was looking down. Were there tears on her face?

Primus took a moment to look her over. The girl had changed since she first came to Possum Kingdom. Most of the fear was gone from her eyes. She carried herself tall now, not like a hunted thing. Possum Kingdom had been good to her. Hadn't the town gifted her with her courtiers, the black dogs?

Primus wasn't exactly sure what to think of those dogs. He didn't think they were devil-spawn, like some of the folks in town seemed to. That was just plain ignorant. There was nothing evil about the Girls. He could see the goodness shining from their eyes, the innocence of their simple souls. They were just a bunch of sweet-natured pup-dawgs, who had the strange habit of following Rose Heron everywhere.

They were supernatural, of that Primus had no doubt. The unseen world was as real to him as the sidewalk beneath his boots. For some reason, these witchy dogs had been born into Possum Kingdom, and bonded with Rose. For some reason, their happy, sunshine-colored auras blended with Rose's own when they were together, as if they were all parts of one creature.

The dogs. The girl. The paintings on the walls of the Holy Blood. What did it all mean? Primus grinned; he had absolutely no idea. He was looking forward to finding out, though.

For some reason, Robbie Jo Ridgemont's smiling face flashed into his mind, and he frowned.

Rose almost bumped into him. "Oh!" she cried. "Good evening, Reverend Reylark. I didn't see you there."

"My fault," he smiled. "I was lost in thought. Evenin', Miss Rose Heron. How are you tonight?"

"Just fine, thank you." She was lying, of course. Something weighed heavily on her mind; Primus could see it in her face.

He took her little hand in his own, much to her surprise. "Miss Rose, if there's ever anythin' you'd like to talk about, you know you can come to me, don't you?"

"I—well, I, um, thank you, Reverend." She was blushing. "I'm sorry I haven't been back to church—"

"That doesn't matter a whit to me. The Holy Blood's not for everyone, that's for sure. I was put on Earth to help folks, not make sure they listen to my sermons ev'ry week. Okay?"

"Okay." Her smile was real this time.

"Excuse me now, Miss Rose. I've got to get this food back to my wife before she gets mad and makes me cook the supper. That would be a sorry thang indeed."

She laughed a little. "Goodnight, Reverend Primus."

"Goodnight, Miss Rose Heron."

He watched them go, the girl and her escorts. He wondered if he were missing something important; something he wouldn't fully understand until it was too late.

ROSE IN THE PRESSURE COOKER; ROBBIE JO IN THE OVEN

*J*ust a little while later. Rose sitting across the table from Naomi, a steaming mug of hard apple cider in her hands. Owen had taken a broad hint from Naomi and gone upstairs to read.

"He wants me to marry him!" Rose wailed, unwanted tears spilling over yet again. "What am I gonna do?"

"You don't like the idea, honey?" asked Naomi gently.

"But I do! I love Michael. I love him so much." She sniffed, looked down into her cup.

"Say yes, then."

"Naomi, I'm eighteen years old! My life's just beginning! How am I s'posed to know who I should spend it with? Besides, I just gave Robbie Jo all kindsa crap for marrying Sam, and now here I am, thinking about…" Her face crumpled.

Naomi stroked her hair. "Michael Yeats isn't the same kind of man as Sam Dunwiddie, honey. They shouldn't even be called the same species."

Rose nodded. "I know. He's such a good man. Too good for me."

"Oh, Rose, you're such a wonderful girl! Whatever would make you say a thing like that?"

"I—There are things in my past—Naomi, I'm really screwed up." Rose bit her lip.

Naomi's heart ached for the child. She knew Rose hadn't told her the truth about her family. She'd known for a long time. But she figured that Rose would tell her the real story when she was good and ready. "We've all got somethin' in our past that we'd rather forget, honey. Ever'body makes mistakes.

Bad things happen to people who don't deserve 'em. That doesn't make you a bad person."

Rose heaved an enormous sigh. "I lied to you, Naomi. You gave me food and love and a place to live, and I lied to you. I'm not taking a year off before college. I ran away from home. My mama's been dead for years and my dad—well, he used to, uh, used to hurt me. So I ran. I'm sorry. I'm so sorry." She started to sob.

Naomi got up and took the girl in her arms. "I don't blame you for not tellin' me. You didn't know us from Adam's off-ox. But honey, none of what happened to you was your fault. You're as good a person as they come. If you and Michael should decide to get married, well, I think you'd be equally yoked."

"Really?" Barely a whisper.

"Of course. You've got enough love in you to keep a happy marriage for a hundred years. Enough love for a dozen babies." Naomi kissed Rose on the top of the head.

"Babies...oh my God, Naomi, I'm not ready for babies. I'm not ready for any of this." Her tear-streaked face looked so young.

"You can say no, sugar."

"But it'll hurt him so much! And what if I say no, and he was really the one? What if I say no, and I never find anyone who'll love me that much again? Naomi, please, you have to tell me what to do!" There was panic in Rose's wide green eyes.

Naomi rocked the girl gently back and forth. "I can't do that, baby. No one can do that but you. But I can tell you this much. There are two parts to pickin' a husband. The first is whether or not he's a stand-up man. Can he provide for you? Will he be there for you and your kids? You already got that one answered, Rose. Michael's strong, responsible, and so very kind. He's got all the fixin's to be a first-class partner. And then there's the second part."

"What's that?" asked Rose, cheek resting on Naomi's chest.

"Love, of course, you silly thang. You gotta love him more than anythin' else in the world. You gotta love him enough to get through whatever horrors and hardships fate is gonna throw at you. And you gotta be sure that he loves you that much, too."

"But how will I know," in a tiny voice.

"Just think on it for a few days. Pray, if you can. If you're s'posed to be with Michael Yeats, your heart will tell you so."

Rose looked up at her. "Did you know right away with Owen?"

Naomi grinned. "From the moment I saw the fool. But you got better judgment than I do. You think hard on it, and I know you'll make the right decision."

"How am I gonna do this?" Rose sat back down miserably, took a deep drink of her cider.

"You're gonna do it like you do ever'thin', Rose Heron. With intelligence and honor." Naomi kissed the girl's fragrant hair.

"I love you, Naomi."

"I love you too, child."

Rose spent the night thinking, agonizing, crying, dreaming. Robbie Jo spent the night making love with her new husband in the retort of the Sweet Hereafter's crematorium.

The whole thing seemed to rattle Sam a bit. He kept glancing at the gas jets nervously, as if he thought they'd roar to life on their own, roasting him and Robbie Jo like a couple of scrawny, sweaty turkeys in a superheated pizza oven. In fact, watching him squirm was almost more fun than the thrill of fucking in an incineration chamber.

It was too uncomfortable to sleep in there, of course, so after washing the ashes from their sticky hides in a long, hot shower, they eventually snuggled up in Sam's big bed. As she rubbed her bare skin against expensive satin, nestled her cheek on a fine feather pillow, Robbie Jo knew that she would never live in poverty again in her life. No matter what.

THE POSSUM'S PLAN; SIMON'S SIGNATURE (CUPCAKES, BIRDSEED, AND BLOOD)

Robbie Jo left Sam still sleeping and headed off for school in the morning. The fog hadn't burned off yet, and it swirled between the trees, ghost dogs chasing their tails around and around.

Instead of taking Main Street, Robbie Jo left through the back entrance of the Sweet Hereafter and walked through the woods toward school. Sometimes she did that. Sometimes she did it because she wanted time to think. Sometimes because she was in a bad mood and wanted to be alone for a little while. And sometimes, like today, she did it just for fun. Slipping through the woods made her feel like something feral, a sleek, light-footed predator among the sheep. And wasn't that what she was?

Robbie Jo was deep in her own head, so she jumped out of her skin when a voice called out to her from the shadows.

"Robbie Jo Ridgemont! I must speak with you!"

"Who's there?" she asked, although she had a fairly good idea. It was a pleasant voice calling her name; deep and rich, sincere, a little velvety, a little sexy. A preacher's voice.

The big possum who called itself Reverend Meshach Reddingale emerged from behind a tree with a self-important waddle. It stared up at her with unblinking, wet black eyes. Its fur stuck out all over its body, unkempt and wild.

Robbie Jo laughed. "I thought it was you. What the hell do you want, possum? And how did you know my name?"

"I dreamed of you," said the possum. "My dreams told me it was you who brought me back from death. Thank you."

"Well, that's awfully generous of ya, considerin' the fact that I turned you into a goddam possum instead of a human bein'. You're obviously suckin' up to me. As I said before, what the hell do you want?" Robbie Jo considered kicking the possum like a furry football, seeing if she could clear the big maple a dozen yards in the distance.

"I want you to place my soul into a human body," the possum said. It grinned, showing acres of sharp, pointy teeth.

"Even if I knew how to do somethin' like that, which I don't, why the fuck would I? I think you're kinda divertin' this way."

The possum clambered up on a log. It was clumsy, as if the reverend hadn't quite got the hang of controlling his new body. "You will help me, Robbie Jo, because you and I are destined to change the world together."

"Yeah, I've heard that one before. Fuck off." She started to walk.

"Wait! You *must* help me! It was foretold! I painted your picture on the wall of the Holy Blood!" Robbie Jo grinned over her shoulder.

The agitated possum stepped from foot to foot and drooled. "And the other signs are there. The black dogs who move as one. The other girl—in my dream, her name was Rose."

Robbie Jo cocked her head. "What's Rose got to do with it?"

"Two girls, their hands dipped in blood. Two girls who have taken life will give new life to the world," the possum intoned.

"Now, just wait a second." Robbie Jo squatted down next to the creature. "You're right about me. I've taken life. Several human lives, to be exact, and I got no intention of stoppin' there. I'm tellin' you this, you understand, because you're a fuckin' possum, and no one's gonna believe a damn thang a fuckin' possum has to say. But Rose, she's never killed a damn thing. She prob'ly tosses spiders out the window instead of squishin' em. She just isn't capable of hurtin' anybody."

"You'll help me, then?" The possum brightened, which didn't help its looks a whole lot.

"I didn't say that. Give me one reason why I should."

"You'll get to kill somebody."

"Well, holy mudslingin' Jesus! Why didn't you say that in the first place?" Robbie Jo patted the possum on the head, making it bare its teeth. "Who do I get to do?"

"We'll get to that when the time is right. First I must see the girl, Rose. If I can look into her eyes, I can see if there is a seed of murder in her soul. Take me to her."

"You didn't say 'please,' preacher. But I'll take you to Rosie, if you'll tell me what you were tryin' to do the night you were killed."

The possum sighed deeply. "I suppose I must. Better now than later. You see, like in the time of Noah, the people of the world have grown evil and corrupt. It became clear to me that mankind, such as it was, was not worth saving. So I fasted, and I prayed. I met with spirits light and dark. I danced until my legs gave way. I pierced my flesh with thorns. I—"

"Yeah, yeah, yeah, holy shit, get on with it!" Robbie Jo griped.

The possum glared. "A solution was revealed to me in a dream. A solution so perfect, so complete, so utterly final…it blinded me with its brilliance."

"What *was* it?" Robbie Jo asked through gritted teeth.

"It was, you see—"

A high-pitched scream, jagged with horror, ripped through the morning air. The possum stiffened and fell off the log.

Robbie Jo nudged to possum with the toe of her sneaker. It didn't twitch. "Well, sheeit," she muttered. There was another volley of screams, louder than the first. Robbie Jo trotted off through the woods to investigate, a little smile of anticipation curving her lips.

There were five girls, all members of the high school's Glee Club, standing outside Effie Granger's bedroom window. There was nothing unusual in that. There was an old hunting trail that kids who lived in the north end of Possum Kingdom used to walk to school, and it went right by Effie's house. She'd been bitching about it for years. What was unusual was the fact that they were all screaming, crying, and clutching each other. Mista Tidwell was barfing in Effie's azalea bed.

"What's goin' on?" Robbie Jo asked. No one answered. M'Lynn Carbo managed to point into Effie's window. Robbie Jo gently shouldered past the crying girls and took a look for herself.

Her first reaction was anger. Her eyes narrowed as she stared at Effie, spread-eagled and blood-drenched, a gaping, sticky wound beneath her many chins. Another killer in Possum Kingdom? The fucking nerve of it all!

This town ain't big enough for the two of us, pard'ner. When I find out who you are, I'm gonna fix your wagon. I'll mail you out of the Kingdom in little bitty boxes. I'll—

That was when she focused on the lumps on Effie's torso, squinted, and realized that they were Hostess cupcakes.

Simon.

Robbie Jo began to laugh. She covered her mouth and managed to make it sound like crying, but Robbie Jo laughed so hard she nearly wet her pants. She had to limp doubled-over around to the front of the house to avoid blowing her cover.

Robbie Jo rested her forehead against Effie's living room window, tears streaming down her face, trying to stop giggling (or at least slow down some).

That's when she saw the parakeet.

She fell to the grass, laughing like a Bedlamite.

ROSE'S CHOICE; ROBBIE JO'S WARNING; EGGS, KETCHUP, AND EVIL AURAS

The animal clinic was just out of earshot from the screams. Rose heard nothing but the pounding of her own heart as she opened the front door and walked in. Michael was behind the reception desk, glasses down his nose, papers in his hand. He looked up when Rose entered the room. His mouth opened, then shut. He licked his lips, swallowed. Hope and terror shone in his eyes.

Rose took a deep breath. "Yes," she said.

Michael let out a great whoop and vaulted the counter, taking Rose in his arms. He lifted her off the ground, spinning her around and around. "I love you, Rose," he said, kissing her. "You'll never regret this."

"I'd better not," she said, laughing. There was a thrum of fear somewhere deep in her belly, but mostly, there was overwhelming joy.

Robbie Jo didn't like to be late for school, but some things just couldn't wait. She strode through the woods to Simon McCray's pitiful little house. She had to find out what was going on in that boy's head.

He was asleep, mouth agape, blood still crusting his bedsheet shroud. Fresh needle holes in his ankles.

Robbie Jo shook him. "Wake up, you stupid shit."

Simon jerked awake, screamed. "Demon! Monster! Get away from me!"

"That's not what you said the last time I had your dick in my mouth."

Simon scuttled backwards like a crab until he hit the wall. "I didn't know. I thought you were human. I thought you were my…my angel…" he started to cry.

"Oh, shut the fuck up and listen, Simon. Ever'body knows it was you that splattered Effie. You left a line a' cupcakes on her belly, for shit's sake! You better get outta town unless you want lynched."

Simon's head rolled back and forth like an angry rattlesnake's. He bared his teeth. "I cannot leave Possum Kingdom. I've been shown what I must do. I must cleanse souls, then save them. I have no choice, demon."

It occurred to Robbie Jo that the boy was completely, irretrievably batshit. "Well, you do what you have to, but I'd move outta this house if I were you. They'll come lookin' for ya before too much longer. They want your blood, boyo. You'll be lucky if you make it to the sheriff's in Jonesborough. People are sayin' you're demon-possessed."

Simon bristled. "Me? Not me! I have holy blessings upon me! I work for the Lord!"

Robbie Jo squatted down so she was eye to eye with him. "Yeah, sure, what-the-fuck-ever. You listen close now, Simon. You can go slaughter ever'body else in the Kingdom if you want, and their little parakeets too, but you stay away from me and Rose Heron. 'Cause if you don't I'll split you from crotch to throat and strangle you with your own intestines. You understand me, boy?"

Simon blinked. "Get thee behind me, Satan."

"Yeah, I'll get behind ya and shove a red-hot poker up your ass. You stay away from Rose. Got it?"

She stared into his eyes until he blinked, grimaced. "Yeah," he mumbled.

"Good. Now git, Simon. They're gonna find ya sooner or later, but it doesn't hafta be right now. Get out." Before he could answer, Robbie Jo turned and walked away.

Damn, she thought. *I hope I didn't miss my math test.*

After school, when Robbie Jo came into the back entrance of the Sweet Hereafter, she found Sam talking with Jimmy Liggett and two other people; a tall, scrawny woman who looked an awful lot like a buzzard, and a short, gray-haired guy with coke-bottle glasses and tiny little puckered lips.

"Hi, sweetheart!" Sam called cheerfully. "C'mere a minute. I want you to meet our new embalmers, Chuck Tully and Cynthia Ragin. They'll be startin' the first week in November. This here's my beautiful bride, Robbie Jo." He beamed.

"Pleased to meetcha," said Robbie Jo, shaking their hands vigorously. The woman's long, bony hand was dry and cold. Chuck's was moist and damp as the underside of a cow pie. Cynthia's eyebrows had shot up to her fuzzy hairline, probably at Robbie Jo's age. Chuck just seemed to look perpetually baffled, like a lobotomy patient.

Robbie Jo turned to Jimmy. "Afternoon, James. How are you today?"

"Just fine, Miss Robbie Jo." As usual, he looked a little bit afraid of her. Robbie Jo liked that, because it was good to be feared. She also didn't like it, because it meant Jimmy Liggett knew, or had figured out, that she wasn't just a sweet little girl. She made a mental note to kill him, maybe.

"So why are you hirin' new people, honey?" Robbie Jo asked, after the two embalmers had left the room. "Some days you barely have enough work for ol' Jimmy."

Sam beamed, as if he had been waiting for the question. "I've started advertisin' in other towns, sugar. And I've put up a website. We'll be takin' overflow from at least three other mortuaries. I've ordered new equipment—a high-volume embalmin' machine, a brand-new scissors lift—I'm bringin' the Sweet Hereafter into the twenty-first century, baby. Your hubby's gonna be the biggest businessman in Tennessee."

"That's wonderful, sweetheart!" Robbie Jo threw her arms around Sam, thinking how pathetic, how boring he had become. Whatever had been wild in him was gone; he was just another whipped dog. Robbie Jo had never found dogs to be very interesting, and she sure as hell never wanted to fuck one.

The next afternoon, Robbie Jo and Rose had lunch at Possum Pete's café. Rose had been nervous about telling Robbie Jo of her engagement, after giving her friend such a hard time about her own wedding. But Robbie Jo didn't seem the least bit upset. If anything, she was maybe a little amused, which rankled Rose a bit. But she let it slide. She was too happy to be mad at anybody.

Robbie Jo told her all about Sam's improvements to the Sweet Hereafter. She was going into lurid detail about the embalming machine until Rose asked her to kindly stop before she yakked up her ketchup-coated omelet. Rose told Robbie Jo about Michael leaping the counter and taking her into his arms.

They talked about what Rose wanted her wedding to be like. Would she wear white? No, purple. Would she marry in a church? No, in the woods. Robbie Jo unsuccessfully tried to convince her to be wed at the Holy Blood. Wouldn't snakes make great bridal wreaths? The Girls could be her bridesmaids, in hideous foam-green dresses with puffy sleeves. They laughed themselves silly over that one. Rose did want Reverend Primus to perform the ceremony, though. There was something special about him. Robbie Jo agreed. Besides, his snake tattoos were cool.

Rose was happy. Truly happy. Possum Kingdom, strange as it was, had become her home. Robbie Jo was her best friend. Michael Yeats was her husband-to-be. Her father (she almost never thought of him anymore) was far away, and he'd probably forgotten all about her, or drunk himself to death. Rose was safe. Her life was a shimmering bubble, surrounding her with joy and delight.

She had no idea how soon it would explode in her face.

Reverend Primus Reylark was on his way to pay a call on old Harris Cowper, seventy-nine years old and housebound with the flu. It was a gorgeous day; clear but chilly. He strolled down the street, whistling "Bringing in the Sheaves." He happened to glance up at the door to Possum Pete's, and Primus Reylark nearly collapsed in his tracks.

Rose Heron and Robbie Jo Ridgemont emerged from the café, hand in hand, laughing and talking. They were still surrounded by that awful, jagged, bloody aura that arose whenever they were together. It was disturbing, of course, but Primus had grown used to it. But then Rose's pack of dogs ran up to greet them, circling the two girls' legs, grinning and wagging their tails. And when the dogs came close to Robbie Jo and Rose, well, something awful happened. The dogs' good-natured golden aura merged with the two young girls', and became a hellish tornado, surrounding them all.

Primus squinted. He had never, in all his days, seen anything like it. Angry reds, bruised purples, poison yellows, and vicious spikes of impenetrable black whipped around the giggling girls and the prancing dogs.

Something terrible was going to happen. Soon. Something awful, unnatural, irreversible. And there was nothing Primus could do to prevent it.

Of course there is, said his brain, with chilling calm. *You go home, you get your old deer rifle, and you shoot Robbie Jo Ridgemont through her evil little head.*

"No," he whispered. *I'll never do that. Never.* He just had to hope that once it had begun, whatever it was, he would have the strength to stop it.

THE POSSUM'S IMPROBABLE TALE

Robbie Jo finished saying her goodbyes to Rose. She waved at Reverend Primus, who was standing in the middle of the street like a jacklighted deer, for some reason. Then she stepped into the woods behind Pete's, where Reverend Meshach Possum had hidden himself away to watch.

"Well, you saw her," Robbie Jo said. "Harmless as the Easter Bunny, right? She'll never dip her hands in blood."

"She already has," said the possum.

"What the hell are you talkin' about?" Robbie Jo picked the animal up and glared into its furry face.

"Rose Heron's hands are already dipped in blood. She has already committed murder. I saw it as clearly as I saw your name in my mind's eye."

Robbie Jo let out a little laugh. She didn't believe the possum, but she didn't quite not believe him, either. "Well, I'll be damned," she said.

"Undoubtedly," said the possum.

"Who asked you, Rat Fink. C'mon, we have some serious talkin' to do." She clutched the possum and trotted off into the deep woods.

Robbie Jo and Meshach Reddingale sat in the pretty clearing not far from her house. Red and yellow and purple leaves rained down on them every time the breeze stirred. The possum was perched on a tree stump; Robbie Jo lay on her back on the ground, watching the sky.

"Now," she said, "Who exactly did Rose knock off?"

"I don't know that," said the possum. "I only know that she has the taint of murder on her soul."

"Mm. Now tell me what you were doin' the night you were killed, before I skin you and nail your ratty hide to the wall."

The possum bristled, bared its teeth, and spoke. "I was attempting to purify the human race, before it was too late."

"Oh? And how, exactly, were you doin' that, Adolf?"

"Who?"

"Never mind. Talk, you ugly furball."

"There's no need to be so rude, Miss Ridgemont. I was in the process of swapping the bodies and souls of humans with those of animals." He puffed up with pride.

"What the fuck does that mean?" Robbie Jo sat up, irritated.

"It means I was changing all of the people into animals, and all of the animals into people. Animal souls are pure, you see. But the magic was too strong, and I was not strong enough."

Robbie Jo yanked the possum's tail. "You're crazy. You're fulla shit, and I have half a mind to cook you up and eat you. What do you say to that?"

The possum boldly met her stare. "It's true, Robbie Jo. The process had begun. It changed every man, woman, and child in Possum Kingdom that night. It would have kept going, spreading across the world, if I hadn't had a heart attack before the spell was complete."

"You died of a heart attack?" Robbie Jo was a little disappointed. She had hoped for spontaneous combustion.

"Yes. Weak hearts run in my family. I felt a crushing pain in my chest, and I collapsed. In my weakened condition, I could not protect myself from the magic, and I began to change, into a mountain cat. Then my heart stopped. As I died, the magic ended. But you, Robbie Jo, can make it happen again. Restore me to a human body, and you and I will change the world!"

"A mountain cat? Sheeit, rev, I'd say you got demoted some." To her satisfaction, the possum grimaced.

She patted him on the head, making him drool. "Now back to this changin' shit. Are you sayin' that ever'body in the Kingdom is descended from—from animals?"

"Yes. That's exactly what I'm saying."

"So I'm—"

The possum squinted at her, as if trying to read fuzzy newsprint. "Fox on your mother's side. Rattlesnake on your father's."

Robbie Jo started to laugh. Then she remembered Reenie Rackham calling her fox girl. Snake girl. *No way.* She scowled. "I repeat, possum, you're fulla shit."

The possum grinned. His tone was soothing. "I realize it's frightening, Robbie Jo. But it's true. And you can help me finish what I started."

Rage flared in her, white and sudden. "I'm not frightened, I'm pissed off. You're wastin' my time, you goddam freak of nature."

"Not nature," intoned the possum. "Magic. Wild magic."

Robbie Jo grabbed the possum by his tail and held him up like a fishing trophy. "Ow!" Meshach screamed.

"Listen up, you. I'm gonna go check out your story right now. And when I find out that you're lyin' through your fifty fuckin' teeth, I'm gonna come back here and gut you alive. You understand me?"

Before the possum could answer, she dropped him on the stump and stomped away.

"I'll be waiting here, Robbie Jo Ridgemont," the possum called after her. "I'll be waiting here, because you will discover I speak the truth!"

THE ROOT WOMAN'S REVELATION
(ROBBIE JO SEES IT ALL)

R eenie Rackham was doing her laundry in the washtub in the front of her house when Robbie Jo the fox girl burst out of the woods like a rabid wolverine. Reenie briefly considered running, but that was ridiculous, of course, because she was older than dirt and the fox girl was a young, vicious predator. Reenie stood her ground, a dripping skirt in her hands.

The fox girl already had her knife out. "Talk to me, old woman. Tell me a story. An ugly fuckin' possum who used to be your boyfriend just told me a tall tale about all the critters in Possum Kingdom becomin' people, and vice-versa. You got any idea what I'm talkin' about?"

Reenie couldn't seem to get enough air in her lungs. *Meshach? Alive? How else would the fox girl know?* The world shrank down to a pinpoint, and black rushed in to smother her.

Cursing under her breath, Robbie Jo dragged the old woman into her house. She hauled her into her bedroom (surprisingly pretty, with lace curtains and prints of wildflowers on the walls) and dumped her on her bed. She took a handful of water from the washbowl on the dresser and splashed it into Reenie's face. The old woman gasped, her eyes flew open.

"You gonna live, you old prune?" Robbie Jo asked.

"Unless you kill me," Reenie grunted. Robbie Jo had to laugh at that. Reenie sat up on her bed. "What did you do, girl? Did you bring Meshach back from the dead?"

"I sure as hell did, honey. But I'm not sure you want him anymore." Robbie Jo started to giggle. "He seems to be stuck in the body of an o-possum."

Reenie blinked, then did something Robbie Jo hadn't expected. She giggled, too. "Well, it's no less than the ol' bastid deserves."

Robbie Jo raised an eyebrow. She was finding it hard not to like the old lady. She put her knife up to the rootwoman's throat, just to keep herself from getting too sentimental. "Do you think you can tell me what I need to know without fallin' on your ass this time?"

"I can if you take that blasted knife outta my face, girlie." Robbie Jo lowered it.

Reenie breathed in, deep and long. She had vowed never to speak of what she had seen that night, so very, very long ago. But Robbie Jo had dug it all up again, in more ways than one. What would happen now was up to fate, up the Lord above.

"I dunno what Meshach tole you, but he got it into his haid that people, such as they were, weren't worth savin'. The only way to keep 'em outta hell was to give 'em fresh, new souls. Animal souls."

"Yeah, he told me all that crap. What really happened?"

Reenie's eyes glittered. "It was workin,' Robbie Jo. All over the Kingdom, people were changed. He'd put me an' Hazel in a circle a' fire, so's it didn't get us. But you could hear the howls all aroun', like the end of the world. Then Meshach, he grabbed his chest an' went down, an' his body started changin'—" She swallowed hard, as if the memory were choking her. "It stopped, then. But it had done its job. Ever'body in the Kingdom was changed. 'Cept me an' Hazel, an' Mary Lou Crispin, who was caught in the middle when Meshach died."

"Caught in the middle?"

"Yep. She was jus' a little girl when it happened. The critter that was turnin' into her—a possum—well, it died. Poor lil' ol' Mary Lou was astartin' to become a possum when the magic stopped, but somehow, she survived it."

"Oh, c'mon now—" Reenie shot Robbie Jo a poisonous look. The girl shut up.

"What happened to Mary Lou, well, a good chunk of it was my fault. An' she was so afraid, poor thang. Her mind, y'see, it wasn't all animal, but it wasn't all people, either."

"What about her soul? Was it human or animal?"

"Who knows? Maybe both. Anyhow, I took care of her. I set her up in a lil' empty house, an' I brought her food ever' day, 'til she was big enough to go fetch it for herself. I kep' her away from ever'body. Even after they wasn't crazy anymore, the folks of Possum Kingdom prob'ly woulda killed her, lookin' the way she did an' all."

Robbie Jo shook her head, smiling. "Uh-huh. So what happened to her?"

"You ever hear of Possum Woman?"

"Shit yeah, every kid hears that ol' story. You ain't sayin'—"

"That's zackly what I'm sayin'. Mary Lou, that's Possum Woman. That stuff about her eatin' babies an' such, that ain't true. She'd never hurt a soul, if you ain't a muskrat, that is. But she's real. She's out in these woods right now."

Reenie stood up, walked stiffly to her dresser and leaned on it, as if for support.

Robbie Jo shook her head and grimaced. "Okay. And what happened in town, after ever'body was suddenly swapped with critters? Life just go on as usual?"

The old woman gave a bitter little smile. "Not zackly. The new peoples had some of the memories of the folks they was s'posed to be, but they also had animal thoughts. The animal thoughts was stronger than the people thoughts, for awhile there. Blood was spilled. It was madness, screamin' madness, for a time."

Robbie Jo's irritation rose. "Uh-huh, sure. So all the critters in Possum Kingdom, they got human souls?"

"Well, not anymore, I don't think. Their souls have changed to fit their bodies. But they did have. There's nothin' like seein' a deer standin' there, an' look in its eyes, an' see somebody you used to know, somebody you talked to ever' day, lookin' out at you, trapped an' petrified…" Reenie shuddered.

Robbie Jo sneered. "Okay, then. That's about enough horseshit for one day. I think I'll kill you now." She coiled and leapt at Reenie, silver fang hungry for blood.

Reenie pulled her hand out of her dresser drawer, faster than Robbie Jo would have thought possible, and threw some kind of dust in her eyes. And then she was blind. And then her legs and her arms stopped working, and Robbie Jo crumpled to the floor.

She couldn't see. She couldn't speak, or move. But she could hear. Robbie Jo could hear the old woman kneel down beside her. She could smell her; homemade soap and chamomile tea. She could feel Reenie's breath on her face. She knew she should be afraid, but instead she was boiling with rage. She blinked her sightless eyes again and again; it was all she could do.

"You don't believe me, snake girl? Well. We'll jus' give ya a look for y'self, how 'bout that?" Robbie Jo felt something wet sprinkling into her open eyeballs. Then just like that, she was somewhere else.

Main Street. Different, older, but clearly Main Street, Possum Kingdom, U.S.A. People everywhere; screaming, running in circles, biting at their clothes, at their own fingers, at anyone who came near them.

It was fairly easy to see who was who. The predators were raging. They prey were cowering, running, hiding. An enormous bear of a man lumbered down the street, roaring, bellowing in terror and fury. A skinny, rabbity man darted in front of him. The bear man struck him with one enormous fist, knocking him to the ground. Then the bear man was on him, ripping out the rabbit man's throat with newly blunted teeth. Inside her own head, Robbie Jo started to laugh.

A group of skinny teenage boys who had once been coyotes chased a slight mouse of a girl, and that wasn't lust in their eyes, it was hunger. A round muskrat man grabbed his seizing chest and died. A weasel girl bit and slashed at anything that came near her. Blood coated the lower half of her face like a highwayman's mask. A puma man sat atop a deer woman, slashing and slashing at her belly with his blunt fingers, unable to understand why her intestines wouldn't reveal themselves. He didn't even seem aware of the wolverine boy gnawing away at his lower leg.

Robbie Jo laughed and laughed. *Beautiful,* she thought. *Oh, wonderful, wondrous, beautiful.* Inside her mind, she writhed in ecstasy.

Reenie Rackham stared down at the girl on her bedroom floor. Robbie Jo's face was stretched into an unholy grin, her eyes rolled up like a rabid dog's. Drool ran from the corners of her mouth. Hair wild around her head like a halo of fire. She was laughing somewhere deep in her chest, uh-uh-uh-uh.

Reenie Rackham had never been out of Tennessee in her long life. She'd never wanted to leave. But she gathered all of her money and the few things that were precious to her in an old but sturdy carpet bag, and started walking to the highway.

She regretted leaving her house, but someone else would find it, she knew, and someone would live there and love it.

She regretted leaving Mary Lou, but the Possum Woman was old herself now, and wily in the ways of the woods. If anyone in the Kingdom would be all right, would survive whatever taste of Hell was coming, it would be her.

She regretted leaving the girl on the floor of her bedroom alive. Reenie knew she should take the knife from the girl's flaccid hand and plunge it into her chest until her poisonous heart stopped beating. But it wasn't something she could ever, ever do.

Reenie Rackham walked to the highway, and caught a ride with a long-haul trucker from North Carolina. She never saw Possum Kingdom, or Tennessee, again.

POSSUM WOMAN

Robbie Jo's sight came back before she could move. She lay paralyzed on Reenie Rackham's flowered rug, staring at the ceiling. Her heart was still pounding from the sheer, savage joy of what she'd seen.

Slowly the chill worked its way out of her limbs. She rolled over onto her belly, got to her hands and knees. *Fox girl.* She grinned.

When Robbie Jo could walk again, she searched the little house for Reenie Rackham. Evidently, the old woman had the common sense to get the hell outta Dodge.

Robbie Jo went around to the back of Reenie's house, and searched the woods until she found what she was looking for. A path, mostly overgrown, no wider than a dog trot. Robbie Jo followed it.

As she walked through the woods, Robbie Jo felt a strange lightness in her belly, lifting her, as if her feet were barely touching the ground. She sang under her breath; "Downstairs at the funeral home, by myself but I am not alone..." She was profoundly happy.

Everything had changed. The world was a very different place than she had thought it was. If people could turn into animals, if animals could turn into people, anything could happen. Absolutely anything.

"I see spirits dancin', bodies movin'..." The colors of the forest seemed brighter, details sharper. Dew drops hanging on the underside of a toadstool. The glitter of a squirrel's black eye, the fiery flash of his tail. "...good God, now the aspirator's pointin' at me! Got a call, gotta get into the wagon, a spirit in the night, to a—"

Robbie Jo's breath caught in her throat. She couldn't believe she'd never come across the house before, in her long, restless prowlings of the woods. Maybe it was because the house was outside Possum Kingdom, and the Kingdom had never let her see it before. Or maybe Reenie Rackham had cast a spell around it, a glamour, to make it invisible. But Reenie wasn't here to protect it any more.

It was a strange little house, spindly and out of place in the deep woods. Narrow at the base but two stories tall, with an attic. It must have been painted at some point long ago, but now it was silver-gray with age, ill-kept and overgrown. Windows broken, shutters hanging. The front porch had caved in, leaving a jagged-edged, yawning mouth right below the front door. *If anyone lives here, they sure as hell don't come in and out that way.* Maybe Possum Woman was dead and gone.

Robbie Jo's eyebrows shot up. She'd just spotted the strangest thing about the house. *If I'm not mistaken, there's a fuckin' tree growin' right through the middle of it.* She let out a little laugh.

Thick, twisted limbs reached out through the upper floor windows, spreading their leaves to the sun. The moss-covered roof was cracked in places, fractured, where great gnarled branches had pushed their way out like skeleton arms escaping a shallow grave.

"Well, I'll be damned," said Robbie Jo. She crept around to the side of the house and rubbed one filthy windowpane with the sleeve of her denim jacket.

It was dark in the house; a dirty, brownish dark pierced by shafts of sunlight. The only piece of furniture appeared to be a couch, legs furry with moss, cushions black with slimy mold. Tall, pale, unhealthy-looking toadstools like the eye stalks of albino slugs sprouted from the ancient fabric.

There was indeed a tree growing through the center of the house. It had gone right through the first-floor ceiling, through the second-floor ceiling, and up through the attic. The floors had long since sagged and mostly collapsed. Robbie Jo could see light from the holes in the roof, two-and-a-half stories up.

She frowned, rubbed another window pane. Trees didn't do that. Not natural trees, anyway. But Mother Nature seemed to have little power these days. The old girl had been overthrown by wilder, more savage forces, capering agents of chaos who didn't give a shit about the way things ought to be.

Robbie Jo squinted. Her eyes were adjusting to the darkness inside now. She could see the ceiling beams on the ground floor where they had fallen, the house's lath bones showing through where the plaster had fallen off like decaying flesh. She looked up at the tree, the impossible, awesome tree. It looked like some kind of oak, but not one Robbie Jo had ever seen before. The thick, rough trunk shot straight up, then exploded into muscular branches halfway to the ceiling.

The center of the house, the crotch of the tree, held a darkness so black and thick it seemed to be alive.

Holy shit. It is *alive.*

Something in the crotch of the tree was stirring. Something was creeping along one of the heavy branches. It was big; human-size, but not human-shaped. It was thick, slow. Fuzzy around the edges; was it covered with fur?

Of course it is. 'Cause it's fuckin' Possum Woman. Robbie Jo was marginally aware of the fact that she was grinning ear to ear.

The thing on the branch crept into a patch of sunlight let in through a gaping hole in the roof. It stretched, arching its back, straightening out a long pink tail as sinuous as the body of a python. It held on to the branch with long claws at the ends of pink hand-paws, but its limbs didn't bend like a possum's. They bent like a human's. The thing yawned, and its whole long, pointed head seemed to split in half, revealing an impressive array of long, jagged teeth. Canines like daggers.

The thing *(Possum Woman, you know her name, it's Possum Woman)* looked up to the hole in the roof, then cocked its head to scratch one of its big, leathery black ears. Its eyes were blue; sky blue, human eyes, sleepy from a long, satisfying nap. Possum Woman began to clean her front paws with her curling pink tongue.

Robbie Jo realized that the hairs on the back of her neck were standing up. She had never in her life seen anything as beautiful, as amazing, as Possum Woman. She shouldn't be, but there she was, by God. There she was.

"I'll never hurt you," she whispered to the monster in the tree. "You're special, you're so special..."

Possum Woman was crawling along the branch now, heading for the window. Robbie Jo silently fled into the woods before the creature could see her.

"Take care of yourself, Possum Woman," she said, as she slipped through the trees. "Stay away from the highway, you hear me?" She giggled, shook her head. "Possum Woman. God damn. Possum Woman."

THE POSSUM AND THE FOX GIRL
STRIKE A DEAL

Although hours had passed and it was nearly dark, Meshach was still waiting on the treestump. He was napping again, curled up, pink nose resting on his scaly tail.

Robbie Jo was in too fine a mood to scare him, or even push him off the stump. For the moment, she was in love with the world.

She knelt down next to the sleeping possum and stroked his fur. It was soft, like a fine fur coat. She lowered her face and breathed in his scent. To her amazement, the critter smelled good, like ripe fruit and rich earth.

He woke up with a jump, black eyes bulging in his ghost-white face. He seemed frightened to see Robbie Jo so close to him. His jaw dropped open wide, and he let out a hiss. That gave her a giggle.

"Don't worry, I'm not gonna bite ya. I know now you were tellin' the truth, Rev'rend, and I aim to help you." She patted him between the ears.

The possum grinned. "I knew you would see the light."

Robbie Jo sat down in the crunchy autumn leaves. "Okay. How do we go 'bout this?"

"There are some things which we will need," said Meshach.

"Oh, shit. I don't guess we could get 'em from the Piggly Wiggly in Jonesborough, could we?"

"No. The most important element is the body of a healthy adult male."

"A body? A dead body?"

"No. Alive."

"I see." Robbie Jo brushed a spider from her knee. "And you're gonna take over this body, like Invasion of the Body Snatchers?"

"No," said the possum. "The body—the man will be sacrificed. The magic will use his body as—as raw material, shall we say, to make me a new body."

Robbie Jo grinned. "You talkin' human sacrifice, boah? That's mighty un-Christian of ya."

"It's for the greater good, Robbie Jo. Our sacrifice's soul will go straight to heaven."

"I'm sure that'll be a mighty comfort to him. Does he have to be a young feller?"

"Any age will do, as long as he has reached his eighteenth birthday." The possum began to groom his scaly tail.

"Gotcha. So tell me, Rev, how the hell do you find out all this stuff? In some demonic fuckin' cookbook or somethin'?"

The possum sneezed angrily. "There is nothing demonic here. I communicate with the spirit world. I can speak to the dead. I can speak to Indian gods and Christian saints and—"

The possum cut himself off, his long jaw snapping shut.

"And what else, Rev? What were you gonna say? You haven't been talkin' with Ol' Scratch, now have you?" Robbie Jo whisked a finger at him.

"Of course not! I can speak with older things, that's all. The spirits that have dwelled in the Earth since long before mankind. Old ones who have slumbered for millennia, but have awakened to act as my counsel. Because they know what I can bring about." The possum glared down at Robbie Jo.

She rolled her eyes. "Okay, Mr. Lovecraft, let's not start pattin' ourselves on the back just yet. What else do we need to get started?"

"Well," said the possum, "We will need the disinterred skull of a suicide."

"Shit!" yelled Robbie Jo. "I just reburied one!"

Robbie Jo decided to put off digging up Justin Raffkin's ill used remains until last. She spent the next few days gathering up the items on Meshach's list. It was the same kind of weird shit that the resurecshun spell had demanded: A fertilized chicken egg, forty-four spiders (that took awhile), hair from the mane of a black horse, a bushel of acorns, a lizard skin, and so on, and so on. In the time it took her to locate the stuff, Simon McCray killed a tobacco farmer and his wife, a transient from Jonesborough, and the high school principal.

The F.B.I. was called. Posses of Possum Kingdom's finest citizens swept the woods, looking for the killer. State police crawled all over town. This was irritating, of course, but also pretty damn funny. Simon McCray, sineater and serial killer. Who knew the kid had it in him?

ROBBIE JO

You're prob'ly wonderin' why the bloody hell I'd wanna help the batshit Reverend Meshach Possumboy Reddingale turn ever'body in the fuckin' world into critters. Well, try this on for size: Why not?

What the hell is so great about people the way they are now? Sure, you get the occasional Mother Teresa, but you get a lot more Jeffrey Dahmers. And those are just the extremes. Mostly what you get is a whole lotta self-centered morons livin' their lives with their heads so far up their asses that they never see daylight. Folks who slink through life with their heads down and their tails between their legs, never doin' anythin' much; nothin' bad, nothin' good; hopin' that nothin' bad happens to 'em before they can retire and play golf until they croak of a coronary from eatin' one too many Big Macs. Folks with all the self-awareness of a sea sponge. Dull. Domesticated. Bored and borin'. What, I ask you, is so goddam special about that?

Not that I think that the Big Swap'll make 'em any better. I mean, all a' Possum Kingdom is just a few generations away from bein' critters, but they're just as corrupt and stupid and *common* as ever'body else on this god-forsaken planet. Rev'rend Meshach says that's 'cause they didn't have his leadership to shepherd their innocent souls to the Lord. Personally, I think he's fulla shit.

Those poor critter souls were doomed the minute they got human bodies. Y'see, if it looks like a duck, and it walks like a duck, and it quacks like a duck, pretty soon it's gonna turn into a fuckin' duck.

And what about the animals in the Kingdom? The ones who started out with human souls? Are they more greedy than reg'lar critters? More violent? More selfish? Who the hell knows, I don't speak Muskrat. But since they haven't been buildin' cities or cellular communication networks or nuclear warheads, I'd say the effect was pretty minimal.

People will be the same as they are now, after the fur flies and the dust settles. So why am I helpin' the Rev?

Because, for a little while anyway, it's gonna be a fuckin' good show.

And when it's all said and done, after the Rev domesticates his new flock, maybe...just maybe, I'll kill him. And then I'll rule the fuckin' world.

HA!

ROBBIE JO AND SIMON WITH THE ANGELS

obbie Jo in the graveyard; digging, sweating, and cussing up a storm. "Goddam you, Justin! Why do I hafta dig your goddam dead ass up *twice*? Why didn't you tell me I shoulda taken your stupid skull? Sure, it's got a hole in it the size of an elephant's asshole, but I bet you were stupid to begin with, weren't ya. I'm comin' to get ya, Justin, you dead motherfucker!"

She rested the shovel on a root for a moment, and heard something. A sigh. Robbie Jo climbed out of Justin's grave and slipped through the fog, looking.

Simon sat against the towering gravestone of Landon MacAllister, tobacco king, dead since 1887. Simon was still wearing his filthy sheet, twisted around his body, stuck down with mud and blood and sweat, decorated with sticks and dead leaves and bits of human tissue. Tears left shocking white streaks on his dirty face. There was a rubber tube tied around his arm. His works lay in front of him; there was a full syringe in his hand.

"Whatcha doin' Simon?" Robbie Jo surprised herself by feeling very sorry for him.

"Robbie Jo," he said, and his eyes met hers. The blue-hot spark of madness was gone. There was only emptiness now, and sorrow. Sorrow so deep it seemed bottomless.

"Are you killin' yourself, boy?" Robbie Jo knelt down next to him.

He nodded. "I don't know what happened, Robbie Jo. I guess I was demon-possessed. But I killed folks. A lot of 'em. And I just cain't live with what I done."

"Simon—you got no idea why you did it?"

"No." He shook his head miserably, and Robbie Jo realized he had forgotten all about eating her sins.

"They're lookin' for ya, Simon. There's lawmen all over town."

"I know that. People always hated me, Robbie Jo, and feared me. Now they got a damn good reason for it." He touched her cheek with his black-crusted fingers. "But I'd never hurt you. You know that, right?" She nodded.

Simon rolled the syringe between his fingers. "I know I gotta pay for what I done. But I'd rather do it myself. I just don't think I could stand to be arrested, to see all those people who want my blood..." his lip trembled.

"That's prob'ly best," Robbie Jo said gently.

He held out the syringe to her. "Would you do it, Robbie Jo? Would you do it for me?"

"Sure." She took his skinny arm in her hand, lined up the needle.

"I love you, Robbie Jo," as the syringe blossomed red. "I love you."

"I know, sugar." Robbie Jo kissed his forehead and pressed the plunger home.

Simon's eyes rolled up, and he slumped against the headstone. It took him a little while to die. Robbie Jo waited with him, holding his filthy hand.

When he was gone, she rummaged around in her pack until she found a slightly squashed Three Musketeers bar. She broke it into pieces, and placed it on Simon's sunken belly. She waited a moment, then picked up the candy and ate.

There was a gush of sin. A flood. A goddam firehose of sins Simon had eaten, sins his father had eaten, and his father's father before him. Sins horrific and petty, unspeakable and insignificant. The sins of every man, woman, and child who had died in Possum Kingdom for the past sixty years.

It should have been too much. It should have filled Robbie Jo to overflowing, to bursting. It should have shorted out her mind like a plug-in radio dropped into a bathtub.

But it didn't. The dark, alien thing that was Robbie Jo's soul drank the sins like a thirsty sponge. It absorbed them, embraced them, made them her own. The sins of Possum

Kingdom were woven through her nerves, wrapped around her heart, pumped through her veins and arteries and into her heaving lungs. They became as much a part of her as her slender hands and her fox-colored eyes.

Robbie Jo slept for a little while, as her body worked the sins into her bones. At last, she opened her eyes, and saw the dying sun, the forest of gravestones, and Simon's cooling corpse.

She blinked her eyes, licked her lips.

"Delicious," Robbie Jo whispered.

SAM GETS A BIG OL' SURPRISE

R obbie Jo was in a foul mood by the time she got home. Her shoulders ached from digging up Justin Raffkin's skull (which she had in her school backpack), and she had just about frozen her ass off washing in the creek. Then there was the bit with Simon. She felt sorry for him, and that irritated her. Worse yet, she felt a nettle of guilt, and that really pissed her off. If Sam was going to give her any shit over being so late, she was more than ready for him.

But he didn't yell at her. He whined, which was worse. Where have you been, I was so worried. You should really call if you're gonna be late (like there was a fuckin' phone in the cemetery). You gotta think of me, Robbie Jo, I'm your husband now, I love you I love you I love you--

She kissed him to shut him the fuck up.

They had sex in the embalming room. Robbie Jo wanted to be washed with pleasure, to forget about everything but her crotch for awhile, but Sam just wouldn't shut up. I love you, Robbie Jo. I need you. We'll be together forever and ever and ever.

She started thinking what a fine sacrifice he would make. He had plenty of raw material to go around.

Robbie Jo closed her eyes, tried to ride away on the hot wave that was building inside her, but Sam kept rattling on and on: We'll build a life together, we'll have kids, six or seven of 'em, we'll grow old together, you can help me run the business, I love you, I love you, I love you.

All by itself, her hand crept out to the big scalpel on the shelf. Before she really knew what it was doing, her arm swept up in a vicious arc. The knife connected with Sam's throat, and there was hot red rain.

ROSE'S RAPTURE; ROBBIE JO'S WHITE TORNADO; JIMMY'S CLOSE CALL

As Sam's blood was erupting from his severed carotid, Rose Heron and Michael Yeats were entangled on the floor in front of his fireplace. The Girls decorated the house like sculptures of jet, draped over the furniture, lining the hallway.

Rose was naked, skin warm in the firelight as she traced the fine muscles of Michael's back with her fingertips. She was secure in his arms, and safe, so safe.

"I love you," he whispered, as he entered her for the very first time.

Rose gasped with nothing but pleasure. She nipped Michael's ear. "I love you too. I always will." Her head fell back as he began to rock his hips, so slowly, so sweetly.

No fear. No worry. Rose's father was nowhere near her thoughts, as if he had blipped out of existence, as if he had never been.

The world was Rose and Michael.

"Shit! Fuck! Goddam-sonofabitch-SHIT!" Robbie Jo dipped the sponge into the bucket of bloody water and scrubbed the ceiling. The walls. The floor.

"Stupid, stupid, stupid. You're losin' it, girl. You really are." She scrubbed faster. Jimmy Liggett would be back from his supper break any time now.

She'd already stripped off her bloodsoaked dress and blasted her skin and hair with hot water. She'd mostly cleaned up the amazing amounts of bloodspray in the embalming room. But there was the little problem of Sam himself.

She'd managed to get him up on the embalming table with his new scissors-lift gurney. She'd rinsed the blood from him (not that there was that much; the bastard had sprayed most of it all over the room like a goddam Rainbird lawn sprinkler). And there he was, lying on his back, with his marble-white face and his wide-open, surprised eyeballs staring at the ceiling. "Fuck you," Robbie Jo said to him as she dumped the bloody washwater down the deepsink.

She stared at Sam. "Gotta burn ya," she muttered. She took one of the lightweight blue body bags from the closet and began to wrestle his limp cadaver into it. It was hard work; almost impossible. Sam weighed much more than she did, and he was—well, he was dead weight. Robbie Jo ended up sitting on the end of the table, feet on Sam's shoulders, gripping the bag in both fists as she used her legs to shove him in. A zip here, a zip there, and his stupid, pale face was gone. She clambered over the lumpy blue bundle and used her sneakered feet to shove him off of the autopsy table and onto the rolling gurney.

Robbie Jo had nearly made it to the crematorium door when Jimmy Liggett came strolling out of the woods.

Jimmy stopped in his tracks. The last thing he wanted to see was Robbie Jo Ridgemont coming toward him in the twilight, wheeling a corpse.

"Evenin', Roh—Mrs. Dunwiddie," he said. The girl's face was in shadow. Was her hair wet?

"Evenin'," she snapped, pushing the body past him.

Jimmy wondered why it was in a body bag instead of a cremation carton, but he wasn't about to ask. "Um, would you like me to help you with that?"

She stopped, looked at him. All he could see of her eyes was a couple of little red pinpoints. "I'd be much obliged," she said finally. She held the crematorium door as he pushed the gurney in for her.

She threw open the door of the retort and took hold of the body bag. She sure seemed to be in a hurry.

"Um, if you don't mind my askin', why isn't Sam helpin' you with this? It's not gen'rally a one-person job." Jimmy hefted and dragged the bag onto the steel conveyer belt. *Good sized guy*, he thought.

The burners ignited with a whoomph. Jimmy jumped. "He ain't here," said Robbie Jo, adjusting the temperature control. "He's at a mortuary management convention in Florida. He'll be back next week." Jimmy barely got his hands out of the way before she hit the button and started the conveyer belt rolling.

Jimmy watched the bag being drawn into the raging fires, like a damned soul entering the mouth of Hell. He knew, in that instant, who was inside the bag. There was no doubt in his mind at all.

Robbie Jo put her hand on his shoulder, and he cried out.

She patted him. "You need to cut back on the ol' caffeine, Jimmy."

"I guess so." He could feel tiny beads of sweat popping out on his forehead. His heart began to pick up speed. Jimmy realized that he was scared. No, not scared. Terrified.

"I'm gonna be in charge while Sam's gone. That okay with you?" Robbie Jo stood too close to him, her russet eyes locked on his.

"Just fine," Jimmy whispered. Robbie Jo cocked her head. *Oh Jesus. She knows. She knows I know.* Jimmy's stomach rolled. He gritted his teeth to keep from vomiting.

"Good. Good. Now Jimmy, I'm thinkin' of givin' you the evenin' off. There's no business tonight anyway, 'cept for this dead fucker." She slammed the retort door shut. "What do you s'pose you'd do if I sent you home tonight?"

Her eyes only left him for a moment, to sweep the room. *She's looking for a weapon,* Jimmy thought. *She's wondering if she could take me out right here.* He pulled himself up to his full height, like a crippled bird fluffing up its feathers to look big when a weasel's about to pounce. "I...I guess I'd just stay home and read," he said, fishing for the right answer.

Robbie Jo's body tightened, as if she were preparing to spring. *Oh shit, talk fast!* "Or maybe I'd, uh, go out of town for a few days, I could use a little vacation—" Jimmy's words cut off as his dry throat constricted.

Robbie Jo's shoulders relaxed, ever so slightly. "Why, that's a fine idea, Jimmy Liggett. Things are really gonna pick up once Sam gets back and those two other embalmers start. Why don't you just take a little time for yourself before then?"

"Thank you, Mrs. D.," he said, backing toward the door. She closed the distance between them in the blink of an eye.

"You're not thinkin' of makin' any phone calls tonight, are ya, Jimmy?"

"No!" He all but shouted the word.

"Good. We wouldn't want anybody gettin the wrong impression, would we. Besides, my mama always said it's wrong to carry tales." She was so close he could feel the heat from her skin. Inside the retort, fat from the corpse started to sizzle.

"No, Miss—Ma'am. I wouldn't dream of it."

"'Course you wouldn't." She patted him on the arm. The touch of her fingers made him want to scream. "Have a good trip, now. Drive safe."

"Thank you," Jimmy said. He fumbled with the doorknob for an eternal moment, then threw it open and ran out into the night.

PRIMUS AND JIMMY; HEREAFTER
HOODOO

*R*everend Primus Reylark was in town that night, helping to decorate the elementary school for the annual Halloween party. Unlike some of the preachers he knew, Primus had no problem with Halloween. It may have once been a pagan holiday, but somebody had to come before Jesus's time. It had been a Christian holiday longer—the Feast of All Saints. Now it was a night for children to dress up and play pranks and eat way too much candy. Was it a celebration of evil spirits? Primus didn't think so, but even if it was, evil spirits were a part of life. If a soul was never tested by evil, how could it ever become stronger?

He was thinking about all this when Jimmy Liggett came running down the sidewalk toward him, as if the Devil Himself were on his trail.

"Evenin', Jimmy," Primus called out.

Jimmy Liggett stopped dead and stared at Primus, not seeming to see him at first, like a panicked animal caught in the headlights of an oncoming truck. "You okay?" Primus asked. He set his hand on Jimmy's shoulder.

Jimmy started, as if Primus had come up from behind, instead of standing right in front of him. "No," he whispered. "No, I'm not okay."

"How can I help you?" Primus smiled, hoping to set the young man at ease. He knew he made Jimmy nervous. Most everybody in town knew that Jimmy Liggett was an atheist, or at least an agnostic. Not that he boasted of it, but he was never seen in either church, and his reading material of choice was anything but sacred—tales of men who built rocketships and went to the stars; of exploration and adventure in the name of Man alone; of alien skies devoid of Heaven or God.

But Jimmy Liggett was a good man. Primus knew of his kindness to Simon McCray, the sineater, the poor miserable rabid puppy who had recently begun to sink his fangs into the citizens of Possum Kingdom. Thinking of Simon hurt Primus's heart. The boy was a lost soul if ever there was one. Primus had no idea what could have driven Simon to madness and murder, but he felt he had, in some way, failed the boy. He should have reached out to Simon. Coaxed him into the light, where the people of Possum Kingdom could have seen him for what he was—a lonely, motherless child. Should have taken him under his wing, protected him from whatever evil spirit or demon had beset his innocent mind. Primus had gone out on all of the townspeople's searches for Simon, hoping to find the boy before the angry, bloodlusting mob could string him up like a catfish. But it was as if Simon had become smoke, and melted into the woods.

It was too late for Simon (at least for his earthly life—Primus still held out hope for his soul). But not for Jimmy, Jimmy Liggett, who had been right there swinging a hammer when the town got together to rebuild the Maplewoods' house after the big storm of '04. Jimmy Liggett, with his shy eyes and polite manners, who had once helped to repaint the Holy Blood, despite the fact he had never once set foot inside. Who was now staring up at Primus with the expression of a man who had just been handed a death sentence.

"Jimmy?" Primus shook him gently. "Jimmy?"

The embalmer's chocolate eyes snapped into focus. His voice, when he spoke, was a frightened rasp that made the hair on the back of Primus's neck stand up. "You believe in evil, don't you, Rev'rend?"

Primus nodded. "Of course."

"Well, let me tell you somethin'. There's evil in Possum Kingdom. A big, nasty, oily blot of evil, in a sweet little innocent-lookin' package."

"Do you mean Simon?"

"No! I mean—never mind what I mean. It doesn't matter. You can't change it. But somethin' worse is comin', Rev'rend.

Somethin'—" Jimmy shuddered all over like a spooked horse, and bolted down the street. Primus called after him, but Jimmy didn't even slow down.

With a sigh, Primus turned around. And gasped. Almost screamed.

The Sweet Hereafter Funeral Home was surrounded in swirling, pulsing, venomous black light.

PRIMUS INVESTIGATES; JIMMY RUNS LIKE HELL

*P*rimus Reylark was afraid. As he walked up to the darkened front step of the Sweet Hereafter, he shivered, a bone-rattling tremor that seemed to shake him to the soul. He hadn't been this frightened since he was a little boy, sitting on his Gramma's knee and listening to tales of the Creek Devil.

The Hereafter loomed before him, black and shadowed, a crouching spider waiting for prey. The sickening aura pulsing around it made Primus's skin crawl. This close, he could almost swear that the aura was putting out an odor, like the smell of a week-old cadaver beneath a thick layer of perfume. The darkened windows had the empty look of a corpse's eye. Primus shivered again.

"Fool. You're actin' like a jumpy little girl," he whispered to himself. The building looked the same as it always had. It was just too dark. Ephram and Ruth had always kept the front porch light on, all night long.

Primus thought of what had happened to Ephram and Ruth Dunwiddie, and he had the sudden impulse to turn and run. Instead, he rang the doorbell. He could hear it ring, echoing inside the apparently empty house like a church bell. "Bring out your dead," he whispered, for no reason at all.

He waited for a minute, then two. He rang the bell again, and waited some more. No one came to the door.

Sam and his new bride must have gone to Jonesborough for dinner and a movie, Primus decided. He'd talk with them in the morning. It was with no small measure of relief that he turned and walked away from the Sweet Hereafter, striding down the street faster than he really needed to.

Primus looked over his shoulder, just once. For a fleeting moment, he thought he saw a rust-colored glint in an upper bedroom window, the glitter of fox's eyes. Then the window was dull and dark again.

Primus sniffed the chill autumn air. There was something on the breeze—something much different from the smells of folks cooking supper and jack-o-lanterns burning. Something faintly sweet, like overcooked bacon, and the sharpness of burning hair.

That's when he noticed the curl of smoke coming from behind the house, from the Sweet Hereafter's crematorium.

Jimmy Liggett packed fast and sloppy, his heart aching at the thought of leaving behind his books. There were a few he had to have, of course. A few he'd never think of leaving, like *City* and *Childhood's End* and *Slan*. But most of his collection he left on the shelves for his landlady to find, and she would probably throw them in the trash or burn them as demonic propaganda.

He threw his clothes into a duffel bag (they all fit—he wasn't one for fashion) and wrapped his Metropolis and Star Trek models in paper towels and set them carefully on top. He started stacking up his favorite videos: Contact, 2001, Close Encounters, Alien, The Day the Earth Stood Still. He got to Hellraiser, and dropped them all.

Jimmy sat on the floor and cried. He knew he should call the police. He didn't suspect Robbie Jo had murdered Sam and stuffed him into the oven, he *knew*. Knew it like his own name, or the color of his mother's eyes. But he was afraid.

Afraid of a little teenage girl, his brain taunted. *Yes, scared shitless, damn straight*. He should go to the police, of course he should. But if he did, she'd find out. She'd be long gone before they could catch her—the girl was slippery as a watersnake. And then she'd find him. Wherever he was, she'd find him.

Jimmy had no doubt that Robbie Jo Ridgemont was evil. He'd always known; he realized that now.

He'd never liked the girl—she made him uncomfortable. He was ashamed to admit to himself that part of it was her looks; her reddish eyes, the same as her hair, like some weird forest creature. Or one of the Fairy Folk, the Sidhe.

The bad ones.

He couldn't understand how people believed her nicey-nice act. She reminded him of the little blonde girl from that old movie, The Bad Seed; gooey-sweet candy coating over a poisonous, molten core. Only Robbie Jo was smarter than that kid had been. She'd hidden her inner monster much better. Jimmy suspected that the only people who knew her secret, other than himself, were dead. He didn't believe for a moment that Sam was her first. She'd been far too cool for a first-time murderer.

Robbie Jo was a creature of nightmare, and just like a bad dream, she'd find him while he slept. He'd wake up to find those weird dried-blood eyes of hers staring at him, just before she rammed an icepick through his eye, or slit his throat, or gutted him like a gasping river trout.

"Fuck that." Jimmy hauled himself up from the floor and grabbed his videos.

He shoved his few bags and boxes into his vintage VW bug and tore out of Possum Kingdom, drove like the hounds of Hell were on his trail. He hit the highway, and headed for Alabama, where he was born, where most of his family still lived.

Because more than anything, Jimmy Liggett wanted his mama.

Primus's whole body tensed as he walked around the side of the Sweet Hereafter, toward the crematorium. It was pitch black out, and he nearly tripped more than once. "I have faith in thee, my Lord," he whispered. "Give me strength, Lord." *Because I'm scared to pieces*, his brain added to the end of the prayer.

But God knew that. He knew everything. And if it was His will, Primus would return to his wife safely on this night.

But who can know the mind of God?

Primus swallowed hard, and reached for the doorknob of the little brick building.

The door was locked. He peered through the small, diamond-shaped window, and saw that the crematorium was dark.

Except for the oven, of course. Bluish light from the gas jets glimmered beneath the oven door. Someone was cooking in there, all right. Someone was well done, and then some.

"It's how they make a livin'," Primus murmured. "It's a funeral parlor, not a flower shop." He walked back to the street, trying not to picture liquid flesh falling away from blackening bone.

HALLOWEEN HOOTENANNY
(RETURN OF THE SINEATER)

*W*ednesday morning, October thirty-first. Halloween. Robbie Jo got up before the sun rose. She dressed carefully, in a dark purple sweater and jeans, her long hair pulled away from her face in a perfectly respectable twist. She took some documents from the top dresser drawer: her marriage license, her birth certificate, Sam's birth certificate, their latest bank statements. She tucked them into Sam's new leather briefcase (three hundred dollars, by mail order) and grabbed the keys to the hearse. In the gray morning half-light, she drove down Main Street and out of Possum Kingdom.

Time was of the essence, she knew. Her lame-ass story about Sam going to a convention wouldn't hold up for much longer. She didn't think Jimmy Liggett would tell anyone. She had terrified him, she thought with satisfaction. But other folks would notice Sam's absence, and those new stiffs (ha!) were supposed to start work Monday.

And then there was the blood. Despite her frantic scrubbing, if a cop were to spray Luminol around the embalming room, the whole place would light up like the fuckin' county fair on a Saturday night.

But Robbie Jo wasn't worried. Not a bit. Because if everything went right, none of it would matter after tonight. Not one goddam bit of it.

She swung the hearse onto the highway, and headed for Jonesborough.

Robbie Jo was gone a good hour and a half before Primus Reylark rang her front doorbell, knocked at the back, peeked in the windows, and finally went home.

But she got back just in time for three local boys to bring her Simon McCray's wasted corpse in the back of an old Dodge pickup truck.

Robbie Jo had the guys pull the truck around back, to avoid a scene. She started to go get the gurney, but Seth Greeley, a brawny farmboy with acne like road rash, threw Simon over his shoulder like a sack of beans. "Boah stinks," he grunted as he stomped through the back door into the embalming room.

"Dead folks tend to do that." Robbie Jo gestured at the steel table, and Seth dropped Simon with a repulsive, meaty thump. Simon was past rigor mortis, and he fell in a tangled heap, bony arms and legs sticking out in ways they really shouldn't.

"C'mon in, boys." Robbie Jo beckoned to Tommy Longyear and Lumpy Bohoon, who were lurking in the doorway with identical nauseated expressions. Reluctantly, they took a step or two inside.

"You tell anybody you found 'im? The FBI fellas?" Robbie Jo addressed Seth, who seemed to be the least likely to barf.

"Well, no, Missus Dunwiddie." Seth rubbed the back of his meaty neck, looking embarrassed. "Y'see, we was in the cemetery smokin' a little ditchweed when we found ol' Simon. We didn't wanna 'splain what we was doin' there. 'Specially cause there was a grave dug up, as well as the daid kid. Y'spose he done that too, Rob—Ma'am? Dug up a grave?"

Robbie Jo looked at Simon's pathetic little corpse. "I s'pose if he could slaughter folks in their beds, he was capable of anything, Seth. Anything at all."

"He sure don't look like much,' grunted Lumpy. "How'd a lil' fart like that keel anybody, anyhow?"

Robbie Jo regarded Lumpy; hulking, soft, and slow as a crippled ground hog. "You ever see a weasel take a big, fat muskrat?" she asked him. "Some of the fiercest critters in the world are the little ones, y'know."

"Nothin' holds on like a weasel," Tommy had to agree. "My Uncle Smitty stuck his hand in a log one time, and a weasel chomped onto it and wouldn't let go. He hadda cut its haid off."

"Did it let go?" Robbie Jo asked.

"Nope. The weasel haid was still bitin' 'im, even without no body. He hadda go home and have Aunt Nanner pry it off with a spoon."

"Hmm," said Robbie Jo, "that's a weasel for ya. Lemme ask ya somethin', boys. You plannin' to go to the Halloween dance tonight, over to the high school?"

They all agreed heartily that they were.

Robbie Jo nodded. "I kinda thought you might. But if I tell the FBI that I've got Simon's body, they're gonna tear up this town. They'll grill ever'body up one side and down the other. They'll spoil Halloween. They might even cancel the dance."

There were grunts and squeals of protest.

"Now just hold on a minute, fellas. I know what to do." Robbie Jo patted Seth on the hamhock-sized shoulder. "You keep quiet about this. Come tomorrow, I'll tell the law that somebody dropped Simon's body off at the back porch, I got no idea who. That way, we still get Halloween, and nobody has to know you were smokin' fatties in the boneyard."

The boys declared Robbie Jo brilliant. She clapped them on their backs as she escorted them through the Sweet Hereafter's back door. "Don't tell a soul, y'hear?"

"We won't, ma'am," said Seth, tipping his baseball cap to her.

Robbie Jo watched them pull out of the driveway, fat heads lined up in the cab window like balloons in a shooting gallery. She knew they wouldn't keep their mouths shut. In a few days, one or all of them would get all liquored up and start bragging about how they found Simon McCray, the psycho killer. The story would grow and mutate like a monster in a 1950s science fiction flick. Hell, they'd probably end up saying that they killed Simon in a fight to the death. They'd probably say they saved a busload of nuns and orphans from his evil clutches. Robbie Jo chortled.

They'd never have the chance.

All she needed was to keep the cops away from her until tonight. After tonight, none of it would matter.

Robbie Jo sighed as her eyes rested on Simon once again. She untangled him from the filthy sheet and put it in the hazardous waste container. It wasn't hard; he weighed next to nothing. She washed his milk-pale skin, scrubbed his hands, brushed under his nails. She washed his hair, picking out leaves and brambles and bugs. His hair was always so pretty, pale as the moon, soft as a baby's. She brushed it straight back from his face, which made his sharp cheekbones and sunken, half-closed eyes even more prominent.

"Oh well. You ain't s'posed to look that good when you're dead, are ya, Simon." She stroked his icy cheek, and squeezed his eyelids shut. No reply came from the slack, open mouth. Everything that had been Simon McCray was long gone; his sweetness, his sorrow, his little-boy sins.

Robbie Jo didn't embalm him. Simon had been a creature of nature; to wire his jaws shut and pump poison through his veins was just wrong. Instead she went upstairs and found a soft blanket to cover him with, and two silver dollars to place on his eyes. Then she moved him onto the gurney and rolled him into the cold room, where she left him. She'd worry about what to do with him later, after it was done.

She closed the door, but she could still see Simon in her mind's eye. His stupid, innocent face, filled with utterly trusting love. Tiny nettles pricked at Robbie Jo; slivers of guilt, even a single thorn of regret.

"God damn you, Simon McCray," she murmured. But it was even too late for that, because Robbie Jo had eaten all his sins. Robbie Jo had given his sweet young soul wings, and sent it flying straight up to heaven.

ROSE ACCEPTS AN ODD INVITATION

ose smiled as she worked, updating the files in Michael's huge old wooden filing cabinet. She couldn't take her eyes from the sparkle on the third finger of her left hand. It winked at her every time she moved, as if they shared a happy secret. Rose had never cared about diamonds, never thought about them, really. But this one…it was incredible, beautiful, like a tiny piece of the stars fallen to earth.

Rose held the ring up to the light. The oval stone flashed multicolored fire. She marveled at the craftsmanship—tiny leaves and twists of ivy surrounded the stone, delicately crafted in luminous white gold. Michael had slipped it on her finger just last night, "to make it official." Her smile became a grin.

"Whatchoo got there, woman?"

Rose jumped half out of her skin. "Robbie Jo! I didn't hear you come in!"

"My, my." Robbie Jo grabbed Rose's hand and held it up for scrutiny. "Looks like somebody's got a gen-yoo-wine diamond engagement ring! Did it cost Mikey two months' salary?"

Rose laughed. "Nope. It was Michael's grandma's, and then his mama's. Isn't it gorgeous?"

"It sure is." Robbie Jo turned Rose's hand, making the stone catch the light. "A lot nicer than this tacky-ass thang Sam gave me." She stuck her hand out, showing Rose a huge pear-shaped diamond set into a thick gold band.

"Wow!" Rose blinked. "How many carats is that?"

"I dunno, six carrots and a tater, who cares. I think it's ugly as sin. But yours—well, that's a work of art."

Rose grinned. "It is lovely, isn't it. But yours is, too."

"Sure, if you're the trophy wife of a middle-aged used car tycoon." She yawned, stretched, tugged on Rose's finger.

"Guess Mrs. Yeats musta been wearin' that ring when she died in that awful accident...good thing her hand wasn't mashed."

Rose yanked her hand away. "Robbie JO! That was an awful thing to say!" Her gut clenched. She had somehow managed to avoid thinking about that obvious fact. Until now. She glared at Robbie Jo, more than a little hurt.

"Well, sorry, sugar, you know me, I just say whatever pops into my head. I didn't mean anythin' by it." She reached up and rattled one of the chains of paper skeletons hanging from the ceiling. "Besides, it's Halloween. It's okay to talk about dead folks and haints today."

"If you say so." Rose shoved her left hand into the pocket of her jeans.

"Oh, sweetie, I'm sorry." Robbie Jo leaned across the counter and gave her a hug. Against her will, Rose felt herself start to smile.

"Oh, it's okay. I'm just a little freaky about the whole thing, I guess. It seems so weird...the idea of me bein' married." Rose kissed Robbie Jo on the cheek. "Speaking of married, how's your new hubby?"

"Oh, he's fine. He's off doin' some business in Jonesborough. That's kinda why I came by to see ya."

"Oh yeah? Scared to be by yourself on Halloween?" Rose leered.

"Petrified. So I was wonderin' if you'd mind joinin' me for a little Halloween celebration tonight."

Rose frowned. "Well, I've just gotten Michael talked into goin' to the Halloween dance..."

"That's fine. You can just break away for an hour, can't you? Then go right back?" Robbie Jo batted her eyes. "Purty please?"

"Anything for you, girlfriend. What are we doin'?"

Robbie Jo grinned, showing all her white teeth. "It's a surprise. Meet me at ten o'clock tonight at the Wounds of Christ."

Rose groaned. "I dunno, Robbie Jo. The last time you had me meet you there, it was such a big surprise I nearly dropped dead of shock. You're not marryin' anybody else, are ya?"

"Hmm. That's not a half-bad idea, Rosie. A whole harem of boytoys, all doin' my biddin'…but no, I couldn't stand all the goddam dirty socks all over the floor. So, you gonna be there?"

"Sure. Michael too?"

Robbie Jo shook her head. "Not this time. This is a girls-only event."

There was an unnerving, hot glitter in Robbie Jo's eyes. Rose wasn't sure she liked this much at all. "But at the Baptist church? Why? Robbie Jo—this isn't illegal, is it?"

Her friend laughed. "Nope. Not even immoral or fattenin'."

"It *better* be fattening. I'm expecting some Halloween candy. And no goddam candy corn, either. I want chocolate." Onyx, on the floor at Rose's feet, groaned softly. Rose patted her head. "You tell 'er, girl!"

"Don't worry, Rosie. You'll get treats aplenty." Robbie Jo patted Rose on the shoulder. "Listen, I gotta go get ready. See you tonight!"

"See ya!" Rose turned to her filing. In the back room, she could hear Michael repairing cat cages. A bark; the Girls out playing in the tall, dry grass behind the clinic. She put the file in her hands on the counter and plopped down into the receptionist's chair.

Rose was ashamed to admit it, but she was nervous about meeting Robbie Jo at the Wounds of Christ tonight. She was more than nervous—her stomach was filled with spastic butterflies, and the hair on the back of her neck was standing up. What in the hell could Robbie Jo be planning? Onyx whimpered, and shoved her black, cold nose into Rose's hand. Rose stroked the dog's heavy skull and silky ears.

"It's probably some stupid prank," Rose murmured to Onyx. "Some dumbass small town thing that they do every year." Onyx kissed her palm.

Rose wished she hadn't agreed to this, or had at least talked Robbie Jo into letting her bring Michael.

"Oh well," she sighed, petting her dog. Whatever it was, it couldn't be that bad. Hell, it'd probably be fun. Nothing to worry about. If there was one thing Rose was certain of, it was that Robbie Jo would never do anything to hurt her.

ROBBIE JO MAKES READY; SIMON'S FINAL GIFT

Robbie Jo hummed to herself as she left the animal clinic. Rose had started to slip away from her. She was all wrapped up in Michael Yeats; everything else had paled in her eyes, even her best friend. Robbie Jo knew she should be upset about this, but she wasn't. It didn't matter. Not the least little bit. Because after tonight, after Michael had become a muskrat or a raccoon or some damn thing and left a gibbering doppelganger in his place, Rose Heron would be all hers.

The black dog licked the hand of her mistress, breathing in her warm, beloved scent. Something was going to happen, she knew, and very soon. Something huge and unavoidable, like birthing her puppies, but bigger. So much bigger.

Onyx was half filled with the desire to run, to just tuck her tail down and run and run until she dropped. But that wasn't possible. She had to protect her mistress. Nothing else mattered, including her own life, or even the lives of her pups.

Besides, there was a part of her filled with anticipation, like the scent of fresh meat caught on a summer breeze. A part of Onyx *wanted* the thing to happen. Hungered for it.

But all she could do, for now, was wait. Wait until she was summoned.

Onyx rested her muzzle on her mistress's warm knee, and closed her eyes.

It was risky to slip into the church in the afternoon, but if she waited until sunset, the streets would be crawling with little trick-or-treaters. Robbie Jo shifted the heavy duffel bag on her shoulder as she slipped through the woods, as quietly as possible.

She tried the back door, and was grateful to find it unlocked. Not that she couldn't have picked it, but it was one less thing to slow her down.

She set her bag down, and pulled out the jar of Halothene she had stolen from the animal clinic earlier in the week. It was risky stuff—if the "patient" got too much, he just might choke on his own vomit and die. But it was a better bet than whacking him upside the head. That could kill him outright, or if she didn't smack him hard enough, he might turn and fight. The Reverend Thomas Rye was soft and out of shape, but he was a big galoot. Robbie Jo didn't relish the idea of a brawl with him, when the objective was to take him alive. Now, if she'd planned to kill him, it would have been a different story. Robbie Jo smiled, imagining beating the reverend's head to a pulp on the marble floor of the chapel.

"'Nuff of that," she whispered. Rag in one hand, jar of animal anesthetic in the other, she crept through the darkened church. *The Rev should be here*, she thought. He always spent Wednesday afternoons in his office, reading the bible, planning his sermons, organizing his rarely attended church activities. Robbie Jo knew this, because she had been watching him for some time now. Boring work, but necessary. A dry appetizer for the feast that was to come.

The door of the office was ajar, and the room seemed dark. Robbie Jo frowned, and pushed it open, just a little, with her shoulder. Empty.

"Shit!" she hissed. *He has to be here, goddamit, he just has to!* She scanned the church with narrowed eyes. *There!* The door to the choir robe room was open, and the light was on.

Robbie Jo grinned. "Gotcha, Rev." She moved quickly, quiet as a cat. She peeked around the door, ready to pounce.

The choir robes aren't supposed to be red. Why are they--
"Shit! Fuck! Sonofabitch!" Robbie Jo hollered. There was the Reverend Rye, all right, lying in the middle of the floor, eyes and throat wide open, Ju-Jubes dotting his chest like colorful cancers.

"Simon, you little bastard! You arrogant little fucker! Eatin' the sins of a rev'rend, huh? Well, I hope they were fuckin' delicious! Yum yum YUM!" She kicked Reverend Rye in the ice-cold slats. A yellow Ju-Jube popped off and rolled along the floor. Robbie Jo had to laugh at that. Pretty soon, she had to laugh at the whole thing.

When she was done giggling, Robbie Jo sat down in a pew to think. She had to find someone else, and fast. The ceremony was locked and loaded. Nothing was going to stop it, not the dead Reverend Thomas Rye, not Simon, fucking with her from beyond the grave. Possum Kingdom was full of men. It wouldn't be hard to lure some dumbass redneck to the church with the promise of sex.

Or better yet, with a tale of a damsel in distress. Robbie Jo started to grin.

ROSE AND THE WOUNDS OF CHRIST
(ONE HELLUVA PARTY)

*M*ichael hadn't wanted to let her go. He'd been worried when Rose told him she had to leave the dance, just for a little while. "People go a little nuts on Halloween around here," he'd said. "Let me at least walk you there." But Rose had talked him out of it, kissing him on the mouth, promising to be back in an hour or less. They shared one last slow dance (Michael would only dance to the slow ones), and then Rose slipped out into the night.

She was sweaty, and the cold October air made her shiver right through her denim jacket. The band from the Holy Blood was playing, and could they tear it up! Even though Michael wouldn't join her, Rose had felt the music in her bones and just had to dance, spinning and shaking and careening off her new friends and neighbors. Michael watched her, grinning, clapping. She'd get him out on the floor someday. She knew he had rhythm. Rose smiled, felt a warm flush creep over her as she remembered him moving on top of her.

Yep, she'd get him to dance the fast ones with her, eventually. She had years to work on him. She had their whole lives.

Onyx and the Girls, waiting patiently outside the high school gym, fell in line behind Rose. She welcomed their silent company.

The wind rose and fell, dry leaves swirled down the street, danced in the air, skittered mouselike along the sidewalk. The night sky had been clear when Rose and Michael entered the dance. Now black, oily clouds were forming over Possum Kingdom.

The little ghosts and goblins had mostly gone home to bed by now. The ones who were left were the big ones; frying-size boys and girls whooping and hollering down the street. Probably soaping windows and putting blazing bags of dogshit on people's doorsteps, the little monsters. Then there were the teenagers (the ones too cool or too shy to go to the dance), tearing down the street in battered pickups, laughing too loudly, roaring drunk in rubber masks and old bedsheets.

One pack of redneck punks hooted at Rose from their pickup and threw a half-empty beer bottle on the sidewalk a few yards from her feet, where it exploded in a spray of amber liquid and glass. Onyx snarled at them, chased the pickup a few yards before turning back and returning to Rose. *Maybe I should have let Michael walk me, after all.*

But it wasn't that far. She was at the Wounds of Christ before she knew it. Rose stopped at the walkway, and looked up. *That's weird.* The clouds seemed thickest over the church, roiling in the sky like living things. Flashes of yellow light illuminated them from within like dark Chinese lanterns. Heat lightning, folks around here called it. There was a distant rumble of thunder. Rose pulled her jacket tighter around her, and walked quickly up the sidewalk.

A tiny sign on the front door said, in Robbie Jo's loopy handwriting, "around back." Rose sighed. The Girls followed her to the back of the church.

It was dark inside, and she couldn't seem to find the lightswitch. "Hello?" Rose called. No answer. She could smell incense, musky and wild, more suited to a Buddhist temple than a Baptist church.

She walked down the narrow corridor, past the closed door of the reverend's office and the robe room, to the end of the hallway. The Girls padded along behind her, so very quiet.

Rose paused outside the unmarked door, hand halfway out to the doorknob. She was expecting some sound; music, spookhouse noises, satanic chanting, even. But there was nothing. Perhaps because of the silence, Rose was getting mightily creeped out.

"Which is exactly what Robbie Jo wants," she said to Onyx. "We'll show her we're not scaredycats, won't we,

Girls." Onyx woofed softly. Rose patted her head, and opened the door.

It opened onto the front of the church, off to the side, near the pulpit. Stars, all she could see were dozens of flickering stars.

Rose squinted, letting her eyes adjust. Not stars, of course. Candles. Robbie Jo had decorated the church with a bazillion candles. They were everywhere; dripping on the pews, stuck to the pulpit with thick puddles of wax. There was a skull on the pulpit too, a fat, dripping purple candle stuck to the top of the cranium, leaving dark streaks like tears down the bony cheeks. Very Hammer Film, circa 1968.

"Shit," Rose muttered. "What a mess."

Then she saw the rest of it.

The raw, bloody-edged animal hides tacked to the back wall. Squirrel, muskrat, mouse, cat, weasel, rattlesnake. Black dirt scattered over the floor. A tin bucket of what looked an awful lot like blood. And the centerpiece, on the stage behind the pulpit: a shrouded corpse. With a possum on its chest. Just sitting there, grinning, like some kind of ridiculous, drooly gargoyle.

"Oh, for shit's sake," Rose grumbled, trying her best to convince herself she wasn't afraid. "Robbie Jo!" she yelled. "Get your butt out here!"

She heard a laugh from the shadows. Robbie Jo stepped into the candlelight. "You like it?" she asked, gesturing to the scene at the front of the church.

"It looks like the set of a Dario Argento flick. Rev'rend Rye is gonna kick your ass when he sees this wax all over the place."

A smile. "Oh, I don't think he'll mind."

Rose's fear, which had been steadily rising like mercury on a summer morning, took a quick detour into anger. "What the hell is this, Robbie Jo? Some kind of dumbshit séance? We're a little old for Bloody Mary or Light as a Feather, y'know."

Robbie Jo chuckled, driving Rose's irritation a notch higher. "Not Bloody Mary, sugar. This here's the real thing."

"Goddamit! The real *what*? Who is that under that sheet, Sam?"

"Not Sam," Robbie Jo said.

"And he's gonna pop up and scare the shit outta me any minute, right? You better move the possum first. I'm outta here, Robbie Jo." She turned to leave.

"Do you trust me?" Robbie Jo's voice hissed through the air, tickling her ears. Rose turned to face her.

"You know I do."

"Then stay. We're gonna do somethin' special tonight, Rosie. Somethin' incredible, that's never been done before."

Rose sighed. "Oh, c'mon, Robbie Jo, you don't believe in all that occult bullshit. You told me you don't."

"I didn't used to. Rose, has it ever occurred to you that anythin' can happen? Lit'rally anythin'?"

Rose frowned. "Well, sure. I never imagined I'd end up in a place like Possum Kingdom, or meet anybody like you or Michael..."

"Not just odd twists of fate, Rosie-baby. I'm talkin' genuine weirdness. Ghosts. Miracles. Monsters." Robbie Jo was grinning like a jackal. The possum stirred, shifting from foot to foot.

Rose crossed her arms. "Hell no."

"Well, maybe you should open your mind," said the possum.

Rose blinked, stared. She grinned. "Now that was cool. How'd you do that, Robbie Jo?" She moved closer to the possum on the shrouded figure's chest. The Girls, in a half-circle behind her, followed.

The possum licked its pink, rubbery lips. "No phonograph, Rose Heron," it said. "No radio. It was I who spoke to you, of my own free will." It stood up on its back legs and grinned.

"Jesus Christ!" Rose tripped over dogs in her backward scramble. "Holy shit! That thing really talks! It talks, Robbie Jo!"

Robbie Jo laughed, loud and long. "That's not an 'it,' Rosie. That's the Rev'rend Meshach Reddingale. He just had a little detour on the road to reincarnation, that's all."

Rose realized that her legs were about to give out. She sat down on the floor. She remembered a phrase she'd heard somewhere; some old comedian or something. *Everything you know is wrong.*

"You—you're Meshach?" she asked the possum, feeling foolish and frightened.

"Yes. Robbie Jo summoned me from the sleep of Death." A string of drool ran from between its jagged teeth, onto the white cotton shroud.

"Oh, my God," Rose said. The Girls crowded around her. She put her arms around Onyx and held her like a teddy bear.

Robbie Jo had moved behind the body on the floor, squatting next to the possum. "It's a real mind-fuck, ain't it?" she grinned.

The possum shot her a disapproving look, then turned back to Rose. "We couldn't have done it without you, Rose. Your presence here, in Possum Kingdom, was the catalyst for my resurrection."

"No," she said, not knowing why.

"Yep," said Robbie Jo.

"And now, Rose, you must help me return to human form. It won't take long—the ceremony is ready to begin. And when I am a man once more, Rose Heron, a change will begin. A change that will redeem the corroded soul of Humanity."

"Collective soul," Robbie Jo clarified, patting the possum on the head. It snapped at her, and she laughed.

Rose's head was jammed with strangeness. She wanted this to be a dream, but she knew it wasn't. "I—I don't know what you're talking about—" She scrambled to her feet, ready to bolt.

Robbie Jo leapt down from the platform and put her arms around Rose. When their skin touched, there was a shuddering crash of thunder. Rain began to beat down on the roof. "Now look here," she whispered in Rose's ear. "The critter's tellin' the truth. We're gonna pop him into a human body, and then, you an I will be witness to an honest-to-pizza miracle. Somethin' will happen—well, I won't spoil the surprise. But when it's done, you and I will…"

"What?" Rose said, numb and shaking.

Robbie Jo took Rose's face in her hands and whispered, "We'll rule, Rosie. We'll rule the goddam world."

"This is crazy." Rose put her hands over Robbie Jo's. The other girl's skin was hot, feverish.

The possum began to sing. It had a deep, melodious voice, but Rose couldn't understand what it was saying. Then she realized the words weren't English. Some were Latin; she recognized that. Some were Spanish. And something else; something that sounded Native American, something that sounded West African.

And the Girls began to dance. They filed up to the body on the floor, and encircled it. They moved around it, slowly at first, heads swinging to the throbbing rhythm of the possum's song. Then faster, as his chant picked up speed. They pranced, they turned. They rose up on their back legs and walked like humans.

Robbie Jo clapped her hands in delight. Rose just stared. It was amazing, and wonderful. It was also kind of horrible. Dogs didn't do that. It wasn't natural. It was kind of like a newborn baby looking straight at you and saying "good afternoon." It made you want to laugh, and then run like hell.

"Now Rose, this may be a little hard for you at first," Robbie Jo hissed into her ear. "But sometimes, in order for somethin' wonderful to happen, you have to make a sacrifice. In this case, it's just one person. I'll make sure it doesn't hurt him any."

"What are you saying?" Rose was finding it hard to breathe. Robbie Jo didn't answer. She bounded onto the platform and took a foot-long hunting knife from behind the pulpit.

At that moment, the shrouded figure on the floor began to struggle.

THE SERPENTS SPEAK;
ROSE REMEMBERS

P rimus Reylark was in the back pew of the Church of the Holy Blood, reading the Bible by the light of a camping lantern. He was there to keep the church safe from boisterous teenage tricksters, and to protect his snakes. Last Halloween, somebody had broken in and tried to steal Wigglestick, the big timber rattler. The culprit had lost his nerve, evidently. *Lucky for him,* Primus thought. He'd found the lock snapped on Wigglestick's box, and the big old fellow curled up in the bottom, sleepy and amiable as usual. Wigglestick was a mellow critter by nature; seven feet long and thick as a little boy's thigh. But if the thieves had snatched him up, well, who knows what would have happened then? Primus probably would have had a missing serpent and a Baptist-boy corpse on his hands. He didn't aim to let that happen.

He raised his head, eyes narrowed. He heard something, above the roar of the rain and the crashes of thunder. He set down his Bible and cautiously approached the front of the church, where the noise seemed to be coming from. It wasn't long before he knew exactly what it was; he'd heard it many times before, but never without provocation.

The snakes were rattling. All of them. At once.

"What are you doing?" Rose wanted to shout, but all that came out was a whisper.

"One life," Robbie Jo shouted over the thunderous roar of the rain. A crash of thunder shook the church. "Just one life, Rosie. A little bitty trade-off, for the salvation of humanity. Right, Rev?"

The possum didn't answer. Froth dribbled from the corners of its mouth as its song rose in pitch and cadence. The dogs' dancing grew frenzied; a blur of shining black fur, rolling eyes, lolling tongues. The body on the floor *(person, it's a person)* thrashed hard enough to nearly throw the possum off. Still singing, it crept backwards to sit on the figure's legs.

Robbie Jo slid through the kinetic ring of dogs to stand beside the body. In one smooth motion, she crouched down and pulled the shroud from the figure's upper body. Skinny arms, bound close to the sides to ring-bolts in the floor. Dark-skinned hands clenched into fists. Heaving chest, thrashing head covered in a rough cloth sack.

"Come up here, Rose!" Robbie Jo hollered. Lightning floodlit the windows, the big knife in her hand flashed. "Take your place in the circle. Stand beside me!"

A single thought lit Rose's brain like neon. *Robbie Jo is going to kill that man. She really is.*

"NO!" she screamed. "You can't, Robbie Jo! You can't!"

Robbie Jo sighed, stood up. "Oh, don't be so prissy. The good rev'rend here tells me you've done it before." She jumped over the man on the floor and headed straight for Rose.

Rose felt prickly all over; hot and sweaty, cold inside. "Done what?" she screamed. The world flashed red.

Robbie Jo had almost reached her. "Murder," she said, eyes glittering scarlet.

"No! No, I—" The world went red again; red on the walls, red on the floors, red on Robbie Jo's grinning face.

Rose screamed. The sound ripped up from her soul, escaping her mouth in a wretched, tearing, alien howl. As her body stiffened, as she fell, as she began to convulse, Rose remembered. Rose remembered it all.

Six a.m., graduation day, and Rose is getting dressed, quiet as a mouse creeping past a sleeping cat. Dad is sleeping, of course. She can hear him snoring wetly through the thin wall that separates his bedroom from hers. How often she had wished it was a brick wall with no door, a steel plate a foot thick. She had first seen "Dracula" when she was eight. She had wished with all her heart that she could sleep in a coffin like Bela Lugosi; a coffin that locked from the inside.

But Rose was happy today. Tonight she would be a high school graduate, and in a few short months, an adult in the eyes of the law. Then she would be gone, gone, gone, and she would never see Dad again. Never again hear him opening her door in the middle of the night. Never wake up with his body on hers, wishing she were dead.

Rose had a new dress. She had saved up money from her job at McDonald's for months to buy it. Deep, celestial blue satin, sleeveless, the material flowing around her body like water. She had no party to go to after graduation, and no one to celebrate with, but she would wear her beautiful dress under her robe anyway. And she would wear it the day she turned eighteen, and left Miami forever.

Now she slid the dress over her head, and the cold fabric against her skin made her shiver. Rose admired herself in the mirror; something she almost never did. She usually avoided her reflection; the guilt and pain in her own eyes made her cringe. But today she saw herself with new eyes. She could see through the chrysalis that surrounded her, the hard shell she had constructed to keep the world from seeing what was inside. Rose looked through the shell, and saw herself growing wings.

There was no school today, of course, but Rose would go there anyway, and spend the day in the library. Mrs. Gurley would let her in; she always did. She wouldn't even see Dad until after the ceremony. Best not to think of that now. Instead, she twirled in front of the mirror.

Her father seized her around the waist. She hadn't even heard him coming. He ground her against his body, his erection prodding her in the back. "Good morning, sweetheart," he said into her ear, and his breath stunk like putrification.

"Dad no," she said, teeth gritted. "I'll be late!"

A sharp cuff to her ear, and the world rang with pain. "Don't lie to me. You don't have school today." His hand was under her skirt. His alcohol-poisoned sweat soaked through the fabric of her dress.

Rose had long ago learned that you never say no to Dad. Not if you don't want to get punched in the gut until you puke, or get your thighs beaten bloody with his belt. But today, she said it. She screamed it. "NO!"

"Give it up, you little cunt," he growled. He rammed two fingers inside her. With his other hand, he ripped her lovely new dress from her body.

The world slowed down then. Rose watched the shredded dress flutter to the floor, a dying butterfly. Saw Dad's fingers curl around the waistband of her panties and tear them off. Watched him pinch her nipples, slap her bare behind; watched, but didn't feel. He slammed her up against the wall, lifted her up, intending to impale her on his cock.

And then the world went red.

Rose howled, bared her teeth, and plunged her thumbs into Dad's eyes. He screamed; a hideous, agonized shriek, high-pitched and wailing. His fist lashed out and caught Rose in the mouth, cutting her lip on her teeth. Drops of her blood hit the wall as he fell, her thumbs left his eyes with a wet, sucking pop, and then she was on him. She leapt on his chest like a panther, her knees cracking ribs, her hands become claws, ripping and tearing at his face. His screams began to bother Rose, so she sank her teeth into his windpipe. That helped a great deal.

The rest of it was a red-soaked blur. She remembered something about a hammer, a hacksaw, a barbeque fork. And the scissors, of course. And the drain cleaner.

When it was done, when it was all done and all that was left of Dad was a pile of harmless, sticky meat, Rose, slick and crimson, got into the shower. She scrubbed her skin raw, washed her hair three times. When she got out, she was very careful not to step in the blood, or any of the other bits. She dressed in jeans and a t-shirt, and her mind was a beautiful blank.

Rose's conscious mind dropped its periscope and dived deep. Some other part of her brain took over; some old, cunning part which was determined that Rose would survive. It packed her bag for her, found Dad's booze money, carved up his neck with a steak knife to make sure there were no teeth marks left. On autopilot, Rose left her apartment for the last time, walking the eight blocks to school.

She gradually awakened in the school library, curious as to why she couldn't remember the morning, but unconcerned. Rose's mind sometimes went on short vacations. Especially during Dad's visits. Her plan to run away after graduation was fully formed; Rose thought she had been planning it for weeks. She was happy, excited, terrified.

Rose took a volume of Shakespeare's comedies from the shelf, and began to read "The Tempest." She remembered a dream she had last night of a blue dress; a lovely thing of satin, something she would never have the nerve to wear.

She hoped Dad wouldn't come to the ceremony.

Ten hours later, she was on a bus out of Miami.

CRITTERS CONGREGATE; PRIMUS FOLLOWS THE SERPENTS; ROBBIE JO GETS A HELLUVA BIG SHOCK

*R*obbie Jo grumbled curses as she dragged Rose up onto the platform by her armpits. The girl seemed to be having a full-on fit; she was vibrating like somebody had run a high-voltage wire through her, and she was frothing at the mouth. Robbie Jo noted with amusement that she now resembled the possum.

The Girls leapt over Robbie Jo and Rose, slipping easily around them like water rushing past stones. Robbie Jo knew that Rose had to be in the circle when the change started, if she didn't want her best friend to be a chipmunk.

She laid Rose down by the sacrificial meat on the floor, and knelt down beside her. "C'mon, Rosie," she yelled, slapping her. "Wake up!" Rose continued to tremble and foam. "Shit," Robbie Jo growled.

One of the church windows broke, exploding inward in a shower of glass. Then another. Robbie Jo jumped to her feet, eyes narrowed. Rain slashed in, soaking the pews and the carpet. A deer thrust its head through the shattered window, eyes wild. A raccoon leapt in through the other.

Robbie Jo ran to the window. She began to laugh. Animals surrounded the church six or seven deep. Bears next to possums, mice on the backs of coyotes, snakes thrashing in the mud, deer and muskrats and squirrels and birds. They all seemed unaware of each other, and of the rain pounding their fur and feathers and scales. Their focus was inside the church. Robbie Jo was reminded of a crowd of glassy-eyed teenagers, waiting for the Boyband of the Month to come onstage.

"Just hang on a minute," she hollered at them. "Your new bodies will be with you shortly!" The animals didn't seem to see her at all. With a giggle, she ran back to Rose, who was trying to sit up.

Primus's eyes narrowed. The snakes were no longer just thrashing and rattling. They were pounding their snouts against the inside of the boxes, desperate to get out. Leaving red streaks on the plywood. Primus's stomach rolled.

"Damn fool things'll kill themselves," he muttered. He was very frightened. He threw open the boxes. The snakes boiled out like fishing worms from a tin can. They poured down the aisle, a slithering river. They slipped around Primus's boots without seeming to see him at all. The door slammed open on its own, or maybe, Primus thought, because the snakes commanded it to. Angry rain whipped in as the snakes poured out.

Primus Reylark stared at the open door, and shivered to the marrow of his bones. Then, without a second thought, he plunged out into the storm and headed for Main Street at a dead run.

"How ya doin', Rosie," Robbie Jo hollered as she lifted the stiff, singing possum from the sacrifice's chest.

"Oh, God," Rose groaned, fists to her eyes. Robbie Jo set the possum down not far from the body on the floor. It didn't seem to notice. It was lost in the dark magic it was summoning. It occurred to Robbie Jo that what she'd set into motion couldn't be turned back. The thought made her smile.

"So who'd ya grease, sugar?" she asked.

"Daddy..." Rose whimpered.

"Well, hot damn! Good for you. I've always been a strong advocate of patricide, my own self." Robbie Jo squatted down and hugged Rose tight. Rose was limp in her arms. As she pulled back, she saw that light had surrounded the two of them; deep, blood-red light, crackling with electricity, shooting off vicious spikes of black.

Robbie Jo smiled, pressed her cheek to Rose's. "You see that? We're sisters, Rosie. We're better than the rest of 'em. We're bonded in blood. We were born to kill together."

"No..." said Rose, trying weakly to twist away. Robbie Jo grabbed Rose's face in her hands, hard.

"Now you listen up, baby. You're gonna be right here while I carve this guy open. If you try to leave this ring o' pooches, I'll smack you upside the head and hogtie you. I won't like it, Rose, but I'll do it." Rose blinked, said nothing.

Robbie Jo patted her on the cheek. "Now let's get on with it, shall we?" She yanked the sheet from the man on the floor, and straddled him. He still had a croker sack over his head, so Rose wouldn't have to see. Robbie Jo grabbed his old-fashioned white cotton shirt, and ripped it open.

Robbie Jo scowled. There was some kind of pressure bandage on the guy's chest. She hoped broken ribs wouldn't fuck up Meshach's body thieving. She grabbed the hunting knife and sliced through the wrapping.

Revealing small, flat breasts.

"What?" Robbie Jo screamed. "What the FUCK?" She yanked the bag from Owen Tanner's face. "You're a woman, Owen? You're a fuckin' girl?"

"Surprise," said Owen, baring white teeth in a humorless grimace.

Robbie Jo rammed her hand under Owen's waistband and rudely groped. She found crisp, curly hair, and a cleft just like her own. "Fuck!" She yanked her hand back. "Fuck, fuck, FUCK!"

SHOWDOWN AT THE WOUNDS OF CHRIST, PART 1

R ose awakened shivering to the roar of the rain. Even after she opened her eyes, she wasn't sure where she was. Her brain wasn't working right. All it would do was drone the same phrase, over and over. *I killed Dad. I killed Dad. I killed Dad.* She felt no horror over this, she felt no guilt. In fact, she felt nothing at all.

And what was Robbie Jo doing, with a possum and a man on the floor?

Robbie Jo said something to her, but Rose wasn't sure what. She opened her mouth to ask, but what came out was "Daddy."

Then Robbie Jo was there right next to her. As Robbie Jo's arms went around her, Rose felt something like an electric shock. There was red all around her, all around Robbie Jo; pulsing, living red.

Robbie Jo was talking to her, but the words didn't make any sense. Then, finally, Rose heard something clearly.

"We were born to kill together."

No, Rose thought. *I've done all my killing. I'm done.* "No," she managed to say.

Then Robbie Jo had her by the face and was threatening her, saying she'd hit Rose and tie her up if she tried to leave. Why would Robbie Jo say that to her? Rose wanted to ask, but Robbie Jo wasn't there anymore. Where was she?

There she was, sitting on the guy on the floor, tearing open his shirt, and she meant to kill him, damned if she didn't, because she had a huge hunting knife in her little hand. Rose knew that she should jump up, should stop Robbie Jo, but she couldn't seem to make her legs work. Rose's face twisted when Robbie Jo started cutting the guy--but no, she wasn't cutting *him,* she was cutting the bandages on his chest, and hey, it wasn't a guy at all. And Robbie Jo was cursing, ranting, screaming, and the Girls were dancing and spinning, and then Robbie Jo yanked the bag from the head of the woman on the floor. And it was Owen. Owen Tanner.

The fog began to clear from Rose's mind. It was replaced by scalding anger.

Rose struggled to her feet. "Robbie Jo!" she screamed. At that moment, six more windows exploded. Animals tumbled and jumped and flew in from all sides. The possum stopped singing, although the Girls kept dancing.

"Find another!" the possum bellowed, pink tail lashing. "You must find another living man NOW!" Thunder shook the church.

"Oh, shut the fuck up," Robbie Jo told him. Rose saw that the crimson aura which still surrounded her was connected to Robbie Jo's by a rope of light, like red neon. She tried to sever it, but her hand passed right through.

"You were gonna kill Owen!" Rose shouted. "How could you, Robbie Jo?"

When her friend bounded over to her, Rose took a step back. Robbie Jo looked hurt. "I'm sorry, Rosie. It was s'posed to be Rev'rend Rye, but Simon killed him, the little asswipe. Owen was just handy, that's all."

Rose grabbed the sides of her head. Robbie Jo couldn't be saying what she was hearing. She just couldn't. "Owen— Owen's like a father to me. A real father. He and Naomi took me in and treated me like their own! How could you—"

"Shit, Rose, I said I was sorry! I'm doin' it all for you, y'know!" Robbie Jo's eyes were narrowed, her face tight.

Rose's fists clenched. "Doing what for me? Whatever it is, I don't want it!" The aura around them flared like a sunspot.

"You will when you have it," hissed Robbie Jo, with a scary smile. She took a step toward Rose.

"No! Don't you dare! Don't you dare commit murder in my name!" The air around Rose crackled with power.

Robbie Jo grinned, wolfish and angry. "Calm down, Rose, or I'm gonna have to—"

The front door burst open. Reverend Primus Reylark stumbled into the church, eyes wild, soaked to the skin. A riptide of rattlesnakes poured in after him. He froze, eyes wide, staring at the front of the church. The dancing dogs. The possum. Wild animals everywhere. The candles. The hides. Owen, Rose, Robbie Jo. "What in the name of sweet Jesus Christ is goin' on here?" he bellowed.

"Help!" screamed Owen.

"Get him!" screamed the possum.

"Run!" shouted Rose.

"You'll do," snarled Robbie Jo. She grabbed a head-high brass candleholder and flipped it over, holding the weighted base over her shoulder like a sledgehammer.

Primus held up his big hands. "I don't know what you're doin' here, Miss Robbie Jo, but it isn't too late to call it off. You're messin' with things you don't understand."

"I understand perfectly, Rev'rend." Robbie Jo came down from the platform, started to circle Primus like a hyena searching its prey for weakness.

"You're puttin' your immortal soul in danger," Primus said to her, sorrow and shock in his coffee-brown eyes.

"My soul." Robbie Jo laughed. "Tell you somethin', Rev'rend. If I've got a soul, it's already sittin' on the Devil's shoulder, wigglin' its pointy little tongue in his ear."

The Girls raced down from the platform and danced around Primus and Robbie Jo, like schoolkids cheering on a playground fight. "Stop it!" Rose screamed, at Onyx, at Robbie Jo, at the raging storm. No one listened. The rope of light, stretched to a string but bright as flame, still connected her to Robbie Jo.

Robbie Jo, who was trying to brain the Reverend Reylark. She swung the candlestick in a vicious, whistling arc at his head. He jumped back, quick as a cat.

"You're fast for a big fucker," Robbie Jo grinned.

"Put that down, now," Primus said gently. Robbie Jo swung the candlestick again, missing his chin by inches.

The possum came bustling up, climbed on the back of a pew to see. "Don't kill him yet!" it shouted.

Primus's eyes cut over to it for a split-second. "Good heavens," he said. "That critter spoke."

Rose wrenched herself out of her shock and charged Robbie Jo. She threw her arms around her best friend's waist. "Don't!" she howled.

Robbie Jo lowered the candlestick, not taking her eyes from Primus's face. She flipped it around, hands choking up on the weighted base. "I'm awful sorry 'bout this," she said, and smacked it into Rose's forehead. The world turned a funny sort of gray, and Rose fell to her knees.

SHOWDOWN AT THE WOUNDS OF CHRIST, PART II

*O*nyx froze. Her daughters leapt over and around her. Her mistress had been hurt. She wrenched herself from the savage call of the Dance, and rushed to the mistress's side. Her mistress was on her knees, and then she collapsed to the floor, and seemed to sleep. Onyx stood over her, protecting. She snarled a challenge at the Fox Girl, but it went unanswered. The Fox Girl was intent on hurting the huge Man, who smelled of rattlesnakes and kindness. Onyx would have liked to help him, but she wouldn't leave her mistress. Not for anything, even her own life.

Primus let out a little cry when Robbie Jo hit Rose in the head with the candlestick. Robbie Jo's head snapped around to look at him, her reddish eyes laser-bright. "Now look what you made me do," she hissed.

Primus was crouched like a boxer, hands still raised, palms out. He was pretty sure that if he caught Robbie Jo, he'd have no trouble holding her. She was a wiry little thing, but his biceps were bigger around than her thighs. Catching her, though—that was the problem. The girl was quick as a greased weasel.

Primus nearly lost his balance, jumping back to avoid a nasty swing at his knees. "Robbie Jo! Whatever you think you're doin' here, you gotta stop it. Can't you tell how *wrong* this is?"

Robbie Jo laughed. "Wrong, right, who gives a shit, Rev'rend? Ain't we havin' fun?"

"Get him!" screamed the possum. "Hurry!" The church shook with the force of the storm. The animals, quiet until now, went berserk. Squirrels and muskrats chittered and raced up and down the pews. Coyotes howled. Bears roared. "NOW!" the possum shrieked. Robbie Jo opened her mouth, probably to yell at the critter, but nothing came out. Her eyes widened, and her jaw dropped. She was looking past Primus, at the front door of the church.

He shot a glance over his shoulder.

"Dear God," Primus said. Fear clenched his gut and stiffened his spine. There was a *thing* standing in the open doorway. Human sized. Covered in rain-soaked gray fur. Two legs, two arms, huge rat-pink tail, gaping, drooling jaws.

"Possum woman," Primus whispered. A sense of wonder swelled in his chest, like he hadn't felt since he was a little boy.

The back of his head exploded in pain. There was a white flash in his eyes, and he was falling.

The last thing he heard was the possum, on the floor beside him, starting to sing.

"Finally!" Robbie Jo grabbed the knife from the floor where she'd dropped it, and pounced on Primus Reylark's chest. *Excellent. He's still breathing.*

"Not for long," Robbie Jo muttered, ripping open his shirt. At least he didn't have tits. The man's chest was huge, broad, thickly muscled. Robbie Jo paused to admire the enormous white rattlesnake tattooed into the chocolate skin of his abdomen, matching the ones on his arms. *Kind of a shame to split it open. Oh well.* She raised the knife high, in two hands. It would take some force to get through all that muscle and bone. Even more to pry out Primus's still-beating heart.

"NO!" Rose hit Robbie Jo with the full force of her body, knocking them both to the floor. The knife flew out of Robbie Jo's hands. Rose sat astride her, green eyes blazing. Robbie Jo thought her friend had never looked more beautiful.

"No! I won't have any part of this, Robbie Jo! I'm not gonna let you kill a man right in front of me!" Onyx, the dog, growled at Robbie Jo over Rose's shoulder.

Robbie Jo hooked her ankles over Rose's shoulders and threw her off, hard. Rose went sprawling on the carpet. As she clutched the purpling bruise in the middle of her forehead, Robbie Jo jumped up and retrieved the knife. She went for Primus.

I said NO!" Rose's voice was loud, carrying over the storm, the singing, the animals. Robbie Jo felt a bone-aching weakness wash through her. She spun around. The aura she shared with Rose was still there, but changed. The light surrounding Robbie Jo had gone watery and weak. Rose's light blazed like a bloody sunset, surrounding her with crimson fire.

Robbie Jo didn't like that. Not one bit. She flipped the knife in her hand and charged Rose, intending to hit her in the temple with the heavy wood and brass handle.

Onyx roared. She was in the air before Robbie Jo could react. Her front paws hit Robbie Jo in the chest, knocking the air from her lungs. Then the dog was on top of her.

The other dogs, the Girls, broke from their circle and attacked Robbie Jo in a snarling, biting mass. Hot, ripping pain on her ankle, her arms, her shoulder, her face. A blur of white teeth, black fur, red tongues. Smelly dog breath. *What a stupid way to die*, she thought.

SHOWDOWN AT THE WOUNDS OF CHRIST, PART III (THE FATES SEVER THE THREAD)

As Onyx sprang at Robbie Jo, Possum Woman ran wobble-wiggle down the aisle, shredding the carpet with her long, sharp back claws. As the Girls attacked, Possum Woman seized the howling Reverend Meshach Reddingale in her arms.

"No!" he bellowed. "Put me down! It must be finished!" She tucked him under her arm like a football. Grinning her huge, wet, toothy possum grin, she trotted through the front door and into the pounding rain.

Rose threw herself at the ravening Girls, who covered Robbie Jo in a furious landslide of dogflesh. "NO! NO! NO!" she roared. The red around her flared. The dogs whimpered, and backed away. All but Onyx, who stood next to Robbie Jo and growled.

Rose took Robbie Jo in her arms. Blood oozed from dozens of holes and gashes in her flesh. She even had puncture marks on her neck, and a long, jagged tear down her perfect jawbone.

"Robbie Jo!" she cried. "Robbie Jo, I'm sorry!" Rose held her close, crying.

Robbie Jo opened her eyes, blinked. "That sucked," she said. Rose hugged her fiercely, loving her, hating her.

With a little help, Robbie Jo stood up. "Where's the Rev—the talkin' possum?" she asked.

"Well, a, uh, giant possum-lookin' thing carried him off," Rose said. It occurred to her that Robbie Jo hadn't cried out while the dogs were savaging her. Not even once.

Robbie Jo glanced at the still-unconscious Primus, at the fiercely struggling Owen. "Hmm," she said. "So much for that idea."

Tears, hot and bitter, rolled down Rose's cheeks. "You need help, Robbie Jo," she said. "You—" her throat constricted, and words failed her.

Robbie Jo took her by the shoulders. "What I need is you, Rose. We're done with Possum Kingdom. Come with me."

Rose shook her head. "Come with you where? What are you talking about?"

Robbie Jo's eyes sparkled. "I'm talkin' about us, Rosie. We're sisters. We're bonded, for this life and whatever comes next. We're the hunters, Rose, the wolves. They're the sheep." She nodded at Primus. "Wolves stay together."

"No." Rose tried to back away. Robbie Jo held fast. "No, I'm not—"

"You are," Robbie Jo said, into her face. "You're different. You're a killer. Just like me."

Bile filled Rose's throat. "I'm nothing like you! I'll never be like you!" She shoved Robbie Jo away. Robbie Jo landed on her back, and as she hit the floor, the rope of light connecting her to Rose snapped. Her scarlet aura fizzled, faded, disappeared. Rose's remained for a moment, then popped blinding-bright and was gone, like light bulb's explosive burnout.

Robbie Jo stared up at Rose from the floor. Her face rippled through emotions; shock, disappointment, love, rage, hatred. Her russet eyes narrowed, filling with tears. Her features crumpled in on themselves in outraged grief.

Robbie Jo staggered to her feet. She wrapped her arms around her belly as if she had been gutshot, and ran from the Wounds of Christ, ran into the silver curtain of rain.

"Robbie Jo!" Rose howled after her. There was no answer, just a rumble of thunder.

The animals began to file out of the church. They still seemed unaware of each other; their exit was as orderly as a wedding procession. The Girls sat here and there, wagging and worried. Onyx pressed herself to Rose's legs.

Primus groaned and stirred. Rose knelt down to help him.

"Excuse me," said Owen, polite as he always was. "Would somebody mind cuttin' me loose?"

Rose found the knife where Rose had dropped it, and severed the ropes around Owen's wrists and ankles. She helped him to his feet, pulled his shirt around his chest without comment. Then he and Rose went to see about Primus, who had blood matting the back of his hair, and streaming from his broken nose. Rose watched Owen's rope-burned wrists as he gave Primus his handkerchief, told him to stay sitting until they could get the doctor. Not for the first time, she admired Owen's kindness, his compassion, his quiet, unshakable dignity. *Owen's just about the finest man I've ever met,* she thought.

Even if he is a woman.

It was just about then that Michael Yeats burst into the church, calling Rose's name. As he took her into his arms, the rain slowed, and then stopped.

WHAT HAPPENED AFTER: PRIMUS AND OWEN

*P*rimus was okay. He had a cut on the back of his head and a concussion that kept him in bed for a day or two, but his wife Jerianne took wonderful care of him. Doc Poteet reset his nose. Primus prayed for Robbie Jo Ridgemont's soul every night.

Owen was okay too. After Doc Poteet and Jerianne came to collect Reverend Primus, after Michael escorted Rose and Owen home, the Tanners and their young boarder sat quiet and shellshocked around the dining room table. Steaming cups of coffee grew cold as Owen and Rose recounted their improbable tales.

Owen's was simple. He was taking an evening stroll, only partly to make sure no Halloween pranksters broke into the store. He heard someone crying in the shadows, near the Sweet Hereafter. He went to see, and someone clamped a cloth reeking of chemicals over his face. He woke up roped to the floor of the Wounds of Christ.

Rose told her story, sometimes whispering, sometimes crying, yelling once or twice. It was as raw as an open wound, and yet it didn't seem real. Robbie Jo wouldn't do things like that. But she did.

When Rose finished, they sat in silence. At last Owen spoke, voice quiet but steady. "Robbie Jo tore open my shirt, Naomi. Rosie saw."

Naomi's hands flew up to her face. "Oh," was all she said.

Rose didn't know what to say, so she smiled, to let Owen know it didn't matter. "You won't tell anyone?" said Naomi, voice shaking.

"Of course not." Rose took her hand. "You, um, you had children..."

"Oh, yes," said Naomi. "We adopted. Five beautiful babies. It was much easier back then, you know. The state couldn't get rid of black babies fast enough. Three boys, we raised, and two girls. They're wonderful people, all of 'em. Aaron's a lawyer, can you believe it? Jeph is a housepainter in Georgia, Mary's a midwife, Sally..." Her voice trailed off. Her face twisted. "I almost lost you," she said to Owen, and tears rolled down her plump, smooth cheeks.

He smiled at her, kissed her cheek. "But you didn't. Stop blubbin' old woman."

Rose wondered if Michael would love her that much, when they were old. "Um, your kids," she asked. "Did they, uh, did they know?" *Oh Christ. Why did I ask that?* She started to blush.

"Oh, no," said Naomi. "Owen was always just Daddy. Nobody in Possum Kingdom has ever known. We met in Kentucky, when I was just a girl of sixteen. Owen came through town, workin' with a tinker. He was the handsomest thing I ever saw." She beamed. "He took to courtin' me, and I fell for him, hard. When he told me he was—when he told me 'bout the way he'd been born, I didn't believe him. He had to show me."

"Naomi, please," said Owen, looking embarrassed.

"Hush. Anyhow, it didn't matter to me. I knew Owen was the love of my life. When I told my mamma we were fixin' to marry, she was mad. She didn't want her oldest daughter marryin' a tinker, a drifter. Then...well, one day, my sister came across us in the barn...she told. She told everyone. We had to run away together that very night, or they woulda hurt Owen. Or worse. We ended up here, in Possum Kingdom, nearly fifty years ago." She held his hand tight.

"She gave up ever'thin' for me," Owen said. Rose saw the love in his eyes, and knew why.

"I never saw my family again, if that's what you mean," said Naomi. "I didn't mind. My mamma had a foul temper, and my little sister Cherry was always a spoiled brat." She smiled.

"She just says that to make me feel better," said Owen, smiling back. They were wrapped up in each other for a few moments. Then Naomi turned to Rose.

"What are you thinkin' 'bout, honey?" she asked, worry in her dark eyes.

"I'm thinkin' I wish you and Owen had been my parents," said Rose. Naomi burst into tears, and took her into her arms.

"I killed him," Rose whispered, into the softness of Naomi's breast.

"Killed who, honey?"

"My Da—my father. He used to…do bad things to me. One day…I snapped, I guess. And I killed him." It was surprisingly easy to say it. Rose closed her eyes, and waited for the horror, the disgust, the rejection.

Naomi patted her softly on the back. "Well sugar, some folks just need killin'."

WHAT HAPPENED AFTER THE KINGDOM

*P*ossum Kingdom was okay, too. Oh, there was some damage from the storm, to be sure. Late-season crops washed out. Fallen trees crushed fences and walls. Shingles blew loose, and houses leaked all over town. Some folks said it rained frogs that night, or fish, or blood. Some folks claimed they saw the Devil's yellow eyes in the roiling black clouds. Some said they saw Possum Woman walking right through the middle of town.

But even for the less gullible, there was plenty to talk about. What really happened to Sam Dunwiddie, for instance. It was said that he left Robbie Jo for a dancer in Florida. Or he took the money from the Sweet Hereafter's accounts and left the country. Maybe he and Robbie Jo fled together. Or just maybe, Robbie Jo killed him and burned him up in the Sweet Hereafter's crematorium, which overheated and exploded that night. It was everybody's favorite topic of conversation, next to Simon McCray and the horrible things he had done.

It caused some confusion when Simon's body was found washed and shrouded in the Sweet Hereafter's cold room. Had he been in on something with Sam and his white trash bride? There was plenty of talk about Satanism. The desecrated grave, the murdered Reverend Rye, the evidence of a horrible ritual in the Wounds of Christ Baptist Church—what else could have been going on? Everyone knew that Simon didn't act alone. Satanists always ran in packs. For awhile there, the people of Possum Kingdom were eyeing each other with newfound suspicion. There was a sudden upswing of godliness.

A new preacher came to town from Jonesborough, to take over for the late Reverend Rye. He was a young fellow named

Jeremy Spindle, with freckles and fiery red hair. His foot-stomping, spit-spraying, roof-raising, Hellfire-and-damnation sermons packed the Baptist church each and every Sunday.

And then there was the mystery of Robbie Jo Ridgemont herself. Opinions on the girl ranged wildly, from cold-blooded murderess to innocent victim. She had taken the hearse and left town; that much was common knowledge. But the extent of her involvement in the weird events leading up to Halloween was a subject of much speculation. Possum Kingdom talked about it for years to come.

When Robbie Jo's mother was found bloated and stinking on her kitchen floor by Red Cross volunteers, there was tongue-clucking and head-shaking, but little surprise. Lureen Ridgemont had been drinking herself to death for years. Just another facet of the legend, now.

Repairs were made. The town pulled together. Neighbors helped neighbors. Roofs were mended, fences rebuilt, windows replaced. The congregation of the Holy Blood helped clean up the Wounds of Christ. The congregation of the Wounds of Christ helped catch new rattlers for the Holy Blood.

No one was sure what to do about the Sweet Hereafter. The Dunwiddies had left no kin behind; there was no one to take over the business. So the furniture was covered, the windows boarded up. The funeral home became an object of terror and delight for the children of Possum Kingdom. Ghost stories were told; kids crept up to the front door on Halloween night, rang the doorbell, and ran screaming and giggling away. But not even the bravest Halloween pranksters would venture behind the Sweet Hereafter at night, to walk among the blasted ruins of the crematorium. When a little boy got close to the scorched earth and shattered brick, the hair on the back of his neck would stand up. His skin would crawl. Before he knew it, he was backing away, then running like hell.

It was said that the Sweet Hereafter was haunted, but the crematorium was evil. Cursed. And it was best not to talk about curses, or even think about them much.

Perhaps for the same reasons, Owen, Naomi, Primus and Rose never discussed what happened that night. It was their silent consensus that some things were better kept secret. No one even knew they had been in the Wounds of Christ, except for Michael Yeats, Jerianne Reylark, and Doc Poteet. And they wouldn't tell, either.

WHAT HAPPENED AFTER: ROSE AND MICHAEL
(AND ALL THOSE DAWGS)

Rose Heron was not quite okay. It wasn't the realization that she had killed her father. The memories were horrible, certainly, and it was disturbing to know that she had been living in a world of her own creation for months. But Rose felt it unsettlingly easy to forgive herself. She had hated her father with all her heart and soul. Knowing that he was dead lifted a massive weight from her heart. To her surprise, being a murderer was much less horrifying than being a victim.

It wasn't the fear of being caught. Naomi drove Rose to the library at Jonesborough one harsh November morning. There, with her heart pounding and her mouth dry and coppery with fear, Rose looked up her father's murder on microfiche copies of the Miami Herald. They had to know. Or at least suspect her.

What she found instead were more ugly secrets about her father, John Ross Heron, who was not only a child-rapist but evidently a drug dealer as well. Rose smiled, she shook her head. She'd never even known. He had been nothing but her tormenter. Anything outside that role had never concerned her.

The police believed that John Heron's murder was the result of a drug deal gone wrong. A desperate junkie (or several of them, some thought) had torn the man to pieces, and either kidnapped or killed his only daughter, Rose. There was her picture, not as the prime suspect, but as a missing person.

Rose started to laugh. It began as a giggle, then a chuckle, then a full-throated howl which bubbled up out of her as unstoppable as a waterfall. She covered her mouth, tears rolling down her cheeks, as Naomi led her from the library and the glares of patrons and librarians.

I'm free, Rose thought. *Free of Dad, the fitly monster son-of-a-bitch. Free of suspicion for his murder. Free.*

I Got Away With It.

But her mirth was bitter in her mouth, and on the ride home her laughter began to choke her. Soon Rose was quiet, and before long, she started, softly, to cry.

"Why are you so miserable, honey?" Naomi asked, eyes crinkled with worry.

It was Robbie Jo. Her friend had been her lynchpin of security in the strange, swirling waters of Possum Kingdom. In one bizarre night, Robbie Jo had changed from sister and confidante to a vicious, unknowable stranger. Rose wondered if the death of her mother and her marriage to a beast like Sam Dunwiddie had driven Robbie Jo to insanity and attempted murder.

Or had she been that way all along?

Rose's heart ached every time she thought of her friend's smiling face, her sparkling, rust-colored eyes, her sharp tongue and fierce affection. She missed Robbie Jo like a severed limb.

Possum Kingdom was a dark and strange place to her now. What had seemed eccentric and charming was now just small-town creepiness. Rose was lost. The Girls seemed lost too; after Halloween night, they had stopped following Rose in their neat formation. Now they were just a bunch of black dogs. Beautiful, sweet dogs, but the magic had drained from their golden eyes. Only Onyx continued to shadow Rose, but in the way of a good dog, not a supernatural protector.

Rose spent long days and nights in her room at the Tanners'. She felt she no longer knew herself. And if she didn't even know herself, how could she marry another?

Michael was silent, sad-eyed when Rose came to his little home to talk, as if he already knew what she would say.

First, she told him about her father, and what she had done to him. Michael cried, held her close, sorrowing for the years of torment that had brought Rose to a single, terrible act of violence. When he looked at her, his eyes held no horror, just infinite love and sympathy, which made it so much harder to say what she had to.

"I still want to marry you," Rose whispered, his face in her hands. "Just not right now."

They talked it over. Michael didn't try to change her mind, although she could tell he wanted to. Rose would start college in Memphis next quarter. Michael insisted upon paying for it. She would take Onyx with her; the Girls would stay with Michael. He'd visit her on weekends, sometimes, and in the summer she'd come back to Possum Kingdom.

They made love that night, first slowly and tenderly, then with a near-desperate passion. Fear shimmered in the depths of Michael's eyes. Rose knew he was afraid that she would decide, once she was out of the Kingdom, that she didn't really need him after all.

She hoped with all her heart that he was wrong.

AND, OF COURSE, ROBBIE JO

Yeah, I'm fine too, thank you ever so fuckin' much for askin'. I admit, I was pretty flustered. Okay, flustered ain't quite the right word for it. I was runnin' down the street, howlin' like a baby stuck with a diaper pin, tears and snot all over my face. I made a beeline for the Sweet Hereafter, and hopped in that big ol' hearse. I already had a suitcase in the back, for when me and Rose were gonna head out together, outta Possum Kingdom and into the Brave New World.

Rose. My Rosie. How could I have gotten it so wrong? I guess my mistake was this: I assumed that if somebody committed murder, she must've enjoyed it, even if she didn't remember it for awhile. I thought that when Rosie woke up and smelled the blood, so to speak, she'd want more. Just like I did. But those lessons we're taught from birth stick to us tight as pine pitch.

Thou shalt not kill.

And if you do, you better have the good grace to feel guilty about it.

Those lessons stick, even when they're taught to us by evil rapist monster motherfuckers in the shape of a Daddy. They get pounded into us over and over, by a two-faced culture that worships ever'thin' exotic and violent and strange when it's boxed in by a TV or movie screen, but turns tail and runs when it comes face to face with the real thing.

Poor Rosie never had a chance.

I know now what I should have done dif'rently. I shoulda introduced the idea slowly, dippin' her in a little more each time, like turnin' the heat up on a lobster in his kettle. By the time we got to a boil, she woulda been ready. She woulda split Owen right down the middle, just for an appetizer, then helped me make Rev'rend Primus the main course.

Owen. Heh. Now that was a helluva note.

Anyway, it's too late now. I cut my losses and ran.

I traded the hearse along the way, to a fly-by-night used car dealer in Georgia. Yeah, I know it's a crime against nature to trade a custom 1958 Cadillac funeral coach in cherry condition for a babyshit-green VW microbus, but what's a girl to do? The old dame was just a little too conspicuous. Sure, I know a van just screams "Hey! I'm a fuckin' serial killer!" It's all just a little too Norris Bittaker for me. But I can sleep in it, if I hafta, and with those ratty orange curtains over the windows, I can hide just about anythin' in there. I can do just about anythin' in there. It's all good.

I headed on down to New Orleans with my fugly van and all of Sam's money. It's the fuckin' Wild Frontier out here, post-Katrina. Record-keepin' has gone to hell. It's the perfect place to start a new life.

I cut my hair short and dyed it black. I bought myself some brown contact lenses. I think I look a little bit like Winona Ryder now, 'cept my ears don't stick out as much. I don't know if anybody's lookin' for me, but if they are, they aren't about to find Robbie Jo Ridgemont.

I bought myself a fine little Toshiba laptop computer, and bought a whole new life on the Internet. Birth certificate, driver's license, high school transcripts, the whole enchirito. Now I'm Annabel Lee MacGuire, ever so pleased to meetcha.

Turns out Annie's a straight-A student, and a whole year older than I am. She's startin' at the University of Louisiana next semester.

I intend to study law. I think I've got the makin's of a fine lawyer. And I intend to finish, unlike that fuckin' French-fried loser Ted Bundy.

So, you can see, I'm okay. I'm doin' just fine. Oh, sure, my pride's a little wounded. And my heart's a little dented. But I'll get over it.

Besides, I haven't given up on Rosie. I know I'll see her again someday. I know it like I know I'm gonna take my next breath. I'll get another shot at her. It's our destiny.

Maybe I'll be a hotshot lawyer by then. And Rosie'll be a vet'rinarian with her own practice. Maybe she'll be married, with a coupla kids. Wouldn't that be a kick in the pants? Maybe she won't even recognize me the next time we meet.

Or maybe she will.

Sometimes I miss Possum Kingdom. But mostly not. But I miss Rosie. I miss her so much it hurts.

But if I kill somebody tonight, I'm sure I'll feel much better.

For a little while, anyway.

Lorelei Shannon lives in the woods outside Seattle with her husband, two boys, and various other unruly creatures. She is the author if *Rags and Old Iron*, *Vermifuge and Other Toxic Cocktails*, and co-author of the *Blood of Father Time* novels. She spends her spare time sculpting, gardening, playing with her kids, getting tattoos, and driving her 1947 Cadillac hearse, Annabel Lee.

Cover art and author photograph by Holly Burke.

hollypossumangel@gmail.com